Sins Of Our Imagination

WILLIAM FRANKS

Order this book online at www.trafford.com
or email orders@trafford.com

Most Trafford titles are also available at major online book retailers.

Printed in the United States of America.

ISBN: 978-1-4269-6595-1 (sc)

Library of Congress Control Number: 2011906123

Trafford rev. 06/16/2011

 www.trafford.com

North America & international
toll-free: 1 888 232 4444 (USA & Canada)
phone: 250 383 6864 ♦ fax: 812 355 4082

Contents

The Sins of Our Imagination

My name is Nigel Peters; some of my friends call me 'Tuesday,' yes, Tuesday, as in the third day of the week. Don't ask me how I came by the name, I've always assumed I was born on a Tuesday and the name found laissez faire or what I may call, common acceptance, after a joyous member of the family called the name Tuesday; which is common in the part of the country I'm from.

I'm a Teacher by day and part time House Detective, and all-other-things-that-are necessary, to make the Excelsior Hotel run well at night in the 'Big Easy,' yes, the Big Easy, as in New Orleans, even as the immaculate Saint Louis emits, *sanctum sanctorum*....

For the past seven years, I've been married to a French Creole, five feet five, 110 pounds, sexpot, an important work of an artist, par excellence, who makes everyone else in a room look less important.

Jamie does not believe in work, not if it does not involve pleasure; *'dolce far niente,'* reincarnate. Her favorite exit, when questioned about when she is going to get a job, is always: "Let's just say, I grew up in an environment, where pleasant idleness, sweet doing nothing, sweetly and softly, was the norm." She never believed in the adage that you earn what you get just as surely as you are what you do. On the other hand, living well was what was uppermost in Jamie's mind, which if I may say, is a contradiction in terms.

Jamie doesn't mind staying home to take care of her manicure, pedicure, and yes, her hair. She had an obsession with her hair. It was either cut too short by a gay man who hates women, or kind of uneven to losing its color. In most cases, it takes my playing 'Doctor' and administering 'therapy' to calm her and help recoup her lost *amour-propre*, her self-image.

A vegetarian, *bon vivant*, Jamie loves to cook. She believes the proper food enhances lovemaking, so she stocked the kitchen full of oysters, avocados, mangos, apples, yes apples. It was an idea she got from the Romans, for their worship of the apple as an aphrodisiac. Champagne, candles and soft Jazz music were necessary enhancers. Cooking gave Jamie the opportunity to walk around the house in her briefest lingerie or nothing at all, which according to her, helps build sex drive and expectation to a desired end, a incredible crescendo.

The closest Jamie ever came to working, was as a part time model and voice-over artist; yes, she had a sweet voice that caresses the senses, like petals of flower caress the ear lobes. She was, in the true sense of the word, an Aphrodite, who was too aware of her physical beauty and the power she was able to generate with it, and there were many victims; even with all the signs reading *caveat emptor*.

My friends used to wonder how I was able to sustain Jamie's extravagance and our yuppyish lifestyle on my teacher's and part-time detective income. We did manage for a while, until Jamie, *enfant terrible*, outgrew my combined salary and walked out on me, one fall day in August, while I was at work, the teaching part.

The note on the cocktail table read "Dear Nige..." one of the many nicknames she had for me. The note continued: "...What we had was beautiful, truly wonderful, but it does not do it for me anymore. I need more, Nigel..." I will hasten to remind all concerned, that Jamie's dissatisfaction was Economic, not sexual. She continued: "don't try to find me, I'm gone, gone, gone, you hear me, Nigel... gone!" The gone, gone, sounded like the pounding of a nail on its head long after it was already settled in. The is not always pleasant, nor does it offer one the setting for thinking rationally. If anything, it produces, *ad nauseam.*

So suddenly, I found myself single again after seven years of a blissful, sexually and culinary satisfying marriage. This was even though we lived on the edge of bankruptcy most of the time – remember; Jamie never liked to work. She made up for it with her large appetite for sex and good food. This could go on all day and night, in our own little world, oblivious to the rest of humanity - At the library, the green room, the Clubhouse, the swimming pool, Jacuzzi, sauna, under the bridge, at the pier or under the Gazebo, in the mode of *carpe diem.* An absolute insatiable escapade of orchestrated sexual binge, that creates its own geysers of aroma - gushing with smiles of raptures.

I was brought back to life by the shrieking sound of the telephone. It was like a messenger, who after long gone, creates a powerful presence, a super facsimile, all on its own. To me, at this very moment, it was nothing but an agent provocateur. My palm was balmy, my mouth dry. I could not recognize my own voice. I believe I sounded, "Hello," I must've drifted off to sleep....

It was Charlie, friend and night auditor at the Excelsior. All I could hear was Jamie's voice, calling: "Hey Toot," (short for 'Tootsie,' as in Tootsie Roll, she loved tootsie rolls) or "Toot, could you pass me the glass of wine?" "Yes, Toot, that feels good, yes, my backside too, Toot? My Doc. says to rub on my boobs, hard, to make it firmer, harder Toot, blow on it, softly - yes, that feels real marvelous..."

The thoughts remained, and lingered, and as hard as I tried, they refused to go away. They went back to the first time I met Jamie. It was in our advanced Advertising class. This was my first time coming back to school after a semester layoff. She was coming back from a hiatus of over two years, the better part of which she spent on a sojourn to the San Fernando Valley, in Southern California; bringing with her, all the elements of a true valley girl, plus, but not limited to her elocution.

School started in August, but Jamie didn't register until September - late for every of her class. This should have served as a warning sign, but it was not. It could have been the unconventional me, the one that hated the past, because the past had come too often to haunt the present, bringing with it romantic deaths, which were sudden and unsavory to the flesh. Pushing life, testing it to the edges of one's existence, the extreme outlines of man's basic identity - when only the immersion in cold water is the only way to get rid of the false notion, the delusion of one's invisibility, man's invisibility. When this deception might be halfway your fault, especially when you live in a city like New Orleans, a city that trembles with the energies of love, love made on wide brass beds with down comforters washed white by the moon, somewhere, in most cases, between dusk and dawn.

When she waltzed into the class; almost half an hour late, it still was not warning enough for me. All I saw was a five foot five gypsy goddess, her full flowing skirt, tight tops and brown suede jacket to match. An oversized bag strung over her shoulders, looked like it contained all her life's belongings. A hat, which she pulled to one side, covered the better part of her head.

A silence fell on the class - even the professor, Ms. 'what's her name,' had to stop briefly, to acknowledge the new breeze. She walked to the vacant seat next to me, her firm breasts (the hard nipples visibly aroused), undulating, sat down. Meticulously, she put her bag down between us, took off her jacket and Ray-Ban Way-fairer Sunglasses; rearranged her hair and flowing skirt, making sure her long smooth legs were showing, not really acknowledging anybody - It was lust at first sight.

There was this aura of street-smart about her, a '*je ne sais quoi,*' but in a larger sense, a cosmopolitan way, one can feel it, all one has to do is stay close enough. She moved deliberately and decisively. With a determined walk, to hear it was to know already that she was not easily deflected - A heel-to-toe walk that requires a good rotary action of the elbows and a vindictive moral purpose - a 'woe to the vanquished' aura about her. This was still not enough warning to me.

Even after the thought occurred to me, time after time, the thought of how many men she must have laid, their hair made grey, having wasted them thin. Leaving them constantly perspiring and scandal infested. These thoughts were still not warning enough for me.

Thoughts, imponderable thoughts - There had to have been numerous times when she had used sex to get an advantage. I suspected she used it in cold calculation, leveraging all the obvious assets. Sending out the message: 'Suitors beware, there is nothing but a body for you to take; my thoughts and heart are mine; you'll share none of them.' I ignored all the warning signs. Then, I thought to myself again, (of what use I do not know, since the bait towers larger than the logic), that there got to be philosophers and no doubt psychiatrists and mystics as well, who would loudly refute any notion of a distinguishing line between our wishes and their external counterparts. If this is so, their doctrines will have to extend to humans. If this further proves to be true, it then means that humans, those who refuse to heed the warnings of those ever present external counterparts; that natural self-preservation coat, would be subject to full responsibility for their acts, the act of not paying attention to the outside parallels, especially the similitude or vagaries of modern living. This in turn, imposes on us, a distressing situation: responsibility for and to our creations. Adventurers, dreamers, strivers; who purpose to be lithe, swift and tireless. Tacitly replacing the external counterparts with youthful frenzy, visualizing unlikely stunts. Thinking the battle is over before it ever started. A projector of smoother waters and long prosperous peace of mind, before the battle began, all because he refuses to pay attention to the natural protective coat - the corrector of things going bad. Despite these restrictions, I fell prey to Jamie, because I had never possessed anyone so fully, nor wanted anyone so urgently. Visualizing her full creaseless body, the moist ovens straining through membrane of silk only added to my lust, and her susceptibility to my own progeny, my seed, and our seed. Was I ever in big trouble, which was to be proved?

To me, love has always been timeless, and elusive of sequence, in the realm of the 'ever faithful, my way of living or getting along.' It evolves beyond the customary branches of our activities, in certain half-lit clouds from which day animals are excluded; occurring when the soul, in some unfathomable way, is more sublime than the most beautiful firmament, and everything that the eyes believe illustrates the inner globe, the world within, 'no more beyond, not after one reaches the ultimate,' was always my motto, and clocks were set to them, I was a stickler as can be.

After class, I summoned enough courage to ask Jamie to tea at the Student Union. She said: "Why not." If ever there was anything like supreme bliss, this sure came close to it. The talk over tea was amiable and seductive. I found out that underneath, Jamie was a pussycat. Just like any other intelligent animal, she reacts only when she is threatened, and there was no visible threat over tea. There were the usual student talks and actions - worries, fears and aspirations. I could feel eyes boring through us, inquisitive eyes. Questions whispered, *sotto voce* - wanting to know more about this new couple. One recently back from Europe and Africa, and the other a Valley transplant. Students are no different from other people - as if it needs reminding. They care about invaders, new entrants to their territory. Jamie and I were cognizant of all this, and to a degree, empathized with them. Plans were made for that weekend: a movie and a walk in the French Quarter. If time allows, the old Spaghetti Factory or Georgie Porgie, in the warehouse and garden district respectively, 'pro tempore.' That was that.

How many steps can one take through a seeming mine field and keep landing on petals of flowers? How many steps? I will tell you, only a few. In the city called New Orleans, with its sex traps and seekers of decadence and false security, how many times does one search for the ultimate companion and find the package called Jamie? I will tell you again, almost none.

Factoring into the equation the fact that we are talking about the external dimensions and not the internal aspects of this package; and all the other things in between, vis-à-vis the misinformation or disinformation the outside of the package may have communicated, whether this was purposeful or inadvertent is of no import. What is important is keeping the date, being on time and playing the proper role, the role befitting the messages sent out by the external counterparts of the package, the package known as Jamie.

I was ten minutes early for our date; Jamie was just getting out of bed. This also should have served as a caveat, but was still not foreboding enough for me. Watching her get ready was music of its own. The smooth supple body, not full, not thin, just right. Complimented with a fine neat waist and strong legs. The firm breasts enhanced by the well-sculptured bellybutton on a flat stomach. The burgundy hair was luxuriant, and when let go, falls on a shoulder and firm breasts that would make Cleopatra blush, *au naturel*. All of which helped cloud the warning signs, in this *affaire d'amour*. She made no effort to hide anything, totally uninhibited - and I would have been content if we had just stayed home so that I could feast on the menu before me. I did not push it; I could not push it, 'Patience, Nigel. Patience, all in due time...'

Jamie decided we should go see Bizet's 'Carmen' at the Orpheum. This came as a surprise, not because of any dissimilarity between Jamie and 'Carmen,' the cold-hearted seductress. I just never thought this gypsy beauty was into Opera. Even though the Opera is really not my first choice of where to spend my leisure time, or for that matter, where I would go on a first date, I said: 'Sure, why not.' Borrowing a leaf from Jamie. Who is fast turning out to be, *an 'au fait,'* or *'au courant belle.'*

The first hour, the theatre decided to dedicate to the Video rendition of 'Carmina Burana.' This was their opera week. It quickly turned out, after the first ten minutes of Carmen, my patience had reached its zenith. I watched as the Matador taunted the bleeding Bull, his red cape appropriately and gracefully maneuvered to tease in this 'ancien regime' game. The Bull's moves were slow but precise. Charging, slow but steady, just as it had been trained to do. The Matador elegantly played the role of the quintessential Bullfighter, a classicist who knows his trade. Then, the finale of the *bete noire;* the sword piercing of the Bull, which is supposed to lead to a quick and painless death, *a coup de grace.* It should be remembered, that, the bull had no vote in this, he never even saw the ballot. To the Bull, *a coup de grace* means death, and death alone - Everybody held his breath! Is the Bull going to meet with a quick and painless death, or is it going to be condemned to one of agony, because of a *faux pas,* all because the sword piercing Matador was not so harmonious after all, and missed the proper target? Then one asks, is the death really painless in this '*de rigueur*' scenario? Or is it just a fixed idea, an obsession in an *haute monde,* if not the *beau monde* of the ancient regime?

Alas! It was Bravo! Bravo! Bravo! That resounded throughout the colossal Arena. The spectators had not been disappointed. The sword-piercing classicist was on target. The Bull, slowly, slumped to the ground, met with a quick death, '*a fait accompli,*' and I am quite sure, not a painless death.

The glee of the spectators was resounding and contagious. Some of them trooped to the center of the field. The master of ceremony pulled the sword from the point of entry, wiped it off of blood and handed it to the Matador - a worthy trophy. The Classicist, with a big grin, raised his hands and the sword high. He took the usual circular, but elegantly engineered bows - which further sent the crowd into frenzy - a multiple verbal orgasms, in the highest level of debauchery. To me, a vulgar act, of a time long gone that smells of atavism.

The crowd could not resist the significance of the moment; they carried the classicist on their shoulders and paraded him around. After all, he had just performed a rare feat. Not too many classicists make it on a first go, the quick and painless death of the Bull.

The spectators could just imagine the mob scene that would have followed, if the bull had met with a clumsy death.

I watched as the bull was dragged by horse-driven carriage towards; I was quite sure, the consummation of other rituals, before its final resting place. My endurance quickly wore thin, for this non-pastime activity, and subtitled movies are really not my first choice.

Jamie slowly turned her head to me, making sure the silky hair brushed against the side of my face. The whiff of new coiffure greeted me. With her unblinking eyes on me, she asked if I liked it.

What does she mean do I like it? Not really sure of what she was talking about, the movie or the person asking, I asked her what she meant.

This modulated with a soft calculated voice, a voice devoid of any threat, again befitting the role of a responder to the message of the external counterparts of Jamie.

'The movie, silly, what else?' She giggled.

'Oh! It's okay, only that it's lost its initial tempo, you know, the Matador, the red cape and the Bull. It was fun; later parts just dragged. You know, 'ad nauseam,' Opera movies are really not as good as the real thing. I mean, the stage presentation."

She stared at me, still with the unblinking eyes, and since I was not done with my critic, I continued.

"It would even be more okay if one likes animal cruelty, the brutality of animals for fun."

She just gazed at me, the face showing no emotion, one way or the other, as I showed my prowess as a movie critic.

'It is their culture Nigel, for the Bull to die, just as you and I have our own cultures, and things happen in our cultures they also may not get. Got it?' She asked, with a voice laced with mild exasperation. She continued.

"The bull is especially bred and trained to be killed in this fashion; it is the way it has been from time. It is to meet with a quick and painless death, or something is wrong."

"Either way you cut it; a spade is a spade, is a spade. So, the whole charade is nothing but animal cruelty, a brutality. I thought you loved animals?" My gut feelings told me to back off, that I had taken the critic of the movie as far as I could go, without doing permanent damage to the evening, was now treading on delicate grounds.

"Do you want us to leave?" She volunteered, again without any emotion.

"No, not if you're enjoying yourself, I thought we were just evaluating the entire movie? Sorry for shooting my mouth off, I don't care too much for killing as sport, nor do I like the free flow of blood, even if it's that of animals. I am sorry." I was hoping the caring and sensitive personality would impress Jamie. It seemed to.

She planted a soft kiss on my cheek. I counted to ten and took a deep breath, happy that this first lovers' quarrel ended without any bruises.

From here on, it was my vision of what I anticipated. Jamie, for the first time put her hand on mine and clasped her fingers with mine, all five fingers. Constantly, glanced at me with smiling eyes and soft parted lips, occasionally showing a moist rouge tongue: 'patience is a virtue, humility brings it rewards, in love games,' were my unspoken thoughts.

We walked to the French Quarter after the movie, holding hands, stealing occasional kisses on the cheeks. We darted in and out of T-shirt and gift shops. Visited antique shops, Art galleries and museums. Museums are truly, as they say, the most wondrous of aphrodisiac. We went into the Saint Louis Cathedral, and with the expenditure of a quarter each, lighted a couple of Votive candles and sprinkled some holy water. We decided against the confession booth, for no sins had been committed, not yet.

At the Spaghetti Factory, all eyes were on us. It is safer to say, all eyes were on Jamie. On the dance floor, Jamie who is a student of Ballet and Modern Dance, strutted her stuff; and if I must say, we did complement each other, for I, Nigel Peters, do have a few moves of my own - translated, I am known to have a natural rhythm, quite able to hold my own on a dance floor. As if we made a secret pact not to dance with other people, Jamie refused all the advances of other suitors. She won my respect and affection, by her demure and polite rejections extended to other suitors.

Her thoughtfulness remained as I saw her to her door. She studied me closely before taking my head between her hands and kissed me on the lips. Suddenly her mouth opened, mine took a cue. The kiss became intense, and I felt an unfamiliar mound plying against my thigh. There was this warmth, and I felt soft hair slipping against silk as she pressed more rhythmically. She whispered 'Nigel,' and I heard a squeak, and wondered if she had been hurt somehow. Her head twisted, her neck pressed against my lips. With confiding fingers, she handed me the keys to her flat. With her eyes closed, whispered: "Take me to the bedroom, Nigel."

The day after - I got up cautiously, considered the unfamiliar environment I found myself in. My head felt like the head of anyone who ever overindulged the night before. I decided to move slowly. I limped cautiously through the door to the living room. It was in a mess. Our clothes were strewn about the furniture and shoes scattered about the floor; wine bottles and glasses in front of the coffee table; the telephone was off its cradle. We had touched all the places on the agenda and more the night before. We discovered we were not only compatible dancers, but also complemented each other well on the bed. I tiptoed back to the bedroom.

Jamie was lying on her side; her breasts pressed together, stretching, like two pointed spheres. Her burgundy hair fell over her face, which was buried in the pillow. The top sheet was draped across the lower half of her body; a leg protruded, revealing the sun-darkened flesh of her inner thigh. Watching her, I felt the provocative stirring in my groin. I wasn't sure what to do. Would this sex fiend wake up and decide it was all a mistake last night and decide to throw me out? I inhaled deeply for a few moments, excited by the sight of her breasts, her exposed legs and the burgundy hair that partially covered her face. I took the bait and the necessary steps toward the bed - I acknowledged the person in the bed.

She rolled over on her back. Her face was attractive in that innocuous California style. Pert, evenly suntanned, the features all too well coordinated to find any blemish. Her large breasts separated, the sheet fell away, displaying her pubic hair and the swell of her thighs. I moved to the foot of the bed and pulled down my boxer shorts and lowered myself on the sheets.

Jamie opened her eyes; she did not throw me out. She also still remembered who I was. She smiled. When she spoke, it was with the same signature soft modulated voice, this time laced with sleep. Which I found out later in our relationship, is more than a regular pastime. She enjoys her sleep just as much as she enjoys her sex and food. Jamie was always quick to point out that; 'isn't sleep a pastime for us all?' She wanted to know if I was okay. I said I was, and asked her if she was.

"You banged me like a ram last night, Nigel, first time in a long while, but it was a fulfilling ecstasy, I loved it. I could make you the happiest man on earth, Nigel." She moaned. She loves me rotten, I thought.

"I am already," I replied, thinking love was the measure of our potential, a bridge between what we are and what we can become. After all, how often do we meet total love; I mean real love? Once in our lifetime if we are lucky, twice if all your sins are forgiven and you are Jamie, with all her paradoxes, evasions and insoluble collisions, she was the eternal survivor who used man's follies as vehicle for accomplishing goals, her set goals.

I crawled beside her and she brought her hand to my swollen erection, cupping it gently. I reached for her nearest breast; the nipple was taut under the pressure of my fingers. She moaned and began pulling on me in short swift movements - a very developed sexual partner, who needed very little priming.

"Don't stop Nigel, make me feel warm all over, like last night don't stop...bang me Toot, fuck me, come on fuck me." She whispered.

I buried my face between her breasts. She parted her legs, inviting me to enter into her. "Let me get on top Toot, let me do the work." The caressing lips, provoking and setting me on fire. I pulled her head into my groin. She moaned the familiar moan and spread her legs; all was sweet wetness and soft flesh. I grabbed her under her arms. She was parallel to me. Her breath came in quick, loud throaty groans. Being on top, I would later find out, was a controlling trademark of Jamie, performed like a tigress.

"Oh, Nigel, you're something. Oh, you're, the all-time best."

Her whole body began to writhe. Her whispers now bordered on screams. Which I also later found out was a trademark, when the sex is good and long, hard and satisfying. The neighbors can go to hell.

"Oh, Nigel, you're driving me crazy, you're the best, the best there ever was! Never anyone like you. Now, now toot."

After brunch, a movie and dinner, we came back to her apartment. Over linen, candles, chalices, and plate, she talked about the world and its riches, love and the search for happiness and the gift of life; and I listened like a favored pupil, listened to every word, but remembered almost nothing but her smile and the beguiling softness of her voice - The virtue and the acts. She was my constant; I rotate but she is still. With that, I exploded inside her, totally drained. This woman is a man-eater, I thought to myself. Even this was not warning enough for me. The repetition of history and the folly of the man sexually, psychologically trapped. In the Big Easy, especially in the Creole community, it's called a man that is being pussy-whipped. I guess I was pussy-whipped and more. Then it becomes love as a destiny. As a calling and a lovely agony. Out of the air, from the undefined edges of that magical moment, I discovered that, or should I say, I believed Jamie was the chosen one, the one destined to become Mrs. Peters.

In retrospect, I must say, I was not pussy-whipped, neither was Jamie the chosen one; my experiences, relationships with other women had played a bigger role than I had realized in my infatuation and subsequent hypnotic entanglement with Jamie. What had drawn me to Jamie was my hatred of the past, my hatred of convention; the conventional wisdom and norms that I embraced: ('Nigel, you always do the right thing,') and the blind acceptance of the restrictive and voluntary imprisonment of the soul. The past was my enemy, has always been. Looking at her then, I thought it was the past that was in ruin and not the future, which again brings to mind, how history repeats itself? Lust, while it's lovely, doesn't really last the whole drink through.

With all said, it was really inevitable not to have fallen in love with Jamie, even though it was really lust *prima facie*.

Then I remembered what Charlie once told me: That in our thirties we pay for what we did in our twenties, and in our forties, we pay for what we did in our thirties. How logical and true - but in a sense, karmic. Charles is a philosopher.

Then it occurred to me that Jamie, although she was petit, and exhibits childish demeanor when she wanted to, was very sexually experienced, and I wondered about the rows and rows of early lovers and the stupid excuses she might have invented to go to bed with them. Did she use them much? Did they put her on their laps? Did she want or like them, or did she just let them take her to bed out of boredom? Was it anything to move the smoggy air of the Valley or the Big Easy? Would it be out of curiosity? Men to prove her power, men to avenge herself against other men, or against other women, against her sister or mother for that matter. She once told me her sister 'screwed' an ex-boyfriend after a drinking bout. Was that it, punishing men for the sins of her sister? Could the insatiable appetite for sex and men be out of politeness due to sheer bone weariness at men's persistence?

As a student of the theatre, was it the casting couches, the use of men to break the tension or to create it? Okay, she has always sought father figures, would it be men to inform and politically enlighten her, 'in loco parentes?' Appointed to explain to her in bed the nuances she could never get her mind to comprehend from books. Those three minutes lust, like the one that attacked her right after our first date, the one that subsequently leaves her lonelier and more desperate than ever. Was that it? Is it to free some demon in her? Is it because she couldn't hold on to the men? Was it about being a mistress and the dynamics that come with it? Could it be the curse of a lecherous housemaid? Was it the incestuous sister? Maybe for just being a gypsy slunk in from the streets? Five bucks a bang and free bath after? In the zone of no holds barred. It's apparent they all ended in failure. So, if it was none of these, what was it?

The Hired Killer

"Nigel, are you there? It's almost 10 p.m., you were supposed to be here an hour ago!"

It's like watching one's life go by in a kind of bewildered free fall into enemy territory. I thought to myself: So this is what it's like. This is badland and these are my feet spinning towards it like a sycamore twig. I experienced this incredulous detachment and isolation. Then the thought became more reinforced, this really got to be badland. Where one prays, prays hard that in consciousness, the whole darn thing had just been nothing but a bad dream. Another voice rears its head – telling me, 'Face-up, this is reality my boy, welcome to the real world.' Jamie, it turns out, is that girl, who never gets out of a man's heart, she stays there like a heavy meal: because, some memories are harder to forget than others....

The room took on a different configuration, becomes very low, windowless and over-lit. Strange voices are saying: 'Hit him while he is soft.' Weird thoughts, questions race through a once solid mind. Is there time to say goodbyes to the neighbors, or to send flowers for Michelle's birthday? How about the cat? Do I have time to send it for safekeeping? This weird scenario plays itself out; one in which you become afraid of certain thoughts, because they were so bad, that the mere thought of putting them into words or images could turn them into truths, into some self-fulfilling prophesy.

Someone once said that suffering is an unexpected benefit: That we have got to suffer deeply to overcome suffering. That if one does not suffer, how on earth can we create? Then, I thought to myself, has this person really suffered? Does he really know about the genesis and dynamics of this ill-social matrix, which is really hard to define? What does he know about suffering, its categorizations, and its different levels? Does he know that there is a dissonance between what's in our heart and what's being projected for remedy?

'For my soul has had enough of
calamities, and my very life has
come in touch even with sheol...'

'they have surrounded me like waters
all daylong. They have closed in upon
me all at one time....'

'you have put far away from me friend
and companion, my acquaintances are
a dark place...'

I had to summon my reserve, the reserve of my dwindling
willpower,
I knew I had to get it together, 'get off your elbows Nigel, race
through wet streets if you have to, and get your ass to work in a sober
state.' I prayed for body and soul not to fail me, especially voice. In
a slow voice, I said; "Yes Chas, I'm here. Sorry my alarm did not go
off, I'll be there in a jiffy, please cover for me."

I was quite sure Charlie wasn't buying my defective alarm story, and
if I could see through the fiber optics or whatever lines this telephone
uses, I am sure Charlie's reproving eyes would be boring through
me. Charlie and I have cultivated over the period we've worked
together a relationship based on trust and reciprocity. We do know
how to look out for each other, especially in times like this. A sigh
of impatience, followed by that of frustration, like a liquid click in
the roof of the mouth, followed by a decision not to breathe, done
on air, not food; Charlie hung up. There had been other cases in my
lifetime, naturally, even before I met Jamie, but not before I clocked
thirty-something, that my professional life had been regularly turned
upside down by one terminal, heartbreak or the other, but never this
excruciating and close to middle age.

If you've ever seen a mummy or Zombie, like the ones featured in
those black and white 'B' movies of old, with Boris Karloff, yes, like

those ones. That was how my movements from my apartment on Seagull Lane, overlooking Emerald Lake, were that late night.

See, Jamie chose the Lakeview flat, so she could watch the sunset from the huge windows overlooking the lake, with the thick ivory curtains pulled to the sides. Sunset, as she relates it, helps clear the mind. Lakeview also afforded her the space to suntan right in front of our flat - In her briefest two-Piece French bikini, that barely cover her torso and the part of the body between the navel and the upper thighs, al fresco.

The gods must have cursed the night. Gusts of rain followed by thundering winds greeted me as I stepped out of the flat. I made it to my car and headed to work, which is just ten minutes away. I had to deal with the heavy rain and thunderstorms that tore across the windscreen of the car, as if the gods were really angry about the sins of the world; and that only those without sins, who pay heed, and who can make it to the 'Ark,' are exempt from the deluge. I made it to work all right, and that was when the fun started.

My arrival at work did not extricate me from my daydream or the retrospective-ness of it all. It may, in actuality, have heightened it. I was lucky to have made it to work safely; as short a distance as it was, I must have ran two or more traffic lights, with irate drivers shouting all kinds of unprintable things at me - And these were not slip of the tongue.

I was happy to fall into the comfort of the hotel-lobby-sofa, when Charlie's voice thundered from across the counter...

"Snap out of it, Nigel."

"'The year of the Angst!'" That's what he said, the year of the Angst." I said, in a state of shock. It was as if I had been in a state of denial all day. All of a sudden, resurrecting the memory of a cold-blooded killing I had witnessed, and the single statement of a killer that afternoon, the memory, which was totally obliterated by the jarring and odious moves of Jamie and all that her 'dear John note' contained.

'Who said?' Charlie interjected.

"The hired Killer, the man dressed in black," I shot back. Was this premonition or clairvoyance? No. I have never been a prognosticator. If not, what is then responsible for the reemergence of this particular memory at this time? Does it have anything to do with Jamie and her shock treatment? Was this an escapist move on my part? Why did I call him the 'Hired Killer?' What do I know about the man? What connection does he have with Charlie? I found it to be a *'Non sequitur.'*

"What about the year of the Angst?" Charlie persisted, the weight of my second statement not registering yet on him, unless he was just trying hard to avoid it, pretending not to have heard it. His body movements and his eyes betrayed his guise. Charlie knows more about the killer than he lets on, I thought.

I went on. "Okay, Charlie, the Year or Age of Angst, is believed to be the feverish millennium – where in an all-out apocalyptic realm of thinking - Nuke wars, rivers of blood, plague, pestilence, or the ever present threat of being invaded by aliens from outer space, becomes reality. This is a general view. There are those who have a slightly different interpretation." At this point my patience was running out and I wanted a response from Charlie about the 'Killer' and so I asked if he was trying to ignore me.

"The Hired killer, let's talk about him." Charlie stared at me, frozen in the harsh mechanics of my reproach. The words, the weight and mode of dispatch, he had never heard from me before. "The Hired Killer, let's talk about him."

If Charlie was trying to scare me, or inhibit my plans, vis-à-vis the 'Mysterious Killer,' I will say he was on the right track. His accounts about the 'Silent Guy,' as others call the killer, were chilling. This was not part of a regime I was used to. My past training did not sufficiently prepare me for the content of Charlie's story, and what was to follow. The surprise was that, I was still resolved, even after this frosty narration, to pursue this adventure, most analysts would consider futile.

I went against the grain. I became more assured in my conviction, that more knowledge about this killer was necessary. Because, before this point, my actions were based on emotion, never considered the lay of the landscape, the terrain and its actors. Future dangers were never factored into the matrix.

More than ever before, I was determined to get to the bottom of this story; and do something about it, anything, anything at all - Clues that would at least unearth the origin and the main characters of this unknown outfit; the genesis of the killings, and if a wrong had been committed, the rule of law allowed to take its due course.

Was history on my side? Not sure. I do not have any precedent to follow or consult. If time wasn't on my side, history will have to be my saving grace, or providence will have to align in my favor.

I was not to know that at this point, that my 'premonition' was right, that the 'Hired Killer' was just that, 'Hired.' That there were more powerful people behind him, benefactors, men who sit in deep chairs and have their fingers ready to press some color-coded buttons.

So, as one can already see, I will have to fight a two-prong war, and if I may say, two-prong wars are not the easiest to wage. They are full of unanticipated contingencies. The gadgets of the opposition, the gimmicks, the lies and Gila monster of the opposition - That single shapeless fog, which I will have to cut through to see the far beyond: the success of my mission, without sowing the seeds of my own destruction.

What I have to learn, I'll have to learn fast, for this project into which I have thrust myself without the requisite due diligence, not weighing the consequences and the realities of the purpose. I needed to be cognizant of one important fact, the fact that I am a one-time spy, and a one-time spy is just that, one-time-spy. He lacks the currency of the game, for the tools are ever evolving. I have to do research on the killer, his backers, and his quarries, especially those who will become expendable within the next forty-eight hours, in this frantic game, which I suspect is the handiwork of all those who stand to gain in maintaining a perpetual cold war or wars of any kind.

In this new game, the silent killer has an edge on me. He is current on all things, especially on gadgets and technique. Technology. He has been in the field, the past five years without a vacation. He knows the Quarry, I don't. That becomes the paramount thing to find out, giving it a-find-it-out fast code color.

The killer also has, to his advantage, the big machine and the sophisticated high-tech network of his benefactors. This requires infiltration, but by whom? How do I find a plausible mole? Find an operative who is willing to risk it all? This operation requires personal contact, live assets. Tracking his electronic footsteps won't be easy without triangulating their system.

More than anything else, his vicious and elusive method of operation makes the killer an adversary to not take lightly. I needed to act fast, and Charlie's story was becoming too long. Became too long. The enemy was gaining ground; I was marking time, entranced by Charlie's monologue.

"That guy across the street is the silent killer, everyone knows about him in the neighborhood, but no one dares come forward." I was shocked. The killer! That man across the street is the killer? What do you know? Perhaps I do have the power of premonition, after all. Why is all this happening now? What is responsible for the sudden resurrection of this memory?

I jumped up from my seat, and took a close look. Charlie was right. The man across the street, dressed in black, was the same monster I had seen earlier in the day, kill an innocent man in cold blood. I needed to remain calm. I also needed to take a systematic approach. Ask questions, many, but get answers. I need answers.

"What neighborhood?" I interrupted, trying to shorten his narration, and get him to the outcome, the main points. "I want specifics of a very short version, please. The luxury of time does not favor me." I was firm, but polite. Politeness never hurts. In most cases, it acts as the oil, to soften tight lips.

"The community of security agents, and if I am not mistaken, to which you, Nigel Peters, once belonged, in one capacity or the other." Charlie starts, but he forgets about my very long absence. In the game of espionage, which is called spying by others, currency is important in the secret intelligence service, for the tools and methods are regularly updated to meet with the cascading events of the new and improved world order, blinking into the light of day. I let Charlie continue.

"There is a new twist, a new and more sophisticated clan, a weapon for those who want to hide their illegal activities, at the expense of unsuspecting victims' lives. The prospect of a global rapport, a byproduct of the demise of the cold war, is making these people edgy. The killer is their mercenary. He became a gun for hire after he was purged from our special unit. These men found usefulness for his special skills.

They are now rearing their heads again, at times recklessly, in their zeal to protect and preserve the status quo. The oath they had taken to nurture a perpetual cold war remains nonnegotiable, until a replacement of equal value is found. This becomes absolutely necessary to feed their war frenzy and war machines, and by extension, their pockets and those of their immediate allies, while the resources for human-faced causes are neglected and mismanaged.

There is always a need to find a new enemy on their part. This need accelerated especially after the demise of the old monster, the evil empire that self-destructed, an old enemy now singing the tune of an ally.

From their point of view, there would always be a need to find new enemies, even those considered small players in the old scheme of things. This is a predetermined two-pronged approach on their part – it feeds their war machines, the military industrial complex, and it is politically expedient, say, in an election year. See, the populace is known, expected to rally behind their leader during major crisis, especially in wartime. I suspect that if the situation does not improve, I can see history repeating itself, in a scenario where internment and restriction of civil liberties could be employed. In a fascist mentality, without the brown uniforms."

His words were jarring, emit the eeriness of a graveyard at 3 a.m. Charlie was doing his best to scare me, or at least impress the gravity of this non-thought-out-adventure. I have been away from this cat and mouse game of waiting, worrying and intrigue, known as spying, for so long that I now consider myself a neophyte again. See, the tools and methods have undergone major makeovers - they have been refined and upgraded, as the field needs demand. There is so much I have to learn, so much to know, and new acquaintances to make, which is the most integral part of the game. Everything you have ever heard about the perils and pleasures of spying are true - The turf wars with diplomats, the failures, defections and defeats, and I need defections to my side.

I was not ready to concede, that this nation, a centrally good and attractive country, the single most important nation on earth, had fallen into a vulgar realm, ugly in spirit, encouraging every horror to rise from the sewer, a part of a plethora of pain inflicted upon it by the selfish benefactors. "If these dimensions are as dramatic as you claims," I asked, "then how come the intellectuals are not occupying the barricades?"

"They are all too apathetic." Charles said. "We live in a situation that is terribly confusing - Too much information to consume, from too many sources - e-mails, social networking and instant messaging. Doing much communication in many ways. It has brought information fatigue. No one really knows anymore who the true enemy is, or if we even have an enemy. Then there is the identity crisis. Do they really identify themselves with this society, the group that it had an impact on? Do they consider themselves part of us?"

"Isn't that the one reason, the most glaring excuse handed to them on a silver platter? Which is all that the intellectuals need to deal with these topical problems?" I retorted.

"They are all worn out. There's no fire out there any longer. Main reason I think we are headed towards fascism. Who will stop or block this free-fall? Forget about the intellectuals, they have been crippled by the internecine strife that divided them into groups, fighting the irregularities of the old order. It was the classic case of divide and rule method employed by the enemy that led to this defeat. They have never truly recovered from it." Charlie answered.

"So, whom do we turn to, if all the instruments of checks and balances are all in the hands of the enemy, possibly in burnt-out mode? Who does one turn to, to right wrongs and all the injustices of the society?" I asked.

"The problems are too extensive, too big for any one section of the community to grasp. We need more than segments of its parts. In the end, all we have is a single result: apathy, and nobody knows the solution anymore. Intellectual confusion ensues. The veneer has been broken; the intellectuals have been exposed for who they are, a group who once represented the bigger society from the middle, in the middle. They are now found out to suffer from self-righteousness, self-pity and a huge dose of hypocrisy, and the tendencies have gotten worse day to day. We see some of them complaining all the time... only no one listens to them, because they are now recognized for the whiners they are, or that they have become.

It is this that makes society realize that the nation never really had intellectuals — intellectuals who concerned themselves with social issues, without something in it for them...the few who did were not major players, not like the ones one finds in other societies of equal range of development like France for instance. In some instances, we find some intellectuals, even scientists are now hired to promote or skew research to benefit a corporate outfit - a new kind of corruption."

Charlie continued: "If I may hazard another guess again, I would say, doing otherwise tends to get in the way of research and research grants - If you are too angry about something, that is the quickest way to get pegged as a troublemaker. No more talk of research grants. No more invitations to punditry on the national evening news. So, when they write, they abide by the old maxim: a good book is written through irony, not through rage."

"Are you saying that the intellectuals are afraid or unwilling to touch controversial and socially relevant subjects, because that may affect their pocketbook and fame, that they decide developing into opportunists?" I cut in.

"It's still a free country, Nigel, you can make that accusation, and you might be right. It is just too hard for me to judge it, at this time.

As you know, I happen to be one of them, an intellectual, and I am in the middle of it. I can only assert from my own experience that it is harder and harder to say who the real enemy is."

"Come on Charlie, you know the consequences of this resignation! In a few decades, intellectuals of your ilk would become insignificant - accepted by society, spoiled, but without any influence?"

"Precisely, but there will be a good side to it, albeit selfish, that is, future serious intellectuals will work on projects they really enjoy, because that is what they really want to do, without having the illusions that they will make a living from it - unless they sell their expertise to the highest bidder, and it might just be to those small players in the old scheme of things, who are now daring to acquire the tools that made the former 'big bad boys' what they were. They will hark back to 'The metaphysical club, the Saturday night club of selfless doers, who meet to ponder the issues that affect the nation, and proffer, from their deliberations, solutions for the greater good."

"Okay, I like the idea of the Saturday club gentlemen, God knows we need that, but my question is, what will the culture develop into with these symptoms, without the intervention of those that fit the mold of the metaphysical club?' I was very much intrigued by the dimensions of what Charlie was suggesting...

He was quick in responding: "Into a hideous culture of television, videos games, facsimile, voicemail, and computers, both mobile and embedded in mobile devices like cell telephones, the ones called smart phones: all impersonal gadgets – we have arrived at that state, and the results are visible. If you live with a goat all the time and this goat just 'baa-ed' in your face all the time, all the time, all the time, after a while you would become rather stupid yourself, and you would act like a goat as well. These gadgets are turning our kids into non-learners and slackers."

"Are you saying that this society is turning into a nation of sheep?" The thought exasperated me. He was talking to a diehard patriot, who was not ready to concede the goodness of this fine nation to the enemies of good. I stared at him awaiting his answer.

"Goat, sheep, whatever word you use; either way: a dull beast. Yes, yes, the society is less attractive than it used to be. The people are getting leveled out." He responded with equal seriousness...and the more I talked to Charlie, the more I realized he knows a lot more than he is telling me, because Charlie has never been this vocal about the ills of the society and those at the vanguards of reforms - the checks and balances players.... it was scary, but I had to know more, because there were questions begging to be answered...

"Okay, Charlie, enough of that already, if you, a symbol of the old intellectual social critic, now claim that that entity is as attractive as worn out furniture, what hope remains that others of your ilk won't start to think the same way?"

"If it's of any satisfaction to you, you may as well know that, I never did relate well with those you so eloquently equate me with. I don't draw hope from them, but as odd as it seems, from another source: the end of the cold war, yes, the end of the cold war is going to introduce some very interesting problems for our economic system that demand a fundamental reassessment because the nation's economic system has lost a dear old friend," Charlie said flatly.

"Wait a minute, you sly devil, are we thinking about the same thing here, the old monster, the big bad Bear, the evil empire enemy, the war machine it helped create and its attendant largess fueled corruption?" I asked.

"Exactly. The campaign against the 'the evil empire' kept us knit together a little more tightly than our natural inclination, and now that this pressure from outside is no longer there, we are on our own and there are going to be growing disagreements.... It's not as simple as Adam Smith versus Karl Max anymore. The war-machine spewing greenback period is gone, and it is making the benefactors very edgy. Nigel, my old friend..." Charlie's voice trailed off for a moment...

Charlie continued. "Don't tell me that, that is the man you're planning to case and confront." The change of subjects was sudden and direct. It was in the mold of a shock treatment. It sounded more like a warning than a question.

"That man is known by different names and faces in the community. The 'Assassin.' The 'Paid killer.' - And other more esoteric names. There're some aliases he uses only as a diversionary tactic, the classic misdirection. The fact that ordinary citizens like me could publicly state that they witnessed his exploits, even to the point of naming him, would create havoc, to a level unprecedented in the annals of secret service due to other 'players' that could be smeared. Whenever anything close to that has happened, he just simply moved up his schedule a notch."

Charlie continued: "He is the lord of the community - he is the hired killer. I saw him shoot a man between the eyes on a bright sunny day, in the presence of spectators and walk away cold-bloodedly." This did not come as a surprise. I had also witnessed it first hand, albeit unknown to Charlie, but I needed to play the role, the role of someone who needs answers to many questions. In an environment like this, playing dumb gains more yardages.

"Get out of here," I said

"Get out of Town," Charlie responded with equal sarcasm.

"I don't get it! Are you saying you saw that man in black kill somcone?" Was it John Buchanan who said: 'The success of playing a part is to put yourself into it?' This needed all of me, but I could no more check myself than if I were resisting an urge to vomit in this supposedly self-renewing period of compromise and doublethink. I needed to externalize the secret affinity between the new age, and me, and assert my enhanced understanding of this emerging new order, what it stands for and the nature of its ultimate triumph. To be at the center, and not shoved to the bleachers where I had been for so long. No more sitting by, watching the wheels spin. No more standing by and watching other people live. For once in my life I would take a stand, a stand for good against evil, a stand for wholesome humankind activities - painted all over with human faces - yes, that's going to be my new motto! The one I hope will jumpstart me to action.

Charlie clasped his hands together. He sets them, still clasped, on the desk to indicate, whether I like it or not, he was still speaking.

'Yes," responded Charlie. He then rubbed his chin, his expression rueful but undefeated. He turned to me again.

"Do you know that psychiatrists from the opposing camp, during the war, assembled a rather disturbing profile of that man? What they found was a serious strain of controlled instability. There is a paper out on that subject, Nigel, please read it." Charlie was overrunning himself and couldn't stop.

'Do you know that that man made the most subtle pass at my wife the last time he was here? I don't begrudge him for that, my God no, she is a beautiful woman. What I mean is, this man is everywhere without being anywhere. He is all over the place, without being at any place. His cool and subtlety, his disappearing acts and the so-called infrequency of presence is just a veneer. Unless he has people who double for him. When he speaks, his voice is as cold as clarity and as late in arriving. I have always assumed that all businesspersons are crooks, especially those who stray into the espionage realm for the money, but this guy is an oddity. He's a stone killer, a very cold-blooded one."

He glanced around, as if to make sure the 'killer' was not within earshot. I figured there is just too much inside him and that he needed to put it somewhere. It was no excuse. So I said:

"Tell me my name is still Nigel Peters, and you're Charlie Hughes, and that you're not pulling my leg?"

"Yes, Mr. Peters, anything else, 'Sire,' for I've work to do.' Charlie sputtered, while gathering his pens and pencils for the night's audit. Charlie had never talked so much, not about so heavy a subject, anyway. I felt he was doing it all for my sake. Trying to ply me to the straight and narrow road, which leads to infinite life, but would I listen...

"It's unreal, it's illegal and it's a crime, no matter which way you phrase it, no one has the right to walk to another and shoot him through the eyes, no matter what time of day it is. The man needs to be behind bars, or worse." I was not done yet, I continued.

"Very soon, the young men and women of our armed forces who took part in the wars, will be coming home. It's not going to be the same. Questions will be asked. The tone of questions will indicate - an immediate response needed. They would indicate by words or actions that their patience has run out. Because they, and the rest of us want the dividends from the war we fought and won."

"It is here, the old guard, in its infinite wisdom will endeavor to throw a protective shield over its investments and secrets. Because someone has just thrown a spanner in the machinery they have constructed, and have in motion. That is what you're really saying, isn't it Charlie?" There was a long pause, and Charlie looked up at me, in an almost melancholic state, he said:

"There are those who would lose from the stability that prevails, those who profit from a nurtured cold war or any other war, who are now caught flat-footed and not knowing what to do; not knowing how to act or react. It is a period of inertia, the silent killer is their only hope, can't you see? You have not been listening to me, Nigel. They have to keep those they want silent, silent." What is Charlie talking about, I asked myself. Keep those they want silent, silent? Are they playing God here? What gives anyone the right to play God? When whatever is going on is more than halfway the fault of their game of deceit and double talk - Impostors manufactured in media labs.

"I bet if they had not been an elitist society passing as an egalitarian entity they would not have to worry about any of this. Charlie, the new society wants actions with a human-face. There is enough for everyone, enough to go around. It was for them to win, and it was for them to lose. They chose to lose."

"They are caught in their own web. Like the spider and the miniature boulders, and the task of making sure they remain as they are, as against being removed by the opposition - See, the spiders need the pebbles and miniature boulders for anchor and maneuverability. They have to be removed to make their logistics inoperable." I wasn't quite sure Charlie followed my logic, but he was bent on educating me as to the Silent Killer, a subject he apparently knew more about than he earlier acknowledged - He continued:

"When the Hired Killer came to the neighborhood, as a green recruit in the spy-game - no one expected him to become this dominant, as in an all-time all-timer. He worked his way up, learning and improvising - finessing, but not saying much. Others said he brought a better knowledge of the art to the neighborhood: the agency; along with they say, multiple athletic skills. He can run and shoot - knows when to shoot, when to draw the quarry, how to get his rest and at the same breath, find time for total privacy. He matured! At his own pace."

"He embodied the reputation of intelligence men for high living, and was a student of the female form divine. In the beginning, he worked exclusively with beautiful female spies, who he deployed to lure enemies into spilling their secrets, in this powerful instrument in the early struggle against fascism and bolshevism.

"One on One, he's the best in the world. If there is any part of his game plan or totality I would like to integrate into mine, it would be what he does at clutch situations - Improvisations of split second make." Charlie was impressive, but I needed more.

"Charlie, I am sure that reasons abound for wanting to reduce this burden of unnecessary conflict, because as a student of history, I am sure you also know that the mechanics of these unnecessary conflicts are expensive and difficult to engineer. The difficulties are further compounded, if the opposing sides require that the methods of operation, which the hired killer totally ignores, be accomplished through explicit mutual agreement - that delicate nuanced arrangement in the operational 'Workbook,' for every nut and bolt, an ABC of Do's and Don'ts of espionage."

I was not so sure if my diplomatic analysis was consistent, or for that matter, appropriate to the ongoing discussion. I was resolute in my determination to downplay the prowess of the 'Hired Killer,' and the expectations of his Benefactors - the men behind the veil - that thick screen of deceit. So I continued to play the part of the pseudo political pundit, commenting on what attitude may be necessary to win in the new age, the age of the emerging world order, and how I saw what needs to be done and what may be expected from the pseudo egalitarians, those now wounded lions.

"Listen up Charlie" I said, "we have all experienced the changing trends; the frantic and cascading political order, the dizzying pace of the unfolding events. Those who are able to adapt will survive. History has shown that. The thing is, these benefactors have lost the ability to adjust subtly to this unanticipated changes, Charlie, and their own contradictions have caught up with them, the totality of their being, leaving them to go on view, in their true colors. Their exposure has led to a substantial decline in status. Increasingly, they come across obstacles of unanticipated nature, and they are unable to react effectively. They are in the new era, the Emerging Society. The only option left to them is change or find themselves following the popular trammeled path of their past pathetic minions." I continued:

"Naturally, since it is not in their nature to do so, they would resort to such boisterous acts of Saber rattling, confusing logic and other diversionary tactics hoping to fool the people once again, admonishing a demonstrative need to stop all unconscionable acts on either side, which in essence, is another desperate act to deceive – they would devise new slogans, and even champion the call - 'Freedom for all'."

Since they believe, the people have short memory, and not as savvy as they are, they may even start preaching and asking people to aspire to noble aspirations and a desire to be good. They would condemn the relentless rivalry to dominate. They would ask people to eschew greed and embrace selflessness, all because the media men said it is now fashionable to do so, because it might win votes and sell more products."

"Charlie, my good friend, I hope you do not take offense at my ongoing analyses. My intentions are genuine and honest. All I want to prove is that the 'Killer,' as you call him, is expendable, as are his Benefactors; everyone has his or her insecurities. Eventually, his Benefactors will have to get rid of him because he would have known too much. They just cannot afford to live under his ghost for the rest of their lives. The only alternative to all participants is this resolve I touched on earlier, which is now being accommodated by his benefactors, the resolve to aim for noble aspirations, a desire to be good, taking the air out of this relentless rivalry to dominate and pursue the credo of greed and selfishness."

"To be in this game, one has to be a strategist and these men are strategists, and Strategists are trained to be astute and perceptive, with a knack for seeing beyond the immediate. Thinking long term and global - not small minds." I continued –

"We are at the end of a tumultuous decade and the beginning of a new Age. New power blocks are formed, are being formed. Its an emerging era that wants actions, again, actions with human face on them." It was definitely my turn to gloat over my knowledge of these changing times. I was not done yet. I continued:

"As I indicated earlier, those with the ability to adapt, the ones able to step outside of themselves and grasp the broad historical sweep and significance of this epoch times, are welcome to this next stage of human history, provided they are able to seize this perspective beckoning in the horizon, and not contrive to destroy themselves first. Viral clips, news, have made it possible to stream, be picked up, and disseminate information like at no other time. Reaching more people for ill or for good. Sometimes able to deceive easily - Wearing an image that has underneath, the total opposite."

We were so engulfed in our talk, and me, earlier transfixed by Charlie's talk on the killer, had streams of cold sweat trickling down my spine, we did not hear the entrance of the stocky man, dressed in black, walk in. He had a Catlike girt about him. Yes, I must agree, he really does exude fear.

The Philosopher

I found myself unable to unfold this beguiling story of non-belief. Non-belief because I do not believe that anyone has the right to shoot a defenseless human straight between the eyes, in front of spectators, without the full weight of the law applied to right the apparent crime or total disregard for justice. To say I was being turned in two would not be sufficient to describe my mood. A part of me is saying to back off, while the other is saying: "you cannot chicken out now, Nigel." I became progressively drawn to the latter, and ventured deeper and deeper into Charlie's account of the exploits of the Hired Killer.

Each feature of his face was refined and each coordinated with the whole, producing a striking, yet cold demeanor. He had almost rectangular eyes, their gaze steady. They were the eyes of a confident animal that portrays the owner to have a quick and unpredictable response. His sculptured head, covered with a glistening crown of blond hair, reflected the light of the overhead lamps, producing the appearance of a pale-yellow ice.

His walk was measured, sending out signals of strength and precision. He looked at me with an emotionless quick glance, producing unease – what does he know about me? I worked to keep my mouth from drying, and keeping my outside appearance as pokerfaced as possible - I looked at Charlie and saw that he wasn't faring any better - and realized I couldn't depend on him for support.

"I believe I have a reservation here," he uttered and pushed an American Express black card towards Charlie. For once, I was glad that I was not the one on the other side of the Counter, and that I could observe them both without giving too much of myself away. My inner turmoil would have shown through, would have been an easy giveaway. This is a guy who uses fear as the key. It is obvious that he employs the element of fear to intimidate his opposition. A strange feeling crept through me; it was as if this guy was already onto me before I even started. I had to convince myself that my fear bordered on paranoid logic, that it is the tediousness that comes with believing in delusion.

At that moment, I resisted the temptation to throw out names, things, some trial balloons, to get some reactions, which under the circumstances would be suicidal; so I took consolation in the fact that, logistically, I was positioned to view him without making it too obvious. The acoustics also favored me.

Meanwhile, all sorts of thoughts ran through my mind - possible scenarios and plausible action plans. Unlike in the case of the classicist and the bull, there's no laid down script. I have to learn and upgrade my game as I go along. The killer is not an ordinary adversary.

"Yes, Mr. Delaney, we do have a suite for you," Charlie responded, I must say with some stutter, as he handed 'Mr. Delaney' the key to his suite. I watched him walk to the elevator and out of sight. A relief came over Charlie. Everything had gone well, considering the unexpected nature of the elusive killer's visit.

"Now, do you see what you are going against, Nigel?" It was time for Charlie to gloat, "You have to balance your perspectives, I hope bright lights, big city aren't affecting your concentration. What happened to that integrated individual I knew?"

"Now, Charlie, I am not sure how much of that endorsement I deserve; appearances can be deceptive you know." This was said more to slow down Charlie than anything else. First, I have been out of the game for so long, there got to be some rustiness. Then, what does he know about the integration of body parts – or of body and soul? What makes him an expert all of a sudden? What is he really hiding? He has said a lot, more than I had bargained for, but has not really provided me with pertinent information - what I want to know right now – operational information on the so-called killer. Charlie was not to be denied this opportunity to rub it in.

"Nigel, you have to realize that everything has its proper place in the grand scheme of things." What does that have to do with anything? Why don't he just come out with it? Injecting Aristotle or Galileo was of no import to me as we stand here. All I need are answers. Charlie was not done. He continued.

"I do not know what exactly you are trying to accomplish here, in this foolhardy project of yours. One thing you need to know is that there is no absolute reality or for that matter, absolute anything, all things are relative in the grand scheme of things; the only permanent reality is not in the individual but in the death. This game you are injecting yourself into without proper preparation, I may add, is as old as time, and it will continue long after you and I are gone. Be careful Nigel. Don't be a martyr." This was getting too heavy. Charlie was doing his best to prepare me for what lay ahead – the perils and especially the pitfalls. I was shocked by his concern, but it impressed me. This was another side of Charlie I had not known, a new Charlie.

Charlie was dogged; he was like a kid with a new toy, he knew he was making an impression, and he was going for closing the deal, and the rest of the neighborhood kids would have to salivate and beg to touch this wonder machine because it took him forever to persuade mama and papa to procure it.

He continued. "Now, let me return to that perverted and convoluted theory about the year or age of angst, if ever there was one. Angst, as you know, is an affliction of fear or anxiety, has origins in Germany – could have to do with activities during the wars they initiated, but the angst thing came into general consciousness in the mid-eighteenth century. The present realm of thought, again, if ever there was one, never did categorize angst as a syndrome, valued officially. Mass angst, is generally believed to have happened between 1914 and 1945. Left to me, I would say it is a concoction of a sick and depraved mind, Nigel. It never happened."

I had to demure. I then politely said: "That was quite good, Charlie, I never knew you could put words together like that, not to talk of intellectualizing an idea so succinctly as you just did; without the accountant in you taking control. You could've saved the tirades; I'm not a believer in the angst thing, as you called it. I was merely repeating what I heard or eavesdropped on."

"In that case, be careful information gleaned from eaves dropping, gotten out of context, that has possibly much of the meat or body missing, giving out false impressions. Please, don't broach or consider the utility of information without it fully researched or vetted. Could create future problems." He said, almost inaudibly, as if out of breath after a hill climb. I thought he must have fallen back into one of his melancholic moods. I was mistaken. Charlie was only feeling pity for me, not understanding my avowed need to confront the 'Hired Killer.'

"Why Nigel? Why this elusive killer of all people." This was a complete turn around. Charlie's reluctance to discuss the Killer has segued into an unbridled enthusiasm to try to save me from what he considers an untenable adventure. Was this new tact his genuine concern for my wellbeing? Is there something more sinister, lurking underneath that Charlie is not telling me? All I could do was shake my head in answer to his question, not knowing what to say. Am I too absorbed to focus on what's in front of me? Is this preoccupation an outgrowth of Jamie's shock treatment - my escapism, and to what unknown?

If only Charlie knew what I felt at this particular moment, a feeling of pure relief, a paradoxical one. It is the kind of relief one experiences after being spat out of the mouth of a Dragon and landing on a bed of feathers, the superhuman exhilaration of being shot at and missed. I have just come face to face with the Hired Killer without any apparent giveaway of my intentions. Have I gleaned anything from this initial contact? Did it make me the wiser? They say what makes us wise also makes us rich. Am I richer by this experience, or am I running out of imagination?

This whole thing is eating at me, and I am trying very hard to not let it run away from me; but it keeps feeling like a Chinese water dropper, dropping and eating away at my conscience, egging me on to do something - and the ghost-face of the helpless man killed earlier in cold blood, while begging for mercy, is the Chinese water dropper....

How can I possibly explain my obsession with 'Mr. Delaney' to Charlie, without giving too much away? Charlie is my best friend and confidant all right, but the Killer has an affect on people. Charlie, the new 'Philosopher,' tends to talk too much. He also likes Cabernet Sauvignon and beautiful women, just like the 'Hired Killer.' This is my predicament. It is easy to say what red blooded man doesn't like good wine and beautiful women? The catch is - that may turn out to be the ultimate caveat, when the killer decides to trap either of us, or get to me. This is a risk I can ill afford at this nascent stage of my plans.

In a much somber demeanor, more than I had wanted to display, I said – "There is so much going on I do not know, there's so much I may never know, there's so much I would like to know, but answers are not easy to come by."

"What was that?" Charlie asked.

"I was just thinking aloud." I responded. Which was the truth; I was caught expressing my private thoughts in words. It came out sounding like a statement, a statement one makes when invited to a funeral, in a symphony of mixed emotions. At the end - you want to know that proper protocols had been followed through and through. No faux pas of any kind. Especially when sensitivity is an issue.

"I bet if he had told you to lay an egg, you would've asked what color?" That was a low blow, even from Charlie. Because I figured he might have been trying to lighten the atmosphere, my response was not as caustic.

"That's not true, Charlie.' That was that. Charlie's worn out cliché did not merit more than that. It is always easy for those on the outside looking in to have a wrong interpretation of a situation and become prisoners of speculations, just as those inside looking out are not immune from the same vice. I was not ready to engage Charlie in this cliché-infested line. I have to think. Any question I pose to Charlie would have to produce necessary insights into how to approach this task.

The calm and deliberate manner in which I handled myself during the brief but captivating meeting with the so-called Mr. Delaney, elicited praise from Charlie. He thought I was stealthy, even while I was obviously out there.

"I must say you exhibited an incredible sense of subtlety, and if I may say more, I believe it will aid you and be a good tool in your endeavor."

"Thank you, Charlie, I may need your help as I go forward; but in this particular instance, the sheer desire to succeed, and a desire to right a wrong is the main driver of my emotions. I have to rein in any undue outbursts or unnecessary pronouncements, including actions of a physical nature." I said, pleading for his help.

"I will try my best to provide you with the bits I know. Be careful, my dear friend. This is not an ordinary adversary." Charlie advised.

"Again, thank you Charlie. I will take that to heart. Especially because of the uniqueness of the opposition and his benefactors, who dress up human savagery in ideological uniforms." I said.

"Just be sure this is not motivated by a desire to block out your own pains or fears, by taking on other people's problems. Try not to make everything out to be a conspiracy. Be sure it is from the guts and you truly believe in the mission, that this really has nothing to do with Jamie's shock treatment – otherwise the psychological aftermath might not align well, for all concerned, including me."

"I am mindful of all that, Charlie," I said.

"Just be careful"

"Come on, Charlie, enough of the 'be careful stuff,' I thought I just laid it out, my plan the approach and all I need to do. I do not want to discuss the problems; I want to focus on solutions - all which would help me as I go forward. I don't care about anything else, and your 'be careful' admonition is starting to bug me, if you do not know what a bug is, I will spell it out for you, a distraction, someone who may become my Judas, a mole, a stoolie, take your pick, I am getting tired of your questions and no answers, I wonder if you are not already a paid traitor." I exploded on Charlie. I appreciate his concerns and they are valid, but he is still to provide me with any valuable knowledge about the killer.

"That is a jaundiced view, Nigel. It is preposterous for you to even think of me in those terms. You should be ashamed. If you must know, I wasn't trying to be smart Alec about anything. My concerns for your wellbeing, moreover mine, since I would make some contribution, in kind or otherwise. I need to make sure I am not putting my ass or that of anyone associated with me in jeopardy or thrust into the vortex of viral media. These are the only drivers. I just want to be sure, that's all." Charlie said; trying his best not to sound like the picture I had painted of him - of a possible Judas. He was eager to explain his motivation in all of this.

"My first impression after listening to you was to assume that you might be seeking a dramatic end, the so-called Hollywood ending. Knowing you, one has to expect anything, and it could be anything. If you really want to know something, I will tell you, I hate when people try to over dramatize a situation, people who try at every chance to make technical every buzz word that jumps at them." It did not make sense. I have not done what he is accusing me of – he must be confusing me with another person. I was concerned about the direction this was all going. So I said.

"What are you accusing me of, Charlie?" I asked, exasperated at the implied insult, though maintaining equilibrium. He truly believes what he is saying.

"I am not accusing you of anything, Nigel. I must warn you about a familiar habit, one of your habits, and which I had just noticed. When you talk shop with others of your ilk, knock your socks off. Just don't try to be too elitist."

"Elitist? You call me elitist, I'll tell you what elitism is - I'll say the most elitist thing is to hold your audience in contempt, like when you use some of those accounting terms of yours, which sound more like Einstein's E=Mc2, when simple terms will do."

In fairness to Charlie, I must admit that I do have the habit of verbalizing my thoughts in solitary strategizing sessions. What I always take to be a by-myself-mode, forgetting sometimes that others are within earshot. I talk things out during these periods. I had just had a replay right after the departure of the killer. Charlie's response was quick.

"Spare me the dramatics, Nigel; you are way off this time, that was definitely a bad answer, more like an invitation to a stroll in the mud. Being smart Alec isn't going to cut it, get serious about this adventure of yours. These are just some wise words from one friend to another - Whether you still take me as a confidant or not, I am your friend and I do not intend to betray your trust. The Hired Killer is a formidable adversary, please reassess your priorities and don't let Jamie do this to you." I have never known Charlie to be cryptic, either by nature or by profession. People, even friends, say the strangest things in the heat of an argument.

"Charlie, time and resources may not be on my side, but I do believe history is. I also believe the killer and his Benefactors have more to worry about than I do. As the eminent poet-playwright-statesman, once said, a system such as the one propagated by the hired killer and his benefactors is: 'Essentially doomed to become finally the victim of its own lethal principle and mechanics…thanks to the absence of any impulse within its own structure, that could, as it were, make it face up to itself…in trying to paralyze life … paralyze themselves, in the long run, incapacitate themselves…It may be a long process, but one day it must happen: The lid will no longer hold and will start to crack.' That is what he said, Charlie. I could not have said it better, my good friend… we should not give credence to freakishness masquerading as originality, nor enthusiasm pretending to be vitality."

Charlie remained solemn and speechless, I hoped because he knew the gentleman-scholar was right. Who could ignore history, without paying a price? Charlie is a philosopher; and he is my friend…He conveyed seriousness through his face. The face and his behavior, I have always trusted. Generally you get in these fights, and you can't pick your allies. If you had to pick an ally, then Charlie was a perfect person.

It was definitely reassuring to know that I still had my best friend in my corner. Besides, I cannot afford to make new enemies, nor lose a valuable friend, who has served as a source of rationalization of the immediate unknown. Charlie is a good friend. There are times, and I am sure it has happened to anyone who has had a best friend, when I do not know what I could have done without him. His distractions and sometime nagging questions do help modulate some of my extreme devised method of operation. The rare circumstance, when a word of caution from a trusted friend, combined with your subconscious, act as a protective shield in barbed situations.

"Nigel?"

"Yes, Charlie.'"

"Just remember, Life's never always the way you want it to be, but what it is, and what you make out of what the universe serves you.

It's just the way it is, always has been - it's the true essence of being. The best songs usually come from every day life - because life makes songs." Charlie philosophized.

"Thank you, Charlie - But let us remember, that in the end, in a more primordial sense, what motivates all of us is that comparative edge, that little advantage that keeps us going and sane - Cultures may differ from here to there, but we all do things for one reason, yes, for one singular reason and nothing else - which is mostly for self-preservation; and as our self-consciousness evolves, we become, might become seekers of balance, truth, fairness – it is then that we might seek to more fully inhabit our lives and the world in which we live them, and hoping that if we more fully inhabit these things, we might be less likely to destroy what we have taken so much interest in preserving. At the end of the day, Charlie, we all have the same wants - Family, happiness, love and money, yes money, that all encompassing green paper and all the same insecurities and anxieties that come with life, living – they may not necessarily be in that order, but that is life, in a very short presentation." I continued.

"To me, at this particular moment, the only absolute reality in an agent's life is that; it is better to over estimate your enemy than to under estimate him or her. It is here that it also becomes essential to watch out for nuances, the indiscreet remarks, that little slip, the one that escapes so fast most people miss it. They are the ones that make or break assignments - The ones that bring down most giants, who are infected with hubris, thinking they were born with Teflon shields. My goal now is to search for that weak spot, the soft heels of the benefactors and their agent, Mr. Delaney, if that is really his true name, and expose in strong terms their toxic inflated sense of entitlement and the distorted sense of priorities."

"You have it all figured out, eh?" Charlie cuts in. What does he mean? Has he been listening to me? I paused, and seriously considered what Charlie had just said. It has been all innuendos, questions and no answers. Does everything really have a price? Can Charlie be bought? Can I fully trust him? It begs for me to develop calm in the presence of all the confusion. I put aside these nagging questions and answered Charlie.

"I am not sure what you mean, Charlie. But, I do know that these guys are impervious to the logic of reason, but sensitive to the logic of fear. Concerning the search for their weak spots, it is axiomatic, opportunity favors the prepared mind – and luck is the man who did his homework. In this case, a good opposition research on the enemy would go a long way in actualizing the objective. I may want to add at this point that as organized and integrated as you may think I am, for the most part, I'm still trying to learn more about myself, aimed at finding out who I am, why I am here, where I'm going and what my responsibilities are - to humanity, to the world." I said to Charlie.

Charlie was quiet, so I continued.

"I have never strived to predict the future, Charlie, if anything, I loath punditry - the chattering class, especially the Sunday parade of talking heads and their ilk, who may or may not truly know what they are talking about, but who on the other hand, try to make us believe that one shoe fits all, and that their words are coming from a divine source. What I do allow myself - as events unfold, is act and comment, in a modulated, hopefully in a balanced and impartial tone, on the moments, and hope that maybe clues from them might give insights to the future, and possibly answers to some elusive contemporary problems. Again here, you allow the listener to connect the dots and find answers without any dogmatic influence from me – no black and white rationalization, for there are many shades in between. It's how to keep the eyes down, Charlie, even when you're looking at the sun, a 'John Q. Public,' if ever there was one. A John Q. Public, who wants to make a difference with less trumpet,"

Charlie allowed me to go on without interruption. I took it to mean he had respect for what I was saying. I went on.

"I tell myself: 'Nigel, you're a smart guy, you got to be here for some reason, right? – Put here to make some contribution, in whatever measure, in whatever capacity to uplift humankind - using your smarts and creative wherewithal to do good – human-faced deeds.' These are the thoughts, questions I wrestle with that never seem to go away. On another dimension, there is this other question about whether I am doing enough, about the possibility that I could end up like one of those geniuses who become brutishly famous in death? Would I have to slice off my ear to get attention, mimicking some recent historical fellows who revert to slicing off their ears in desperation, because no one took notice of their creations, dying in poverty from the neglect and scorn of an ungracious fellow-countrymen; who, in a twist of perverted irony later reap millions from their works in death?" "Do I need that fifteen minutes or is it fifteen-seconds of fame to be able to achieve my goals and the common good? Hoping that when mine comes, the fifteen minutes that is; it is tremendously, positively, ecumenically with enough bangs for the efforts. If by chance the fifteen minutes or seconds make a substantial difference - that's not too much to ask, is it? I know what you might be thinking; that this is a contradiction, no, no, no, this is not a contradiction – this is neither out of the left field or right field. It is just what it is - An organic, hopefully holistic approach to dealing with issues of such nature and magnitude." Charlie was still quiet, so I went on.

"So Charlie, my good friend, I do intend to go after the killer; if only to satisfy my conscience. Please be reassured, it's not an ego trip as you earlier insinuated. Here, I must also add that I can use all the help I can get from you; what you might offer, if only as an information bank, as the guy who has an ear to the ground, for me. Who knows, we might just share those fifteen minutes together my dear friend, as long as it is for humankind deeds, for this new and improved world order. You never know, you just never know, Charlie, my good friend."

Again, there was no response from Charlie, and I took his solemn and blank look for an affirmation. Hoped I was right.

The Professor's Insights

It was early dawn. A warm fog hung over the graveled driveway of the Excelsior, leading to the 'B' parking area. The late fall humid air of the Big Easy was no help as I walked in this semi darkness. I needed to think, clear my head. I needed to think this whole thing through, after the lecture from Charlie and my longwinded response. The question becomes, what line of approach should I take? Should I recruit other allies besides Charlie? Does the killer have vulnerabilities I can exploit? I remembered Dr. Fell, Chair, Political Science Department, U.N.O. I was his Research Assistant for two and a half semesters. I once came to him with a project I was working on, and sought an appropriate approach. He responded with his usual question for question approach, that makes you think harder, thinking how foolish you were in first place for asking the obvious. I remember Dr. Fell asking me, in these words: "What is the difference, in essence or morality, between the all encompassing anarchic criminality of the artist, which is endemic in all fine creative minds, and the artistry of the criminal?"

I was expecting, hoping for a straight answer, and he gave me his usual question for question response, and the only response I thought was appropriate was a vigorous protestation as I can muster – mind you, appropriately delivered in jest, so as not to appear confrontational.

"That won't do prof.' I responded. 'Can't accept that, I'm afraid. You thesis contains too many long words, sorry about that," I joked, even as I realized his drift. He, as usual, never got my joke, or may have just decided to educate me some more for my irreverence. Then the professor continued to expand more on his thesis - About the folly of blind trust and assumptions, about human behavior vis-à-vis the state and its machines.

He said: "Hell Nigel, the cardinal point to remember here is that we're all licensed criminals – corrupt as hell, but preaching to the rest of world about fiscal responsibility and corrupt practices, while unable to rein in our own excesses. That's what I'm trying to tell you. What is our racket? Do you know what our racket is? I will tell you. It is that we place our larcenous natures at the service of the state. Which invariably turns around and blackmail us, taking advantage of our gullible nature. The gist is this, why should you feel different about the protagonist, just because he got the mix a little bit wrong? Nothing has changed except you both landed on different sides of the fence."

"Got you prof., I must admit I truly get the essence of what you are trying to say. It is about individual responsibility and the consequences of our actions. In this case, the decision is his and the repercussion he should be able to accept – which is not too different from, as you sowed so shall you reap. Which is appropriately about karmic influences. That is, if he decided to cut it and run. Leaving his wife, kids and work, and just step into the blue, the unthinkable. Only problem is the protagonist is not a very thoughtful man presently. Amazing, just amazing prof., thanks a bunch.'

I took off. Happy. Thinking that the professor is the most analytical mind I know able to break complicated subjects into simple perspectives. Now, the only thing is, the professor is not here to act as my sounding board. Should I go above or below the line? The professor once said that in every operation there is an above the line and below the line move. Above the line, he said is 'when you do it by the book.' Below the line is 'how you do the job.' How do I do this job when I can't even agree on the right approach and tools? My long inactivity in the game of spying, espionage or covert operations, whatever name you want to call it, has taken its toll.

After the walk and meditation, I headed back inside, to the air-conditioned suite of the CEO, who is out somewhere in Europe this time of year. What happened next should go into history, if not the larger history of the killer's affair, then at least into my own exasperating personal chronicle of seeing everything with perfect vision and being repeatedly haunted by my past – and they have not been pleasant. This time, it came in what I would call a welcome interloper – and when memory is viewed as pain, one does whatever is necessary to help the healing process. And since memory is not easy to forget, you try harder, because you know you must forget, because memory is pain – haunting, poignant and evocative – if the basis is always true, the emergence of an interloper, especially of a pleasant nature becomes a welcome development...because in this sphere, memory is in abundant supply...and the more the memory, the more the pain...and life is simpler with less memories...and there is a time under the heavens for every purpose....

Michelle: An Erotic Interlude, An Unlikely Ally

It is said that cultured people use defensive weapons to be prepared for the unexpected. And flexibly adapting to time and change will make them rise above the unexpected. With this in mind, I took a no questions asked, no excuses, no apologies and definitely no explanation posture with Michelle, a take it or leave it, combined with strength in balance – because I needed the scenario in front of me to play out, as someone being careful of virtues, but who builds up the small to lofty grandeur. The shock of seeing Michelle in the CEO's suite was of such magnitude, that this was the only logical approach I could think appropriate. So many things raced through my mind. Memories – lusts and fantasies suppressed, because

Michelle was Jamie's best friend - Am I going to experience those fantasies never experienced because of Jamie?

The more I looked at Michelle, and her body expressions, it became evident I would experience all of them from this ex-placid beauty, now turned seductress; whom I used to shun and not shun - who would turn me on and never really turned me on. It was a paradox I never was able to reconcile until now - a diversion, not an improvement, a temptation, and a peril. I needed this temptation.

Michelle is a beautiful Chicagoan, who deemphasized her beauty by the activities she got involved in, in a turn-on, turnoff routine. The ultimate adventurous woman, she prefers navigational outfits, with legs that would make any man the true animal he really is.

As it became, it was in Michelle, the most unlikely source that I would find all that I needed to know about the Hired killer. Although it has been some few years since I last saw her, the memory was still fresh. I remembered the accolades Michelle heaped on me to get my attention, and how she sometimes coerced my affection. See, Michelle was Jamie's best friend, and Jamie was a very jealous lady, and made sure Michelle and any of her other friends understood that I was neither for sale nor for hire. To Michelle, it was not much of a deterrent, because, the Chicago in Michelle never cared much for the New Orleans in Jamie. So at any chance she got; when Jamie was not around, she did what she had to do - All blamed on the Chicago in her - because, in her words, you have to make a distinction between the act and the historical perspective or you lose the rationale.

So, of all the hotels in the big easy, Michelle chose the Excelsior as her nesting ground, for a two week working 'vacation', which by its nature, timing and the dynamics of prevailing circumstances, turned me into an accidental tourist, because I needed her like I had never needed anyone before, in a situation of using the past to effect a cure for the present.

Even with the vortex going on within, I made an effort, as naturally possible, not to show it; and when I did show any acknowledgement, I made sure it was opaque, so as not to be completely rolled over. Her stories, devised to break the ice, were as erotic as they come, without a hint of remorse for her actions.

She said to me: 'Don't jump to conclusions, now, Nigel, for we must crawl before we walk, and walk before we can run...but as they say, you cannot hold onto the past and expect to ride into the future... our future...you cannot hold on to the past Nigel, or allow it to affect the present. If my research is correct, Jamie is gone, done with you. So let's try not to waste valuable time by playing to a non-existing gallery." Now, that's a fine delicate phrase, I thought.

Her stories, leading to the hired killer, an erotic adventure not for the sexually fainthearted, and definitely not for the under twenty-one...

Not For The Under Twenty-One

When I walked into the room, they smiled, and naturally, I smiled back - The shock not quite registering yet. I looked from one to the other; the mini scarves that girded their loins, their bodies glistening in the aqua blue psychedelic track lights that covered them. They were seductively postured on a king size lavender futon, not trying to hide anything, totally uninhibited. Their smiles meant to disarm. I found my defenses weakening and lust taking over. Unknown to them, I recognized it for what it was, a relief made for my present situation, a complete stress reducing, sexually satisfying orgy, done on a binge, with an implied agreement for everyone involved to unequivocally forget everything and anything that is beyond the limits of this master bedroom – and the same flowering voice I had come to know said -

"'I have an eye for things that make women look good, and Jamie recognizes that.'" Those were your last words to me, the last time we met." The voice and arrogance were recognizable, it was definitely vintage Michelle, a trademark which still follows her.

As mesmeric as their presence were, I managed to utter: "Hello Michelle, did you know I was here when you made your reservation?" It was a question uttered more from not knowing what to say than as a conversational piece. The distraction was just too strong; Michelle's friend was even more tantalizing and seductive. I was lost for words.

"No, but as fate would have it, I found you out before you found me, and me and my friend here, did our homework, and knew that you come to the presidential suite when the CEO is out of town. He owes me a favor. Do you like what you see?' 'It's for you to take with no strings attached."

"Like what I see?" She got to be kidding or just plain teasing. This placid beauty turned seductress; who does she think she is, or for that matter, what does she think I am. Even wood or stone would wake up to view this, it was that good. From past experience, Michelle is very innovative with her hands, like a tongue gently caressing an ear.

They were that good. I am known to be very discriminating when it comes to picking my women - This was easy choice, presented on a platter. I looked from one to the other - the message was the same. The eagerness and willingness was evident. How many times does one get this lucky in life, digging for coal and strike diamonds?

"I will take it," I heard myself say. Michelle raised a glass of Champaign already chilled and served on a silver tray and said -

"What do we toast to?"

"What would you say?" I replied.

"To all the successful seducers and the games they embark on," Michelle volunteered, ever the belle feminist.

At that point, I wondered if she was reading my mind. My intentions, unknown to her, was to seduce her; not just for the sex of it, but for everything that I can extract from her about the hired killer. The recruitment began even without my trying.

Michelle slowly let drop the skimpy scarf that girded her loins, revealing an inverted-pyramid of curly black pubic hair above swollen moist lips. It was an act, an invitation I could not resist, and I joined them on the futon - calmly and meticulously trying to satisfy my hunger and create the right equilibrium for body and spirit. There was the throbbing member which was bursting out of the seams of my pants and was evident to Michelle and her friend, who looked with anticipation with their lips ever slightly open and eyes beckoning.

I moved toward Michelle and took her outstretched arms; our lips met, our tongues deep in each other's mouths and our pelvises grinding hard against each other - my lips alternating between the two well-rounded breasts. I squeezed her firm backside and she reached for my throbbing manhood - there was a soft hissing sound as I entered into her, and she whispered: "you fill me up Nigel and I love it. May I climb on top as Jamie does?" Did Jamie tell her that? Was it a tidbit from women's night out gossip forum? That was a question for another day. She climbed on top and continued to ride me, borne of experience; the 'Tigress in the sac,' she was. The rest, as it's said, became history...

I woke up to a Sun flooded room, piercing through the screened window, with blinds partially drawn. I saw Michelle spread-eagled to the far corner of the futon, bare breasted, with the thin cotton quilt etched between the crack of her buttocks. Her mysterious friend -

maybe a nine to fiver, had left, hopefully a happier woman. I never found out her name. I hoped she believes in reciprocal support and mutual discreteness.

A quick look around the room, the new fixtures, Michelle's articles of fashion and the content of her handbag, that was carelessly tossed to the east end of the suite, indicate one reality - that of brute economic and political strength. Michelle seems to have fallen into some insane money and political clout - a comparative advantage. How does she know the CEO? Are they lovers? What is the relationship? What is it based on? For the CEO to give her his suite for such rendezvous tells a lot. He has never done so, not to my knowledge.

I couldn't help but reminisce about our clandestine meetings before she moved back to Chicago - Our frequent meetings in the library, her office in the French Quarter, the studio she rented in the garden district or at Seagull Lane - using any of her numerous excuses as a passport to visit me when Jamie was at her mother's. We would talk, drink some of her potent homemade margaritas; receive and give massages, and not make love and say goodbye, keeping in mind the 'Shadow,' or 'Antenna,' code name for Jamie. Last night was different, very fluid and lucid, with an aura of levity to its magic – because we were free of the shadow.

I watched as Michelle yawned and stretched, kicking the cover off her bare body. Scanned the room until she saw me. She then turned on her stomach, raised her legs and rested her chin on her palms.

"Good morning Nigel, please pass me my cigarettes." One of her habits that constituted the turnoffs of that bygone era, our past – Michele is a smoker. She has not kicked the habit as she promised. As I watched her, I saw a totally different person from the Michelle of last night. She was calm, relaxed, with a certain demure, almost of one who needs or misses her father. She blew her smoke towards the ceiling, looked straight at me with those sparkling big eyes - a tint of seriousness to it. She said -

"Any hope for us, Nigel?" I shook my head and returned the look, not knowing what was really on her mind. What does she mean - any hope for us? When did we get serious? Was it over the last forty-eight hours? Should we be planning our marriage? This woman is really pushing it, I must say, a little too hard. This is not forever, one day at a time will just do nicely, thank you. These were thoughts I could not utter, because I needed her more than I had ever need anyone before.

Then she said, "Remember this story? 'Relationships are relative in the global and ecumenical sense of the word. In their multifaceted categories and subcategories - political, economic, personal, or business - relationships built on a solid foundation and mutual respect and trust can be very rewarding. Yes, the relationship has to be built on trust, mutual respect and understanding - with many stroking and exchanges, if you will. Each helping the other grow to its full potential. This applies to all four variables in their infinite. Eradicating negativity. Abhor its discussion in its perceived state. It is possible to talk about negative subjects, like the good and the bad in everyone and everything, without sounding or being negative oneself - as in the day by day, moment to moment observations and comments, having the potential of shedding insights into the future and geopolitically elusive answers without predicting it.'"

Michele continued:

"That was the mini lecture you gave to my question on relationships. I regretted asking the question. You were ever the analyst and diplomat. You answered me without answering me. I kept wondering what it would take, or what I had to do to have you. What Jamie possibly had that was absent in me. The answer eluded me until very recently, when I stumbled upon some information about you, and the subsequent demise of your union with Jamie, gleaned from a mutual friend in London - It does take sophisticated sexual, political and economic empowerment, but not necessarily in that order, but more sexual than anything else, right "Mr. vague," to have you?"

It was good to know that I was not the only one reminiscing, though not really helpful. Who is the mutual friend she is talking about? I refused to ask. My demeanor was neither one of agreement nor that of disagreement. It was a blank look that said: 'Whatever turns you on.' Then, knowing Michelle, even if I had said my thoughts aloud, it wouldn't deter her from pushing ahead with her agenda. It is the Chicago in her, not necessarily the Al Capone stuff, and not because of the chilly wind that blows across Lake Michigan, but because a Chicago girl is a Chicago girl.

"If you're going to learn to shave a woman, Nigel," she said with a wink, "you've got to learn how to rub the soap in first. It's high time you learned it's not polite to mention one woman to another. If you don't learn that, you will always waste your advantages. Duplicity means you please one person at the expense of the other." What does she mean, learn to shave a woman? Duplicity? I never pursued her while with Jamie. Giving and receiving massage is not the same thing as infidelity. There had never been any exchange of fluids between us.

Why is she talking about duplicity! What does she mean? Is she confusing me with someone else? I have not even said a word, not a word, and the woman doesn't even give the man time to breath. I may have to make a dash for the next exit - As if reading my thoughts.... Michelle rose elegantly to her full height, one leg, then the other, and having fixed her long curly rebellious hair behind her ears, wrapped the soft cotton comforter around her olive smooth bare body. It was a disarming spectacle, easy on the eyes. After this, everything seemed to flow in one unstoppable direction and all she had to do was sit close enough to me, pull her full hair back, making sure there is enough whiff to emit her woman smell and let the current carry us...As Charlie would say: 'however the wriggle along the way, it was one jolly stream.'

In my memory however, she is anything but one jolly stream. She is tall, soft haired, vital, with large misty eyes and an air of flounce about her stride. Nothing happened slowly with Michelle. I remember it must have been a summer when we first met on Seagull Lane, overlooking Emerald Lake. Her lips were swollen, her jeans tight and faded. I remember how I longed to see her naked, and devoted the better part of that afternoon to contriving it. Michelle must have guessed it somehow; for later that afternoon, she suggested, even with Jamie present, saying if we needed to save time for the show we had planned to see, we share the shower - to wash off the chlorine from the swimming pool.

Jamie, a little buzzed, and a stickler for time when it comes to ballet or opera, agreed. Unknown to Jamie washing off the chlorine meant stripping off the wet garments. Michelle stooped, naked, and let me watch while she reached for the knob, I'm sure she did, and she turned towards me and said – "Well Nigel," showing me her wet spread hands – "let's see how accommodating the bath water is, without thinking of impure thoughts." I am sure she said that too, and there were much thinking of impure thoughts that afternoon. I felt refreshed and freed of an intolerable burden – knowing that Michelle had the same thoughts as I did, and that left alone together, those thoughts would be actualized. Michelle, one can see that she was alight with pious optimism. There was something in her smile and alert eyes that told me, somehow she knew we would be doing this again... and we are doing it now, and I am sure we would do it repeatedly before the night is over.

Michelle realizing its been a long time since breakfast, decided it was time she told me the story of how she met and became Mr. Delaney's lover. It started with a blind date she had arranged between Anna and Hakeem, 'the Jew and the Arab,' who were mutual friends of hers. That was when she found out that love and compatible sex can bridge political and religious boundaries. At dinner, and tea that followed, the Jew and the Arab hit it off great. They could not stop talking nor were they able to take their eyes off each other. There were footsies and hand holding under the dinner table and some stolen kisses. Michelle, finding herself to be the odd-one-out, decided the smooching and the heat it was generating was getting out of hand, decided to do something about it...

She assured me that she was polite when she asked Anna and Hakeem, the Jew and the Arab, to join her for a walk on the beach. It was there she met Barack, an 18-year-old hunk who was training for the Olympics, as a boxer. Michelle had seen this young man sneak peeks at her as she suntanned on the beach, hiding none of her well sculptured body. She does not understand why people fight against nude sunbathing. Anyway, after a couple of chance meets with Barack, the young man offered to help wash her car; an offer Michelle said, she found tempting, but which she declined, because of what her neighbors might assume. See, Barack is not only well built for his age, but is very popular in the neighborhood, especially among the young women.

Given the present situation, and the explosive heat generated by the activities of the Jew and Arab lovebirds, Michelle threw caution to the wind, and was almost, obtrusively too eager to oblige Barack of a tour of her new beachfront condo. She allowed Anna and Hakeem to wander off and satisfy their lust. As she walked off with Barack, Michelle wondered, 'A Jew and an Arab,' maybe she should write a story about that, it would make a fascinating love story. Another 'Romeo and Juliet' kind of story maybe, she thought to herself...if only she can just get rid of this heat and excruciating urge to rip off her clothes and those of Barack...right there on the sandy beach...'Oh, damn the nosy neighbors...' She cursed, under her breath. These were her very words.

As Barack and Michelle ascended the staircase, she slipped. The impact of the fall coupled with the cool summer breeze, helped hike her already too short dress; exposing the fact that she had nothing under her dress. Michelle, like Jamie, makes it a point not to wear underwear in the summer, especially New Orleans summer. Embarrassed about the fall, she looked up only to find Barack looking down at her. At first she did not know what he was gazing at. Then she followed his gaze, and realized it was her hiked dress and nakedness. She then meticulously pulled her dress down and slowly closed her wide-open legs. It was at this point that Barack offered his hands to pull her up, and in the process, planted a kiss on her lips. He carried her the remainder of the way.

Barack gently laid her on the soft Persian rug, and put a pillow under her head. Michelle did not offer any resistance, blaming it on the heat generated by the lustful acts of the 'Jew and the Arab.' As she liked to say: "You can't beat a little sex for breaking the tension and removing social barriers."

Michelle and Barack made love on the Persian rug. She was surprised at how strong and sexually experienced Barack was, considering his 'tender' age. Michelle wanted more, a take-charge mode. She tugged at his dark blue abbreviated French shorts. He drops to his knees and pulls her to his mouth. She can feel the scratchy stubble of his young beard as his tongue and hers begin their courtship. The rhythm of her breathing changed: Bone melting heat, a rush of blood. 'You're doing well for a young man," She told him, "You're good, you know. Did the others tell you how good you are?" Michelle pushed him back onto the floor. "Just lie there. I'll put it in. Don't move. I'll do it. I said I'd do it." She is sitting on it, thighs locked against him, holding his hands down, watching his face, his eyes closed. He is smiling. She lifts herself, riding it, rubbing herself against him, trying to come. "Suddenly he grabs me, holds me still. Thrusts against me, deep and hard – makes me gasp. We're really fighting now." "I want to do it Barack, I want to fuck you..." But he is stronger. I can only keep control if I make him give in to what I make him feel. Now I'm squatting on him, my knees pressed together hiding his face, one hand behind me holding his balls in a little neat package, lifting slow, falling hard, turning the tension tighter, so close to coming, so close and then, mean bastard, he pulls me off him, throws me onto the floor again. "You can't do that," "I am crying," "stop Barack. I'm the one." "He twists me over onto my face, both hands grabbing my ass, pulling it toward him, shoving into my cunt from behind, deep and deliberate. I lose my breath with every bang."

Am I too naked too quickly, she worries, knowing that there is no gentle ambiguity, nowhere to go but the soft Persian rug. Michele continued:

"There was so much of his mouth, so much softness and pressure, so much insistence of tongue, from a youthful body. I could not remember how we made it from the staircase to the living room and Persian rug, or how we got out of our clothes. Did we fold them, hang them neatly or rip them off with abandon? I felt the curly hair on his chest. My obsession took over, what I call submission fantasy cock, enormous, feeling the hardness pressed against my thigh. Tongue and mouth everywhere, teasing, biting, sucking, and insisting. His young strong hands kneading, pressing, hands that hurt, soothe, caress, and hurt again, using my breasts in some new merciless pattern of pleasure and pain. Everything was happening to him at once and too fast, tuned to pure erotic response - a simple predictable instrument. Writhing, pulled towards, pulling away from, shock, coming apart under his fingers. Soft young fingers inside me: twisting and pressing - rude violation so good. I cry: "Put it in, Barack" and wonder why he doesn't give it all to me, now! "Now, Barack. Now!"

"He would not, the young sadist. He wants to do it his way, deliberate and slow. He wants to do everything to me. He holds me down. Wants to kiss me, pinch, rub, and lick every part of me. To me, it feels like we have been doing this all-day, he is just only now putting his mouth between my legs, in the celebration and native ritual of the virginal, and I am suspended far and away in space, in clouds, where no one has ever ventured - floating, tumbling, exploding and coming apart again. Insatiable me, I come back for more because I am enjoying it so much. He stopped. I opened my eyes. He rests his face against my thigh, face red and wet, mouth displaying all our mixed juices." Michele was not done:

"I woke up the next day with my mouth surrounding his cock. It was the taste of myself, and I liked it, realizing why he and others stayed there so long before putting it in me. The smell and taste of his come and my wetness mingled together. I wondered what he likes, the teeth or no teeth pressure or just teasing licks - Watching him watch me, I hoped he was pleased with my mistress-fullness." She continued: "I looked into his eyes, and said:"

"'I love to feel full, Barack. No one else has ever filled me so full. It's really all the things you do. I am sure you know that, and the others say them to you...don't they?'" "Really expecting no reply, in my preoccupation, my obsession with the magical instrument, trying unsuccessfully to encircle it under the head with my thumb and index finger, I can barely encircle it, purple-ribbon with jagged distended veins...'"

This was the meticulous and methodical fashion with which Michelle related this erotic story. She has never opened up this much to me before, which begged the question: was it to make me jealous? It was a throw back, the Youngman and this narration, reminding me of the 'Damascus experience' - in the 'bigger landscape,' where all things happen - here we all are, the faithful and the sinners, the virtuous and the profane, the sublime and the arrogant, the lions and the Christians, the snake charmers and those who are kings and queens for a day...but Michelle told it like it is, in her own unique trademark fashion.

This love fest between Michelle and the Adonis went on for the better part of the summer, until this older woman became an obsession for the younger man. One day, Barack had introduced 'Mr. Delaney' to Michelle as his boxing trainer. The meeting was casual, and without any fanfare. A few days later, Mr. Delaney paid Michelle a call and warned her to stay away from the lad; that she was contributing to his many distractions. That was that.

Ordinarily, Michelle would have told Mr. Delaney in what direction to fly his kite. It was not so in this case. She found this man, not only fascinating, but something about him, made her tingle in a funny way, as she always says. There was this eeriness that has always attracted her to such men, the mystery factor, she would say. She knew that this Mr. Delaney was no ordinary man. She was curious about this man, who was always dressed in black. So Barack became expendable. Michelle had to let him go the best possible way she could, without breaking too many bones or heart. Unknown to Michelle at this time was the fact that Mr. Delaney had total control over his students. So, the exit of Barack was quick and without any fuss.

So, Michelle became Mr. Delaney's mistress and student. She cooked for him, gave him massages and catered to his large sexual whims to relieve his tensions, and in return, he taught her about the art of self-defense - martial arts - Judo, Karate, with emphasis on the art of espionage and the tools of its operation.... last but not the least, philosophy, the human-face dimension, as seen from the eyes of an all-involving apprentice, in activities that were hitherto beyond her - observing, learning and putting into perspectives human rights and human failures - and why things are the way they are and have been. In her mind, what might be necessary to make it more human-faced, all couched in mindfulness and self-awareness.

"He was my teacher and my lover Nigel, and I am ready to bring all I've learned to you, and make myself available as your sidekick. Just to be your sidekick is good enough for me, and if I must tell you, it's a powerful force too. This offer comes with many hardware and software - the latest in relative technology, the works. These are all that you need and more. They would bring you current, up to date, my dear. It never gonna be a dull moment."

I chuckled, "Never gonna be a dull moment, eh?" "After last night, I believe anything you tell me. You are in, but it's absolute loyalty, and you have to wait for my instructions and signals, for the good of both of us."

She said, "deal," and planted one of her 'marathon woman' kisses on me. I said to myself, "Why can't I get enough of her..."

"What's my first assignment boss?" She surprised me.

"Slow down my dear lady, one step at a time. I will think of one." I responded - and she pulled me to her, and it was a repeat of the night before, and more...

I was surprised at how much this formerly placid beauty had changed; progressed may be a better word. I couldn't help but reflect on the advice she gave me that first day, after being anointed my sidekick; incase I found myself one on one with the killer -

"Remember'" she said, "you're the amateur, and he is the professional. Use that position; turn your liability into an asset. The amateur does the unexpected, not because he is clever or experienced but because he doesn't know any better. Apply the unexpected rapidly, obviously, as if confused. Then pause and wait. A confrontation is probably the last thing he may want now. If he does want it, you might as well know it. Shoot. You should have a silencer; we'll get you one in the morning. I know where. If questioned during the procurement of any of the tools you need, you're to lie indignantly but not arrogantly, and never in a loud voice. That kind of anger triggers hostility, and hostility means delay and further questions."

Even though I had lived through this in a previous life, a life I thought I had abandoned for good, the life of waiting, worrying and running that is called the Spy-game and have gone through this kind of orientations countless times, I listened to Michelle with respect and awe. Not just for how much she has learned and knows, but the sensitivity and concern that came with every word she said.
"I'll tell you something about cover; something you'll learn soon enough yourself. Never volunteer information. People do not expect you to explain yourself. After all, what's there to explain? When in doubt, play it by ear. When going from point A to point B of a long distance, a gun is to be dismantled, its barrel separated from the

handle, the firing pin removed. These procedures generally satisfy the men in blue. Inoperable weapons do not constitute a threat; so do not concern them. If they object and decide to confiscate, let them; another can be procured. A couple of blocks before the meeting place, you're to immediately reassemble them; using the toilet stall of a men's room. Always act like the politician at the scene of a disaster, naive yet foot sure, like being thrown upon your natural resources when the cards are stacked against you, got it?"

"Got it." I said.

why do you want to come inside,
when you've a firmament,
a large firmament to play in,
a firmament almost without
restrictions - knowing when you
come inside this abode of mine,
you'd be caged, harassed, terminated,
disposed off unceremoniously -
enjoy your freedom you pest...

The story of the pest,
a fly outside my window

The Confrontation

Michelle's stories have given me so much insight into the working mind of Mr. Delaney. Her offer to be my Sidekick, and occasional troubleshooter and lover was acceptable and most heartedly welcomed. The food and wine were good, the sex excellent. The stories were aphrodisiacal and seductively delightful. Why can't I get enough – why do I feel there is something missing? Why do I have this feeling of not being adequately prepared for this mission? Could it be the fear of the unknown? Is it due to the long period of inertia? Does it have to do with my past? Am I being haunted by the fear of it? Is it my feelings towards Michelle I am afraid of? What is it? It was hard to fathom - I just could not put my finger on it.

I was still in my boxer shorts, and a trip to the bathroom would do me some good, after the night's activities, activities Michelle described as - 'A blissful, binge-full, sexual delight. A total ecstasy producing monument to womanhood, and you gave it to me Nigel Peters, my first real orgasm.' Michelle is not known for her humility, so this came as another surprise, baring her heart to me. Telling me those other guys never really did it right, even the boxer and football players, and others of their ilk, and then, thanking me for it? It never fails to make a man feel good.

"Stay with me tonight." I heard Michelle say. I could not help but think this is really the time to dash for the next exit, what is this woman trying to do to me?

"I can't," I responded, while holding on to the door handle. "I have work to do, and I expect you to understand."

So for the next twenty-one days, the Killer's 'Girl,' became the mole, my mole - planted in his *pied a terre*; with implicit instructions. He was monitored on his sleep patterns, how much time he spent in the bathroom - subdivided into time spent in brushing, flossing, under the shower, and for shaving. The patterns of his faucet running water were timed to the second. Then, there were those 'Water Spies,' the skimpily clad girls who engineered chance meets and peeped through the blinds.

The information gathered from Michelle and the other 'information research officers,' prepared me for so much, but I was not completely sure I was ready yet for a meeting with the killer. Even the task force put together for me by Captain Banks, of N.O.P.D's finest, was unable to constitute a rallying point for my brewing fears. I was reasonably begging for guarantees, and in this business, there are none. You are trained to think like the enemy. Taught not to react, but to initiate actions, even if they are just trial ghosts. It is better to treat your enemies as you treat spiders, by destroying and removing the miniatures boulders - The spider needs hard or semi soft objects to weave its web. It is the cardinal response - the miniatures must go. The Spider must be rendered powerless, neutralized into perpetual inaction, using its own medicine. Michelle and the young boxer are gone, but are those the only agents he has? The unknown agents are the most dangerous. They have to be found out - heightening the already stratospheric crucible of emotions.

Michelle's preparation was in essence, an *avant courier*, but it did not prepare me for the fact that Mr. Delaney reserved a flat at Frenchman's Wharf.

This unexpected, unsolicited, and unprepared for meeting, was unnerving and exhilaration busting, exhilaration from Michelle's reappearance. The nagging questions I could not get rid off were: "Why did Delaney kill all those men and the inadvertent female victims, the ones caught in the crossfire." "Why did he kill the last subject, the one I witnessed; the one that became the motivational fuel in this adventure to stop or 'educate' him, without ending up becoming a victim myself. Hoping the use of a different approach, with new mechanics and platform, would open up new horizons in this convoluted game.

Then, above all else, how come Michelle did not tell me about the fact that, 'Mr. Mueller' or 'Delaney,' maintains a flat or flats, overlooking the Canal, here at Frenchman's Wharf?' Is Michelle a double agent? I have always taken Frenchman's Wharf as a place for renewed energy, renewed faith and the desire to accomplish the works and dictates of the 'bigger picture.' It is a place for rejuvenation after the harsh hours at work and play - A therapeutic piece of property in the Lake Forest subdivision of the Big Easy, east. The perfect play ground, ten minutes from the French Quarter, the Warehouse district and CBD. I am sure everyone has his or her own version of what Frenchman's

Wharf represented to me. With its Emerald Lake and Sailboats, the Lagoons and Fishponds, the bushes and manmade dunes and hills - The lush greenery and Piers; the huge Lighthouse-deco Clubhouse and its facilities; Frenchman's Wharf was the nirvana, my nirvana. It has been invaded and violated, and I don't like it. Michelle definitely has some explaining to do.

He did not bat an eye, not even after the few name drops I proffered, which were intended to distract and confuse and hopefully expose some vulnerability. I realized right away the need to go to Michelle's playbook - from the steely calm eyes; I was for all intents and purpose a cornered quarry. I either talk my way out fast or face the consequence of a curious Cat. His powerful shoulders were hunched forward inside the familiar black jacket and he carried nothing but an apple, which he quietly rolled from one hand to the other as if to maintain circulation. A dark-haired girl, and I am thinking this is Michelle's replacement, waited at his side, one hand lightly on his arm. She was serene and very beautiful, and she stood directly beneath the light. From my vantage point, I could see, with the acuteness of perception, which accompanies sudden shock, the bold imprint of a love-bite on her lower neck. All of a sudden, I was hearing nothing but the sounds of love and battle, the whispers of longing couples, of morality, love and family, where each has his own private hell to go to, when all else fails. Vertigo almost seized me. He dismissed the beautiful damsel, who had now moved a few steps and was now silhouetted against the light pole. Her face locked in the tension of uncomprehending resentment. Was it resentment of my presence or the resentment of being dismissed by her 'master'?

I could hear her saying, without words coming out of her mouth: 'you are without nobility, without any scrap of decency or moral fiber or human compassion. You haven't got any instinct that is remotely human or honorable. I know that you're a brute. Why don't you admit it? You wouldn't recognize God even if he punched you in the nose.' She did not say the words; she couldn't have said the words, for saying them would be detrimental to her health. I must say again, he does know how to pick his women, if nothing else. Then, also without words, I said: 'you don't fool me lassie. Women like you like fighters, the brute in them. It's the 'Tyson-Givens syndrome,' why should you expect nobility, decency and moral fiber, which do not mix with the brute in him?' It is a contradiction in terms, to say the least. I grunted and shifted one arm in a restless motion, with my mind alert and working fast.

"I have been expecting this, waiting for it to happen, not knowing when it would; hoping that when it does, I am prepared and ready for it. Now that we are here, lets make the best of it."

This, I took to be thinking on one's feet, a strategy of taking the offensive, hoping if I put him on the defensive, it would not only help buy me time, but hopefully convince him that I have done my homework and have specific data and resources to back me up. He was not daunted, the steely calm eyes said it all – he was not touched nor fooled. His eyes disturbed me as they continuously appraised my every move. They were too truthful, undefended and too clear. It made me fear that I may have pegged him incorrectly, a naiveté that exposes my security. I also realized that it was imperative I continue, or face the possibility of being taken for granted.

"Why did you kill that man?" I shot out, more of a lead-in question than contrived neuro linguistic programming, a bon chic, bon genre product, totally home grown.

"He had something that belonged to me."

His response was quick, to the point – he was not in the mood to waste words, a reputation that precedes him. This reputation is commonly associated with him - that he has a quick mind, but says very little. There were no contraventions to that fact yet. He did not ask me which one; he figured I was talking about the last victim, or any one of them for all that it matters. I am sure they all had things that belonged to him or by extension, his benefactors.

"What thing?" I ventured.

"I do not see that as any of your business." He replied. This might be a first for him, being confronted like this, questioned like a common criminal. He was true to his reputation, he did not say much - utilizing a mathematician's frugality with words. I have to make him open up, make him go beyond one-line statements. How can I make this stone-faced, cold-eyed killer lighten up? I have to know about his inner working mind, to help me refine and upgrade my strategy and tools of operation, Michelle's latest in relative technology gadgets not withstanding.

I decided to take a different tact; maybe a play on friendly or humanitarian motivation would do it. So I said: "If you don't tell me how can I help you, the Police and other law enforcement agencies are on the lookout for you."

"I do not need your help." He said with finality.

I have to continue, I cannot give up now, if just to buy time. It is already obvious that he is an egomaniac – do I need to massage his ego a bit? Clearly, if I am to extract any secrets, even the smallest body language - both conscious and subconscious secrets, I will have to use subtlety. Watch the eyes and look out for the soft or hard body speak, when different movements in the body are significant statements – these are strategies I have to employ If Michelle is to be believed. So through clenched teeth, I continued -

"You are regarded as the best in the community, an invisibility of some sort, they were quite wrong, wouldn't you say?"

"Being the best is insignificant in this particular situation we have just found ourselves. All your homework may not help you now, so get on with it."

This, I took as a step forward. He has graduated from a one-liner to two-liners. I have to make him expand a bit more, just a bit more.

"If your humility is genuine, and you are really the best, you got to have smarts." I paused, took a deep breath and continued. "If this particular object justifies the taking of a life, you must have treasured it, I would think." I quickly realized this approach was not cutting it.

"Shut up, my first response was metaphoric." The killer said, surging towards me.

"Who said the object is mine?" He continued in his predatory mode, "I had to kill him to get paid, so in a way, he owed me. You've involved your self in matters that are no concern of yours. You'll pursue them no further."

I couldn't help but notice the coldness with which the statement was uttered, coupled with a sinister and absolute command of tone. It is said that one can study the eyes of a professional soldier and not see the resentment or temptations behind them. It was true in this case. I can't quite decipher what is what, temptation, yes, resentment? That's a different story – It was all written all over him, and resentment can be very toxic, and make the owner do unpredictable things. We're getting somewhere, if I can keep it flowing out of him.

"You do not use badness to correct bad, nor evil for evil correction, who is doing the paying?" I asked.

His slow predatory advance was still in progress. It was as cunning as the man himself, an inch-by-inch encompassment. What was that about the missile one sees coming at him, from a distance, not killing he that sees it?

I summoned enough courage and said – "If you do not tell me, I'm going to have to blow this thing wide open, make the dossier I have on you available to the law enforcement people – and I do have enough on you, trust me." It was a gamble. His response was quick as usual, delivered with no hint of fear or concern. He is the ultimate poker player. This time, he was more expansive.

"By the time I finish with you, there won't be enough energy left in you to do anything, if I were you, I would imprison that curious mind of yours. The only solution is to not reopen the 'Zebra' file, or you might be hit by a tsunami or swirling manhole. Stay away Tuesday!"

He knows my name. I tried hard to hide the shock of this revelation. Was it Michelle? Even Michelle does not call me Tuesday, nor does she know of it. How did he find out? Have I been careless, compromised myself in any way? If this was meant to dislocate me from my keel, I will have to play it as cool as humanly possible, and pursue my search for information, one stage at a time.

"What's in the "Zebra File?""? I demanded.

"You don't want to know, but if you must know, not sure how this concerns you, it was a low intensity operation conducted in a European country some few years ago, not that this is going to help you. It remains classified for another fifty years. Your clearance does not extend to that level."

I am sure he told me all this, knowing that I have no hope of getting out of this place alive, if he has a say in it. He would not say more about the 'Zebra' affair. I left it at that.

"What did you call me?"

'Tuesday! That's your name isn't it? Is Nigel preferable?"

"Only a few of my friends call me by that name, who are you?"

"I like to stay ahead of my opposition. I fingered you the first time I saw you. There was an aura of betrayal all around you. Your body language was utterly revealing. The signs, they were all there, I had to check you out, 'Teacher,' and it's not from whom you think. She is a deluded young woman. I'll deal with her in due time, I have her and she is why you lasted this long." He continued.

"She thwarted all my moves, a trusted ally she was. That double agent and insatiable nymphomaniac, she will pay for it."

A sudden apprehension struck me. I suddenly was afraid of any lapse, any form of inadequacy stemming from my long period of inertness. I felt a strange anger welling up in me just looking at him, in his calm demeanor. I wanted to reach out and strangle him, which was wishful thinking, nonetheless. What has he done with Michelle? My tool and possibly only tool this very minute, may just well be talking. There is so much I have to find out. Outright confrontation may not yield the right result. The operative word is subtlety. Knowing Michelle is not a double agent is helpful and reassuring.

For a man paid to kill, he was cool - He is someone who would make you question your instincts and preparation. I did my best to stay focused. Think, think, and think, I kept telling myself. Good writing as is said, is in the rewriting, so recreating the past few days events would be helpful. The more I listened to this man - the more I looked at his bland emotionless demeanor, the more I realized he just may be a chump, his reputation notwithstanding. It is also true that he may, in actuality, genuinely believe in the validity and altruistic cause of his benefactors and their ideology. It became tempting, the thought of cultivating a friendship with this monster, and reeducating him, I thought, may not be bad for humankind; in the new geopolitically emerging world order. He is a tool, has always been a tool of those behind the veil of secrecy. Utility - yes utility, why not use him, his vast knowledge and tools of the trade in bringing to justice the real and true culprits in this macabre operation of a Machiavellian outfit.

So I said – "I do not pretend to know your motivations or those of your benefactors. All I know is that innocent people have gotten killed and that you have been the tool of some unknown people who have a lot to lose from the stability of things. They are engaged in selfishly perpetrating a perpetual cold war, to further their ideology and ill gotten profits. They use you as a weapon to silence those they want silenced, to cover up their activities. In short, you're their pawn, their 'Oliver North,' expendable, when you've outlived your usefulness, can't you see?"

Emboldened by his silence I now undertook a closer examination of his massive frame, pondering the perils and possibilities that lie ahead. I kept my observations to myself, but continued in my quest to reeducate and realign his affiliation. Hoping that his natural sense of value would be too strong an answer to mere materialistic temptations. I had to make him believe that a man is judged by what he looks for and not necessarily by what he finds.

"To them, you already know too much, to them you're arrogant and impetuous, a loose cannon whose exploits border on insanity. For all we know, they are already grooming a replacement for you. So teaming up with me and exposing their obscene and decadent activities would make you a hero instead of the goat. You've only been a mercenary who got involved for the money; but a repentant 'Watergate burglar,' what's his name? The bald headed one."

"Gordon Liddy, but you meant to say, Chuck Colson, the one they say has turned back to God, some kind of born again" he interjected. He knows his history.

"You do know your history." I said, surprised and embarrassed at my lack of memory. I gave him time to digest this new approach, hoping it would mollify him.

"It's an unfair business." I added sternly. "You've had a big responsibility and secrets thrust on you. You didn't ask for it but you can't Un-know it. You know enough to hang men and probably women in powerful positions. That places you in a certain category. It comes with obligations you can't escape." I concluded, trying to make him aware of my concern for him. His response was quick as usual, but this time a surprise, a pleasant surprise. This is what is called a nightmare client in the business. I was beginning to feel I had lit a fire inside him, and that there is no knowing how it would spread or who would put it out. He said -

"There is also someone else, more powerful, with a gun to my head, how do I explain it. Most importantly, there's a room vital to all that you want to know, the computer room - How do I get you into the room without raising eyebrows? I may have misjudged you. You're crazy, crazier than I had thought. I can not for the life of me comprehend why you've chosen to spend your time on the edge of someone else's web, a web that spreads from one end of the world to the other - New Orleans, San Francisco, New York, Chicago, Benin City, Brussels, Paris, Amsterdam, Ghent, Antwerp, London, Frankfurt, Tokyo, Shanghai, Beijing, Qingdao, Shenzhen and other smaller spots not even on the map - you will have to cover these areas and its vast network of agents, double agents and cutthroats. I will take you to the computer room, follow me.' Just like that, as if from an unseen signal, the young damsel vanished into the shadows. He has them well trained, I must say. It occurred to me that he had been mulling all this, his decision to take me to the computer room while spewing all the reasons he could not do it. He is a contradiction in terms, a true enigma.

He walked across the grass, beating his pockets for his keys. He entered a side street. He stopped momentarily, reflecting pensively. As someone would do, who has been underused for twenty years - and has a sudden chance to shine, knowing that this is a once in a lifetime lucky opportunity that should not be blown. Was it? Is it another trick or track covering? He vanished from view and I followed softly after him. The house was a wedge, narrow on the street, broad at the back. He unlocked the door and closed it behind us. He pressed the time switch and began climbing the stairs, keeping an even pace because he had a long way to go. I decided the wisest thing was to do the same thing he did, a step-by-step replication of the killer's moves. To get my oh-so-many talents working in one direction, and to make a fresh start that would get me clear of all the fresh starts I had made before, during the era of Jamie and my long period of inactivity.

Hoping conclusively to put away this guilt and shock treatment Jamie just inflicted, and not feeling responsible for both halves of every relationship that has collapsed on me. Hoping to make a new clear and understandable beginning. Because, "Before anything new can be created, all things old will have to be destroyed." I said this, knowing that even the most careful make mistakes. Then, mistakes are part of the corrective nature of life. What is important is being able to learn from them, hoping that at the end, they would not only make one better, but also make one stronger. Leading to an appreciatively finer way of life - of doing things.

and the days of your mourning
will have come to completion....

The computer room was filled with all kinds of exotic gadgets for eavesdropping, filtering and voice analysis. There was this continuous humming of the mainframe, that makes the place feel more edgy than it looks. At this point I was more interested in the database. I wanted names, dates, figures, places and times - Illustrations if possible. His face was a study in desperation. He ran from one module to the other, pulling buttons, switching on the different monitors. For a moment, I found myself feeling sorry for him. His decision to bring me here caught me completely by surprise. He never even got the benefit of seeing the look on my face when he made the decision. I am not sure of what to think, he was acting as a man possessed, whether from panic or vengeance, either of which doesn't make for rational reaction. Guilt does breed fear. Fear in turn leads to distrust. Finally, distrust gives birth to violence.

The room was deserted, which was either a good sign or a trap. It was not a trap. It was a carefully planned room but bleak and without sympathy. This guy who is known not to talk too much is spilling his guts, a way of unloading a perpetual load that came with waiting, worrying, in the game of spying. He peered around him. Letting everything greet him in its own good time. What greater freedom than not knowing where you are going and why. What was certain was that the place had just been scrubbed so glowingly it was a shame to tread on it. He began turning the remainder of the content of his pocket on the surface of the nearest console, stocktaking before a shift in personality and premises.

The sight and touch of the place intrigued me. This is where the killer and his benefactors conceived, analyzed and put into motion their decadent plans. All the data is within the limits of these walls. This might, probably, be the most unselfish thing the killer had done in his entire life. Is it perhaps that we have to do a thing to find out the reason for it, and that our actions might just be questions instead of answers? No evasions. You take the role of the male bee and play it to the hilt. You do it once and die - A satisfying death, knowing that you have done the right thing and done it well to the best of your ability. In the process, humankind might benefit.

He took up a pen, then a single sheaf of paper. He scribbled some lines. Whatever may have come to his head? His hand ran smoothly, not crossing anything out. He had no reason to. He was a man possessed by a new spirit. He grunted under his breath.

"Sometimes, Nigel, we have to do things to find out the reason for it."

I nodded because the less I said, the better.

Again, one by one, with a red pen he numbered each document on the top right corner of the desk, and then entered the same numbers at the appropriate points in his computer text by way of reference.

With a bureaucrat's neat manners he stapled the exhibits together and inserted them in a file marked 'Nigel.' Closing the file he stood up and gave an unrestrained relief and thrust down his arms behind him like a man slipping off a harness. The ghostly formlessness of adolescence was over. He was in a new mode, the mode of selflessness and the desire to make penance, do good for the sake of humankind, in this new emerging era - where actions with a human-face are taking precedence over senseless obscene greed and man's inherited, selfish desire to dominate.

Lightly, very lightly, almost on tiptoe, almost as if he were afraid to give our presence away to some occupants in the next room, he peered through a peephole. Smiled a sardonic smile. Paused on his way back at the desk and read the decoded message again, that for once he had not bothered to destroy. He may have been satisfied with what he has done.

"I would for once like to get out of the land of innuendo and the assumption that straight speakers go to hell - straight speaking is not for sinners Nigel, I'm ready to make amends. It is to be hoped that it's not too late."

I had no quarrel with this. I have never been an enemy of authority, and all that is good. On the contrary, I do have some authority in these areas myself. Especially as a former wavering soul, Mr. vague, I do know that power and justice are the same. For someone from the other end of a divergent spectrum, he is inspiring and perhaps more. He has shown me the official and unofficial versions of his identity. Two sides of the same coin...

He has taught me to respect his complexity and to reckon as much with his secret world as with his overt one. It was as if the privacy this computer room presented, allowed each player to reveal his many cards, fake or real is of no account; that would compromise the whole aura. I was prepared for everything except for the pace and urgency of this intrusion or invasion, and the possibility of being caught red handed by a group who believes the taking of a life is necessary to preserve their obscene deeds. Then one might ask - does everything have to wear a disguise to appear real? A writer, someone once asked: 'It's a monarch, who should look down with love upon his subjects, even when the subject is his enemy.' My obligation, from my translation of the above, is to relate or recount the story as unbiased as humanly possible. There really shouldn't be any special affection or love for the protagonist - or should there?

"Your version of justice may not be too different from mine, Nigel. Let things be. You're looking for a more rational explanation or solution, there isn't one, can you give me one? I may still have to kill you yet - for my own sake. I have much more to lose by supporting you, the public may not see it my way."

What does he mean, 'for his sake?' I wish he had known the elaborate plans I went through with the police task force, the SWAT team, in preparing Michelle as a mole in his domain. I am sure he would not have brought me to this control room. I am also sure he does know that I am not a government agent, nor a representative of any of its organizations. I do have many explaining to do to my people, especially to Michelle, who had risked her neck and so much, to get me this far. This would seem a 180-degree turn to her and others. I still believe it's the right move, for the benefit of humankind - The bigger landscape...

"What's your real name? I hate calling you the 'Hired Killer,' and I know 'Delaney' and 'Mueller' aren't your names. What is it?"

"I do not think it's in your best interest to know my name, or for that matter, be associated with me - especially not after our invasion of this computer room. Those I work for are not the most civilized when it comes to people who breach their security. The central role of secrecy in their operations cannot be overemphasized – it's a reaffirmation of traditional tradecraft in an era of leaks and the pressure for ever greater disclosure. To them, secrecy is not a dirty word - secrecy is not there as a cover-up - Secrecy plays the crucial part in keeping the organization safe and secure." He continues.

"If their operations and methods become public, it would weaken their game plan, and won't work when you shed the traditional cloak of their trade. No members of the group are supposed to be identified in public, and their movements are not widely publicized."

"It's illegal and abhorrent under any circumstances," I cut in. "We should do nothing to be enablers of their evil deeds, in what they would like us to believe is a conflict between safety considerations and perceived operational need depicting their group as caught between the need for information and the manner of its acquisition and usage." I added.

"These are not abstract questions just for philosophy courses or searching editorials, they are real, constant operational dilemmas and fears borne out of primordial self-preservation," he said, "sometimes there is no clear way forward. The more finely balanced judgments have are made by the top leaders themselves." He continues.

"As much as this would demystify the aura, the urban legend that have been built around me, that of a cold blooded and unfeeling monster, I warn you to do all that is humanly possible not to be associated with me, or the invasion of this computer lab. It would do nothing but hasten your elimination. For the sake of plausible deniability, I would rather you be in the shadows with no hint of ever knowing me. It would cause you nothing but pain, trust me on this." I reminded him that pain is my business and that elimination comes with the spy game, and that if one has been killed as many times as I have been killed, one gets used to it. I also reminded him, lest he had forgotten, of why we are here, who the true enemies are and their vulgar capabilities....

"Your benefactors, the people you work for as you put it, adore crisis - they feast on it. They spend their lives dividing and conquering

- quartering the globe in search of crises to revive their flagging libidos. Remember, uninformed speculation is the true enemy within. They need to be exposed and facts are needed for the avoidance of speculation or doubt." I said to him.

"These are not normal people, they are not the kinds of people who believe in the saying: 'no leader wants to go down in history as the one who destroyed his country in an afternoon.' They have a narcissistic objection to suicide. Remember, the laws are too often governed by precedents - which by themselves are all too often imperfect. The leaders and their operatives are very good at using the law, exploring it, manipulating it to suit their needs and advance their goals. They are adept at taking advantage of every loophole available. It is in their best interest to do so." He responded.

All this could very well have sprung from a precise desire for instant self-isolation or selflessness, but with that edge to succeed evident in his voice and piercing eyes. His methodology was his elusive weapon. Michelle was his student all right – a good information research officer, who has proven her loyalty to me. I very much hope she is okay. Although I was somewhat taken by his new attitude of talkativeness and willingness to do good, for the greater good, I still needed to be on my guard, if only to detect a dishonesty in the making, an impostor. So I said:

"I am grateful for your change of heart, trying to help me and all that, and it would be easy to say: let's call this whole thing off. No, I do not intend to do that. The goal of exposing everyone and anyone involved in this insane and senseless killings, for whatever reason or rational, goes on, with or without your help." His response was solemn, and his tone very uncharacteristic of the man and legend I have come to know. He said:

"The thing about that, and I have to warn you, on what to keep in mind as you execute your action plans - is that the organization itself is not easy to get rid of. It is very amorphous in its constitution. It is more like the specie of animal, which when you cut off one part, they grow another part, a replacement. In this case, when you think you have eliminated them, exposed or whatever, they reconstitute and morph into something else, more nebulous and innocuous on the surface but deadly in within…what I am trying to tell you is that, there are always others to take their place – Sleepers, who are activated by those whose information is not even in the database, but who monitor the situation, the activities of the organization from the shadows. You might still want to consider calling this whole thing off. On my part, I promise there would be no more killings, not from me anyway. I will clear my desk, give my files to a government agency in Washington, who is equipped to deal with such matters, take what is left of my account in this country and retire to an isolated Island, where I will meditate on my sins for the rest of my life. I hope the Big one above forgives me. This is all I can offer."

'Impressive, but how do I trust you, and for that matter, how do I know you won't drop dead the minute you step out of here? If your description of your former benefactors is true and to be taken seriously, and I am more inclined to believe they are true. What I want is some form of evidence, some information, preferably computer printouts that would hold up to scrutiny. What you would get in return from me are unbiased comments and analyses that are followed by actions – actions that either put these fellows behind bars or at least exposed for what they truly are. If by chance, there are any moral lessons, they were not intended, but you can take credit for them or use them for your rest-of-your-life meditation. I do not strive to moralize and point fingers, but would allow the words, actions and characters involved in this macabre series of events to be the true messenger. As an eminent philosopher once said - 'Let the long logic beneath the story, which is so secretly kept, very carefully crafted out of view, dictate the pace and why - thoughts about life in the ecumenical mode, not an episodic event that is totally amplified, that the message is lost - more like writing plainly and unmistakably.'"

He did not interrupt me, so I continued. "This is my only offer, in this attempt to foster the cause of justice. It is more to help you in your retirement. Foods for your meditations - spiritual food that deserves attention, which is also thought provoking, if you may - a catharsis, that ultimate cleansing process - It's my offer, my gifts, take it. Do not be arrogant in a situation that doesn't call for arrogance. It's utter stupidity, and I would say it borders on unforgivable greed on both sides, your latest moves notwithstanding, and they are no less than treason. Take it from me, in this endeavor, accommodations can be made between people of all stripes, and different purposes; what is needed is teamwork. Together we can accomplish more for our individual causes than we can separately. Michelle trusts me, you trusted her and you can trust me. More like A equals B, B equals C. A therefore equals C."

I was hoping this would reach a place in him, that place that exists in all of us, when things become clearer, because we have grown some, from events of yesterday and from the events of the seconds and minutes and hours and days before then, opening up new vistas to solving issues we disagree on, thereby creating trust, trust that produces a more cooperative attitude because we have seen it all on our way through Damascus. I was soon proven wrong. The killer had not gotten to that place yet. His words were emphatic.

"Don't bother me with your morality," he said, "enjoy your faith, practice it, but don't burden me with it. I've enough to contend with in just trying to stay alive and make amends, if I can. I'm trying to think, I cannot do so clearly when you proselytize. I would tell you everything I know if no one else was listening, but take this folder, it's part of the solution, but it's not all. This place is gonna become crowded shortly..."

With that he disappeared into the night. I called after him – "I want to help you, can't you see. Are you that blind?" He was gone. My words were lost in the soft breeze blowing across Emerald Lake. I headed towards the parking lot, trying not to arouse the other neighbors. This was crazy I thought. He is the one trained to handle these kinds of things. He specializes not only in causing bodily harm, but also in producing harmful nervous breakdowns. Now he has thrown this half dossier at me, expecting me to decode and assemble the profiles of some very powerful men in government and industry.

What motivates him? Was it for want of a greater sea, a larger arena - that he had repeatedly wrecked himself against nature's little pebbles, challenging his creator and benefactors to come up with something bigger or put him to rest? Would he be so headstrong when faced with greater odds? All of a sudden, he presents me with an odd mixture of vulnerability and strength. Whatever pain he had endured or caused anyone over the years he refused to turn into self-pity. He recognized the dictates of his profession; understood that the products come with the territory - And the guilt, the fear and this new eagerness to do good, hound those who choose the path of his past. This inspired a spiritual alarm greater than anything I was prepared for. I was in a useless sort of way, angry with myself, at him and everyone participating in this grotesque theatre of the obscene.

All this reinforced my belief that there is a need for a fitting convergence of objectives, rearranged in time and purpose to accommodate all parties without conflict. Will they listen? Has it gone too far for this to work? The killer must have also realized that he would be held responsible both for what he does, has done as well as for what he does not do.

The Odyssey of Man - it's paradoxes
An Exciting Story

When it comes to the odyssey of man, the paradoxes embedded are well known, sometimes without the truly salient or exciting ones. It is also established that man's sins or screw-ups are partially responsible for his mediocrity, which invariably led to this paradoxes, which in simple terms is really our inconsistencies and illogical truths. Knowing this, how can man's story be told without bias or sectarianism? Will this be possible within the realm of humankind, with all of its imperfections - to tell this story, void of the traits of our a fly in the ointment inheritance? Least of which are the battle between the right and the left. Between the tea party and the coffee party? Between east and west? How can one truly tell this story without raising the ire of one or all the groups?

The answer, as hard and elusive as it might seem, is yes. It is truly possible because cultured people know what is wrong by reflecting on lasting results, and a reflection on lasting results produces less pain or melancholy, and at the end bringing smiles because of truths revealed, lights shed on seemingly intractable problems – revealing that negative subjects could be discussed without sounding negative, because they were expressed with respect for all parties. In the process, all participants realize that all beings may be different; their concerns are similar. Resolving from there on to guard deliberately the speeches they make, and moderate their assumptions, knowing that they are playing assigned roles bestowed by the universe for the greater good, at least, without the camera to pose for. Making the day-to-day actions and comments dictate insights into the modification of all behaviors. Using reasonableness, and endeavoring to not be too dogmatic, but commenting on life's activities as they unfold. Working to separate the petty concerns from the main purpose, and highlighting the importance of the bigger picture. Knowing that when there is sincerity, fear is eliminated, because there is broad agreement.

The alternative, a not too palatable choice, is to step away from both – and admit failure. If reasonableness is the yardstick, the attitude of stepping away becomes unacceptable. Because reasonableness helps mortal man refine his inconsistencies - producing a more rational and balanced behavior, even with his imperfections, even under adverse circumstances.

So, it happened, that this adventure of mine, became more complicated than I had anticipated. This is the odyssey of man, exciting, full of paradoxes and questions begging for answers.

Why did the hired killer - (he never did tell me his true name), bring me to the control room, only to suddenly disappear into the night after a veiled threat? Why did he really kill all those people? There are partial answers to that. It is now obvious that it had nothing to do with any political, ideological or philosophical considerations. It had all to do with market economy, the supply and demand of it. The benefactors had a job, a demand - he had the skills, the supply – end of question? May not be as simple as that, because in the core of all humans, there is something bigger than the mere supply and demand of the marketplace. These are answers that are not easy to come by.

The more I knew about Mr. Delaney, the more it became clear to me that I had been right all along, that there are more powerful people behind him, who have their fingers on the buttons. The fear I saw in his face; while in the computer room validates this line of thought. There was, in spite of how much he tries to veil it, a hint of fear and uneasiness, reminiscent of an agent, who is trying to come out of the cold. Would he accept rehabilitation? Can he trust anyone and can he be trusted?

It is possible he may be trying to turn 'Good Guy.' He has in one single swoop, made obsolete my own 'Blueprint,' which took me considerable time and energy and almost non existent capital, to put together. I now have to try another way, for he has thrown a big wrench in my works.

Any new blueprints will have to be improvised on a moment-to-moment basis; there is just no more state of great comfort where time is concerned. It is clear to me, he really was trying to tell me something in that computer room, until time caught up with us, and he sensed things might be closing in, that I am sure of - And that, whatever it was, I need to find out, and find out fast. It is the joy of observing the observer observe. When instant mental calculus in dealing with arising obstacles becomes the value system that drives the goal – in the game of waiting, worrying and running that is the art of spying.

I followed him at an even pace. From the parapets of the gazebo and swimming pool of the Phase one lighthouse-deco club house; through the shores of Emerald Lake, the lagoons and fish ponds through the sprawling parking lot at the Phase Two Seagull Lane 6848 complex, where he got into a black Spitfire Spider.

The Mirage was no match for the sleek and maneuverable Spider, but I did my best tailing him. He went through Dwyer to Dowman Road. Then took Crowder to Lake Forest onto Chef Menteur and over the Danziger Draw Bridge, where he made a quick U-turn and headed in the direction of the High-rise and the French Quarter, by way of Armstrong Park. He had a quick rendezvous at Saint Louis Cemetery, with a dark profiled individual. This must have been the meeting he arranged while we were at the computer room. Items were exchanged. My eyes almost popped out when I saw Mr. Delaney reach into his breast pocket and come out with a silenced gun, and in a hugging position, shoot the dark profiled individual, who slowly slumped to the ground, helped by the killer. He simultaneously cat-wheeled and landed behind a larger tombstone and at the same breath, released a volley of shots, directed at the holder of a telescopic rifle, west of the cluster of the tombstones. The gun and the owner fell to the ground.

I broke into a cold sweat. My stomach was in a knot. I had to fight the urge to vomit. I watched him walk briskly out of the cemetery as if nothing had happened. Did he kill the dark profiled individual because he sensed a betrayal, or is it just the continuation of the senseless killings he had vowed to extirpate himself from? He took

Iberville to Bourbon and Royal streets. He crossed Canal to Saint Charles and headed towards Lee Circle, made the circle and turned back, and headed to the foot of Canal, at the ITM building. None of it made sense. It was more like a wild goose chase, but in circles - Unless the ulterior motive was to shake off some tail. My tail? I wasn't sure if he had caught on to me yet.

He parked the car near the boat entrance of the International Trade mart. He got into another car and drove it to the Riverwalk. Parked the car and turned off all the lights except the taillights. He waited inside the car, for what seemed like eternity. No one came out of the shadows and no one shot at him. He got out of the car. He looked very imposing in his getup.

He took a brisk walk to the Spanish Plaza and walked on to Piazza d' Italia, where he waited as if expecting someone to come out of the shadows and hand him some package or information. This never happened. He then walked to Decatur. Here he met with a young brunette who came out of Jackson Square, dressed in an almost identical outfit.

They walked across to Cafe du Monde and bought what looked like cafe Au lait and some beignet. Now holding hands, they easily blended with the other tourists. Through the Moonwalk, they walked to the banks of the Mississippi, like old companions, they walked silently, surveying the waterfront. A chain of merchant ships straddled the harbor mouth, their rigging drawn in a necklace of lights. The brunette handed the Killer a black pouch and received a short heated lecture in return. They walked to Jackson Brewery and disappeared into an art gallery.

The agony of waiting for him to emerge was worse than tailing his car. Spying is worrying, spying is waiting, and spying is patience, the only antidote to driving yourself crazy. A look at my timepiece indicated an expenditure of about two hours at the Brewery thus far. Panic was setting in. Has he left? I ran to the Kiosk north of the escalator and inquired from the attendant about the man dressed in black, who went into the gallery awhile back. I told the young attendant that he could not have missed him, because of the unique outfit of the killer, and for the simple reason that the exit close to his Kiosk is the only possible departure point.

He said he never saw anyone with that description, and gave me this look that said, 'get away from me Pervert.' I knew to continue the enquiry would be useless. I turned and decided to return to my last vantage point. Then I saw him. He emerged with the mystery woman of the past night, Michelle's friend. They did not see me. They headed to the French Market, where they conversed with a fruit Vendor for a brief moment.

What happened next happened quickly - A Street corner transaction - a willing seller to a willing buyer. The vendor looked behind him, past his shoulders. This, I presumed, was to take the stiffness out of their conversation and make it less conspicuous to anybody watching, or just to make sure no body was watching who is not supposed to be watching. This time, packages were exchanged. He hailed a Cab and got in, leaving Michelle's mystery friend behind. I took the next available Cab and gave instructions to follow the killer's cab.

He was dropped off at Little Italy and walked the rest of the way to the Warehouse District. Here, he went into a secluded Warehouse, with rusty doors. I wasn't sure which of the buttons he had pressed for the release mechanism that opened the door.

I took a quick review of my idea so far, I accepted, I was being guided by ad hoc decisions, and ad hoc decisions at this stage of the game, are never advisable. They are almost never advisable at any stage, unless in true emergency points. So, not knowing whether the killer had caught onto me, I pressed the middle button in the rows of color-coded buttons. The door swung open with a distinctly subdued hiss. I immediately ducked under the bench to my right as I heard the ricochet of shots from a silenced gun.

as for the cowards and those
without faith...

There were more gunshots and bullets ricocheting, producing a deafening orchestra. I could not see who the participants were, but from the sounds movements, I estimated at least three to four people were involved.

I crawled my way to the east end of the massive warehouse, using the double Decker platforms as my new cover. There was a lull in the gun battle, giving way to stone silence. Then some shadowed figure caught my attention. I was frozen by what I saw. Before me stood a pair of massive feet in what looked like eel skin boots, with flat rubber soles. Rivulets of perspiration were trickling down the small of my back. The huge feet made the 'honor guard' round a couple of times, stopped and listened for sound. I was happy he never took any horizontal look at the decked structure.

This has turned into a tale of looking for the obvious, when one should worry about the unexpected. I had thrust myself into this without any preparation. I was not armed, and my Karate and Judo rusty from the long period of inactivity. If I had done what Michelle advised, I would have bought a gun between when we last met and now. To stay noiseless, I occupied my mind by meditating one of my favorite koans, which in a way demonstrated the inadequacies of the logical reasoning that went into this planning.

This quandary, my present helpless predicament of being caught in the middle of the affairs of paid executioners; who wouldn't bat an eye in their eagerness to eliminate me, if I'm discovered; made me think of those people on death row, what must go through their minds, seconds before the axe falls. It's eerie, when helpless in the face of death. All kinds of things race through a once solid mind. The only antidote, again, is the use of internalized meditation to maintain calm, sanity and quietness.

The major worry I had was the possibility that siege mentality might set in. If it does, how do I cure it? Do I just ignore the fact that this problem exists, taking a page from the conveniences of modern great alliances – which to me is, the ultimate kiss of death. That self imposed jeopardy and the possibility of twisting priority, whose only countercurrent is truth as the only justification – at least, truth allows one to see the obstacle and the common denominator – which took me to the story of he who was in search of truth. Did he find truth? Is there really truth? If so, how does truth relate to lie? As Picasso once said, are they the same? In this era when information moves at such a dizzying pace, in spinning vortex; splintered fragments that assail us everyday and every minute, it's hard to recognize perfect truth, or for that matter, find perfect truth or perfect anything when the whole world seems to be going crazy, shifting increasingly to perfidious ways.

Charlie, I love the name Charlie, and Charlie is my best friend. I do miss his words of wisdom now, more than at any other time. He once said - 'One who refuses to heed, lives in a fools paradise, waiting for the earthquake to hit, like the cat who got on the Ferris wheel, only to experience the ever terrifying kiss of death. Such is the terrifying arithmetic, of the nonbeliever, Nigel.' Those were Charlie's exact words. I am quite sure, and they were not for philosophy 102.

Suddenly, all hell broke lose. The Killer, cat-wheeled from the top of one of the double-decked platforms. Raced to the door and onto the open field. In pursuit were two heavy set men, who would pass for Wall Street Stock Brokers – they were decked out in their pinstripe three-piece black suits. There were shouts of: 'don't let him get away, block the exit.' The killer was too agile for them. Swift and graceful; even as the devil reincarnate that he is, one could not help but admire his nimbleness.

The black Spitfire Spider came to a screeching halt, in a cloud of dust. The passenger door flew open. The killer quickly got in. Driving was Michelle's mystery friend, still in her black outfit, but now covered with black headgear. She took off before the door was closed. She spun the wheel, the powerful car swung around on the soft, sandy earth, leaping over ruts on this deserted primitive road and reversing its direction. She slammed her foot on the accelerator, stabbing it into the floor, and then circled the Jaguar XJ12 sedan, in a volcanic Santa Ana. All done with practiced deftness. Bullets chased them from the guns of the men in Stock Brokers' outfits. Unable to stop or disable the Spitfire, they felt their way to their car - the Silver XJ12 Jaguar, which now looked more like a car that had just taken part in a mud car race. They climbed in and followed in pursuit.

I had to kick myself, for being left behind without a car. Then the impossible happened. A cab pulled up, and it was my old Cabbie. I said, "What are you doing here?" "I never left," he said, "I was kind of suspicious, so I hung around, incase you might need me again. This is not the kind of neighborhood to be without transportation, you know." That was that. I never gave myself time to contemplate or logically analyze why a cabbie would wait for a dropped off fare, who never gave instructions to that effect. My main concern was what was happening to the occupants of the sleek high-powered vehicles that just took off in excruciating storms of dust, not for the love they have for each other, but for an obscene hatred and eagerness to kill the truth and anything that stands in the way of their benefactors. Allies turned enemies - A classic example of greed and the selfish desire to dominate - An inherited folly of humankind.

"Follow them," I shouted. It was in pursuit that the Cabbie gave me a synopsis of his biography - that in his regular job, he wears a sky-blue shirt and navy blue pants. Translated, he is a member of the N.O.P.D. On his off days' he moonlights driving his friend's cab. To support a daughter who goes to U.N.O, and a son at Tulane Law School. Several times, I had to caution him to pay attention to where he was headed, due to his habit of turning his head whenever he wanted to make a point, or make sure I was listening. "I know this city like the back of my hand," he told me. I am sure he does, and he is a darn good driver too, but killing us was not part of the bargain, I told him.

Final Solution

and they will walk by means
of its lights...

The two cars had a couple minutes on us, which is quite a lot, considering the comparative advantage of their high performance cars. My initial line of thought was that Michelle's mystery friend and the killer, were headed to either of two places; the computer information center or to Lake Forest. So I was surprised when the Cabbie took Front Street and headed towards Poydras. He said to trust him. "I have very good eyesight, and besides, remember, I do this for a living and this is the area I patrol in my squad car. If they are headed to New Orleans east, naturally, the professional would take the less crowded route to the freeway." I had to resign myself to the thought that, he was seeing what I wasn't, or the length of my inactivity has really taken its toll on my street smarts. I never was the streetwise type anyway.

The Cabbie was right. We spotted the two cars at the intersection of Poydras and North Broad. They were momentarily delayed by the traffic lights. Were now headed south, towards the freeway entrance at the foot of Broad Street and north Claiborne. There were no gunshots. These were 'civilized' men, and civilized people do not do those kinds of acts in crowded thoroughfares.

They were very calm, considering that the killing of each other was the uppermost thing on their minds. Michelle's friend, who is now darkly bespectacled, looked more like a mannequin. The black hair cover and the rouge lipstick, added to the mystique and allure. She had one of those determined faces, irrevocable, a very beautiful sculpture of polished marble – with her very high cheekbones and sinewy, conditioned body. She earns most of her acclaim for the furious intelligence she invests her role. In the psychedelic lights of the previous night, her tall body had reminded me of someone in a recent life. It was lean but not thin, complimented with a fine neat waist and strong legs. Her black hair was luxuriant and when let go, falls on a shoulder and firm breasts that would make the goddess of love blush. Whether clothed or naked, she could make no gesture that did not have its grace - curves of perfection. She is a beautiful woman. The killer knows how to pick them - or do they pick him, as in the case of Michelle?

"What's your name, mister?" This caught me by surprise; I had forgotten about the Cabbie - I was lost in my own thoughts.

"Peters, Nigel Peters." I said.

"Mine is Frank, Frank Delgado. My friends call me Frankie."

"It's nice to meet you Frankie."

"Same here, Mr. Peters."

"Please, call me Nigel,"

'It's a pleasure meeting you, Nigel,'

He was an amiable man, probably of simple means, if not for the kids and the wife, who probably gulp down his paychecks and more. I have to concentrate on the quarries. A thought struck me. Now that I know or think I know where they are headed, why don't I go pick up Michelle from the French Quarter apartment. She does know the logistics of 'Mr. Delaney's' flat and other relevant information I may need. I also needed to tell her about her mystery friend's new involvement and get the true gist on her.

So I said to the Cabbie – "Do you know Captain Banks?"

"He heads the SWAT outfit," the Cabbie responded.

"He is my in-law." I said.

"You don't say. Real swell guy. I can't forget a statement he used in closing a class on SWAT delusions a while back. He said: 'A man who cannot speak clearly cannot think clearly, and self-expression is the companion of logic.' I did not quite get the drift then, but later I realized since SWAT people may have to talk hostage holders out of their misguided missions, it is necessary to be able to think and talk clearly."

Ignoring the temptation to enquire about the appropriateness of the statement in the present scheme of things, I said -

"I will like to take the rest of your day, if you don't mind, going rate, I mean market rate and more." I offered.

"I am much obliged, really my pleasure. As for any more reward, you were more than generous the first time, I am enjoying this as much as you, if you don't mind my quip." He said with a yawn of nervous excitement.

So I called Michelle from a pay phone at the Clarion, and asked her to meet me in front of the Royal Street flat she was sharing with her friend, after she opted to become my sidekick. Going up to meet Michelle was risky, from many points of view. In her serious mode, Michelle's face and the words that come out her mouth are those of a haunting genius, a cool freak with a gift for reading men's mind and a steely contempt for authority. On the other hand, when she is in her playful mode, she is like a lump of butter melting in the sun because it lacked a consistent point of view. I wasn't sure which Michelle would emerge to meet me, just as much as I was not sure if it was Michelle I did not trust, or myself in front of her, alone without her clothes on.

Michelle would never come down to meet me - she would always say, whenever I tell her I got to run, she would say: 'walk, Nigel, don't run.' She believes a calm methodical approach to things reduces the possibility of mistakes - It is why she likes to welcome me without her clothes on. She believes the right amount of sex helps take away tension, sexual or otherwise in the heat of battle - especially in the mix of bad company. This, she says is the key to the killer's successes, for he never succumbs to seduction on assignments. He makes sure he gets the right amount of sex before he leaves home. She believes it was the understanding of the killer to love your profession, at the same time hating the system that perpetrates it. She would look at me with those big eyes – with an intensity that said: 'I'll kill you if you do not love me back,' just as she has reminded me on numerous occasions - 'Nigel, I don't normally switch my allegiance like I just did. There is nothing disloyal in betrayal, provided you betray what you hated for what you loved. I love you Nigel, just as much as I....'

Here, I would give my placating blush and short giggle and touch her lips with my index finger. It works all the time.

Unable to finish the statement, she would plant one of her marathon kisses on me. Is it possible she now hates the killer? Is it merely thinking like a hero to behave like a decent human being? She said we betray to be loyal, and that betrayal is like imagining when the reality isn't good enough. All I could think was that I'm learning a lot of philosophy in a short time from this woman. Then she would raise her face and look at me with the ever big hazel eyes, turn and look out the window as if trying to will away any tears that might be forming in her eyes, then would look back at me again and say:

"This is the Nigel I have known these past years, the Nigel who can't rest until he has touched the love in people, then can't rest till he's hacked his way out of it, the more drastic and dramatic the better."

"The Nigel who does nothing cynical, nothing without conviction. Who sets events in motion and later becomes their victim. What he calls decisions - Nigel who ties himself into pointless relationships, which he calls loyalty. Then the same Nigel who waits for the next event to get him out of the last one, which he calls destiny all because he cannot bear to let anyone down. I can go on and on. I hope this is a new Nigel, the one I love with all my heart. May you never be victim of your own goodness, may you be rewarded for it, my one and only true love."

This would move and touch my soul, as I believe it would any other true red-blooded man. It was a moving testimony of the 'new and improved' Michelle - The Michelle who has really captivated my heart. The blueprint for the bigger picture would preclude my showing it. So I would continue my thoughts on the son of the German immigrants.

By temperament and training, the killer is an agent-runner and captain of men. A determined primitive, just as any one who deals in the vast unsavory quagmire of human nature has to be. A man who would substitute violence or any other adequate vice for the truth, because they believe nobody wants to hear the truth - that truth does not sell. Truth might make them lose their jobs, their self-esteem and vaunted position in the community. Gambling with the fate of humanity. Virtue becomes passé, because they can't change or simply don't know how to change, in this emerging new and improved world order of rapid change. They have locked themselves up in their own paranoia. Experimenting in space and smart weapons, instead of in humankind. Investing in so-called clever toys that get cleverer with every generation, toys that become obsolete a few years hence. There is never enough security on either side. Not for the main players anyway, and definitely not for the newcomers who run themselves up a huge luggage of bombs in their haste to join the club.

Creating unlikely situations and scenarios developed in the labs and computer assisted sources. In this scenario, this particular type of people, develop a situation where a player has such grotesque fantasies about another that he ends up inventing an enemy he needs to justify his belligerency. Exorcising ghosts no one else can see.

> but anything not sacred and anyone
> that carries on a disgusting thing
> and a lie will in no way enter into...

Good voices do not always belong to good faces, but Michelle's voice matched her beautiful face. She was glad to hear from me, she said. I couldn't help but become retrospective about the risk she had put herself in for me. I was glad she was okay. Michelle, the faithful, virtuous and strong - Michelle the brave and beautiful, who even in her own fear had offered to be my sidekick and provide me with valuable information into the working mind of the killer - Michelle who uses her computer virtuoso to burglarize and expose the dark secrets of the killer and his benefactors, exposing corruption in high places, and proving that evil has a long tail, and that the shady fellows on the other side concoct conspiracies of the powerful against the weak – with revelation men who are bent on infernal mischief. She was a natural giver who remembers promises, just as she remembers many other things, with the directness of an unencumbered mind. She has a class, a disarming demeanor only nature can bestow. She has also refined nature's gifts, and with the help of the German immigrant, raised them to the quintessential level, just like the fabled Classicist. All she asks is that we stay alive, long enough to solve the mystery and confront the men who have done this.

Michelle also knows that the immediate malefactors are merely doing the bidding of some higher powers and that her distrust of seemingly harmless old men, which others might see as paranoia, is merely a keen appraisal of the way this dark world works. In today's world, everything is a game. Her presentation and smoldering persona – her rapacity and severely seductive look, is simply impossible not to watch. She's aware of all these, it is why she tries to tamp it down, so people can focus on the substantial part of her presentation, and not the well conditioned body -Because, it would be a shame if the real message is lost because of the superficial outside. This is the alchemy of the story and star.

She has helped me in developing the needed steadying familiarity with the routines of espionage, which have been lacking due to the length of my inactivity. I was proud to oblige her, by throwing caution to the winds for once and not trying to find invisible enemies or other sound excuses for doing nothing, as I would have done in the era of Jamie. This is Michelle's era. She makes sure I do not forget it. She lectures at every opportunity she gets, when she thinks my mind is being clouded by distractions unrelated to the mission at hand - About the art of love, friendship, and devotion - And last, but not least, about the new level to which the game of spying has been raised.

"When you go after a subject Nigel, you've got to move fast while the evidence is still planted on him."

Then, I would say – "What evidence do I have on the killer?"

"I will help you find out." She would say, as she pushes back an unruly lock of hair. "Don't you worry, my little pumpkin."

Knowing how much I hate it when she calls me that. She is the only woman I know, who is bold as to stand close enough to check a man's arithmetic and not bat an eye. Only Michelle would preface this action with one of those fastidious grins, which in a woman always reminds the man of his masculinity, and the need to rescue the belle in....unreasoning ferocity.

Michelle never accepts the precept: 'never go out and play until you have wrapped up the day's business.' To Michelle, it is an aphorism, a twice-told tale of an old song, whose time has come and gone. To her a little sex goes a long way in business and pleasure. When I say, 'Remember women are my vocation, they are my life's study and my consuming passion.' She would say, 'Only when I am the only woman in this love story.' Since in moments of crises our thoughts do not run consecutively but rather sweep over us in waves of intuition, we would do the right thing - which is only natural in humankind.

and he showed me a river of water
of life, clear as crystals flowing...
down the middle of its broad way...

Michelle took my admonition and was waiting by the corner of Royal and Saint Ann. She was in one of her tight faded jeans that enhance her crotch, with enough credit for her backside. This was matched with a light cotton jacket that came to her midriff, exposing her belly button, suggestive of a young woman on holiday, with an evident wanderlust which seems almost genetic, an inbred need to see something more of the world, someplace else, as if to confirm its true existence.

She was leaning against the rusted railing common in the French quarter, searching the horizon, the array of lean-muscled college kids in middle distance, her honey-colored eyes behind blue-tinted aviators, the breeze touching her caramel, flyaway hair – as if reminiscing about soaking up sun in San Sebastian, on the Basque coast of Spain, her last vacation spot, sipping her usual, an Asian bubble tea – her lips, the naked pink of an ingénue.

She saw my signal and climbed in the back seat, which was an art of its own. She had to politely tell off the potential male suitor who kept her company until I got there. She uses men like that - when the need arises - Especially in the French Quarter. As I turned around to exchange compliments, I noticed anger showing on her face. The kind of sulking little kids do when their parents take their lollipop away. The reason was not far fetched. In a voice unveiled of command or dissatisfaction, she said – "Pull over at the next corner, mister."

She said this, as if trying to shake her mind free of its bad thoughts, bad thoughts acquired during our short hiatus. This moving vehicle has to be stopped to achieve this phenomenon. I was quite wrong.

"What would that be for, Michelle?" I asked.

"Come to the back." She answered.

"Not here Michelle, please not here."

"I thought the reason you came for me was so that we can talk, If we are going to talk, wouldn't your coming to the back be the logical thing to do?"

That makes sense, but knowing Michelle, it would not stop there; she has no inhibitions, the epitome of a libber. She once considered running for the local chapter of NOW. I decided to climb to the back of the cab, if only to maintain peace and hoped she had the task of the bigger picture in mind – and she did, surprising me, she went straight to the point, the matter at hand.

"How far does your expertise extend when it comes to cybernetics and the use of cyclotron as boosters?" I took this with a grain of salt, a payback, her way of shocking me into seeing the foolishness of my last rude treatment of her...

"What's that?" I said, not expecting the quick change in subject. My tone was cordial, but expressed the thought that she might have decided to shock me into seeing the frivolity of my earlier assumption, this even when I was not quite sure what charged atomic and subatomic particles have to do with the mission at hand.

"C'mon Nigel, for God's sakes, you're a teacher, you know what Cybernetics is," she said with exasperation.

"I do know what cybernetics is, what I do not know is in what context, and its relative use of cyclotron, which I thought was an apparatus for nuclear energy where atomic and subatomic particles are accelerated by an alternating electric field while following an outward spiral or circular path in a magnetic field, yes? Please be explicit my dear. No need for head games, please. Time is of utmost importance."

"Please! Your humility overwhelms me, and don't 'dear' me," she said.

"Get to the point Michelle, we are heading to the killer's place, who is being hunted down as we speak." I said.

"Since when have you been that concerned with what happened to him, and by the way, his name is uncle Nephilim. Everyone calls him uncle, if it means anything to you."

"That's not what I hear. I have been concerned since I ran into him earlier today."

"What did you hear?" Michelle said, ignoring the second part of my statement, which people seem to do when they really do not want to deal with a particular subject, or are mulling it over, using the time to ready an appropriate response. I find it not only impolite, but also rude. Now in answer to her question, I said -

"That he is the son of an immigrant parent, the Baranowskys."

"Everyone in America is an immigrant or the offspring of an immigrant, except the Indians, Nigel. If it makes any difference to you, the parents came from Sachsenhausen, Germany." She was taunting me now.

Take a reasonable attitude about all this, I said to myself. I have to discontinue the furtherance of similar attitude, the only way I know.

So I reached over and kissed her, allowing our tongues to meet, while I touched her bellybutton and the organ between it and the upper thighs. This works all the time. She reached over and encircled my neck with her arms, returning the affection, she said.

"Am sorry Nigel, I don't know what got over me, do you forgive me. I love you so... don't be too hard on me."

I touched her chin and told her that I know she loves me, and that I do care about her too, but that there is a need to concentrate on the work at hand. Then I said,

"Now, let's hear about the connection between the killer, I mean Uncle and this cybernetics thing." I said, as the words of a president came to mind, he once said: 'If you are walking down the right path, and you're willing to keep walking, eventually you will make progress.'

"Uncle's flat has one of the most sophisticated cybernetic control I know of. He has periodically upgraded them as time and the spy-craft industry evolves – he likes to keep abreast of the game, the tools that is. The interior design of his flat is no different from yours or mine. The differences are the panels innocuously placed, which are not obvious to the undiscerning eyes. There are hidden guns and other robotically controlled weapons, which are strategically positioned to fire at intervals. Only Uncle knows their timings and exact locations. He has perfected a way of maneuvering himself out of the different lines of fire, while trapping potential predators. Besides the cybernetics, there is another remote controlled box in his car, This can trigger gun levers placed outside, which is the domino for timed explosions, while he maneuvers himself to a safe location, logistically impenetrable by anyone else. Please Nigel, take very good note of this, if nothing else, in case you are trapped – there's a false bookshelf in the apartment, south of the library. Locate it when you get in there. It is your escape route when things start getting out of control - it takes you to another flat, and leads you out to the parking lot..." She paused for a moment, and then said:

'It's very elaborate and complicated." Michelle concluded.

"I must say," was all I could muster.

"So be very careful, pumpkin dear," stressing the 'dear.'

Whatever her human faults, and who among us is free of them, Michelle is genuine. I could not find any reason to question her loyalty, love or devotion to this enterprise or me. I had to resist the temptation of being mushy-mushy with her at this moment, as I felt myself falling in love with her as this whole thing progresses – and Michelle is easy to fall in love with. Showing it, expressing it, would have to wait until the conclusion of this mission - If we come out of it alive.

Then Michelle dropped the bombshell, compliments of her mystery friend's computer terminal hooked to Baranowsky's, which in turn had been tapped into the central command of his benefactors, before he became persona non grata. Michelle found out that, 'they' have got warrants and taps running on every telephone he had ever used and now have a blanket warrant for his arrest. Which explained his rushed exit out of the computer room earlier and the activities at the warehouse. They have instructed all their operatives to cancel their leaves and weekends, especially for all the transcribers and eavesdroppers. Surveillance teams have been placed on twenty-four-hour alert. They are questioning everyone who has shared office space with him in the past. Tenants in his block have been evacuated and they have stripped the place from top to bottom, pretending to be woodworm experts, while others are told a story about toxic contamination with deadly consequences. Because of their knowledge of Baranowsky's flat, its fortifications, they have decided to wait him out. It is a trust, very few powerful individuals, using their ill gotten gains, wealth amassed at the expense of the people, now using government as a club against everybody else, specially those who stand in their way. The dice are loaded. The playing field is not level.

There is clear evidence that the benefactors and their allies have amassed heavy firepower in and around the area. The so-called pest control experts and toxicologists have sophisticated weapons hidden under their 'work-clothes.' A television station sympathetic to them is said to have broadcast a cryptic message, target unknown, but which after careful analysis, seemed intended to demonized, scapegoat - turning one group against the other. There are machine gun mounted Rovers, helicopter gun ships and men in army fatigues with painted faces hidden behind the bushes. The operation, it seems, calls for total elimination. This is not a dead or alive mission, it is a dead, dead, command. I became very apprehensive. What does this mean to our mission? So I said:

"Wait, does this mean that my activities have been compromised?" I asked.

"In principle; yes. I really don't know. If I have to follow my hunches, judging from experience, I have got to tell you this, Nigel. Your operation, I believe, is probably so contaminated you wouldn't even want to throw them into your own trash can." She said with a look that stayed on me a beat too long. I wasn't prepared for jokes or sarcasm. She of all people should know that by now. My expression showed my disapproval of her carefree remark, which she may have meant as a joke. To mollify me, she said,

"Don't lose your objectivity over what I just said. I did what Uncle would have done, what he calls a 'last countdown,' but because of its ad hoc nature and the window of time I was allowed online, it was not sufficiently reconstructed to provide me full date, or for that matter, knowledge of the kind of data in their possession, dealing with you a possibility - I lost connection to the command center, when they pulled the plug on uncle's console as soon as he became persona non grata."

"You don't make any sense," I said, I could feel the sweat collecting on my back. "Did you do Reverse Charges?" I asked.

"That's only good for Middle Distance Transmissions, and how did you find out about reverse charges," she asked, forgetting that I was once a part of this trade of waiting, worrying and patience.

"I think I heard Baranowsky mumble such word, when he thought he had lost connection in the computer room, some kind of latent memory?" I lied.

'Sort of, but it did not apply in my case, a satellite - only good for the mother ship consoles. Anyway, everyone knows that if you run any succession of coincidences through a computer, you will discover that everything looks possible and that most scenarios look highly likely. At this point, all I can come up with are conjectures. Trying to piece together probable scenarios from the fragments, pieces of information I was able to gather from the little bit of time I had online. We just need to work hard to make sense out of them. We were made for this Nigel, an analyst and a profiler, between us, we should be able to connect the dots." She said, matter of fact.

It was like asking for the impossible and wanting it by yesterday. I had to control the anger this new information was building in me.

Then out of nowhere, she sprang the most grotesque, and definitely the most startling of her surprises, information I never thought I needed. Which she thought may come in handy if I find myself in the unlikely situation.

"Nigel, I know you may resent my playing teacher to you. You don't have to deny it. I can see it written all over your face. The macho thing and what you've always represented, I mean, having been part of this kind of organization and all that, and now relegated to playing second fiddle to a woman can't be easy. At the end, you will love me and thank me for all that I'm doing for you. You've been inactive for so long. What you don't need is ignorance of past or present methods of operation contributing to your failure." There is nothing wrong with this, who in his right mind would quarrel with such solicitude? Not me.

She continued. "It is possible that during this adventure of yours, you may come across explosives. If you know how to make them, naturally, you will be in a better position to defuse them. So, I'll teach you how to make a simple bomb, the way uncle taught me. Listen carefully."

Listen carefully! What does she mean, listen carefully? I am not so desperate to do what she is suggesting. On a day of indirect hints and hazy suggestions, this was a blockbuster. No, this wasn't the understanding of value the new and improved world order is asking people to trust, never part of the bargain. It is not about people running out the back door while someone is coming in the front door. I am not ready to cede power to these people who invented false science of economics when they knew defenseless people would fall prey to the market forces they helped create. I am not in the market for making toys of mass destruction. It is not compatible with the new order, the liberation of the world from fear. That is the system to be overcome – a system where everyone is afraid of betrayal, loss of freedom and death. The goal: to purge the helplessness beneath its satanic plot; which combines the extreme reaches of illusion and reality - prying into our deepest fears and insecurities, evoking the terror of helplessness, betrayal, and death and of deep psychological consternation. This is not a cry in the wilderness, for John the Baptizer lived in a saner era. Yes, these ills, such as they are, need to be replaced with human-faced deeds.

It is incumbent on all of us to not disappoint those who have rested their hopes on the emerging new order, and the demands it places on its propagators – not to be afraid to tell the good story, even when it contains elements on why the old order cannot be trusted, but establishing what is speculative, what's false and what's grounded in truth. Allowing the citizenry an opportunity to differentiate between speculation, falsehood and what is grounded in truth.

Otherwise, at the end of the day, one may be giving no choice but to succumb to the Faustian legend, if only for self-preservation, within an all-pervasive order, transcending the limitations of one's form, thereby, maybe surpassing Faust himself - Even when it was one's original desire to live in peace and maintain principles congenial to your hopes and desires, without threatening the prevailing order. The two become self-fulfilling, become polar opposites in a sophistic absurdity of social discourse, exploiting the morality that an ordinary human cannot afford or comprehend. Even with all this going on, the benefactors and their minions luxuriate in their usual moral superiority that men in a position of real responsibility cannot enjoy or even espouse.

When caught in this dilemma, what does the self-preserving soul do, a soul who believes that conscience is the internal witness bearer? He naturally reaches for a spiritual and intellectual focus, a place for social self-awareness, a vanishing point where all the ages meet, a seismograph of the times, a place, an area of freedom, an instrument of liberation. These are the arenas in which he must fully achieve his goal of making the other participant members, the true heroes of each piece, participate with him in sorting through the absurd spirals of logic of a world where appearances mean everything and pass for reality. A world thoroughly permeated with hypocrisy and lies, where government that lacks human-face conscience is called popular government; merely because it has a leader, an amiably charming actor, playing the role of the Classicist, who is able to explain things away easily, even when they are so bad and badly managed. A doctor feel-good, if ever there was one. The masses are thereby enslaved by an upwardly mobile mentality that is unsustainable. Preaching fiscal conservatism that is not based in reality, a classic voodoo arithmetic if there was one. A complete degradation of the individual is presented as his or her ultimate liberation and ascension to the top of the ladder.

Deprivation of basic resources, information, and manipulation is called on because of the legal code. The censorship of arts and culture is called protection of young minds. The reintroduction of imperialism or neo-imperialism is passed off as protecting the oppressed and the spreading of democracies; when elections manufactured in human-mind control labs, by media experts, become the highest form of democracy. When people are manipulated in ways that are infinitely more refined than those used by their predecessors - a product of the same professional apparatuses, but whose levels have now been raised exponentially, beyond the imagination of the average citizens - thereby releasing the citizens from all forms of responsibilities. Everyone can sense that something went terribly wrong when in a community where two-thirds believe their children would be worse off than they are, these manipulators are still able to rouse the people to believe in their false notions which if not course-corrected, would produce a community of extremes, with the rich behind gates protecting their kids from kidnapping and everybody else on the other side, struggling to make a living.

This is the familiar odyssey I have found myself, which I have committed to work for and live through, I decided must be founded on truth and the search for deeper connectedness, on a more humane entity in which each individual life can have meaning. A meaningful approach that is not tainted by falsities, and mind control antics manufactured by the professional apparatuses - Instruments that create mindsets and split mindsets, which alone is a dangerous paradox, for the split-mind-set is a confused mind, torn between what was and what is, which is now, a rigidly one dimensional focus built on the status quo. He is a wavering soul, unsure of the dictates of his heart and the teachings of the professional apparatuses. He is unsure-of-his-environment and therefore a dangerous walking time bomb, if there ever was one.

The fence sitter knows what is right. His heart is not so totally dense. He knows the dictates of his heart are the right choice. Then, 'wait a minute,' he says, 'what about the professional apparatuses?' 'What would they and the 'family' say?' This is when he becomes very dangerous, and fear takes over, creating the 'split mindset,' a confused mind, a zombie personality, created by the mind lab of the benefactors system of professional experts - What does he do? One may ask. There is nothing he can do but sit on the fence; just like anyone else you know who is unable to make up his or her mind. He is a fence sitter in the dangerous world that operates on the obscene and vulgar....

So, as much as I was repulsed by the indignities of Michele's new proposal, I found myself helpless in taking a position of non-acceptance, not only to maintain peace, but deciding it is all a means to the end, the bigger Landscape which is bigger than I, bigger than all of us.

So, I allowed her to teach me about bomb making, and the art of dismantling bombs, believing I would never use it, and hoping the situation would never present itself. So I said:

"Whatever you say, Michelle, whatever you say." Giving her a carte blanche, in this climate of fear and revulsion we have found ourselves, hoping we would be careful enough not to lend ourselves to the shameless manipulation of the hated benefactors and their agents, and right before my eyes, my respect and fondness for Michelle as my 'Partner,' in the new world order, was eroding and I was not quite sure I could do anything about it, because violence as a means of problem solving, is not the ways of the new order we are endeavoring to construct...

"You're making things unnecessary difficult, Nigel. What do you want from me? Do you want me as a partner or are you ready to kick me out? Make up your mind. You cannot have it both ways. I can never understand the ways of the world, and of men especially.

Men become increasingly a mystery to me, each time I think I am getting to know them. Here I am, risking my neck for you, only to be paid back with ingratitude, almost a distrust - Your attitude is very unbecoming Nigel, very unbecoming. You should consider yourself lucky that I have fallen in love with you; if not, I would tell you what to do with this attitude of yours. I am already into this up to my eyes; I may just as well see it through. Anyway, if you're interested, this is what you do." Then she continued. "You go to a large supermarket, preferably during its peak shopping hour. Procure a very cheap watch; please don't steal it. Make sure you buy some other things besides the watch to confuse the attendant's memory. Remove the hour hand. Drill a hole in the glass, put a drawing pin in the hole, and solder your electric circuit to the head of the drawing pin. Now the battery: Set the hand as close to the drawing pin, or as far from it, as you wish. Allow, as a rule, the shortest possible delay, to ensure that the bomb is disarmed. Wind up the watch. Make sure the minute hand is still working. If it is, offer prayers to your Facilitator, poke the detonator into the plastic. As the minute hand touches the shank of the pin, so the contact completes the electrical circuit, and if everything is equal, the bomb goes off, if you need it to go off. As you said, you would not need it to go off. Knowing how to assemble it is the counterpart of knowing how to dismantle. Got it?"

"I don't get it." I responded this time. She was shocked. I was surprised she was. I thought this whole thing was unconscionable and despicable. A grotesque product from the tutelage of the killer, or is it Mr. Baranowsky. That she now relies on savage methods to remedy resolvable conflicts, for self-preservation, is beyond me. This cannot be allowed, I thought. In no uncertain terms I made sure Michelle knew my position was nonnegotiable.

"No, no, no, you're blowing this whole thing out of proportion, Michelle. I'm not a terrorist, nor do I plan to become one. I'm also not robbing Fort Knox, for goodness sake. This goes against all I stand for; and represents everything I have fought against all my life. You do not blow up people you disagree with - it's obscene, sinful."

"For God's sake Nigel," she said softly, "go easy, will you? I am just trying to make you understand what you're going up against. You're not appreciative and I'm left heart broken. Do you want to hit me, lover? Do I need that discipline, the one that the fucking bourgeoisie, the same means the shameless benefactors you are supposedly against use to inhibit rude lassies like me? The one you're so much against? Is it just when it's convenient?"

I laughed awkwardly, not really knowing how to respond to this barrage of questioning. The astonishment showed on my face, I imagined. I wanted to reach for her and tell her that I loved her, so much so that I wouldn't mind committing any kind of crime, even that of passion for her. That just one single night spent with her is worth the combination of all of others, including, but not limited to Jamie. I wanted to say: 'I want you all for myself.' I couldn't say the words, afraid that in her anger she would react in contravention. I would not blame her. I saw a seductress with an unspoken unavailability - My actions, to her, bordered on the immoral. Immoral behavior is what calls for new values. Nonetheless, I needed to impress on Michelle my distaste for and aversion to the violence that might one day consume the world.

Man being what she thinks he is; I prayed that I regain my spirit, the spirit of: 'The teacher, the lover and the detective,' all at once. Michelle loves that combination. It is a combination most women find intriguing. Again, she could just be testing the sincerity of my conviction, without allowing the symphonic sounds of a bucking bed in our past liaison to affect her judgment. I did not blame her. She has always thought of me as redeemable. Does she still think I am redeemable? Am I redeemable?

Is it true that what we take from life is what matters? Is it also true that that was how we discovered our outline, our identity, our passion, and our art? These were questions begging for quick answers. Answers that I desperately needed to maintain the necessary equilibrium, for some very unique situations. From the other corner of the cab, Michelle looked at me with a motherly indulgence I found discomforting. Then she kissed me on the cheek, then again on the mouth, the way sisters and brothers do when they are no longer worried about incest. I could taste her toothpaste in my mouth, and the smell of perfume in my nostrils....

Then, privately to myself, without opening my mouth, I said: 'I was at the edge of precipice, and did not tumble over.' I was glad I never said what I had wanted to say to Michelle just before that last action of hers. I had wanted to say: 'Look my fair woman, very soon, you will have taxed me too far and I would be obliged to bolt from this car.' I did not say it; I could not have said it.

See, as softly as she had tried to express herself, I discovered a disguised exclamation of disgust and a look of not being appreciated for - 'All that I've done for you.' Shaking her head as if she could never be equal to the wicked ways of the world – especially a man's world. This latest gesture, her body language, was not making it easy on me, in my attempt to limit the damage from what she perceived as some ingratitude on my part. I decided a calm disposition would be part of my strategy to control this damage. A different Michelle has broken loose inside her and I need to greet this version with caution, lest it explode. She is a good woman. It's the overwhelming stress of the accelerated activities which have produced overheated minds giving way to, as she would say: 'a need to punish me for yet another disappointment.'

In this short lived misalliance with Michelle, a lesson in human nature became obvious, why man and woman act towards each other the way they do, even when the earth is big enough for the wide profusion of all of us. Hoping that we take from it, the fact that our differences can be resolved without resorting to the use of smart toys.

My mission thereby calls for a different calibration. It would reject, because of time essence - the gradualism of structures, political or otherwise - this mission requires action, not cosmetic changes – And they would be actions that have human faces painted on them. Actions that promote trust, because: 'We don't mistrust each other because we have arms, we have arms because we mistrust each other.' There would be no need for arms when the basic culprit, mistrust, is eliminated – Also to be eliminated and rejected would be the so-called operationally expedient indicators, embracing only facts. Where decisions are not irrevocable, because choices do come back. When life must have shared laughter, and when tears accompany them, they would be tears of joy. Where giants, dwarfs, wizards and mermaids share common ground, in spite of obvious differences. Knowing they all cannot be the same, else it would be boring, stale and a tad smug - Where one measures seven times but cuts once. Patience would override the need for hasty decisions and a desire for greed and domination. In the emerging society, the new age of human face activities, smiles replace frowns, and everyday is Christmas and New Year, because if that were so, people will smile more, give more, be more compassionate, love more, and say kinder things to each other and remember the not-so-fortunate-among them...

and there would be no more
public outcry, for they would
be a thing of the past...

I watched as the long dusk turned to darkness and the dim lights of the city reluctantly brighten, telling us what we already know, that the French Quarter never sleeps, and that there is a difference in hue between dusk and dawn - in a significant way; which is really the romance of it all - what brings the night people out, separating them from the day people. It was seven in the evening but the harbor is still alive, emitting distant foghorns. The last clouds of dusk were shaping and breaking like the last day.

As the cab pulled up to the phase two gate, the 'the pest control' workers and the 'Toxicologists' advised us that it was not safe to go into the complex. I argued in a very vociferous manner, that as a resident, I was entitled to go in. I could have been banging my head against the wall for all they cared. Their eyes, tone of voice and stature, gave them away. They were not your ordinary run of the mill pest controllers. So I asked the cabbie to turn around and head back to Dwyer Road, to an area of the wood fence that is removable.

Michelle and I got out of the cab and said our own versions of thank-you to the cabbie, who refused to take any more money from me. I had to decline his offer to tag along and offer his brand of assistance. I politely told him that my insurance was not large enough to cover him and his family. He wished us good luck and drove off. We stood by the side of the road until his taillights were consumed by the mists of dusk.

Now came the tricky part. Identifying the exact part of the fence that has the loose wood panels. It has been quite awhile I have had to use it. I started counting. Was it twenty-two to the left and six to the right? - Or the other way around? I decided the best way to find out was by playing the guess game and literally feeling my way through. It was the sound, the hollow sound that an unattached wood panel makes, that told me I'd found it. I pulled it off its hinge, peered through to make sure the coast was clear; then I said, "Ladies first," to Michelle, who looked at me with apprehension. She stooped over and wiggled her Five Seven, 120lb frame through.

I followed after her, with instructions for her to duck to the left of the fence for some quick survey of our immediate environment. This may have been superfluous. Michelle, student of 'Uncle,' knew what to do. Using the wooded left side as cover, and vantage point, I surveyed the West and North of us. The place was quiet and deserted. Unless the 'workers' were using some wooded areas as covers too. Then Michelle, the ever-handy sidekick, removed from her bag two pairs of binoculars. She smiled, the smile of someone saying: 'What would you do without me.'

Then I saw it. Parked to the northeast of us, was a gun mounted Jeep. The driver and gun handler dressed in army fatigues, faces painted black and green. His binoculars trained on the area of their objective criteria. We decided to maneuver our way, using our basic knowledge of Boot Camp training. After about twenty-five yards under our belt, we were forced to stop by a new discovery. Not quite ten yards from the gun mounted Jeep, was a helicopter gunship - its engine running, its propellers barely emitting any noise compared to the noise from the pest control trucks and that of the generators. I could not understand the need for this heavy firepower. Just for one man, who occupies two flats, in a populated civilian community? Unless, of course, the benefactors really are worried and getting very nervous. They do really want him dead, wiped from existence - seeming, almost with the goal of removing any evidence that he ever lived a life. I turned to Michelle and asked:

"You don't think he is going to show up, do you?"

"With uncle, you never really know." She replied.

"A sane man would think twice." I ventured

"Uncle is not your ordinary sane man." Was Michelle's response.

"You can say that again." I said.

"More like the wolf being guarded by three rabbits." She continued.

"That's a switch." I offered

"Uncle has this mark of heroic determination, especially when his mind is made up, and especially when he believes in the betrayal of a hated group for the greater good, which to me is the existence, fulfillment and recognition of the genius among us, that which precludes equality of men, when equality is the howl of the many-too-many." Michelle, the philosopher espoused, with a tint of sarcasm. All the time, she was the epitome of a well-trained professional, a professional from the school of the son of the German immigrant, one Mr. Baranowsky.

She moved from her knees to lying supine. I could not help but notice the curves made by her faded jeans and the enhanced cleavage. Right idea, wrong place, I conceded. I decided to put all efforts to the task at hand, and put to use the binoculars without being distracted by this inadvertent Jezebel. A student who has by words, and deeds exhibited courage in spite of obvious repercussions from the protagonists for doing so.

Michelle, it seems to me, made a determination; that the moments when active involvement must replace passive debate comes with the territory of the changing times, when active participation takes over from words. She has played the role well. I couldn't have asked for more.

Suddenly, Michelle gasped. Her eyes had been drawn to a speck of faint light, an image of black upon a darker black. I followed her binocular movement. Something. Then it was there. Far away on the man-made hills closer to the Canal, was a shadowed figure, in cat burglar outfit, pressed against the wooden fence. Shape and size indicating female physique. Then a second figure vaulted over the fence and landed on all fours. It was the unlikely visitor, the hundred to one odd. The hired killer, and his mistress, entrancing from the point of non-expectation, while the "'workers'" and 'toxicologists" binoculars were trained on his flat and other obvious points of entrance, he came through the back door. Putting the element of surprise on his side. Validating his reputation.

I had to restrain Michelle from making a dash for them. I told her that it was in our best interest to watch from afar not giving our position away was the logical choice while we figure out what their next move would be. The son of Baranowsky raised himself up a fraction, with his back pressed to the wall his face a mask of stone. He removed what looked like a Mac-10 machine pistol and a Kosh P9S automatic. He knelt back down, pulling up his left trouser leg and inserted the weapon in the crisscrossing calf straps that rested below the back of his knee. Standing up, and from what looked like a hunting bag, he took out a powerful Mauser Parabellum pistol and shoves it into his shoulder holster. That was followed with a sheathed hunting knife resting alongside the gun. He put on a jacket he took out of the bag. He was now the perfect cat burglar, his time measured out in minutes and segments of minutes. He gave a host of instructions to his mistress and then started to the right, to the North end of the Dwyer Canal. Then he stopped. Made use of his binoculars. He saw what I did not see. Pivoting swiftly, he rose and walked gingerly across the short stretch of Edgewater lawn and into the dark parking lot that led to the green alley separating Edgewater from Seagull Lane.

Within seconds, Baranowsky raced out, ninety degrees to the right of his destination; crisscrossing the green alley, hugging the walls of the buildings in the clouded moon's darkest shadows. A lone isolated figure appeared, staggering towards his path, the surprise on his face was the last expression he made, for the killer spun around the corner, caught the intruder between the eyes with the hunting knife. The victim made an unrecognizable noise as he fell to the ground. Then, sensing the approach of others, the killer ran with abandon towards his flat, which was now only yards away; he made a dash for the door, which he opened with the remote controlled mechanism in his hand.

Out of the blue, and apparently responding to the absence of response from his fallen comrade, a walkie-talkie holding 'Woodworm' man or 'toxicologist' appeared, blocking the killer from his flat. The

'Woodworm's' man thrust a bayonet directly forward towards the killer's throat. In a lightening move the blade was deflected; the "workers" then arched it down, slicing into the killer's wrist; the radio fell to the recently mowed grass. Baranowsky then cat wheeled through the open door to his flat, followed by the "workers," who kicked the door shut; the automatic lock clicked.

Gripping his wrist, the killer lashed out his right foot, expertly catching the government man's left kneecap. He stumbled; another steel toe, from the eel skin boot caught him on the side of the neck, then another crashed into his ribs. The killer momentarily lost balance, and the government man lunged, the knife from the bayonet now an extension of his arm, he went directly for the killer's stomach, slicing the black leather jacket, now caked with blood. There was blood on the government man's face as well. The killer fell back to the floor, as he was doing so, he kicked with a powerful force to the jaw of the government man. They both fell to the floor. The killer crawled to the far end of the room, removed the hunting knife from its sheath and delivered a crushing blow to the man's neck.

He looked to check how badly he had been wounded. Tore a portion of his shirt with a blade from his key holder and tied the wound, a temporary remedy. He struggled to his feet; sharp bolts of pain surging through his ribs. Suddenly, the door crashed open, the lock blown out of its mount. Another government man - younger, his thick bare arms bulging in tension, his furious eyes surveying the scene in front of him - whipped his hand beyond his right hip for a holstered weapon. The killer hurled himself against the man, smashing the agent into the door. This freed his right hand to intercept the agent's arm as it slashed down with the blood-streaked blade of the knife.

The killer hammered his knee into the agent's rib cage as he swung the gripped arm clockwise, forcing the agent to the floor. The agent would not release the knife nor relent. Both men parted, crouching, staring at each other, contempt and hatred emitted from both pairs of eyes.

Like two crazed animals, the two massive men flung themselves back at each other, the taking of life, life meaning nothing, not a thing - The only resolution being the final solution, death, death, death and more death. Hating life, their only reason for being on earth. Blood burst out of punctured flesh as ligaments were torn and bones crushed amid throated cries of vengeance and loathing. Finally it happened, the end as volcanic as the initial eruption, sheer brute strength was the victor.

The battle, it seemed was not won by marksmanship, but by the man who had the better skill with the knife. The killer, it seemed, had the vanguard. His knife lodged in the agent's throat, reversed and forced to its mark by the son of the German immigrant.

Exhausted and drenched in blood, Baranowsky pushed himself off the body of his enemy. He looked around the crumbled flat and whispered some words to himself, more likely saying: 'I have to find peace, but before peace and a new order, all things old and obscene have to be destroyed. The battle is not over, not yet.'

Then all hell broke loose again. Thunder - A series of deafening explosions. Smoke. Walls suddenly collapsing everywhere amid the terrified screams of those caught in the destruction. There were shrieks of horror and agony as tons of rubble came cascading down. Helpless men, friends, spouses, fathers roaring defiantly against the cascading hell they knew any second would be their sepulcher. It is the consequence of the choice they made a long time ago, when they sold their souls to the devil, the devil in this case being their benefactors – It is the sins of our imagination.

Baranowsky got to his feet, breathed deeply, and started through the false bookshelf-door, walked gingerly into the flat that leads to the underground, which in turn would lead him to the tunnel and the Canal. The door closed behind him. Though in agony, he must have known to move faster. Any second, the government men would unleash their immense firepower - If he can just get rid of this excruciating headache, he seemed to be saying. His face was covered in blood. He felt his way along the tunnel. He stopped, reached into his breast pocket and removed a piece of cloth. He tore it in half. He used the first half to wipe his blood soaked face, distorted in pain. The second half he applied to the wound on his left shoulder blade. He was wasting valuable time.

Once in his life, he had realized that life is simplest at its most dangerous. When simple things are all that matter - The love of life, the will to live from one minute to the other, the day to day chores, family and loved ones, their significance become so clear - After years of neglect due to the tasks resulting from his pact with the devil. 'In the face of death, one thinks of so many strange things,' he thought. He suddenly realizes, what he should have known a long time ago - that the simple things in life are the ones that keep us going. Time and death become so relative. 'Time and death?' 'What am I saying, the pain in my head must be clouding my thinking faculty, just as it is blurring my vision.' For the first time, the very first time he can remember since adolescence, he prayed to his facilitator for guidance, finally appreciating that he is not invisible after all. Then he thought: 'Is it not supposed to be life and death, master?' A voice in his head whispered: 'what does it matter my boy, time and death, life and death, they are the same, two sides of the same penny. What's important here, is really time, the time you have between penance and absolution or the ever-inviting final solution, which is really shaped by the promises and deeds resulting from our imagination. In simple terms, our destinies all are shaped by the promises of our imagination.'

The killer has never run when he can walk, nor has he walked when he can run. Running is what the situation calls for now, but for the first time, run he cannot. It is more like the soul willing and cognizant of what is necessary in a situation, but the body is weak, too weak from abuse - The limbs and frame beaten into a state of vertigo. So, he dragged himself along, resting every few minutes. He knew he has to get to the Canal, if he is to escape the bombardment coming any minute. Finally, he saw the glistening water of the Canal. His head started to spin again. The excruciating pounding in his brain returned. He is going to faint, from the joy of success, when one is almost at the end of a tedious journey. The joy of knowing one has made it in spite of all odds. He needed to will away this fainting spell. Not now, he begged his facilitator. The humiliation of being captured alive by agents of the benefactors was unsavory, to say the least. With all the energy left in him, he straightened himself up, and one more time, looked around this once familiar landscape perhaps for the last time. Just as he thought tears were welling up in his eyes - about streaming down his face, he dove into the eastbound waters of the canal. All that was visible was the ripples made from the point of entry. With that, the 'Killer,' the son of the German immigrants - the man known as Uncle, a.k.a Mr. Delaney, Mr. Mueller, the 'Silent One,' and more recently, Mr. Nephillin Baranowsky, disappeared.

The Chopper, now airborne and the Rover moved closer for the kill, the final solution - Orders were radioed in for them to move in, all were ordered to unleash their smart weapons, and all the laser guided missiles in their arsenals. 'Reduce to rubble, Baranowsky's flats and all others within fifty yards of it.'

The shock and surprise was evident on the faces of the government agents. The source of this concern had to do with the other destructive acts, of a 'mysterious origin,' the time-delayed explosions and devastation that is enveloping them, which they know were of different projectiles, and definitely not coming from the Apache, nor the Rover gunship. Their state of agitation, nonetheless, had not restricted their zeal to follow through with the order for total elimination, the final solution. The Apache, the Rover, and the men camouflaged in black and green, in a non-surgical move, albeit with precision, moved in for the kill.

The bombardment and carnage unleashed by the Apache gunship and machine gun mounted Rovers continued unabated with the kind of firepower and explosions never seen before in the Lake Forest area. The sky was lit into a volcanic rainbow. The combination of Baranowsky's cybernetics and the devastating arsenal of the gunship created a towering inferno. The flats were brutishly leveled. The killer, did he survive? Was he able to make it through the cascading waters of the Canal to the land of penance and absolution, or was it the ever-beckoning final solution? Even Michelle never knew the answer to this. Nor did his mistress really, just hope. The men in grey, his benefactors: the devils who bought his soul - signed, sealed and delivered -The eminences grises, the ones who sit in deep chairs and their obscene machinations - were they able to make sure he never lived to tell his story? No one may ever know. As Charlie would say: 'That's a sad philosophy,'

It's a sad ending to a brilliant mind who sold it to the devil for some measly comparative advantages he is now in no position to use, when simple things would have just done fine? What a story it would have made if he had been allowed to tell it in his own words. A truism comes to mind: 'what does it benefit man to gain the whole world and lose it?'
The only recourse left to those who would venture into pundit, into the why's and why not of the killer and his escapades, was to deduce slowly the logic behind the secretly scripted manuscript - Mr. Baranowsky's manuscript, his masters' secret ledgers. The one he carelessly tossed into my hands in the computer room Undeciphered. It would be a kind of shadow boxing match with the past not to carefully decode this manuscript, which would reveal his benefactors fundamentally decadent and obscene idiocy that has always produced abject poverty side-by-side with obscene wealth.

The question is, were they successful, even in this changing landscape, in silencing him? Did the son of the German immigrants survive the heap of mangled metal and concrete? Is he laying somewhere in the sun, laughing at all of us?

'You can't get a haircut over the telephone,' a friend once said to me. She was right, subliminal but right. The impossible cannot be made possible. The only consolation is that: 'The seed has been planted, it just needs nurturing.' Yes, the seed has been planted by the killer, an improbable planter at that - it is now left to those who want change to follow through - For the sake of the new emerging order; I hope my friend is right. My friend has never been wrong. But, is she right this time? Only time will tell.

Epilogue
Reflections: A Conversational Philosophy
And A Healthy Proposal.

After playing Jumping Jack Nigel and barely surviving Baranowsky's cybernetic explosives and the needlessly disproportionate fire power of the mercenaries - I dejectedly traced my steps back to the last place of rendezvous with Michelle. Frustrated from my blighted hope, and now sadly disappointed that the son of the German immigrant might have met his demise, I walked on in confused solace.

What I saw was a ghost-town landscape that lay behind me; a caricature of what was formerly Frenchman's Wharf. It had been my nirvana, once the crystallization of the dream of an artist who got drunk on gin and sobered up on absinthe, a Sistine chapel of resort living. Its fabulous, matchless natural setting captured many an imagination - I am sure when the artist stepped back and took a second look, he would say: 'This is not what I had had in mind, this is not the vision I had - what happened to the mind?' He would say this, with both palms pressed to his face, even when the palms are soiled with char, from the remnant of the evil genius's handiwork, creating its own impression on his face. Pulling his hair would not right the wrong, banging his head against the wall would even be worse; what he needs is some tranquil berth, a place to rest a tormented spirit, and if a companion of well-matched promises of imagination is to come along, the merrier the healing effects. 'I need a few bits and pieces to collect,' he would say, 'and I will be on my way,' and his companion would say: 'Where are we going?'

Shouted across from the other side of the Canal... and he would say: 'to a place where the tides rip against the ships, where my soul can finally find peace...'

I found Michelle and her friend crouched at the same spot I had left them, looking like obedient kids, but obedient kids who have just lost their parents. Petrified, apparently by the outcome of the seemingly innocuous adventure turned super-deadly. Teary eyed over the loss of their former lover; the son of the German immigrant, they were hugged in an embrace of mutual consolation. In meditation-tone-like murmurs of the heart, meant only for themselves, they advocated the reemergence of their missing beloved one - The man called Uncle, whom they once truly loved.

It is said that some people wear masks to hide the pains they feel within, while others grow thorns to keep other people at bay. I am not sure to which group this twosome belongs. A sixth sense tells me to tread softly, to carefully navigate myself through their barbed utterances, which I suspect would come, no matter what I say.

Michelle was the first to speak. 'It all boils down to morals and commitments,' Michelle says. She meant the morals of the Benefactors, their excuse for this deadly deed, a response for what she considers a betrayal of her former mentor, the one and only uncle Baranowsky, the killer son of the German immigrants, who selflessly carried out their commands and commitments, only to be rewarded by actions reminiscent of the pronouncements of the demons and liars, a grotesquely vulgar and obscene group of people, who are closer to the animal-kind than humankind.

I told myself, in my private thoughts, thoughts I could not express aloud, if I want to maintain any peace with Michelle or her friend: 'It's fine to mourn the loss of beloved ones, especially former lovers, but whenever people in this trade start talking about morals and commitments, you'd better start sniffing for the fish. Because, by its nature, this is a dog eats dog kind of business and what maybe one man's morality or commitment, can be translated by another as a totally virtue-less deed, where morality and commitments are interpreted as weakness that can pose danger.

In a sackcloth time like this, I took the high road and decided it is better to keep my thoughts to myself, and keep my mouth shut, if I do not have any consolation words to offer these two friends. Being the only man in this equation, my sixth sense told me to tread carefully or I might become meat for two wild cats.

I figured that silence or the mere nodding of the head coupled with a long face would at least convince them that I am on their side, and that nothing saddens me more than the loss or disappearance of the former hired killer, whom I had grown to know and admire, and whom I also found out had some soft sides to him, the former stone killer veil notwithstanding. There is forgiveness and accommodation in the emerging society for the repentant soul, especially for one that went out of his way and his 'sworn-by-death-commitment' to get out of the cold and fight on behalf of the human-faced age, in that regard, all infractions and all sins are forgiven.

> and he will wipe out every tear
> from their eyes, and death will be
> no more, neither will mourning nor
> outcry nor pain be any more. For the
> former things have passed away...
> look, I am making all things new...

Things happen... Michelle's mystery friend became unveiled. Rowena Macaraeg, a product of the Village - as in Greenwich Village, New York - decided it was time to head back home. There was nothing here for her anymore. We did not try to talk her out of it. The determination-look on her face said it all. Michelle and I walked her to the black Spider that was to take her to her apartment in the French Quarter, where she would pack and head home. Flying, she thought would be too risky. Now comes the hard part, saying

goodbye, and in a crowd of three, and the man is the minority...
it is advisable to follow the dictates of the sixth sense... for all the
obvious reasons...

Then I said, as more private thoughts, words enclosed in my mouth:
'Bye, bye, firebrand baby, and welcome home, former firebrand baby,
you were trained to be relative technology experts, equipped to kill
or disarm when necessary, but what now? Do you become sleepers
or activists for the cause of your former lover? What do you do with
all the resources at your disposal, Michelle? Am I going to be a part
of this...?'

A quick analysis of the scene before me, gave me one indisputable fact
- that these 'pseudo widows' have their heels planted, giving every
indication that they mean to be engaging if this private moment of
theirs is broken into rudely. Not wanting to be in the position of the
swimmer who goes back into the sea knowing the sharks are waiting
for him, I knew I had to tread softly, making sure all forms of starch
are removed from my statements, and to have smiles accompany my
responses; even when theirs are laced with venoms. Again, these were
imprisoned thoughts....

I watched them in their embrace, rocking with agitation on the
fulcrum of their butts. At that point, and for the first time, it
occurred to me how close they had been to Baranowsky. Exposing
in the process a brimming distillate of meanness and agitated spite
they could neither dispose of nor retain for their good health. The
question then becomes academic. Do they need to bottle up the spite
they have for the benefactors or dispose of it and reanimate it when
confronted?' After all, is it not true that, to be relieved, one has to
be alarmed in the first place? And, isn't it also true, that the quickest
way to ill health and death is to bottle up anger and hatred?

Even though it was just the three of us, I was getting the feeling of
being hemmed in - claustrophobia of kinetic energy, energy capable
of smoldering anyone who dares breach their limit, their self-imposed

limits. In this bonfire, beaming with barely suppressed anger, hatred - powerful emotions and indignation, I met their smoldering eyes and hoped I live to tell my story. Would I live to enjoy the company of Michelle, the former agent provocateur, whom I am falling in love with as the minutes go by?

Confronting these two women with what I really feel or felt about Mr. Baranowsky, would be a gambit, and would possibly vitiate my already cultivated demeanor. It would be far simpler, though no less fearful thing to do, especially with my new found favor in the eyes of Michelle. Oddly, Michelle's complicity in this regard had added a complication. Any opposite posture from me would have not only humiliated her, but again, invalidate what we had built together this past few weeks. It does not take space science to find out that this twosome belong to the second group, the ones that grow thorns to keep other people at bay - who wear masks to hide the pains they feel within.

Then, what would my failure to comprehend and express that a problem exists do to it? In the end, would it not appear that I have succumbed to cowardice instead of confronting what is in front of me? I really could not gamble this away; Michelle had become too important to me to do so. Above all, I needed some peace after this past-accelerated nexus of events, hoping we all bounce back from all this - See, everybody bounces back from one disaster or the other, they just do not bounce back in the same direction or pace - Michelle, in this case, is my chosen direction - a direction and pace of mutual reciprocity, I hoped...

I could hear the movement of the cascading water of the canal; waves after waves lapped the concrete shores and retreated in a ceaseless rhythm. In normal times it would make music to the ear. These are not normal times, nor are things really equal, in this atmosphere of female bonding.

I stood up and looked up over the fence into the dark beyond, the lips of the canal and the deserted 'day-after-scenario,' there wasn't any doubt in my mind that the emerging order would be secure from harm, if all things old, obscene and sinfully decadent are obliterated, a new situation with human-face will emerge. I felt perfectly and ridiculously at ease with myself - all that have transpired lately notwithstanding, and I wondered how much of humankind or the past should be eliminated to preserve humanity? - A credo of the old that should give way to new thinking - the belief or aims that would guide our actions on way forward.

If there was any moral parallel to be drawn between what had happened some few hours ago between the mercenaries of the benefactors and what is going on now, vis-à-vis, the ex agent provocateurs, it needed to be drawn widely enough to encompass the difference between psychosis and bad attitude - to a chance to do good, a change of heart in an atmosphere of hope - a distance as far flung as the continental geography that separated the world and its inhabitants. In spite of this, I felt an uncanny closeness to the expectations of the people and the realities of the changing world of ours, the new and improved world order. The cascading water of the canal took an inconceivable steep plunge, and the ring of water opened so wide, far enough to lap and foam-wash the concrete walls of the canal.

The Proposal
An Elegant Maneuver And Clever Scheme

It is interesting what a good night's sleep can do for the human psyche and the general physiology of body and soul. Michelle's attitude took a 180-degree turn from the previous night. It was as if she had made a secret pact with Lucifer that says: 'Stay away from me you devil, and don't you ever resurface for I want to put yesterday and everything about yesterday behind me, for today is a new day.'

We ate breakfast like two exhausted lovers even though no sex was involved the night before. She was amiable, hopefully believing that friendship allows for a quiet sharing of intimate problems, for standing together in times of crisis and vicariously experiencing the joys and pains that come with the terrain. Reaching out when the other withdraws - Accepting the fact that friends need others - diminishes independence but can serve to create a healthy dependence. Accepting the fact that people need people, and in little insignificant ways, begin to act it out. When you have it, you know it. When you recognize it, you want others to share its rewards and not acted out in virtual reality.

On these notes, I found Michelle, the former Chicagoan placid beauty, no more just a serene beauty, but a refreshing ally, and the designated executioner of my past, the euthanasia of the albatross that has hung around my neck for so long. Beseeching the Facilitator to give me the strength to change those things within the realm of my human abilities knowing that this emerging new and improved world order is bigger than any of us, and its whims are the promises of our imagination.

Repeatedly, my thoughts stayed on Michelle. She has infused my skin as no other woman has since Jamie; and I do not know how to let go. The question is, do I want to let go? The fear of the past, the agonizing legacies of broken hearts and broken promises inhibit my every move to open up, and pull her into my arms and tell her I love her more than any other woman I have ever known. This becomes a battle between the archenemy, the past and the shadow of sempiternity of the present, which nudges me, reminding me to keep my emotions on an even keel, flashing a misshapen image of Jamie as it does so; a representative metaphor. It is the memories that hunt us, the truths that set us free. Appropriating and neutralizing the symbols of the oppressors, which is not quite the portrait of a man disorganized or in search of his roots, or is it?

I ask myself: Am I the prisoner of my past? If so, by implication, am I the holder of the key to my future? How do I use the key to open the gate to this unknown? It becomes so apt; the cruelest prison is the one we build around ourselves. Would Michelle serve as the key and comforter to this new horizon or is she just another mirage? With its conflicting and contradictory images, hues, smells, voices and illusions, which subsequently end up in complete disorder. All because good, the greater good, always find excuses not to come here, the last great frontier in this over explored planet. Is this earth just a mirage?

In vowing to become my sidekick, Michelle had pledged that in the new environment, the improved-upon emerging era, she would channel her activism into human-faced activities. Because she knows that doing nothing was in itself an act of opposition, negative opposition. Because by doing nothing, we change nothing and by changing nothing, we hang onto what we know and understand even when it is the bars of our own cell - societal and personal jails. Relying on divine intervention or providence for survival, forgetting that the 'facilitator' helps those who help themselves.

I turned to Michelle, and I said to her: "I am enjoying this Michelle, this thing we are building, where we are - the architecture, the mechanism and trajectory. The connectivity. What brought us to where we are. A friendship I never thought I could have again with a woman. As a proponent that true friendship should be based on mutual trust and respect, where discretion is naturally and effortlessly acknowledged as part of mindfulness, because without discretion there can be no true friendship - I believe the dynamics of our present station, if I must say, is in sync with that philosophy. We have managed to infuse those tenets in this union, our partnership. In the new and improved way of things, a lot of discretion, mutual respect and trust are needed - more than at any other time." This comes with great expectations, it emphasizes why people should learn to show love to people when they are alive, not when dead -

exposing the illogical and hypocritical nature of this former logic - building a portrait of resolve, not quite like any other.

"Understanding is also vital," Michelle replied, "because without understanding, you get the silliest ideas about people. When you do not understand them, you just make things up. We are all entitled to our opinions, but we should not be entitled to our facts. Opinions should be based on verifiable facts, not ones put together in obscurity. We should not work nor live in obscurity, we should endeavor to ask for explanation when required." There was no way not to agree with Michelle. It was well enunciated. She succinctly covered all the salient points of the new policies required for the harmony everyone yearns for, the very prominent, conspicuous points; the noticeable and important. So I chimed in:

"In that case, I assume you're entitled to insist that the explainer stand up and declare his qualifications?" I ventured, hoping to get the true course of her leaning.

'No, qualifications are not needed, not paper qualifications anyway, just merits, deeds, antecedents and commitment to the cause in this fast developing and moving times, new urgencies on different fronts," Michelle corrected. "If a participant is required, obliged to prove that he or she has the paper qualifications to back his thesis, apart from being unfair and unwieldy, the whole program might be condemned to a slow and painful journey."

Michelle, the ex agent provocateur, has acquired good expertise in technology, and a sound education in philosophy from Uncle. She was impressive, with an air of character and energy - A daring adventure in intellectual values, and this in not just a crash course on how to skin a rabbit. Michelle, it has turned out, came into town with a good head and a bag full of dollars - It's a community organizer, a local kid made good, in this case, very good.

The room was lit only by watery sunlight that struggles through tinted windows, common in this part of town, as she enumerated the parts she believed participants in the new society should play, when far across the Pontalba, beyond Jackson Square to the south of the river, in a slightly seedy section of the river front, in a down-at-the-heels building that has seen better days but not better uses, Rowena called for our help in this 'hideout,' from the wrath of the benefactors, for the roles she played in the debacle of their hired killer. I pegged it as paranoid logic. It did not make any sense. I do not believe the former backers of the hired killer are that dense, to pursue a vendetta against those who opposed them in the past. That is a war I do not believe, and I am sure they know too, they cannot win. Rowena refused to go into her apartment and ran for 'cover' just because she believed she saw some odd looking characters, who may or may not be peons of the benefactors. When all along, we thought she was en-route to New York.

We helped her see how illogically foolish her fears were, and for the final time, sent her onward to New York. This, we accomplished without the anticipated reprisal of the men behind the veil, 'trailing' Rowena. These men have other more pressing preoccupations. Rowena's departure actually may have helped Michelle rebound from the melancholy of Baranowsky's demise, as well as the mystery surrounding his disappearance into clouds that gathered without stars, in rains of bullets and explosions, in the narrow, sometimes winding green lush alleys and the dim glow of the arc-lights that was Frenchman's Wharf, now a caricature of its former self.

The benefactors, typical imperialists that they are, dashes cunning, false, and importunate and untrusting, have in panic borne of fear and insecurity destroyed the 'peaceable kingdom.' Which goes to solidify the point, that there are times facts are not needed to bring down a man's career, just whispers. Sometimes, when you are under the wrong stars, you pay a high price for doing the right thing....

The sky was calm again, the night warm and sweet smelling. The rain had helped clean the foul air and grime, left by the activities on the river, from the previous night. The lights of the Quarter and the rotating blue and red lights mounted on the slow moving cars of the men in blue, created the sense of security, which, if I may say, the French Quarter gives to tourists and residents alike. Those who live here know that it's possible you can die on the sidewalk and not only would people walk by, but nobody will ask your name. They have been conditioned to avoid unpleasant things - so they walk to keep company with the mind, and drink to hide from it all - Aware that your absolute best may not be the absolute best of society where you are taught and advised on how to do just about everything - how to live, how to love and how to die, if all else fail. I again took consolation in knowing that, in the new era, understanding and accepting our differences will be the norm. *These are the thoughts and aspirations.*

In the solitary moments I take, this even when others are present, Michelle has a way of bringing me back to earth, bringing me to the reality on ground - she would say: 'Snap out of it, Nigel,' telling me 'a prejudiced viewpoint never advances the course of a revolution.' She would tell me this; if she thinks I am straying from any of the forming tenets, the thoughts and aspirations of the new order.

I would smile and touch her chin, sometimes holding it, allowing it to linger. I would think, thoughts that become parts of the other thoughts and aspirations vehicle. Forming. They become the same. They lived in each other, becoming one. In oneness, because what is good for Michelle and Nigel, is good for the engine, the infrastructure that the other thoughts and aspirations were built on. Vice versa. The results from all this, especially the total embrace by Michelle, which creates the premise, that she might well be the key to the gate of the future - all by virtue of her assets and contributions – Yes, she brought a skill and tenderness born of loyalty and true love, a remedy and an aversion to punishment prone desires because of the months and nights of fruitless longings, and because one is in solitary, even when others are present, one sees it all. Her embrace has created equilibrium, a balance and an enabling place to create, to be forward focused.

We looked at each other. It was good to know that our voices remained calm and affectionate during this entire period, which may not be true, because there is always tension in the love zone. There are border guards, umpires. There are referees at the roundtable talks, talks that become negotiations.

I take the whole fight as needless. This us against them, push, push back game. Where an amazing combination of intelligence and stupidity are invested, revealing that a good end does not justify evil means - not when other people's lives and happiness are involved. See, most people, in spite of all the research on mind control, and what big brother, media houses, and advertisers believe they know about the inner workings of the brain and how to make us do things, in spite of ourselves, the programs they bombard us with as a tool, people's consciences, for the better part of society, have not succeeded in making people act like a dog-trained to sit at a corner and resurrect when it's convenient - It is unnatural to ask it to just sit at a corner now to be a non-participant in these worldly games, the games people play. It is not true that you have to pass through hell to get to heaven. My thoughts and reflections lingered, and as we moved into the darkness all that remained were the remnants, alone, all by themselves. Solitary. It is an irony, a metaphor for anyone who cares to listen.

Michelle looked at me again, with those large brown mesmerizing eyes; they always make my defenses melt away. I tried to imagine her body under the cotton housecoat, and I thought, with a face like Michelle's who needs a body anyway? If she were to turn around and tell me she just murdered every member of her household, I would find a dozen ways of assuring her that she was not to blame, that there had to be a reason to the madness. Especially, not after discovering that under the simple housecoat, she was naked, and her eyes asking: 'Would you still love me afterwards, tomorrow, next week, next month, next year, would you Nigel?' Demeanor devoid of reluctance, a departure from set principles and rules, and she gave it, all the same. Imploring me, asking me questions with her eyes. I was not sure how to respond. Trying to steady my mind, I took a sip of the black tea laced with cognac. Working very hard to shed the fear of the past, the all-encompassing jailer of that infinite kind. It has not been easy, but I do report that there is hope.

Repeatedly, I kept saying that to create something new, the old order would have to be destroyed. That also goes for fear of the past, including but not limited to Jamie's era. Michelle, yes Michelle, would be the executioner, the designated destroyer of the past, making way for something new and refreshing.

Then, the past crept up again, showing its head and flashing a toothy smile and said: 'Wait a minute; do not be too hasty, with women you never know. Especially beautiful, intelligent, 'virtuous' women like Michelle; you simply never truly know where they stand. Even when their motives seem obvious.' Could Michelle be up to something? Is she be pining for me, or am I another one of those faces in her crowd? If it's true about what they say about feminine intuition, she must know already, that I am fallen for her without uttering any words. To some women, some men will never be heroes and some heroes will never be men. It's a daily struggle, a daily struggle to nowhere. Would Michelle consider me her hero?

Noticing the easy flow of her body as she stood up, I walked up to her. We were under the chandelier. The pulse of traffic rose from the streets, almost in unison with the pulsating rhythm of the breasts under her cotton coat. I pulled her close, my hands on her backside.

"Do you consider me your hero?" I asked.

"I don't believe in heroes," she said, "for they have a way of letting you down when you least expect - The load, the expectations, sometimes become too heavy for them, and they become victims of their own creations. Remember the great communicator and his minions? How they self-destruct in one false move? I do know that, in an overwhelming way, I do love you and know that you would not endanger me without my consent. The last 48 hours, if it's anything to go by, have proved that to me, I gave you my consent and you decided to tread softly; with respect and thoughtfulness. It is why I agree with you on where we are, what we are building, the infrastructure, the mechanism and the trajectory. I love you more so, Nigel.'

I couldn't help but think that, while I am with this serene beauty turned seductress-philosopher, I would believe that west was east, and that babies grew on mango trees and that rabbits gave birth to squirrels. In just a short time, I have accumulated enough memories from this woman to last me a lifetime. Tears of joy washed my soul clean. She has also shown to me that when you are broke and hungry, everything looks grey - and it's easy to solve with a blow, the dilemma of modern living - Michele has shown me how to fight with my head, not the heart, that one size does not fit all, unless it's made in the lab of the doctor feel-goods, whose barbed parameters measure us against them, as they hop from one macabre act to an obscenely casual execution...

She was watching me, waiting for me to say something, expecting answers to the questions her eyes are asking. Michelle's territory is a safe and easy place, if you know your way around. Do I know my way around? Is it as easy as I think? When I think of Michelle, the love she represents in my life, of the immediate present and future, it falls like rain, washing away, cleansing the grimes and impurities of the past, bringing with it a fresh and calming effect; a security that has been lacking for a long time. Why can't I grab it and run with it? Or, does she have to execute her role, as the executioner of the great burden of my past?

This brought to mind the words of an ancient mariner, a wise man from the East who said: 'there are times when our actions come first and we must consider the consequences, when and only when they occur. If we see the goal clearly, we may advance one step, but if we contemplate all goals at once, we shall not advance at all.'

Then for my own predicament, I said: 'if we cannot execute our past, how can we build our future? A new situation cannot be developed until the mentalities of old have been eliminated. Am I required to eliminate old bags, the mentalities of old before I completely open up to Michelle, or is she, as the designated executioner required to help in freeing me from this burden of the past? Because to be an advocate of truth, of the new thinking and aspirations, requires being an apostle of affirmation. This being what it is, and if it is to be self-fulfilling, if my fear of the past, the past that vitiates the desire to leap to a new situation, the one that would allow me shed the old mentalities - if this is to be realized, Michelle's role as a designated executioner cannot be overemphasized, an executioner committed to redeeming me from the agonizing history of the past, the one who would usher me into the new order. Michelle would be that executioner.

She turned away from me, walked to the window, her silhouette and the side-view of her face cut against the empty sky. I took another nip of the cognac-laced black tea, trying to put the words she expects from me coherently, wanting to say just the right things, the right answers to the unspoken questions of her eyes.

She turned her whole back to me, becoming several women at once. She raised her chin as if talking to the sky, drawing me into her and appointing me her confidant. A half moon appeared above the stars, and a flock of Seagulls settled on the roof across the street. I love you were my unspoken thoughts to her unspoken questions. It's hard to understand that there are times when suffering cannot be described because it is not only subliminal and ephemeral, but because it produces an epicene demeanor, which can be easily mistranslated in our macho world.

Michelle, the appointed executioner, her legs stretched before her, her housecoat tightly drawn over her body, looked over the darkening reflections of the firmament, the moon and stars growing, my thoughts and only concerns were simple and to the point: Am I ready for all these different dimensions? Would the system win because the system always won? Is it possible that all this could be for naught, this entire struggle? It becomes a choice between death by obscurity and death by compromise, and because it is a choice between death and death, one may as well choose the less painful alternative. Then one may ask: 'what! Is that an alternative?' 'Death by obscurity and death by compromise?' It is no choice, really.

There are times we all go into periods of self-denials, for our feelings, desires, strategic objectives. With Michelle, it has been a delightful 180-degree turn. Whether with Jamie present, or absent, I have always wanted to believe my feelings for her were just as plain as she was placid. Until now, I had not realized the strength of her influence over me or mine over her. I thought if we ever got it on, with abandon, overwhelming ourselves, we might be free of each other. It has not been so. If anything, it has been more like a novel that had not been finished, each of us looking to the other to complete the destiny, the last paragraph of the last chapter. She urged me on with her eyes, to be consistent and if necessary, brave.

In the houses across the streets, the necklace of lights on the moonwalk, and across the muddy one, looking towards the gondolas and the distant skyline of the West Bank, home lights were appearing in the windows. Her face was out of sight behind the curtain of her hair.

Then the sky swayed and the evening chill reminded us that it has been many hours since breakfast. Like an icy cloud, it closed over us, even though the sky was dark and clear and replete with a full moon, when it finally kept still, shed a warming glow.

Michelle was the glow, the rekindled faith in a lost love, and love found, of the life lost, not having the same meaning after Jamie's exit. She has rekindled and has helped set ablaze my old passion with subtle manipulation and strong-willed actions, even when some of the actions and questions were unspoken, delivered only with her lushly large eyes. Integrity demands that my response is not based on any particular mold or appeal - especially in a period of calm anxiety and anguished expectations where my own philosophy fits into the totality of the scenario being played out in an intense, tempestuous romance. Is there a chance, the small chance of being consumed or even paralyzed with the rage that threatens to explode any moment? Because after you strip away all the veneer - the aesthetic frivolity, an obsession with leather - what is left is a basic level of anger that becomes essentially debilitating, or with the proper stimulus, evolves into a more palatable performance, by eliminating the poison that creeps into it - loud noises, blood, and half naked people.

After all is said and done, there is this question that begs for an answer: Am I ready to make a passionate declaration of love for this woman I now know I truly love? Would my fear of the past, the old albatross, that perpetual nemesis, the evil genius ruin this embodiment of what I consider rekindled faith and lost love - I gazed at Michelle, and I wondered if I had anything to offer her that she did not already have several times over. A lunge into absolute would be essential in my need to break the tension, but with Michelle, I could find no absolutes to put next to her - which gives a whole new meaning to the value of being at the center of things. Only at a second glance did I recall my eerie apprehension from that morning, producing a smile more like a grimace of pain suppressed, rhapsodically, from a lonely decider.

Then the face of the control officer shot up, and I heard myself say: 'I quit, and I am tired of the killings.'

'I picked up your options,' the group leader responded coldly.

'I never gave you that right.' I shot back.

'Read your contract, Nigel, the fine print, it's there, in black and white, you were away on one of your numerous assignments of late, and were doing so well, your contract was upgraded, an option left open by your producer in the first operate.'

My mouth fell open. Does he have the right to do that? Am I destined to a repeat of the agonizing Cat and Mouse game of intrigue and death that permeate the outfit and those at Mission Control?

Then Charlie's voice, laced with sarcasm filled the air: 'I told you so, once they have you, they won't let you go, they would follow you everywhere, even to the end of the world or hell for that matter.'

'Come back Nigel, your country needs you,' the control officer cried out, but my back is turned to him, poised to storm out of the sterile room.

'Your visa here will soon expire, what are you going to do?' 'They will come looking for you, you've enemies and they are not friendly.'

I say: "so the world is dangerous and full of enemies, what else?" "If I allow that thought to linger, I will be subjected to a perpetual state of inactivity, a neutered realm and a crippling sphere of mind not compatible with the new situation, so long old guy."

It's all a nightmare Nigel, a nightmare that will turn into a dream, the one you will wake up from and then it's not there. The whole scenario makes me feels weak and violated, inviting me to think that the entire system is conspiring to destroy what I had just built. As I pulled the door handle, I turned around and took a final look at the group leader. I sensed something ghoulish and frightening about him, like that of a person who's given up on hope and reason, now of a person only morbidly interested in death or disaster, the face, a make-up on the dying. It is obvious that he has apparently joined the great elitist male menopausal devotion to the greed of the eighties, where stepping on the neck of others to get to the top of the ladder is acceptable - deaf to the brewing revolution inspired by the facilitator - Where only openness, fairness, peace, change, courage and reconstruction of the rejected and demolished old landscape - when all things old and decrepit will give way to a new order.

The group leader's face turned to a crimson mass of pain and embarrassment, with a tint of indignation as veil for its vapid and sinister creation of his benefactors. Not knowing what will happen from here on out like politics, the best side was presented, the chocolate side. Cultures whose myths are manufactured by multinational corporations, in which the consumers of cultures want stories that lie, lull, soothe - victims of the treachery of the Benefactors. A poison that creeps into a relationship, no matter how seemingly close they are. One might ask: Who are the probable victims? The answer is, those who have become bored with contemporary society.

One has to go back to the sixties to find some parallels. At the time, when it became clear that the period was dying and the gains generated were being eroded by a new culture, a counterculture, other groups began to seek inspiration and guidance in other epochs and cultures - anything that would give them some sense of balance, reason to continue - some were not so fortunate in their choices, because the choices were clouded by manipulative big brother and the ever present media bombardments, especially those who thought with their hearts, not with their heads. Then for corroboration, trying to find a point to all that is swarming at them, for as a Chinese friend of mine would say to a proposition: 'what is the point?' If there is no point to anything, a point to whatever one is about to say or embark on, why say or do it? There just has to be a point, otherwise, what is the point? So, you dig deep into the bag of philosophical pundits, burrow through mountains of bookshelves, not caring who said what or who the author is. Bang, you find the appropriate quotes: 'If turmoil is a rich and reliable source of inspiration, the building block of creativity, from this extreme emotion: rage, passion, despair, ecstasy, betrayal – all finding their own rhythm - the dark side of human nature, a weak-minded fascist is produced. A battle then ensues between the two opposing camps. It's like the vented rage of two self-absorbed lovers in an anguished relationship or sadomasochist trysts. Not too different from that of a humiliated leader purged of guilt and self-denial, the icon of human failure, and the almost obsessive born-again fence sitters playing the game of 'let's forget,' juggling themselves into some form of activities.'

These are the forces in society that make things more difficult than they ought to be. When you look to the left, you look to the right; there are always hands, invisible hands that grab you on every side, on your every move - Demons on your track, even when conditions around you speak for themselves.

After a close look at these demons and the unforeseen and unseen forces that come to thwart the grand expectations of all your well intentioned moves, then comes the time to take stock, for reflections and inner-vision. One must gently explore, moment by moment, the spiritual transformation of anger and anxiety reduction needed to exorcize the disappointments and demons that seem to creep up and thwart the well laid plans. This, it is hoped, would create the attitude adjustment needed for the new architecture. The process is not an easy or painless one. It is a gripping journey through mine fields of desires, love, lost opportunities that lead to echoes and tales of disappointments after disappointments, and even when one is one not prone to superstition, one is invited to think that there lurk in the darkness of doors, labyrinths and the sensual atmosphere, demons that are always present, that need to be exorcized. Then and only then can one move forward and innovate - when one has fully mastered the traditions, the terrain and all other blocks in between. It is the nature of hope when all things seemed hopeless - The natural self-cleaning mechanism that is in all of us. Standing up, going and following your initiatives undaunted, fighting for what one believes in, uncompromising, but not quite like the angry man in the box, one needs faith, hope and love, because without these variables, we may as well pack it in....because, what would be the point?

"Yeah, sure," Michelle pitches in, "like a leprechaun, nifty and all that?"

Then Charlie's words rang out: "Hope is not the same thing as joy Nigel; hope is the zeal to work for something because it is good and needed, not because it has a chance to succeed. It's important to note that the superficial variety of the system and its attendant repulsive grayness not be allowed to hide the same deep emptiness - lives devoid of meaning, a facsimile of what the past era was about." Charlie continued: "Because, it is essential, people must transform themselves to change society in any fundamental way, and not wait for a galloping hero on horse back when these things can be done ourselves."

This, Charlie says, is the task that faces us all, every moment of our existence. The big mistake, according to Charlie, is to think that history happens only to others: "Because history, unlike the way some may interpret it to us, takes place universally, and we all contribute to it, in one small way or the other, in making it. Life does not take place outside history just as history is not outside life."

This, I thought to myself, in one of those unspoken thoughts, in my solitary moments, even when others are present - the kind I seem to be having so much of late - would be good for the new and emerging society. What after the runaway train of events that is cascading and enveloping the old mentalities of those behind the veneer, those who sit in deep chairs and push secretly coded buttons to repel invading demons at the gate of utopia - all for letting their imaginations go wild.

Charlie's thesis, I submit, must be accomplished no matter the obstacles the soldiers of change would go through - the tangled web of corruption and deceit from brutal men who hate the idea of change, who use loose cash, twisted relationships and myriad temptations of the flesh. Who, when these intimidations that are so blatant don't work, will cast a deepening shadow over tolerance and the rights of the individual, it's fragile nature, where it's most vulnerable.

The twilight dissolved into a steely predawn, and the sky's grey color turned into a purple blush, promising warmth but not sunshine. The barefoot children with their pets mingled with the tourists, glancing lazily at the horse drawn carriage that wound its way through the narrow alleys and streets of the French Quarter. Laughter applauded the jokes the men outside the cafe exchanged. It was not about the bad and evil dangerous women who are easily recognizable by their orange beehive hairdos, short tight skirts and tattoos, who hide in the back alleys waiting for innocent unsuspecting tourists to rob. You wonder: How come the tourists, even after being warned never to enter an empty bathroom occupied by one that fits the description of the 'evil dangerous women with orange beehive hairdos,' they still go in? Could it be the challenge, the rush one gets from 'the danger zone,' the catharsis acquired from a roller coaster? Then Michelle recalled an incident in one of these forbidden bathrooms:

"I went into one of them Nigel, the forbidden zone," Michelle said, "the zone of the bad, evil dangerous women, women with orange beehive hairdos, short, tight skirts and excruciatingly fearsome tattoos."

"Yes, go on."

"I went in there by myself only to bump into a lassie fitting the description of the fearful evil woman. I said; 'hello,' she nodded while surreptitiously checking me out through narrowed eyes. I must say, in spite of my training and all, I stood frozen against the marble wall, not knowing if there were others hiding in the stalls, clutching my purse, watching her reflection in the mirror, and then there were her rouge-soiled fingers. I was afraid it might be blood."

This was becoming as eerie as the myth surrounding the stories themselves. Michelle continued:

"My freeze frame turned into slow motion as I watched her reach into her bag, stopped, made eye contact and gave me a strange deliberate half-smile that made my heart race, and I thought to myself, this is it, she is reaching for a knife, and suddenly she snapped her bag shut and swiftly strode out, and the freeze-frame-slow-motion returned to normal play, and it had all been a bad dream."

She continued: "I returned to my control officer and I told him that there are no strange people in the alleys and that the stories about the bathroom crimes are not true, that they were the figments of the promises of the imagination polluted by the big city syndrome, of a mind gone insane - from the stress of the trade. He looked at me, not comprehending where I was coming from, but then, he wasn't from the neighborhood."

Yes, Michelle, the former agent provocateur, the former placid beauty turned seductress, turned philosopher, is also a storyteller with a well-arranged prose and sense of humor, I thought to myself, in another of those imprisoned thoughts, solitary moments, even when others are present.

The road stretched dark and long before us. Michelle and I chatted some more, about our anticipation of the new architecture, the new understanding, keeping sleep at arms length. Soon, the moon cast a hypnotic glow on the passing ships; coaxing our eyes to close and the rhythmic hum of the engine lulled us to sleep, telling us that it has been a long time since breakfast, and that as much as we might try to fool nature, it always has the last laugh. And so, in a misty eyed demeanor, we said our 'goodnights' to one another keeping the other hand free for a more clandestine activity - strong fore thrust here, a canny back thrust there, a falsetto squeal of 'uh yeah,' then off to the retired state of sleep, the perfect sleep, a much needed sleep for it has been a long time since breakfast...

Sleep, Powerful Sleep
the heavy hand of sleep
slowly weighed in,
brutishly - the eyes heavy,
the mind in a distant commune,
far and beyond the realm of the
immediate primordial.... it has
to be fought? But how...

The Tap Dancer And The Waiter

The clouds had a quality that deters the prudent from lingering on the moonwalk bleachers, and the bumbling Cafe owner goes to absurd lengths not to mention the dreary heat to his tourist-guests, for that would prompt questions about why the air conditioner wasn't working. The waiter goose-steps in hilarious fashion to the music of Metallica's 'And Justice for all,' and wonders about the complexities of the mix of tourists and their 'Tall orders' of complaints, saying:

'You can never satisfy them.' He eyed a pot bellied tourist and his beautiful young female companion, placing them on the psychiatrist's couch, analyzing such stereotypical traits as arrogance, lying, rudeness, condescending attitudes and sentimentality. I wondered if the waiter would bring this delicate issue out into the open. After all, openness is one of the cornerstones of the new landscape.
I also wondered, did the issue bothering the waiter not border on a mix of suspicion, and envy of 'fat cats,' a School boy fascination that characterizes a waiter's attitude towards tourists, the desire and wont, a dream of exchange of places. So whatever hostility a waiter has is usually expressed in mild jokes and suppressed anger and constant grin or blush, a facade to hide it all. Even when he knows it's unhealthy to bottle up such anger and jealousy. Could it be for material self-preservation? - Wife or husband, and kids to feed?

The waiter, not giving a hoot for the cells that are being destroyed by this anger and jealousy, eating away at him, said under his breath:

'Especially the early rising holiday makers who grab the best our city has to offer and still complain, instead of showing gratitude for not freezing their Asses off in their eastern shores.'

Across the cobblestone, the Tap dancer slanted one eye and gave one of those signs with the directional movements of his hips, a forward thrust, which only the waiter could understand. When translated, says:

'You've expressed a genuine popular concern my old friend, and I share your concern, I've also experienced your pain and agony. These guys think you should roll over and play dead, just because they pump a few bucks into the city coffers, which is also controlled by other 'criminal' fat cats, fuck them.'

The waiter acknowledged his friend, the Tap Dancer - for he could lip-read - a mutually developed talent from years of practice.

As an outsider, and an on the fringe commentator, I found the uproar symptomatic of identity crises rooted in the memory of the slave driver, his subjects and the old hated plantation mentality that now has a subtle reemergence; and more fashionably accepted. In conflict scenarios - when things have really gone bad, economic that is, victims are created, because there has to be scapegoats for why things are the way they are, it becomes us against them; even when the times and events dictate otherwise. And it takes the look of a twilight sphere on the fringe of a new domain, a raft being pulled away into the sunset by the force of change, but which remains kicking and screaming, and even though its screams and kicks grow gradually fainter, has an audience - dregs from the past forgotten period, provoking more and more panic-stricken self-questioning about why the ugly tourists still act in such an ugly fashion, why they have always favored the tendency to just pull down the blinds, shut out the real world, swear at the present and pretend that we can go on just living in a world that is static, frozen in time, as they know it. Even though prevailing elements dictate a new wind blowing, bringing with it a new building block, new situations and mentality - foreboding that of tender, earthly activities on a deadly serious premise of no looking back.

I took cognizance of the barriers that have been broken and those that still need to be brought down - walls that stand in the way of progress and freedom, walls which would, I hoped, collapse under the weight of the will of the people and the emerging new times. The ghosts that linger over this wind of change, because of their irascible hold on the relics of their former glory, are now flapping lazily, weakened by the greater force of a people awakened. It is the departure from one epoch of activities and the entering of another cycle of tranquil events. I Hope everyone has learned a lesson; the impossibility of holding down a people in perpetuity. A rhapsody in terms, one might say.

Michelle said: "There were always, it seems to me, a front seat and a back seat - and the windows on the sides, and the glass in between, in the messages the gatekeepers allowed... Like they say, coal means warmth in life, but with the same token, if you stay too long around it, it means death."

The moral of this was not lost on me. What Michelle is really saying is that retribution has a way of overtaking people, especially occupiers of deep chairs, the self adorned judge, jury and executioners of the past block of events.

And Charlie, who has been quiet all this time, looked up for a change - as if not to be outdone, in this mode of reflections and inner visions, a triune in conversational philosophy, afterthoughts, sins of our individual experience, imaginations and analyses of the past landscape and our contributions to the emerging block of activities - The think tank of the new architecture, if you are to call it that.

Anyway, I would rather deal with the devil I know than the devil in faux Cherubic look that professes a stature of the great and the good. There is no gentle ambiguity here, nowhere but...only when one remembers, that nobility is not a birthright, but defined by our actions, because there are just no perfect men but perfect intentions and deeds...in this never ending struggle against the perversions of nature - on a fast moving train...in full court press!

In a staccato mode, his voice a degree higher than usual but with artificial objectivity, Charlie said, almost as if afraid of where his feelings might lead him if he was not anchored to what he was familiar with, that terrain and possibly the traditions he believes he has mastered - in a studied detachment, a bit too haywire to be classical, he said:

"It is essential and incumbent on the new reformers to not grandstand, rub it in, so to speak, but to search for an appropriate exit line for these discredited benefactors, from a humane point of view, an exit devoid of any unreasoning desire for revenge, for a smooth transition - not unlike a requiem for a lost soul caught in a cascading train of events he can no longer control - a less retaliatory exit is the wiser choice. This would not only save time, but would provide the enabling environment to create and move forward. To do otherwise, is to tell the tale as is, and assail the image that his contemporaries have of him creating unnecessary rancor and bitterness that would further pollute the fragile nature of things with no obvious benefits for the greater good. Like your Chinese friend said, Nigel, what would be the point otherwise?" Charlie paused, then continued.

"It has already been established that the benefactors of the former hired killer and their collaborators having spent the better part of their lives these past decades manipulating and sewing subterfuge, have nothing to offer the new emerging era, and all that is left is for their exit to be done without any of the malevolence of the demon, the liar, and the animal-kind. Even though, it might never have occurred to them that against all sane reckoning they might have made some impression upon their contemporaries that in some modest way compared with the impression they made on them. Knowing that "closet living" retards growth and real freedom, if there is genuine will to repent and be rehabilitated into the new architecture." Charlie was not done yet, and he again continued.

"Because, the new situation would not be for 'the just come along for the ride kind,' would not be for self aggrandizement, or a highly exaggerated opinion of one's qualifications on paper and ideological motives.' Charlie concluded as he took a restorative pull of the cognac-laced green tea. I seized upon the natural break and munched on what Charlie had just said and made an analogy of the activities of the young 'client's' last charade in the restaurant - The 'John Doe' who created such a stir in the Cafe LeMond. He was a young man, idealistic and talkative, and he called himself a disciple of the 'human-faced' architecture. His voice trailed off and on I feared he was engaged in the kind of fabrication which is a thing people do when they are running out of information but want to keep their ascendancy. To my relief, he was only retrieving memories from his store - milking them out of the deep sea of his memory bank, accomplished sometimes, I must say, with some grimace of pain suppressed. His style showed a vehicle of padding points and situations harnessed to unattainable vision, which he believed, would be his contributions to the new era. All I could think of is that, as long as the young man is cognizant that the new era wants genuine partnerships built on human-faced activities not deception, who would quarrel with that?

Since there would be no forced obligations, immaturity and ignorance would be vices consigned to the past and would have no place in the new situation; these and other rules of engagement would have to be sorted out. The sorting out, again, would be done without 'experts,' for according to Charlie, 'experts are addicts who really solve nothing; they are peons of whatever system employs them. They perpetuate not only the system, but also the vehicle that got them where they are. Just take a look around you and tell me what you see. When we are bombarded or tortured by the so-called information age, we are really being tortured by the experts, the same usual experts for the same usual events. When we are sentenced or hanged, it is the same experts who will do it. When the world experiences apocalypse or Armageddon, it is the experts who will destroy us; from the Judge to the inventor of the device, from the man who pulls the switch to the creator of the smart bombs. Translated, the world will be destroyed not by the so-called madmen, but by the sanity of its experts and pundits who make the instruments, the all encompassing smart weapons, and teach the madmen how to use them, by virtue of the ignorance of the bureaucrats, those who close their eyes to the atrocities, since 'they are enemies of my enemies,' in an us against them scenario.

In this discussion, I felt myself in a level of comfort, because they mesh well with my thoughts and reflections, but Charlie's eloquently produced thesis, was not only precise, concise, profound and direct, it was also persuasive without any comedown or comeuppance. Then I realized that after the storm, it is easier for people to sit around the table, reflect and talk freely, motivated by inner vision and the desire to repair and fundamentally change what was wrong with the old, decrepit structure. A philosophical conversation I found necessary and enlightening, where people of different ilk can come together and negotiate out differences without all the saber rattling. It could be a model for the new and improved world order, I said to myself, in one of those unspoken modes, solitary, even when others are present.

Then, I said: "there is no other way; there is no other time, but now. In the past we conducted everything badly and we said they were for the future, and we can see what that future brought us - Hard ware that becomes obsolete before they leave the drawing board. Hard ware that drains the resources meant for human-faced activities, hard ware that siphons the resources meant for our basic infrastructure, doing irreparable damage to the people's psyche; with it despair, excruciating poverty, mistrust - greed, obscene wealth and selfishness. As if these bad behaviors were not bad enough, it is revealed that same hardware would need more money, possibly equal to the price of its manufacture, for its destruction. I am quite sure; this was not factored into the initial equation - the waste, money that is literally flushed down the drain, money that is desperately needed for the greater good, even more so now." I continued. "There is the argument about who won the cold war, and I say the Germans and Japanese did. For while the USSR and the USA squandered human-faced resources on mass destruction hard wares they can no longer use, the Japanese and Germans embarked on producing high quality consumer goods which now dominate the world market; which translated into a higher standard of living for their individual nations - and their people and infrastructure prospered. Because of this, should there be any argument about who won the cold war? It is the land that can feed, house and educate its people that won." I was not done yet, so I continued.

"Now, it is imperative that we do everything right for the sake of the present and future of those not yet born - Because to lose time and the opportunity is to lose everything. For, as we all know, history does not give us second chances; there is no do over where history is concerned. No room for missteps in hope of a chance to recalibrate. When we leap through an abyss, she does not give us the opportunity for a leap back. When we fail, history does not reward us with plums, but with what we rightfully deserve - agonizing pain, because, we allowed ourselves leadership borne of egocentrism, those who never listened and were less discerning of the opportunities and writings on the wall. Above all, there's a need to remember, that we will not triumph in the new architecture without sacrifice, and the needed experiment in human nature, putting words into practice, in the right direction and not useless mouths of polemic rhetoric, because, man may not, as history has come so often to remind us, always be equal to his rhetoric." I concluded.

They all clapped - Charlie, Michelle and Rowena, who is visiting after a long hiatus from the 'Big Easy.' She realized that the Benefactors of her former lover and mentor have more to worry about than her contributions to the ills of her dear uncle. Charlie, showing strong emotion, agreed with me, but added:

"We should also endeavor to break the curse of secrecy by not passing secrets from hand to hand like common thieves like the old discredited benefactors. Because their lies survived this far because of these acts of secrecy - their method of keeping everyone ignorant of this insanity, of its unhealthy nature, and the insatiable appetite to dominate and espouse greed at the expense of the people and other human nature activities - is why great visions crumbled to nasty halt. Secrecy, by its nature, not only does it keep out the light, it makes a caricature of what is supposed to be a near perfect Bill of rights. Translated, and in simple terms - we must endeavor to abhor pseudonyms that invent other lies and secrets when the mechanisms of evasion and distraction, the clever toys that are supposed to make communication easier in the push for global domination have run out."

Charlie stopped, sighed and looked at me with the over bright enthusiasm of a busy man kept waiting in underlying terror. What terror, I could not comprehend. With Charlie, you never know, you just never know. Then with equal emotion borne of contempt, he said:

"The tragedy of past great nations and those who led them is that they had so much talent, they became infected with what comes with imbalance, hubris. Even as these talents begged to be used, so much goodness longing to come out, yet all were so miserably spoken for and misdirected, that one could scarcely believe it was condoned in the old system. But it was, and the story was real, and that is the truth."

Charlie corked and thumped the front rim of his Homburg, for in Paris, even when it rains, you do not carry umbrellas or briefcases.

It is the law. Also, in Paris you do not say goodbye, you just say: 'au revoir,' till we meet again. It is also the law.

Then comes this thought that keeps nagging at me. The thought about the understanding of the times, the spirit, the leadership and the reasonableness it takes to harness the different divergences to create the desired harmony for all and all. Which needs to be done without any or the usual regard for that ever 'fashionable' tag conservative or liberal doctrinaire, nor the ever-present psychosexual analysis and all other divisive stereotypes in between. I thought to myself as I have so frequently done of late, thoughts in solitary, even when others are in the room: that in the new architecture, we would need a silver bullet.

"Say Nigel," said Michelle, "I believe the new architecture is shaping up beautifully after all, I believe we have begun to show that the cold, glacial face for which we were recently known and rebuked for, is ready for thaw - and that also means a less need to say: 'freedom for all?'"

So I said: "Yes, Michelle, the wall, the division, that perpetual chasm interposed between us and the world and humanity as a whole is finally giving way - And for once bringing real tangible and sensitive awareness of others, the different ones among us. If I may say so, if this momentum is to be maintained, a bit of humor would be needed to power the soul, because one really does not have to die first to reach the stars. Humor, I must emphasize, is especially good for serious discussion. Not just for a better equilibrium, but for reminding everyone involved that actions should be based on levelheadedness, which is really long-suffering and self-control packaged in a civilized whole. For the new situation has no need for ideologues."

Michelle brought me back to the prevailing discussion: "Where once there were no highways, and in some places, not even roads, and there was child labor and the exploitation of children and the vulnerable, there would be succor. It would be more unlikely that out of indifference, help would be denied to the child in trouble. We've come a long way, Nigel, the new architecture looks refreshing and the Facilitator must be smiling." She smiled.

Again, I must confess, Michelle the seductress turned philosopher, turned educator, is right on cue. Just as she has won my heart, she has won my mind. I have always said that if a woman cannot engage me in deep discussions, sex is no fun. There has to be more than sex in a man-woman relationship. Michelle does more than engage me, she also enlightens with great insights. And I agreed with her latest thesis, absolutely: "The symbol, and all other unwanted legacies of a world that we would like to ignore - the cold, and at times even glacial world, where in the best of cases, each one thinks about himself and a few others more or less close to him, is giving way to the sense of awareness of the other man." I said.

Michelle looked at me and the smile remained; that all encompassing smile that melts all my resistance to nothingness. It is a gesture that makes me know that my point has gotten approval and that she was in the mood to oblige me for anything, almost anything, keeping in mind that I would not risk her 'safety' without her consent.

Michelle ventured further: "Say, Nigel, this breakthrough has been achieved, a feat that many had believed to be prohibitively difficult, if not impossible, is here. The new era is here, and bringing with it, winds that bring down walls, and people are again more open to express their true feelings, even that of the heart - and, even though the world seems out of whack, sync that is - with all the collapsing walls, nation states, fallen boundaries, and daily revisions of the maps - even with all the anxieties of not knowing what will come next, it's still very refreshing - it's a new wind - those who are able to change with it will be spared, those who resist it, who are unable to adapt to it, will be swept away...."

She snuggled up to me and looked into my eyes with the large brown eyes full of questions, unspoken questions of the heart. It had a melody of its own, even when unspoken. There is no surefire definition of what it constitutes. The unspoken melody of Michelle's tune to me is a good melody - A memorable, hum-able, whistle-able tune, uniquely pleasurable. Since the longing for a good tune spans all levels of taste, sophistication and training, I would respond to the best of my ability - with a rhythmic move that would satisfy her deep longings - and just like in the movies, everyone would be happy at the end. Just because the tonality brought no decline, no rejection, and no bias based on the old system - just form, structure, organization and a need to do good, using the Facilitator and nature's gifts - talent for talent, minimizing our differences, maximizing the goal of the bigger picture. These were and are the aesthetic determiners - particularly after the embrace without the highly cerebral, rigidly complex approaches that had once dominated modern past relationships. Michelle helped prove that expressive possibilities can still be found in the straightforward romantic melodies, again, with less psychosexual analysis and other stereotypes, that were the foundation of the past - enjoying the fresh consideration of the newly vindicated souls.

"I think there's no question that everyone has the feeling of coming out of a kind of purgatory," Michelle said.

I said: "Yes Michelle, I think there is less constraint now about expressing very deep emotional aspirations - in rhythm and melody. If I may say, it has a harmonized compelling aura about it."

Our newfound philosophy in conversation, the reflection of inner visions and the anticipated grand-healthy proposal, soon melted, replaced by the view of the swelling anatomy before me. I found myself savoring the highly melodic body of tunes before me, and not without reason, Michelle was the reason. Her unspoken words, made by the wide, large brown eyes were instructive, and old Irvin Berlin played: 'A pretty girl is like a melody,' which in turn, is not quite like anything else.

The next day was not much different from the previous. Charlie and Rowena were already in the kitchen when Michelle and I made it to the living room. The smell of strawberry cove herbal tea and Charlie's special 'pride' breakfast of mixed vegetables and eggs, buttered croissant and yogurt, reactivated our brains and the conversational philosophy based on reflection of inner vision, began again in earnest. I took it as incumbent on me to open it up. So I thought what better way than to suggest a modus operandi, and I began:

"I believe, for a less tenuous approach, the method of operation, as we move forward, would need to be broken into manageable units, between phases of solutions. This would make the tasks less overwhelming and frustrating."

I stopped, and waited for someone to say something. No one did, so I continued: "It would be essential for there not to be risqué for the sake of risqué highs, no comeuppance, no cipher recklessly miscast for one's political or economic convenience, the old debris should be swept away, those self-certain old demons of the discredited past."

Since there were no rebuttal, and certainly no doubtful looking faces, I took it as an endorsement of my position, an approval I sorely needed, not just for the ego, for ego trips are legacies of the old architecture, but so as not to feel I have wasted my wind. Then I got the sign I needed, they all looked up in unison, meaning one thing, that they have been listening, absorbing and digesting my 'position paper,' and were possibly surprised that I had stopped. Egged on by this, and Michelle giving me one of those approval winks from the wide-large-brown-eyes, I could do no wrong and I felt ten feet tall and resumed my opening speech, if it can be called that. Looking at Michelle in her unbuttoned white cotton housecoat that exposed her cleavage, it could be called anything and there would be no resistance, for Michelle has the potential to melt any resistance. So I continued:

"In the past, there was always a need for narratorial, a 'nameless commentator,' if you will; a 'specialist' on a routine trip from point "A," possible Washington, to point "B," which could be Moscow, only to find the train, and then his destination itself, empty. This time, there would be no such need. Because, as one later finds out as he explores the deserted streets, taking special note of the architecture and the flowerlike scent of the breeze - he uncovers only horrors, horrors that border on the magnitude of a twilight zone, which invariably makes his stomach churn - this, in spite of himself."

I did not mean for this to make any sense to them. It was intended only as a diversion, purposefully inserted to juggle the mind and bring these participants-non-participants into the discourse. A device designed to reinvigorate the dead brains of my non-participants. At that point, I also realized that when your audience starts having long faces and glancing at the person seated next to them, there is a need for strategic change, especially when your lover, in this case Michelle, decides to button down the unbuttoned upper house coat. If that was not cue enough, I don't know what would. The question that pops to mind is whether this is a vision of the afterlife that has emerged, which seems to derive directly from the coexistence of terror and normality that had characterized the old order, which the new situation abhors. I looked at Michelle; the sign of approval has been removed. Charlie and Rowena were now whispering to each other. I was on my own.
I thought: Maybe it is time I pay attention to my breakfast, the 'pride' of Charlie, that was becoming cold from neglect. Again, I looked at Michelle for some strength, some approval, again, there was no sign, none was coming from her, and my heart was broken -

.... Who has woe? Who has uneasiness? Who has
contentions? Who has concern? Who has wounds for
no reason? Who has dullness of eyes? Those staying
a long time with the wine, those coming to search out
mixed wine. Do not look at wine when it exhibits a red

color, when it gives off its red sparkle in the cup,
it goes with slickness. At its end it bites you
like a serpent, and it secretes poison just like a

viper. Your own eyes will see strange things, and your heart will
speak perverse things. And you will certainly become like one lying
down in the heart of the sea, even like one lying on top of the mast.
They have struck me, but I did not become sick; they have smote
me, but I did not know it. When shall I wake up? I shall seek it yet
some more...

Then she spoke! And everybody's head turned towards her, for when
Michelle goes inward, she shuts every bit of her aura to all and all,
and it does not take long to notice, because she has that magnetism,
the kind of presence you want to be around, for it's like a spritzer
whose bubbles have a healing effect, especially for a trapped soul
that fears the past like mine, a soul that longs for that encompassing
emancipator. Michelle is my designated emancipator. I would not let
go, for I cannot let go. She and she alone is the vehicle to Elysium.
These were her words:

"For the sake of the bigger landscape, this new emerging order,
which is too big for any single individual, we should endeavor to
not backtrack, to make sure there is no tolerance for apostates, those
who would choose to mimic our cause, that cannot be tolerated, no
matter what. When it gets stormy, we should be able to stay in the
storm, adjust the sails and continue on; because no one said it would
be easy. In the old order, expectation was low, and at the end, it was
not exceeded. We should learn from that - it's important we do."

As much as I would like to agree with Michelle, and as much as I
believed the essence of the product of her reactivated brain, which
was the essence of my purposefully inserted diversion in the first
place; it was necessary, if only to reassert my self-esteem, so I said;

"The world is moving irreversibly in the direction of openness, and those who learn to operate with fewer secrets will ultimately have the advantage over those who futilely cling to a past in which mass secrets can be protected. The hallmark of a truly great democracy is of maximum possible disclosure, recognizing that democracy can best be preserved only when credibility is truly maintained. I would say, the question before us is whether an artist of vision, perhaps even of genius, ought to be constrained, held legally responsible or ultimately censored because some people find the work in questionable taste or blatantly offensive? I believe this should be unacceptable, should be guarded against at all cost."

I waited for a retort, a rebuttal, anything, there was none of the kind. What I got was approval and the melting of resistance; and the wall that went up earlier, was coming down, even Michelle's buttoned down upper coat, was being loosened, and right before my eyes. It was music to behold and old Irving Berlin's: A beautiful girl is a melody, played again and again, and there was happiness in my soul, and there was hope for that anticipated Elysium, after all.

... And also, do not give your heart to all the words
that people may speak about you, that you may not hear
your servant calling down evil upon you. For your own
heart well knows even many times that you, even you,
have called evil upon others...
All this I have tested with wisdom. I said: 'I will
become wise.' But it was far from me. What has come
to be is far off and exceedingly deep. Who can find it
out? I myself turned around, even my heart did, to know
and to explore and to search for wisdom and the reason
for things, and to know about the wickedness of
stupidity and the foolishness of madness; and I was
finding out: More bitter than death I found the woman
who is herself nets for hunting and whose heart is
dragnets and whose hands are fetters. One is good
before the true Facilitator if one escapes from her,

but one is sinning if one is captured by her.
See! This I have found, said the minister, one thing
taken after another, to find out the sum-up, which my
soul has continuously sought, but I have not found. One
man out of a thousand I have found, but a woman among
all these I have not found. See! This only I have found,
that the true Facilitator of life made mankind upright,
but they themselves have sought out many plans.........

Rabbit Face And The Client

In the game of waiting, worrying and running, that is called spying,
it is fashionable to become part of a duplicitous lifestyle and to
commiserate with impostures or falsities all because it is acceptable in
the line of duty, part of the job, if you may. Instructing surrogates to
give succor in cooked up emergencies, all for playing to the camera.
This is accepted as chic. One's private thoughts notwithstanding,
keeping rendezvous with 'Clients' for a power lunch, even when you
know the 'Client' is not really a client, but an opposition agent or
double agent is welcome, all because the man who sits in the deep
chair asked you to. Compromising your faith and principles, even
though you are scared numb and have a hangover you are trying
to shake off, you still do it, for it is all in the line of duty, and duty
blind loyalty comes first in the game of espionage.

A strange voice, a very strange voice from nowhere, whispers to you,
saying: 'The mother of your bride was right, you are a heathen, and
the Babylonian of your time, and for that reason the system will
always win, because you're part of the web that holds the system
together, you're part of its vehicle.'

Suddenly, you are jerked awake from a stupor, and you question the
strange voice and ask yourself: 'Am I a legal property of the system,

am I really part of it? Is it possible to change it within or without? Am I capable of doing this?'

Then you peer around, very guardedly, at the grimy windows and other 'Clients' as if expecting the blood of your 'client' to come seeping down the cracks of the doors. Occasionally, you allow your gaze to stray to the expected direction of your 'client's' entrance, even if it is done from behind the facade of a newspaper dedicated to printing the 'truth and nothing but.'

All of a sudden, you realize you have been caught in a daydream and panic sets in, in the commonly zoned area of grey, which is a no, no, to a neophyte, for its content of colliding databases that increase exponentially. Out of nowhere a voice from a Rabbit faced Neanderthal, a left foot, right foot hopping kind of guy, who looked too young to be the 'Client' said:

'You are lost?'

Then you think to yourself, as you have done of late, enmeshed in solitude, even when others are within the same space: 'Was that the code word, was it changed and you were not apprised?' How come the 'Client' is not fitting the description of the 'illustration' you have. You say: 'The mother of my bride was really right, I am the heathen and Babylonian of my time, and welcome to the world of espionage, and the high stakes spy game my boy!' Then not knowing what to say to the 'Rabbit faced, left foot, right foot hopping kind of guy' Neanderthal, you say:

'I am not lost, are you?'

This is said in a very calm and deliberate tone. Hoping you were firm enough, that your voice conveyed the right measure of strength without giving away the anxieties that lie within, aware of the butterflies in your belly. Then your worst nightmare comes true, 'Rabbit faced, left foot, right foot hopping kind of guy' is not satisfied, he digs further and looks you in the face, unblinking, trying feverishly to emanate the aura of confidence and the right elocution, he says:

'Do you have some merchandise to sell me, contraband, currencies, or would you like to trade for drugs or women?'

You look at 'Rabbit faced, left foot, right foot hopping kind of guy,' thinking he should have been tucked into bed by now by his nanny and not trying to hustle poor you. An archeologist of human nature could scrutinize and analyze Rabbit faced, left foot, right foot for decades without getting at what must be the complex layers of why he pretends to be who is he not, and remains obstinate in the pursuit. So you say:

"Thanks, I'm fine actually, I'm really very nice as I am, but if you would just move out of the sunlight a little bit, just a little bit, I would be even nicer."

Rabbit face comes from obstinate stock, and he is not giving ground he is in the true sense of the word, a hard sell. He goes on:

"You want to meet some international people, maybe some lavish uninhibited lassies. I can show you the real French Quarter that nobody ever gets to see." He said this with delirious delight in his voice.

Then you look up at the kid, real hard, a good hard stare into his glazed eyes and his feet that he seems to not be able to control, just as hard as he has given you, and you say to yourself in one of those unspoken thoughts, where solitude reigns, you think this must be a botched up set up. Nevertheless, you say:

"Look my dear man, to be perfectly frank with you, I do not believe you'd know the real French Quarter, from the not so real French Quarter, even if it got up and kicks you in the balls." The panic was palpable, even if it was just for a moment – the whir in the air of axes falling, karate moves implemented, the terror commingled with relief, relief that none of his fears came to pass – in spite of the fact that he is now permanently established as one of those who perpetrate the major frauds (specialized in soaking, the colossal swindle of the tourists. Yes, as a truly equal-opportunity son of a bitch, glass eyes, left foot, right foot and those of his ilk are known to pickpocket their own kinds. They call it thieves stealing from thieves) in the quarter, the French quarter; so that today one runs into such comic nomenclatural as glass eyes, left foot, right foot.

I return to my 'nothing but the truth newspaper' and 'Rabbit faced, left foot, right foot' drifts away. I am surprised that throughout the agonizing charade, I was calm in my demeanor and that none of us had really raised his voice. Then to really drive it home, I look around at the weather beaten faces in the crowd. I rub my neck, my face showing nothing but apology for the little commotion of the past few minutes, saying, even when unspoken: 'I share your confusion and I am just as surprised as you all about all this.' Making sure you show empathy, and praying to be assumed into their ranks.

Another panic button sets in, doubts creep into your system. Was 'Rabbit faced, left foot, right foot' it? Was he the conduit? How come no one radioed me? Lingering thoughts persist, squinting into windows and upward at the stubby faces with vile written all over them - No, not him - for goodness sake, not him. They would give me a more decent and decorous 'Client' to work with. For the next half hour I would think of nothing, stare at the paper, but not seeing anything. I would stare at the buildings. I would stare at the girls and the New Orleans girls of summer would stare back at me, their alertness not reassuring me. I would duck back to the newspaper, which became a good investment. Beads of sweat like small marbles running down my spine and the small of my back. It is time to clear my throat, lick my lips, to make sure that I would be able to speak, and then murmur some few words under my breath. Moisten my lips some more to make sure that they are not numb and gummed together. I move parts of my limbs for reassurance - hoping the fear of paralysis was just that, fear and nothing else. That I could still walk like everybody else, and there would be no bone cracking falls headlong down the stairs.

The sun broke clear of the clouds - and just as I was about to give up, the real 'Client' showed up. His appearance made me look foolish - for even wasting my time with the fraudster; for he appeared just like 'Clients' of such 'Setups' are supposed to. I spotted him. He was as precise as he was advertised to be. He was seated to the third seat of the left banister, a V sign flashed behind the newspaper he was holding, very different from the 'the truth and nothing but' paper, but all the same, an object devoted to the macabre etiquette of the trade craft, the sign is the symbol and the symbol decides whether to make or abort the meeting. The next worry, had to do with the hearers, did they hear or really pay any attention to the episode of 'Rabbit faced, left foot, right foot?' I had to, more than ever before be on the qui vive, duty requires it. It was not a sanguine thought – for the anxiety that comes with it, perhaps that is not entirely a bad thing, I thought - as the whole gig might also not have been altogether without purpose.

Not quite ten yards separate the 'Client' from me, but it was more like a test line. Am I walking too slow or too fast? Is it another case of the observer being observed? Is it just a filament of imagination in my racing mind? There is something angular and not quite reconciled with his posture, I thought, which resembles the over-orderly clockwork in a Swiss town. I decided to lift my head - then I struck midway with my truth and nothing but the truth newspaper, now I pull my chair and make way for my guest, my 'Client' or whoever he may really be. All orchestrated as someone else's invention, a mechanical device that is calculating the speed of every movement.

Slurring my pace, I orient myself to the new situation, with diligence. A passive voice asks:

"Sir? I believe we are acquainted. Do we have information to exchange?" It gave off fumes of quiet but deep confidence that can be immensely seductive. I have met men of his physical and psychological type: smallish, Un-athletic in build, wearing expensive yet Un-flashy clothes, nothing dazzling about them. They manage to seem substantial in an unthreatening, even avuncular way. They appear to have a deep secret: they have gotten in on the ground floor, they know how the game is played; should they choose, they could put you on to a few good things. They have deciphered the magic of the spy game, of money and power, even when they do know or comprehend the funny nature of money and power, its fleeting or ephemeral nature. They feel no need to brag, but clearly they have everything under control. Except of course, they don't, not really, because no one really does, do they?

Even when your mouth is about to explode something unprintable, you bottle it all up; what does he mean he believes we are acquainted? I don't even know him from Adam. Information to exchange my butt, that he can say again. Even with all this, you say "yes" and smile sheepishly...visions of the approaching end game enveloped me – the end of the game known as the spy game – hoping the big score from this last transaction, the exchange of 'very important information' that would make the Valhalla possible – Valhalla in this case is a condominium on a golf course in a dull place with warm climate - where, in my peach-colored pants, spiked shoes and chemises polo appear on the first tee promptly at 8 A.M. I would whack away at a little ball, hoping, at the end of four hours' effort, to arrive at the finish a stroke or two fewer than the previous time I spent the morning before. Above all else, I would learn the meaning of the phrase: "dogleg to the left." Definitely.

"Yes," I said again, looking up and making sure there was eye contact from a position of strength. I say to myself: 'this is the code word. 'Rabbit faced, left foot, right foot' was just a rouse from the game plan of an eavesdropper. The information is exchanged and everybody is happy, because there were no gunshots, nor blood rivulets trickling from under the crack of doors - only tracks of pain, fear and worry that accompanied the acts. Moisture returns to my mouth, and my lips are no longer dry or numb. The mission has been accomplished. Only the hunted looks flicking nervously at every passing face. The past architecture was a rape on time, a lesson for the new situation, where everyone will be fed with the truth and nothing but.

A line of streetcars pulled up, the horse and the man flicked cheekily in their wake. Two lovers were embracing at the far corner of the last rows of seats. By the Saint Louis Cathedral, a young woman stood rocking a carriage while she read from the book holding in her spare hand. The expression on her face is as if she is marching into an uncertain world and a relationship armed with all the anxiety and hopes that schooling and life has provided.

The 51 Tram

The breeze from the river washed over the balmy heat, and on the 51 tram, the oriental woman popped seeds into her mouth. The jaws did not move, and I wondered if the Chinese have perfected a new system, the art of chewing without moving the different joints of the mouth. If anyone is in search of something to worry about, in the afterglow of what is the French Quarter, they can definitely find it here - on the 51 tram... an old man looked at me and said:

"This is my buddy," and put his arm around his companion's shoulders, and the 'buddy' expressed a sheepish grin and said:

"Is that right? Then why do I keep looking behind my back when I am with you, especially in a dark alley?"

The old man, with a contrived amazement, said: "I don't know,"

There was quite some laughter. Then he said:

"Don't I only use plastic knives and water pistols in the games we play, don't I?" There was quite some more laughter - everyone thought the two old guys were quite funny, hilarious actually...

The 'Client' has come and the 'Client' has gone, but still you worry about the unknown. The worry imposed by the 'Group leader,' to keep you on edge, to keep one in line. The question is: 'Will I survive this roller-coaster, or am I going to be sacrificed to the angry gods of this dog-eat-dog profession before my mission is complete?' Will the sheep like complacency, which seems to become implanted in the genes of the 'Clients,' often, lead me to make the same monumentally out-of-sync decisions? Decisions that would invariably affect everyone that ever worked out of mission control. How come the group leaders push aside capable 'Clients' whose intelligence or strength promise to equal theirs? Is it fear of their position or what? Is it some form of complex character flaw, like say angst, aggressiveness, egotism, inferiority, sentimentality? Would this be their true psychological portrait? These characteristics, I thought to myself, are of the past and must not be allowed into the new situation, cannot be identified with the future, the new architecture - the emerging new order. Need I go further?

Then I reflected again on the more damaging flaws of the past landscape; for what better place to reflect on such diverse issues than the 51 tram - a tram that takes a full hour navigating between point A and point B, giving the rider, this time yours truly, the luxury of reexamining recent events of the past landscape, its leadership, and their idiosyncrasies. The group leader, when trying to prepare agents for acts of dastard nature, is always fund of saying: 'for the world to function, a thousand things have to go right every minute, and they have to go on quietly. It is why we hire you guys to do things quietly, for the world to function.' It was easier, and more pertinent to the present discussion to think of the less happy ones done quietly: their insensitivity to the feelings of the masses, their obsession with themselves and their strong inclination to self-pity, bullying, and their longing to be liked, a sign of not only weakness, but severe complex of inferiority. Are the group leaders so different from the rest of us?

This concern about the future and the roles or what to do with the 'Old Bosses,' the men who sit in deep chairs, was further provoked by their capacity to overdo things, to kick over the traces and their tendency to over estimate their own capacities. This, the new architecture could very much do without. There would be no place for waste – either in time, human or natural resources. Conservation would be in, because mother earth calls for it. The abuses, producing weather reports never seen before, have to stop.

Then, should the new architecture really preoccupy itself with the old benefactors? Just be aware of them, maybe, just maybe in case they start rearing their heads again.

This then leads one to ask how a cultivated society allowed itself to be brainwashed into barbarism in the first place. If it had happened once, could it happen again? Would this group of people succumb to their past barbaric acts when tested by adversity, major political or economic calamity? How could one tell how they would react in such circumstances, without a crystal ball? Could some of the unhappy characteristics reemerge with just as destructive consequences? The stand and overall message of the guardians of the new order must be unmistakable. A keen watch, removal of the instruments that led to it in the beginning, requiring complete rehabilitation not just for the present unease and the immediate future, but also for what might lie further down the road than we can yet see is necessary. There is a need for cardinal change, to come up with a series of very good results. It's not enough to just say: 'we have taken a certain series of certain measures to correct the certain problems we had.' Then Michelle said:

"I would suggest that managed metamorphosis is a preferred way to go, it's a better choice than a chaotic one, the new world order deserves better - no need to dwell on symbolic fights for fight sake, wasting valuable time." Michelle added.

One does not have to dig too deep, to realize that the activities of the former 'Bosses' had all been too contrived. Could these activities have come from decent human beings? Was it a natural digression, from imperfect memory? Like a hole in time, a big hole to be filled? It could be that when you ignore the shortest distance between two points, making a conscious effort to go slow, producing a heap of suspicion on the huge gap - but no triumph in the other's distress. This was the methodology of the men at the helm of things the last few decades; they moved from point W to Point M and other points in between in the dangerous world of hidden arms deals and murderous intelligence agencies - carrying the game of espionage to a high echelon far and above in the Faustian realm.

Then there were the wild wicked giggles across the crowded room. Could it be from the grinding, hissing, groaning, heaving, sweating, and sighing seething pleasure, of well, making out? Is it related to the frustration of waiting and worrying that come with the game of spying - to relieve the tension?

Where is the noise coming from? You may ask. Is it from the next room? Should I peep? Is it morally okay to do so? Which becomes another war within you. Which you know you really don't need at this time. Which is part of the sometimes-lonely work of espionage, when the waiting game can be as agonizing as the interrogations. 'It should be okay to look when it involves my safety,' it is as good a justification as any? - A mean that justifies the end? The noise stopped! Are they aware of my presence? Is it a decoy? A mind game? Then the noise would start again. Seeping through the cracks of the adjoining door. 'It's going to be soooo good,' the female voice whispered, leading her panting prey, slowly, into an empty walk-in-closet, he is unbuttoning her blouse, weakened by the intimacy...'This is it, this is it,' he groans, hungrily pressing her backward onto the wide solid shelf, his powerful torso melting into hers - the view from the key hole unveils a contravention. This seemingly remote Olympian figure, not known for giving and attending scandalous parties, a moralist of the first order, if there ever was one, who preaches family and the virtues of staying close to God, is just seen committing adultery. This is the same man, who in his royal court, would dispense verdicts that would sever the limbs of subjects for drinking beer, but while in his private chambers drinks champagne and does unmentionable things with the women who flock in and out of his chamber, he is the Sheik - And who says life is fair.

What is life anyway? Isn't it more appropriate to describe it as an apprentice of fate and accident? An instrument, which in the proper frame of mind, that prepares one for the lucky breaks that may come along. Then, you wonder what lucky breaks does one get in this trade? When you are always going against the stream in a senseless game where one can easily be turned into a scapegoat or lab animal, where one dies and no one will ask your name, when lies and fears of the past is always *l'chasseur*.

"When we fear to look at our own past in the face, we have to fear what is essentially to come. All too often in the old order, the fear of one lie only gives birth to another, in the vain hope that salvation from the first lie is a salvation from all lies. Lies cannot save us from lies, it's a given. Lies beget lies, in an endless self perpetuation." Charlie chipped in.

This is Charlie the philosopher speaking, not Charlie the forensic accountant, I thought. It is a new and more reflective Charlie, of a poet-philosopher kind, a Scholar and gentleman, an up and coming accomplished philosopher, just like Michelle.

Then Rowena, who has been less talkative since she returned, broke in:

"The supposition in the old order, that one can walk the tightrope of history and rewrite one's own biography without being punished for our errors and misappropriation of both tangible and intangible human nature resources, is one of the traditional crazy ideas of the benefactors, those who, Nigel rightly calls 'Deep chair sitters.' 'When one tries to do this, he not only harms himself, he also includes all others around him in the share of the pain, for mistakes shared or tolerated, are mistakes halved, for there can be no full freedom where the full truth is not given free rein, if our past is a lie, who is to say our future is not going to be as well." Rowena, her voice calm and subdued, enunciated eloquently.

This did not come as a surprise; if Michelle can do it, why can't Rowena. They both were students and mistresses of uncle Baranowsky, the son of the German immigrant, the hired killer, whose disappearance is still a mystery. Then Rowena and Charlie have spent the past few nights and days together, too close I must say; the philosopher line has a similar ring to it, sounding increasingly from the same lineage, from that of an eminent gentleman-scholar, poet-statesman of eastern extraction.

The sun flitted out from behind the clouds, and monarchs flitted out from wherever monarchs hole up. Colorful in its orange and black. Majestic and enchanting, probably a viceroy for all we know. Who can truly distinguish these magnificent creatures, with their uncanny similarity?

"There's one!" Michelle said.

We all took off down the trail after the delicate creature, swinging wildly, like little leaguers in their first at bat. Michelle got to it first. The Monarch, or a beautiful viceroy, fluttered about inside the white see-through cotton scarf, an improvised net. Michelle, observing the calm, delicate creature, extended her finger, and as if responding to the delicacy of Michelle's touch, it perched on her finger and remained so for several seconds, its lovely orange and black wings spread.

"Now everybody gather around and get a close look before it decides..." but the monarch decided before Michelle could finish, and off it flapped.

The clouds rolled in, the monarchs rolled out. By the time the short hike around the riverbank was over, we had counted two males, two females, one not quite distinguishable and four or five others that could go either way.

"We might have counted the same monarch twice," Rowena challenged. "They are kind of hard to tell apart," she concluded.

There was a pleasant breeze. A purple blue sky rolled in from under the clouds. Right at this very moment, on the muddy bank of the Mississippi, I just wished I could hold on to my present train of thought and fend off the teeming crowds of the French Quarter.

Such a pretty place, such a pretty girl. The burgundy hair, she wears it long and ties it back on the back of her head with a purple ribbon. A few strands dance about her face in the sunlight. She laughs and talks with her friend. She brushes back her hair with her hand. She drinks her beer from the bottle. The last action might not sound too classy. At this very moment, she looks exactly young, beautiful, and brash - A placid beauty turned seductress, turned philosopher - that's my Michelle! A BCBG. Bon chic, bon genre, as they would say in the French quarter of the Big Easy.

It was a mad time. A confusing time, and the vagaries of the French Quarter with its cloudy skies, the balmy and humid air, the pulse of the Mississippi and its breeze and the patches of idyllic beauty, were not much of a consolation for the heat.

You at the big muddy river, a gaze fixed. Because the circumstances dictate a fixed gaze, even when it is done unconsciously. In the trancelike gaze, you might think you saw a small boat founder, any longer than that, you might think you have seen them everywhere - a sail, the hull, possibly the spec of a survivor's head or limb ducking under the river's swell never to resurface. You must go on watching for much longer to find out it was only a mirage, and what might have seemed to be boats were barges and the heads and limbs, those who steered them.

Images of your group leader's lecture might spring to attention. He tells you that the agency has accorded your assignment a full-facility grading, because the men who sit in deep chairs found your work and reports acceptable after a careful going over. Their glee after initial reservations oozes like a tap nothing can turn off.

Nonetheless, you also do your own going over of their acceptance reports and notations that is, and in the process you find out that you can literally make them eat out of your palm. Even with this realization, you still write the ecumenical agreements, based on a firm but fair resolve, because you are a fair man and a sucker for flattery and more than that, because as always you are dealing with very realistic hard-nosed people. Who believe in the credo, nothing ventured, nothing gained in the great standoffs between the superpowers and the not so superpowers, and others in between. This takes courage. Nothing exists in a vacuum.

Every question is as important as the answer in the highest strategic classifications of opposite number to opposite number deals, vis-à-vis the terms and conflicts in the counter spy game where nothing is insignificant and nothing could possibly be left to chance - chance being abstract and therefore not real.

The volcanic color of the fall sun hung over the riverbank ahead of us, making even the muddy Mississippi and the skyline of the west bank of Algiers beautiful. It was all aboard on paradise, with the riverbank and grey gravel to picnic on and everyone oblivious to everything distracting his or her own good spirit. Hoping that all these and other distractions - will shortly belong to the past, while you laboriously fight off the unwelcome singing in your ears. Yes, singing in your ears, that ever present symptom of big city living - that is further compounded by the waiting and worrying that come with the trade of espionage. There is a big fight to defeat the uproar inside your head, an uproar that comes with the sphere of inaction, or the agonizing wait, when the shadow and conflicting messages or instructions of the group leader is not lessening the singing or loud uproar in your ears. You wonder: 'Does this have to go on, how can one free oneself from this theater of conflict?'

Michelle would be the emancipator, the vehicle to the Elysium. The picnic progressed as the sky cleared momentarily. She knelt carelessly behind me, using the small pillow as cushion. She steadied herself with one hand on my shoulder, while with the other she tilted the glass of spritzer to my mouth. I could feel her breast brush against my back. I am sure it was the breast; nothing else could have felt that way.

"Can I share in your pain, can I share in your thoughts, am I welcome - I could be of help," Michelle said.

'Absolutely,' I responded, I did not want to raise any more anxiety, and perhaps to reassure myself.

There was a pause while her eyes considered me: "Nigel, let me in."

I managed a smile, a smile I knew she was waiting for. I smiled some more, a sincere and composed goodhearted smile of friendship borne of mutual love. Charlie and Rowena had dozed off to sleep, smiling from the bubbly and their memories of what had been.

Michelle, apparently not satisfied with the response she has gotten from me, got up and waded into the water in her shorts. She looks more beautiful than ever, even in her wet shorts, and even though she is a little bit preoccupied with what might be on my mind. She scooped some water with her palms, looked to the far horizon. She is the most beautiful woman I know.

The evening arrives, and a tang of fall leaves drift through the dry humid air. It was time to head home, because it's been a long time since breakfast. A pair of pigeons flew over and they might well have been the last two pigeons in the world.

The Daughter Of Eve
And It Might Have All Been In Vain

The young man said: "You know what I will do to people like that?"

His companion, the seducer in a very short, short mini dress and black fishnet pantyhose, said: "What would you do to people like that?"

He said: "I will put their heads against the wall and blow them away."

"Why would you do something like that?" The seducer asked, with her rouge tongue sticking out. Posturing teasingly, she asked for confirmation of an answer she already knows. Her special way of ridiculing a system she finds oppressive to her people, or particular culture.

"Because he is a part of the system, the system that rapes you, uses you, and blows you away," Said her companion, whose demeanor was the exact opposite of hers.

The old man shook his head, and said out loud: 'There is no more respect in the world, it's not like it used to be, I wonder what the world is turning to." The old man, even though they were separated by just some few rows of seats, and almost directly opposite, looked past the young couple, as stone faced, as his aging muscles would allow.

His companion, an equally old woman, wearing a shawl of a very black hue said: "There's need for a return to the glory days, all our efforts and those of our forbears, it might have just been in vain. There is just no more respect," she added, almost in a whisper. "No dreams, no ambition, just decadence and debauchery, and they are the rulers of tomorrow, and he smokes too, in a no-smoking zone. If I could whistle this train to a stop, I would do it. I will get out of this macabre, grotesque, Un-ambitious, dreamless group." Her disposition was a replica of her companion, the old man, who is just as old as she is...

The youth was unblinking, he glared and raised his boom box - glided to the center of the fast moving train, depressed the play button and raised the volume to the highest it would go, and the song of the unknown artist blared: 'Kill them all, kill them all, the users, the dominators, the greedy ones, blow them all away.' With a menacing grin he swung around, and around, and around, dissolving into a whirlwind, the boom box held over his head, he let it fly. It traveled unhindered, through the length of the coach, and at last it found its place, against the glass door-partition. It shattered and vaporized with a hissing sound. The passengers were held spellbound, angst and confusion written on their faces. The silence that greeted it was as eerie as the crash was deafening...

Just then, the silence was broken, the old woman who is just as old as her companion said: 'It could all just be in vain!'

The train came to a screeching halt - the doors flew open. It was time to march out, for those whose urge it is to satisfy the old woman, the old woman who is just as old as her companion. So the dreamers and the ambitious; those working to that ultimate goal, climbing the ladder, the ladder to the top – trooped out to satisfy the ambition that existed in the mind of the old woman, who is just as old as her companion.... She could not see that there are different strokes for different people; that everyone does not have to march to the same drumbeat.

The old woman smiled, a sheepish smile borne of pleasant surprise at the potpourri of characters marching out of the train, a medley of levels of ambitions and choices. She was fooled. She said: "There just might well be hope after all, it could, it just might be possible, it has not all been in vain."

A half moon, draped in showers of mist, hung ahead of us. Occasionally our hands brushed; occasionally our hands grasped each other in a firm embrace. Michelle wasn't speaking, so I wasn't speaking either. It was a mutual moment of solitude. At a crisp pace we marched on. The clock at Canal and Broad read 8:54. I made a consciously officious gesture, and I compared it to my Seiko. The clock was three minutes early. Michelle was angry with me again. She was angry that after the beautiful picnic, I spoiled it by telling her the story of the train and its inhabitants. The train story has had the same reaction on all my women friends, especially when told after dinner, following the ecstasy of a beautiful dinner. I really did think it would be different with Michelle, being a former agent provocateur and all that. What do you know? It goes to show that underneath, a girl is a girl is a girl.

"Where did that happen, Nigel?"

Michelle is talking, the moon lost its mist and my soul does not have to fear Hades, and Elysium beckons. See, when my emancipator is speaking, I listen. Even when I do not agree with everything she says, I still listen, all she needs to do is talk and look at me with those wide hazel eyes. So I said:

"It might have been between Brussels and Paris, through Waterloo. It could have been between Paris and Lyons, or possibly between Victoria station and Heathrow. It's been so long, I don't remember. For all I know, it could have been between Brussels and Antwerp, on a journey to Amsterdam. I will always remember the faces and the participants, they are hard to forget."

"That was grotesque, Nigel, excruciatingly, macabrely grotesque, you made it up, just to rouse my temper, and you should be ashamed of yourself."

See, this is one of our disagreeable moments. In most cases, I would bet nine out of ten times, the real reason lies beneath the surface. How could she accuse me of making something like that up? How could I make up such a thing? Elements might have been rearranged or misplaced, but it was true. Then it hit me. She does believe me. She is just angry because she was not my companion on the mission, and the fact that I deliberately omitted the name and gender of my companion on that mission, did not help. She is waiting for answers to the unspoken questions.

Then I remembered what an old Native American once told me a while back. It went like this: 'Women are not really the weaker sex men make them out to be. It is a concoction of a deluded machismo. Women, if anything, are really the stronger sex. Think about it, they were the first to taste wisdom, and because of that, the wiser ones, for they had a leg-up on wisdom. Eve was kind to share the fruit with Adam, she could have withheld it, and laugh at Adam and his nakedness, even till today. In a way, they still do, in subtle ways - Because Eve discovered her nakedness and the other niceties around her before Adam did, she opened Adam's eyes to the true logistics, infrastructure and other benefits his environment provided, that he never knew about before he tasted the fruit of wisdom, including but not limited to Eve's womanhood. So, tell me, is there any doubt who's the cleverer or stronger sex?'

I looked on with bemusement, not really knowing what to say. Do I thank him for edifying me on a subject that hitherto was simpler and generally accepted? I believed my Bible schoolteacher and the literal interpretation she gave us in junior high. I must confess, that looking back now, my infatuation with her may have prevented my asking the deep and hard questions that could have shed more light on things. Sally Jane was a very beautiful woman. Her voice, even then, did strange things to me - Her beautiful face and perfect body, in a moderately tight fitting dress, reduced absenteeism to its minimum. Many a time, I would raise my hand and ask some sterile question to make her come to my desk. There were times, I believe, she purposely came close enough and allowed her soft thigh to rest against mine. Her face close to mine, and me actually feeling the softness of her luxuriant hair and morning fresh shampoo against mine, she would look straight at me, eyes sparkling, as she explained away, answers to my curious mind, like love bites and the sins of my imaginations as she raises her hand, and tries to put in place an unruly strand of hair, my heart melts, and I always promise my young soul, 'this is the kind of woman for Nigel.' This old man has some profound counter-translation - and if I were not careful, would make an apostate out of me, and vitiate all that Sally Jane represented in my youth. I refused to take sides - at least, not until I hear all of it - so I listened some more. If this old Native American is going to convert me, make me commit apostasy, he had better provide more facts, and not just titillation. I listened some more....

"Another line of thought says it was sex Eve had from the serpent, not an apple. The demon engaged Eve in sexual intercourse, the 'forbidden fruit,' which led to Eve discovering her nakedness and the body part between her legs, which hitherto was only used for discharging unwanted fluid. Thereafter she also discovered Adam's elongated throbbing rod, which in a way reminds her of the serpent and its head. Think about it. Don't they look similar? Anyway, after having tried this forbidden fruit, which she obviously enjoyed. So, just looking at Adam and his naked manhood, she was more than willing to share her newfound lustful secret - which as one can see, was not out of an altruistic motivation. She was in heat; she had tasted the forbidden 'fruit,' which, everyone knows, is the sweetest of them all. It is called lust, which by the way, is also one of the deadly sins. Now, tell me my young man, who is the wiser and stronger sex?" I couldn't argue with any of it. The old man is a son of the soil and he should know but I was not ready to give up my religion yet. I needed more proof. The knowledge I had carried with me for thirty some years cannot just be erased within some few minutes, son of the soil, or no son of the soil, I needed more proof, more information.... The old man continued -

"There is another opinion, a very convoluted one if there is one, goes like this: That the demon caught Eve during her ovulation, and Cain was the result of the conception that followed. Abel was the son of Eve's second sexual partner, Adam. Why else would Cain murder Abel? They were the products of two polar opposites, good and evil. Cain was the true son of the serpent, also called Satan, the devil, and the originator of the first deadly sin. Just don't say I did not warn you, because I did. It is a radical line of thought, but is has its merits, and it's not for the faint hearted, and definitely not for the Jesse Helmses of the world." "By the way, another thing Nigel, men think they are the ones pursuing women, not true. They are the ones pursuing men until they are ready to catch them." The old man smiled, wryly. This was too much. I looked at the old man; he looked back at me. There were no more words exchanged. I walked away, a more confused man unsure if I should wish I had never met the old man. As profound as his elocution was, it was against everything I had been brought up to believe...

See, women, they are a special breed and I love them, especially my Michelle. You just have to listen to them, give what they say appropriate attention, especially the unspoken words. There's no gainsaying the incontrovertibility of their strength and superiority. Just ask the native man; he will confirm it.

"I love you Michelle, I have always loved you, even when Jamie's presence dominated my life. I love you enough to risk it all for you, an acceptable price for the cleansing of my uneasy soul."

Michelle looked at me, surprise written on her face. This was new to her. I can see she believed me, and she knew I was telling the truth. She has to know anyway, she is a woman. The daughter of Eve, the first to taste the fruit, the fruit of wisdom or deceit, which ever appropriates the line of thought you are accustomed to.

It was also new to me. For the first time since I can remember, I was vocally expressing my love for a woman. It had been hard coming out, Initially, I thought I sounded like I had dust in my larynx. It could be that my emancipator had finally freed me from my past and the fear of it, and it feels good.

A slow smile came to Michelle's face, and her lips parted seductively. I watched as her shoulders rise into her neck and stayed there. Her upper torso rose and fell as if she had taken a deep breath of some enjoyable moment within herself - and the dead voice was aroused, and the world was joyful and beautiful again, because my friend is back with me. As they say: 'A man is only as great as his fellow citizen will allow.'

Moot became the hurried walks, the darting looks, and the muffled conversations, signs of people under siege who have been made blind, mentally blind that is.

Her blouse was open and her rich burgundy hair was tousled from the brisk and very hurried walk that got us here. Even behind the chaotic curtain of her hair, the beauty of her face was still discernible, the approval evident.

The apprentice of the hired killer has become heir to the spells of her master, although his magic was more potent than hers, who is on a plateau none of the students has ascended. He was one man alone, but even in death or should I say, in disappearance, he is greater than the sum of his benefactors, those who had presumed to take control of him, dominate him, use him, and discard him when he became expendable. He knew them as the worst of all obsolete weapons and all other vehicles of war and greed and domination before them, because their existence justified their targets.

As for Michelle, she is what, if you are in California: young, articulate, verbal, intelligent and seductive. She has been my sidekick, a 'sometime' lover whose spontaneous, intuitive approach acts as a perfect counter to my cool, intellectual and infrequent bursts of impetuousness - actions that allow me to be more of the true me and not subject to reactionary moves, perpetrated by the enemy - actions that allow me to wait without the over-worry that accompanies it in the game of spying - actions that help me become a reversed man, inwardly reconciled and outwardly fulfilled - eliminating and reducing the perpetual life of secret tiptoes of espionage, even as the neophyte, or just back from the cold old spy - becoming the cool-headed broker between necessity and the far vision, in the all encompassing emerging new world order.

Versions of Truths

The bedside alarm was shrieking, it may have been shrieking for a while. I pulled the linen cover over my head and pulled myself to the far corner of the bed. Michelle said: "Do something, Nigel." It came with firmness unique to Michelle's voice, and I knew it was time to head out and to the control room. The other guys and the group leader must be worried sick by now. The confessions of love had progressed into the wee hours of the morning and I had momentarily forgotten about the group meeting.

An air of thrilled purpose pervaded the atmosphere. All concerned wore the same obediently purposeful expressions on their faces, even when the topic of discussion is centered on a totally cruel and irresponsible thing that is to be done. Completely wrong, whether provoked by the opposition or not, to me it was wrong - creating a sinister umbrella - when it is clear that all and all should pledge to turn a new leaf - inspired by "the beginner's mind," an embrace of the urgent need for optimism and appreciation for all things, guided by compassion and selflessness and our true purpose here

- answering all the philosophical questions the time presents and demands. Instead, they are applauding a war scenario, to further the military industrial machine, and reduce the peace dividend, undoing and sullying the great intellectual and cultural achievements of our forbears by terrible social convulsions, one after another - creating a ship with tall masts and great sails but no keel to keep it upright in a storm, because all the self-correcting mechanisms that the nation is blessed with, that are meant to preserve basic social and political stability, have been decimated for selfish reasons.

The nations social harmony has always depended at least to some degree on its social, economic and political growth and evolution - because it was easier to get along when everyone, reasonably, is getting ahead and not feeling shafted. But when the pie is so much tilted to the few at the top, and shrinking to the rest of society, other groups are more likely to turn on each other - fracturing the social cohesion that have always made it the remarkable classless society - now mostly obsessed by status and money, a far cry from a not so distant past when there was never an identifiable social class that was able to keep the rest out. As this perception grows – of "us against them," that the rich and powerful are intent on getting more and the rest be damned, those outside the gated community would grow increasingly restless. In this atmosphere of insecurity and envy, rumors of and conspiracies theories spread like wildfire, and it becomes easy for regular folks to suspect that those at the helm of things rig the game against them. Even human errors are seen as sinister plots.

The irony of all this is that, the open media that the people have come to depend: the internet and limitless television channels, once seemed to promise more truth, information all the time, from more sources - open, free, unfettered speech, which had usually served to expose the abuses of power and liberate the marketplace of ideas are now viewed with suspicion and indifference. Nothing seems to be working out as envisioned, including the idea that power could not be rendered unaccountable by secrecy. We have gotten more noise and more opinions but not more in the cause of truth. Untruths and gross distortions become more pervasive, and swirl around the internet and supercharged by the cable television bias for hyper-conflict, with the end game being the need for more audience, and by extension, more money. People start believing what they wish to believe, and little lie add up to one big lie, the sort of distortions that can fuel mindless rage. It is hoped that, with the experience already gained, the builders of the new architecture, the emerging, improved order can smell out the phonies and crooks, the power-mad and the truly venal.

I had not gotten enough sleep, but I was glad I had heeded Michelle's advice the night before and stayed out of alcohol's way. I needed to have a clear head to face these warmongers. Michelle made sure I stuck with mineral water with a bit of lemon floating in it, to make it look like gin and tonic. All for the sole purpose of evading anything that would mar the clear-headedness and reasoned ecstasy that is needed to collect myself in this unfamiliar terrain. Taking consolation in the fact that whatever happened you have prepared yourself for it, which are all you can do. Leaving all other contingencies to providence and the will of the Facilitator, who is really the sacred absolute in the center of this swirling vortex - this convoluted and mangled world of spying, and the game of one-upmanship - where the motto is adequate knowledge and preparedness. Finally, as much as you may abhor it, join the short list of elite, who know their first reactions, and the first and last things they would do if their houses catch on fire, in the middle of the night.

Taking a leaf from my philosopher friend, I said: "It's not really a we/them. It's society. We didn't gather here just to hear ourselves speak. We are facing societal crises of global dimension. It requires a great house-cleaning of the mind to prepare for the damage that have been done - hopefully, that would produce a fairness that enables everybody to feel they have an honest stake in the whole society. That's the larger picture here, because it was a humble detail that grand themes wrought their havoc, we need clarified perception in our hopes to destroy the old isms. The old nonsensical fight between the so called good and evil, one ideology and the other ideology, all of which have just fallen dead, with a thud, an almost unheard whimper. Bringing with it immeasurable anxieties, uncertainties and fear of what is to come next, the angst of the unknown. Everything has become so unreal, out of balance - we have all these different competing perceptions working cross currently, who can blame them, the world is a complicated place, and people see the world differently, from regions that have little in common - producing pressures that lead to the tearing of the social fabric. A world, now pushed to do something by the will of the people, a wish borne of a desire to be set free, free from the shackles of repression, unnatural bondage and unnatural national groupings, grouped for the sake of empire building and egoistic arms races that inevitably will crumble. It is unnatural and impossible to hold any group of people down perpetually...."

Now the rhetoric has waltzed underground, into secret labyrinths and chambers of the button pushers - the men who sit in deep chairs, who still dance the night away, long after the music had stopped playing. Their tactic and slogan is new - of a divisive nature - it's us against them - emphasizing ethnic or racial differences to win support - similar, but not quite like the incidents in a not too distant European past, when some privileged group, out of fear of losing their ill-gotten gains at the expense of the poor, instigate actions that led to pogroms. This time, they are subtler, employing high-priced public relations outfits to polish their image, employing coded words to get their messages through - Just because they refuse to acknowledge the new reality, the yearning of the people for a cessation of hostilities and the needless wars. What has become evident is what the yearnings of the people forebode; it worries them crazy, the loss of the comparative advantage, the source from which their illegally acquired wealth come from. With this fear, they ratchet up the slogans - when the news is bad it is propaganda, when it is good, it is news. All this driven and controlled by the obvious, the elephant in the room, the lust for money, greed and the fear of a dwindling influence. Then, one wonders, can they really turn back the hand of the clock, without catastrophic consequences? Would the people tolerate their chauvinistic drumbeat? Especially because, if apocalypse does hit, there would be much to save, because there would be much to lose - In this more globally and geopolitically linked era, there is enough to go around, enough for everyone...

All the group leader could say in response to my analysis was that it's tantamount to a relatively benign situation - but not relative in a scenario where brinksmanship is a feat - in a game that borders on waiting, worrying, and above all, being yourself and assuming other positions as the situations might dictate - in short, being a chameleon changing to blend into the terrain and theaters of conflicts. In you is the desire to live for now, for you might be bumped the next now, where there is no tomorrow, for tomorrow, the group leader would be quick to tell you is an excuse for the weak and the inactive. He has forgotten about the man of tomorrow for today, for without tomorrow, there is no need for man today, or for man's existence... more than ever, we need more men of tomorrow for today.

To the men who sit in deep chairs, there is now or there is no anywhere. Even nowhere is better than the tomorrow of inertia and weak hearts. Which makes it of paramount importance, the necessity to purge the men in deep chairs in ourselves, burn the deep chairs and set our hearts free, which should be the dream of every decent soul, and as hard as it might be to believe, might just be the dream of some certain men who sit in deep chairs. They too yearn for rehabilitation and the unleashing of the forces of sanity, reform and openness of closed minds and dirty chambers. They yearn for these things. They just don't have the courage to face up to them. They need a little push, a nudge, not too hard; enough to allow them keep some of their dwindling ego or power.

A voice thundered; it was the voice of the preacher. The preacher said:

'If you look into a brand new mirror with cracks, what would you see?'

The laywoman replied: 'A distorted vision of imperfection, brother man....'

The preacher said: 'A brand new mirror without cracks would not produce imperfect vision, my dear sister.'

The lay sister replied: 'Oh! I thought you said an old mirror with cracks in it, brother man; in that case, you would see a perfect vision, a perfect mirror to a perfect vision, actually, my eminent brother in holiness.'

Everybody breathed a relief. Then the preacher said:

'Absolutely, absolutely, my sister, yes a perfect vision, it would be.' That was that, and peace reigned in the mission.

Then I thought to myself, as I always do in this kind of situation that warrants private thoughts, solitude even when others are present: I could have sworn I heard the preacher say cracked mirrors! But then, who knows these days in which double talk and word manipulation is prevalent, where conscious hypocrisy is fashionable and finds time slots in the evening news, almost precisely all the time, it just lies beneath the surface...the hidden clues to the logic of why things are how they are, and why some things happen the way they do and what might be necessary to change and produce a perfect vision - the new Un-cracked mirror that would produce the perfect vision, for a new order. It doesn't necessarily have to take elegant maneuvers and clever schemes.

The Vulgar and the Sublime, the Faithful and the Cynical

Sunday is special in the Big Easy, and the French Quarter is part of the Big Easy - and elegant Saint Louis Cathedral beckons to the faithful. They trickle in one by one in their Sunday uniforms, drop a quarter here, light a candle there, scoop some holy water and make a sign of the cross, hoping the sins of the past week will be washed away, and a tabula rasa established for the new week....

The mix of patrons at the Cafe du Monde lingered over beignets and chicory coffee. Across the street, a sidewalk musician played an Armstrong tune, and all seemed well, part of the pervasive facade that is the French Quarter. Then it began to rain, selective intermittent rain is not unusual in the Big easy.

The first big drops splattered over the maestro's horn and fell to the asphalted street, producing steaming spirals, the result of water poured onto a baked earth. Pedestrians sprinted for cover. Within minutes, water rose to the curbsides in places near the Mississippi Riverfront, not even the Riverwalk was spared - but then, the Riverwalk is part of the Big Easy.

In other sections of town, it was worse. The downpour quickly overwhelmed the city's elaborate system of underground canals, levees and pumping stations. Orleaneans in some neighborhood found themselves knee-deep in water that had nowhere to go but up. It inundated cars and lawns and swirled into their houses, turning carpeted living rooms into flood plains... The Big Easy, AKA the Crescent City is a gigantic water-filled saucer that might require the workmanship of Noah and the near perfect Ark to save those without errors. First, they have to be able to make it to the giant boat.

This particular Sunday had not been too different from other Sundays in the 'Big Easy.' The faithful mingle with the curious, the cynical and the hopeful; goose bumps rise and tension mounts, but after the downpour and the relief, beyond the checkpoints the actions begin. The vulgar and the sublime meet in the French Quarter, drawn to opposite poles of the same spy magnet - the vanguard of all activities.

Moments of tension that can freeze the blood, ferocious brutality presented without commentary or judgment, laced with unmistakable moral understanding and vision, from the perspective of a spy killer, whose violent mind is uniquely qualified to pick up a bread knife and hack an already-wounded enemy, with a distanced and uninvolved demeanor, inclined not to believe he has done something very wrong - More of a means to an end really, a way of life in an amoral, limited, tasteless and brutal world of one-up-man-ship. The spy game - selfish impulses devoid of insidiousness and when even the jukebox knows not to make any sound, a levity to unbearable tension - the inevitable consequences of sin.

Everything fresh is poisoned, and all and all has an unwritten rule to make a mess of themselves and everything around them. A conclusion is reached that the next opponent, any future adversary, must be hit with everything at once. Promising to make themselves seem as mad, bad, and out-of-control. It is called intimidation. Eventually becoming a crusade of crude beaten-down zombies, where the lights gradually dim, and dim, until it's all out forever. Like, but not necessarily the same story nor sacrifice, of the candle, the one that gives light to all around it, but burns itself out. Welcome, welcome to the realm of the demon, the liar and the animal-kind.

The Case officer walked in, gruff as usual. He looked around the room as if to make sure no one else was present. He pulled up a chair, sat down. In the field of espionage, secrecy is all, and there is probably no more secretive agency than this one - Even though the deception, treachery, corruption and the dangerously misguided activities to maintain strife, to keep the agency going is well noted - an agency so dependent upon continued strife between the two 'major adversaries' that it must subvert peace and any effort for peace. That is the beastly characteristic in them, they just can't help it; it is not easy for the Leopard to lose its spots, not before the pig learns to fly, anyway...

It is all to maintain and play the icy-cold spy catcher, without engaging any sympathy for characters showing flaws. The aspirations at the heart of the spy catcher's life are simple and understandable - to have money and power, to be respected and feared, to be liked, to be safe. Even though the field hands have to duck through side entrances to avoid crowds, walk through dark corridors - making several turns, and cut through kitchens to finally enter a glitzy night club - to catch that "big fish" - there is never a genuine achievement and any real progress, from the point of view of the case officer, the spy catcher, vis-à-vis the field hand. In the case of the spy catcher, there is absolutely no room for externalizing emotions; that shows weakness. Weakness is a no, no in the spy game known as espionage.

He lives the life of a spy catcher and subverter of peace, the only way he knows to preserve a perpetual cold war, which produces the greenbacks which in turn maintains that particular lifestyle - tip waiters and sit at the Ritz, listening to, 'Take my wife please.' Without batting an eye, he would swap his wife for the comparative advantage known as greenbacks....

The headline on the front page of the *all the truth and nothing but* Newspaper reads: A car bomb nearly killed a French official, Pierre Lucien, early this morning. The sub headlines read: The wife was the victim of a separate fatal attempt two years ago. Police said, Lucien, 46, was hospitalized in critical condition after a powerful bomb demolished his car just after he got inside - suspected work of the Red Army faction...

You say: 'Yeah! Right, Red army faction, in Paris?'

The case officer looked at me, his hands clasped, carefully rested on the solid oak desk that separates us.

"Nigel," followed by a long pause, calculated for psychological effect, to make me feel like a couched patient, then he said, "Your meeting with the 'client' has been reviewed," another pause for effect, and I am saying without really saying it, "get on with it, old man, just get on with it," then he continued:

"There's one disturbing fact we cannot reconcile, it did not add up." I looked deadpan. See, the need to prove that it did not happen as I had stated, falls on him and the agency, and he knows it, and he also knows that I know it. That is why there are more pauses than usual, if I must say... He goes on -

"Your story about 'Rabbit face, left foot, right foot' I believe one hundred percent, but the rest are skeptical, sounds hundred percent true and one hundred and one percent defective, if you know what I mean."

I thought to myself: 'That means you do not believe me, and the men in grey suits want clarifications and modifications for presentation to the upper echelon men in grey, the deep chair sitters,' he continues,

"Our camera shots, I mean the entire audio-video thing was inconclusive, so we might go L.D.T.," Translated, the spy catcher means lie detector test, that all-wraparound wire called polygraph test.

I say: "I can't help that, old man, I did what I was asked to do and 'Rabbit face, left foot, right foot' did appear, his actions and statements and my responses, I have documented, So knock your self out, old man." I stressed the old man part, for the case officer despises any allusion to his true age.

I cannot start thinking negative now, for it has a way of becoming self-perpetuating. You just live your life and hope you get the choices you like, but whether you do or not has no bearing on whether you have a good life. You have a choice: You can be miserable being flung around by the whims of society or the agency, or you can realize spying is just a job and concentrate on being fulfilled and happy...

So, it was agreed that the sooner I take the test the better. I could not be more agreeable, and they were taken aback by my eagerness and non-protest attitude. Unknown to them, my eagerness was influenced by none other than Michelle. I wanted to get the whole darn thing out of the way and get on with my life, my newfound life with Michelle.

The sterile room contained two chairs and a simple table, which harbored the usual gadgets for LDT. One of the chairs, which I assumed was reserved for me, looked more like an upright wooden throne, but with black upholstered seat and armrests. The burly administrator set it handy for the electric socket while the team leader spoke to us briefly, more for my benefit. The administrator is not one bit adversarial, an impartial functionary really; whose machine does the work. 'Give me a break people, just fucking give me a break,' I said under my breath, in solitude, even when others are around.

I looked from the group leader to the burly administrator, and took a quick sweep of the familiar room. It is considered a house of horrors, where savage executioners knock down cognac to help them face another day.

It is where crafty spies leave their portals primed to sow subversion and death in foreign lands, while 'enemies of the people' sit petrified in vans carrying them through other doors that lead to unspeakable pain or death. Activities so secret that every window across the grim facade is shielded by heavy curtains or darkened shades - the training ground for officers in counterespionage who wear smiles fit for charm school, but whose demeanor beyond the primordial vestibule and corridors swiftly changes to that of a mean interrogator in a game of the damned and the doomed.

Then there are the usual barbaric tools of the trade, featured on mantles as a reminder - poisoned needles, disappearing ink, wristwatch cameras, bullet pens, phony mustaches, matchbox radios and other paraphernalia purportedly lifted from the opposing number.

The walls are covered with photos of spies caught 'red-handed' subverting democratic citizens. The group leader never apologizes for anything. The maxim is: never complain, never explain, and above all, never say you are sorry. He never fails to extol the virtues of the agency, reminding anyone who questions his motives that, lest they forget, this is a free society of freely elected parliamentarians, who wrote and approved the laws that guide them, (the agency).

A raspy voice said: "Mr. Peters, would you kindly remove your jacket, it is not necessary to roll back your sleeves, Sir, or unbutton your shirt, thank you. Very easy now, please, nice and relaxed."

With the greatest delicacy, the burly man slipped a doctor's blood pressure cuff over my left bicep until it was flush with the artery inside my elbow. Then he inflated the cuff until the dial read fifty-one milligrams. Why fifty-one milligrams, instead of fifty, I could not tell. But then, in a world going out of whack, anything can happen, and nobody notices. He next fitted a one-inch diameter rubberized tube around my chest, careful to avoid my nipples so it doesn't chafe. The administrator then fitted a second tube across my abdomen and slipped a double fingerstall over the middle ring fingers of my left hand. The stall had an electrode inside to pick up the sweat glands and the galvanized skin response and the changes of skin temperature over which the subject, me in this case, provided I have a conscience, have no control over. The team leader had earlier explained, playing the role of a concerned relative who informs himself in advance about the details of a loved one's surgical operation. To me, it was more of a bad cop, good cop charade, to soften the subject; again, me in this case, and I am not falling for it.

The team leader further explained that unlike other polygraphists, the burly administrator does not require extra band around the head like an encephalograph. That this burly man, whose name I have purposefully refused to remember, does not shout or rant at subjects like other polygraphists. He figures, that many people get disturbed by an accusatory question, whether they are guilty. What a guy!

The group leader further went out of his way to reassure me that 'Mr. Big,' (the polygraph administrator) and by extension, he, by virtue of his conversion to the validity of the lie detector test, was quick to say: "We don't deal on emotions, we deal on facts, and the facts are conclusive as far as the LTD is concerned." It does not take a forensic accountant to see where he was coming from - Far from the quiet leader with loud results.

He remains dogged and ever intense. He is one of those guys who could pin you to a wall without ever holding down your arms.

In retrospect, in one of those imprisoned sayings of mine, I said: 'Look my friend, I may have made a bad impression with the 'client' or 'Rabbit face,' which is precisely natural or human in the intensity and jeopardy that came with the transaction, in this trade we all must die - today, tomorrow, one never knows, but I'd rather it's tomorrow than now...'

The raspy voice said: "Mr. Peters, Sir, I ask that you do not make any movements, fast or slow, if you do make such movement, we (meaning the company), are liable to get a violent disturbance in the pattern which will make necessary further testing and a repetition of the questions. Thank you."

He continued: "First we like to establish a norm, by norm we mean a level of voice, a level of physical response - visualize a seismograph, and you are the earth, you provide the tremors. Thank you, Sir. Your responses should be either a 'Yes' or No' only, please. Always answer truthfully. We break off after a set of questions, of up to twelve. That will be to loosen the pressure cuff to avoid or minimize any discomfort associated with this kind of procedure. While the cuff is loosened, we may engage in normal conversation, but no humor, please, we would not want any undue excitement of any kind. Is your name Peters?'

"Yes, to your question, I do not mean to be rude, or diversionary, but my only goal for the moment is try to get out of this psychological funk - a creation of the task master, and focus on the new reality – if you must know, morale is harder to boost in an atmosphere of anxiety." This was a time-honored tactic, keep talking to buy me some time to get acclimated to this whole gig.

"Do I need to go over the rules again, Mr. Peters? Longwinded answers are not permitted. Do we understand each other?" Mr. Big could not hide his frustrations. My strategy seemed on track.

"All I am trying to say is that you cannot rely on a peacetime general to fight a war, my methods may have been wanting at times, but they are still wanted, the task master is a peacetime general trying to fight a war." I continued on my track.

"Do you have a different name other than the one you have used in the agency?" He ignored me – I take it he is devising a strategy of his own.

"No. Do not wait for your competitors to fall to the ground, it could be a long wait, history has shown that crisis breeds opportunity, ask Obama or Emmanuel, they would tell you, crises are not to be wasted." I am giving him no break, and hoping my strategy would work, ultimately.

"Shall we please stick to the yes and no responses?" Very polite, I must say he was.

"I am trying to get clarity to all this, get some understanding – and get on the same page with you. Do you get me?" I stayed on the offensive.

"This is not a fraternity session, may we get back to the task at hand, and back to yes or no answers. Otherwise, I have no option but to press the intercom button for the group leader. Do we understand each other?'

"Yes, we do. All I am trying to do is to have you understand the emotions at play here; you do need to also understand your emotions. You may be feeling stress, angry, possibly insecure. Get help. Be professional. Don't take it out on your team. It is what the team leader is doing, from my analysis of things. Everyone wants to talk about 'what could have been.' Forget it. Get your team focused on what's ahead." I concluded, and decided to give up, and Mr. Big did the same. He continued without responding to my last words of wisdom.

"Are you a citizen of this country?"

"Yes,"

"Do you carry any other passport?"

"Yes,"

"Have you truthfully answered my questions so far, Mr. Peters?"

"Yes,"

"Do you intend to answer my questions truthfully throughout the remainder of this test, Mr. Peters?"

"Yes, but you must realize that any unusual behavior may have deeper causes. Be more sympathetic and tolerant than usual, to your team that is." I said, still trying to educate burly man on the nuances of field operatives and their travails. He was not buying any of it. Mr. Big is a true company man, in the true sense of it.

"Thank you," said the big man, with a gentle smile, as if reading my mind, while he released the air from the cuff. "Those are what we call the non-relevant questions." He said as though my words were the sound of one hand clapping. Mr. Big is focused, focused as anyone who is performing the valuable, if very expensive, task of demonstrating to his taskmaster that the waters of life are not as pacific as they seem. Sharks are down there, and barracudas, and other scarifying species some of them sell impressive sounding futuristic security gadgets, but really just wait to eat you alive. Life is not going to be a smooth swim, going with the flow, the current of the game, all the way home, is the only option.

"Married?"

"Not at this moment."

"Kids?"

"None that I know of."

"A common machismo answer."

"I am not familiar with that."

"Wise man. Are we ready?" He began pumping up the cuff again. "Now we go relevant. Easy now. That's nice. That's really nice."

There was an open suitcase in front of us, black as usual; the four Spectral wire claws described their four mauve skylines across the graph paper while the four black needles nodded inside their dials. The big man took up a sheaf of questions and settled himself on the other side of the simple table. His face was blank. All of a sudden, an aura of mystery developed, an artificial wall of demarcation that separates the common criminal from the prosecutor. It was working. Suddenly, I became apprehensive of this steel barrier between us.

Mr. Big spoke tonelessly. I am quite sure he prides himself upon that - The R2D2 of his time.

"I am knowingly engaged in a conspiracy to supply untrue information to this country and its allies. Yes, I am so engaged. No, I am not so engaged."

"No."

"My motive is to promote peace in a new world order. Yes, or no?"

"No."

"I am operating in collusion with the intelligence unit of the opposition country?"

"No."

"I am a communist sympathizer?"

"No."

"I am a diehard Capitalist at heart?"

"No."

"I am operating in collusion with 'left foot, right foot' AKA Rabbit man, for the sole purpose of defrauding the government of this country?"

"No."

"Baranowsky is my lover?"

"No."

"Was my lover?"

"No."

"I am homosexual."

"No."

Another break for the non-relevant conversation, and again, Mr. Big eased the pressure. "How does it feel, Mr. Peters? Not too much pain, I hope?"

"Never enough, old boy. I have a large threshold for pain, actually; I thrive on it. It's what keeps me going." What does he care if I drop dead the next second? In an outfit that employs the 3-D's (Deny, distort, and dismiss) more than any I know.

It was as if we made a conscious effort not to look at each other. We looked at the floor, at our hands, or at the beckoning wind - bent trees, the birds and the auburn leaves of autumn outside the window, but not at ourselves. It was back to business, the cozier tone was replaced by the mechanical flatness of mission control.

"I am operating in collusion with the woman Michelle Bond and her ex-lover?"

"No."

"The man I know as Uncle is known to me as a plant of the opposition country?"

"No."

"The material I received from the 'Client' at the cafe du monde had been prepared as an instrument to defraud the government?"

"No."

"The material I received from left foot, right foot was sanitized before it was passed over?"

"No."

"Left foot, right foot is my invention?"

"No."

"I am the victim of sexual entrapment?"

"No."

"I am being blackmailed?"

"No."

"I am being coerced?"

"Yes,"

'By the opposition country?'

"No."
"I am being threatened with financial ruin if I do not collaborate with the opposition country?"

"No."

Without saying a word, Mr. Big started reducing the pressure on the cuff. He scribbled some words on the yellow pad next to the sable machine on the simple table. He got up, took a couple of steps away from the desk, extended the pencil to his lips, in a pensive mood. He walked out of the room not saying a word. I took this as a psychological tool, probably to unnerve me.

Mr. Big returns for round three.

"I lied when I had denied meeting left foot, right foot in Brussels a year earlier?"

"No."

'While I was in Paris I met with the top brass of the intelligence unit of the opposition country to apprise them of our mission?"

"No."

"I am the lover of Anne Boucher?"

"No."

"I have been a lover of Anne Boucher at some time?"

"Yes,"

"I am being blackmailed regarding my relationship with Anne Boucher?"

"No."

"I have told the truth so far throughout this interview?"

"Yes."
"I am an enemy of this country?"

"No."

"My aim is to undermine the military preparedness of this country?"

"Do you mind running that one by me again, old boy?"

"Hold it," Mr. Big said, as he held the suitcase and made a penciled annotation on the graph paper. "Don't break the rhythm, please, Mr. Peters. We have people who do that on purpose when they want to shake off the question. Remember, it's a 'yes' or a 'no.' Do we have an understanding?"

"Yes,"

Several breaks, and the questions droned on, it was clear from then on that Mr. Big would not stop until he had reached the nadir of his masters' vulgarity. For my own part, my "no"s took on a life of their own. Each "no" acquired a deadened rhythm and a mocking passivity. If I was going to go through these agonizing tests, why not give it my best, a creation to match their immoral and obscene methods. I remained seated exactly as they had placed me; I had never been so still for so long in my life. I was even surprised at myself, but there was no true reason to the madness. The toll of it all was becoming evident. My chin was lifted; my eyes closed and I appeared to be smiling even when I was not - Sometimes my 'no's fell before the end of the question. Sometimes I waited so long that Mr. Big had to pause and look up. Struggling to keep pace with both the dials and the papers, he seemed to have the torturer's anxiety that he might have taxed his man too hard. He finally was relieved when one of my 'no's fell again, neither louder nor quieter, just a letter delayed in the mail.

Mr. Big, I am sure, got to be wondering how and possibly when I acquired my stoicism, my no, no to everything and why a man of my apparent intelligence would just sit there and accept all the indignities of the tests. Why not just face up, unless, 'his reality had moved somewhere?' Is that his thought? All that was on my mind now was the thought of Michelle and the future of the love and meaning she has brought into my life. I could careless about the result of their immoral and obscene tests and methods. It was now over, the result they can go to hell with.

The Damascus Experience

A wise man once said: 'the key to making any decision is to start with the answer. Once you know what you want, you just have to figure out a way to get there.' The longer you last in the spy game the less you care about the different danger zones, the more you care about how to avoid them or what to do when caught in them - starting with the answers tucked in your pocket. All this might even make you become more human, the Spy Chief being an exception, for he has a mindset like his bosses, the men in grey. If they were open to the counsel, they would see that starting with the answer brings the human out of us. You become not just Teacher, Lover and Detective, but a philosopher, sociologist and social critic. Able to see the whole landscape, the big picture if you may. You gain the ability to take two extremes and make them work. Some might say it is dangerously speculative, that this ying and yang thing is nothing but a concoction of an eastern mind gone mad; when he was unable to eke out the allegiance he sought from his followers. I say who cares...as long as it works, and as long as it mitigates the offshoot of the sins of our imagination.

I would even suggest that the ability to reconcile or make two extremes work is the acquired responsibility of the spy who came out of the cold, for he has seen it all. By the virtue of being exposed to the good, the bad and the ugly, the dark side of human nature - he is a valid expert, a seer and hearer and active participant in all that is human nature. So he really is the ultimate philosopher, sociologist, and social critic - an all ecumenical pundit - by the rectitude of his experience in the good and the not so good of human nature. It is the

Damascus experience - that jolt of lightening that makes a believer out of an unbeliever.

So the young man with the Damascus experience could not help but reflect on the activities of the deep chair sitters, the men in grey, who usurped his power by playing unsolicited big brother. Bombarding him with political and economic messages that he really did not need - a high-tech device to guide him to what they think is good for him and what is too bad to touch. He reflected on the subtle messages from then to now - information carefully designed to perpetuate a mindset, a mindset only the caliber of a Damascus experience can shatter. The young man decided to explore these contradictions, the double speak, motivated by selfishness, greed and a desire to control and dominate, confuse and misinform. What brought them about, and why had they existed for so long, in spite of our intelligence.

In a time of inner-vision, reflections, solitude even when others are present, reflecting on thoughts unearthed during these cascading events, we realize that perhaps it has always been the case that the waging of peace is the hardest form of leadership, that there's no single formula for success, that through history one gleans that some attributes are universal and are often about finding ways of encouraging people to pool their efforts, their talents, their insights, their enthusiasm and their inspiration to work together for the greater good, our common purpose - in a world of asymmetrical threats. Where events are rearranging the old map of the world; events that have given unsolicited vacations to the mapmakers of the world, for the map as we see it today, may be a different map tomorrow. A nation state as we know it today, may become ten nation states tomorrow.

The young man is curious. His curiosity implicates the broad swath of the cultural crowd, even those who were not active collaborators, but swayed with the winds as they navigate the censorship and repressed freedom, who were not necessarily heroes but opportunistic than evil. Their weakness recalls a trenchant cartoon from the recent past - in a process that reaches further than their intended victims, which later included themselves and those close to them. The young man approaches these conversations as a way of exchanging data as rapidly and efficiently as possible, rather than as a recreational activity undertaken for its own sake. He is formidably quick and talks rapidly and precisely. He has to. He usually does not like things that are just about him, preaching at every point the need to eliminate desire, for that really does not matter in the long run - it has to be more about the bigger picture, the greater good - and this comes with no hint of sentimental feelings, but what other observers might call a thunderously radical vision, and an incredibly powerful one at that. It's a shift from the wisdom of a few, who monopolizes everything, to the wisdom of an enlightened greater majority. Because in the world, we fundamentally parse our universe through the people and the relationships we build - leading to the authentic selves we present, a sense of high purpose, a feeling that the world is changing for the better. Because, we get at most one, and if we are incredibly lucky, two shots, maybe, in our lifetime to truly affect the course of a major piece of evolution, which this is to him. Not one that settles for a lower, less satisfying quality. This isn't a zero sum. His self-control is so total. On this mission, the young man is willing to risk being misunderstood, risk offending, risk failing, he has the courage to try to do more than he or his prose could possibly do, not just told through a linear narrative but through an accumulation of his narrative's odd, the startling, often cantankerous statements that spiral through his presentations in a sort of cubist pastiche of sharp observation and commentary, where the linear narrative assembles itself from these wonderful analyses just a couple of feet, as it were, above their accumulation, not in their sequence.

His analyses do not have any tragic vision in its presentation, and even though there are plenty of the awful, the analyses are rather imbued with a profound pervasive melancholy, a beleaguered, simple unembarrassed sadness over the way things are and over our inability to do anything about it. They progressed in a series of episodes, very thoughtfully conceived and executed, to be understood by the intended audience, even the little mermaids within the society. He is willing to be misunderstood, a price he considers not too big to pay, if that is what it takes - as long as his message reaches his target audience. The point here, to the young man, is this nagging single question: why are the grey suited men against all public displays - theater, art, literature, including educational books he grew up with, that he loved. Why do they want cinema, press, posters and window displays banned, cleansed of all manifestation of the rotting world? What is the rotten world and whose rotten world? What do they know that he does not know? He thought to himself. Does this not boil down to a question of integrity and knowledge? A questioning of one's resolve, a byproduct of 'their credo' to confuse and misinform, which produces fence sitters. As we know, fence sitting is not an ideal place to be.

Do they have some exclusive information, the Young man reflects, some exclusive stone tablet written document, possibly in Latin, Greek or some prehistoric language? He wasn't quite sure about the monopoly of knowledge. What is this cry for the public to be freed from the stifling perfume of modern eroticism disguised as art? He took a closer look at these brands of 'gate keepers,' the men in grey, the Neanderthals who are still kicking and screaming long after the music is over.

The overarching question remained, and refused to go away. What do these men in grey know that the young man does not know? He asked himself repeatedly. The answer was elusive and fuzzy at best. Then he said: 'Isn't this the same group of greedy, self-serving, power hungry, dimwitted, self-aggrandizing, glad-handing, bellicose Neanderthals who would suck anything and everything from a sewer with a straw, if it would enhance their power grabbing egos and enrich their pockets?' The hologram of 'the Senator, the thief-burglar, the Spy, the wife and the mistress,' flashed on the white wall. This brought a flashback, and the young man remembered that the mindset's sole purpose is to vitiate the right of personal freedom, weakening prerogatives that come with individual autonomy, which recedes behind the duty to preserve the 'Clan,' the purity of the 'Tribe,' hoping in the process to appease people of the heartland, who don't quite go to those kinds of 'Things,' for those sorts of 'things' do not sit well with them.

And the old lady, who is just as old as her companion, the young man thought, would say, and he was quite sure the old lady would say it, and the old man would be in total agreement on this one, that - 'It might just have all been in vain,' because in their warped sociopolitical agenda, anything unfamiliar and different is to be viewed with suspicion. The young man made sure he stressed the warped mind, because it has to be a warped mind that produces the disappointing noise, the crude threats - provocative, disingenuous, gratuitous, tendentious, inaccurate, incomplete, filtered information - calculated to mislead. Yes, even the unnerving strategic laugh to drive home key points: He laughs the laugh, allows it to continue for a while, gives a hard look...and the laugh makes a return appearance, signifying a readiness for another of his 'standard negotiating strategy.' You could see it right there, like a mirage, an annoying barrier intended to confuse and misinform and thereby mislead - always on cue, like a push-button model. This is not just an act; it is a capability. It is recorded for future playbacks. Recorded in a way that can't be redacted or removed, while at the same time compressing the timeline radically and permits the universal broadcast virally - building the capacity to dis-intermediate the media outlets - and suffices as a metaphor for the times.

And the old lady who is just as old as her companion appeared in the form of a hologram on the wall, juxtaposed on the young man's vision as dictated by the Damascus experience, and she says: 'What's coming through with the young people is the weird belief that, "we are in, so we might as well get on with it," and she elaborated some more on the thoughts of the younger people: "if we do not get on with it, we're going to be done by the other lot," why don't they just admit it, it is their inability to conform to the sociopolitical norms dictated by the society, (in this case, the men in grey), that is the problem.'

The young man shook his head in disbelief, at the perpetration of this particular brand of mindset, and felt sorry for those who had not had the Damascus experience.

To the young man, they are the descendants of the wild beast with the forked tongue. If they cannot stare you down, they resort to acts of belligerency or polemics, and if that does not do it, to war.

At the core of this strategy and confusion that inevitably follows such an operation cooked in secret, and on a need-to-know platform is the paradox, vis-à-vis the old lady and the young man - whose DNA makeup is so alien to this kind of stratagem, and because he is an offspring of a generation that spent its formative years fighting for freedom of expression, the acceptance of the right to be different, even that of the little mermaids and others like them - deft, daring and unusual for whom a tolerant shrug is still better than total rejection. They have trained themselves to cut down their expectations on how things would be received, not wanting to act like the old order, because it could lead to dissatisfaction. So they invest their emotions into how well the things, the projects have been rendered. The new world order will do without the egos, idiosyncrasies, stereotyping and other forms of negativity that tag on the coattail. You cannot sell your soul every time for a little bounce.

Wait; there is a complication - a dissenting voice. A matter further compounded by the technical wizardry of the darkroom stiff-necks. A strong disapproval oozes from their quarters, and since they are very powerful and can really be nasty, on short notice, in the mode of a vortex of cataclysmic and barbaric dimensions, one has to take notice. The ever growing interconnectedness, the constancy of the twenty-four hour media, a double edged sword, is not helpful, especially since they make themes and moods hang around past their season, which invariably produces the admittedly squishy metrics of pessimism and disruptions - which feels like it started a long time ago. It did. With wounded fury, creating a cloud that has settled over most society, and wrought a kind of seasonal affective disorder on the citizens. To survive, knowing that they have lost some degree of control over their lives, the citizens have no choice but to regulate their behaviors. What is really striking, the young man thinks to himself, is how little the citizenry knew of what was going on inside the minds of these grey men and their chambers, but even after they have learned that what they do not know about them could kill or harm them, they remained transfixed, like a deer caught in front of a headlight. This is not an exercise in fist shaking.

According to the young man, the new challenge becomes a paramount task, to shake off the trauma of the past decades, decades that started with hope but that ended with the loss of control over lives and futures. Winning the minds of the citizenry provides a lesson to be learned from the avarice of the old order. Invoking a need to take all the contradictions and complexities and make sense of their methods and madness. Show ways in which diverse people link up, that is sometimes in linear fashion, sometimes with unexpected leaps such as the epochal events now being experienced. These are unlike any previous, and one thing is certain, it is not going to be dull. He said, again invoking the familiar admonition of Dr. Dorothy Height: "'We have to improve life, not just for those who...know how to manipulate the system, but also for and with those who often have so much to give but never get the opportunity'" He added, 'even though we know our knowledge of the grey men is basically adequate, their nastiness and all that considered, we must not let them throw wool over our faces again, we must regain our sense of purpose, vow not to seek a revival of censorship imposed from the top, but to renounce our reticence and speak out against excess for what it is: a hangover from a long-lost era of uptightness, numb lips and a rigid bellicose leadership, who are still screaming and kicking long after the music had stopped playing. We should not be so dazzled by their technique that we ignore the content of things they have put forward.' If I must say, a staggering picture of a particularly remarkable existence in this brutal yet, above all, beautiful world. Which rings of a certain fierce quality, of people set free, the truth within them allowed to shine, finally.

I tell myself, in one of my unspoken thoughts, that moment-by-moment times of solitude, even when others are present, and even when these thoughts might not predict the future, but with the belief that they might yield insights to the elusive prophylactic to world problems - with the confidence that the young man would agree with me.

The young man, still reflecting on the grey suited men, the ills that got us here, continued: 'We all saw what came out of their fears of change, fears of the different ones among us, of the so-called cultural erosion. Fears, which, if I must say, mask a deeper fear, of the primordial desires every individual harbors to be set free of the excruciating artificial shackles. Which finds us living in an atmosphere where sexual portrayals are abhorred and violent ones glorified - a strange priorities arcade of "Socially redeeming value": This, from the mouths of a tribe of coolly cynical grey suited men, who merely want to outrage, who have no deep social or intellectual grasp of why they are doing what they are doing, and who would as just soon disengage themselves from the rest of mankind and the bigger landscape and retreat into a cocoon of Neanderthals in their zeal to squelch the work of the passionately Un-cynical segment of society, who are deeply outraged by what they see,'

'Sometimes when you are under the wrong star, you pay a high price for trying to do the right thing, especially when you live in a world where the second reason for avoiding the truth is fear; where some people push for what they want, others for what they need. There is a different breed, who pushes until they get pushed back. It is this last group that requires our attention. 'The anti-freedom study in the ultimate sadism of rulers, the benefactors, and why things are the way they are can only be brought to life by the young man with the Damascus experience, in an icily symmetrical composition after another allocates their deeds: Deprivations, hunger, mass graves of dead bodies and of others gasping for air, limbs sticking out, begging for dear life; covered up in 'operations to preserve democracy,' sunken eyes, people forced to eat vomit, pick cans and leftover from garbage, homelessness among boarded houses, crowded classrooms, women who give births on sidewalks and scoop up the child from the afterbirth, surprised, because they never knew they were pregnant in the first place. The coming of the child nonetheless brings a smile to the face, as it would to any mother. This child, is born on the wrong side of the fence, joins the other hungry kids. Drugs, crimes, rapes and executions interposed on obscene wealth - flashy cars, big mansions, · air conditioned dog houses, dining tables filled to the hilt - where the menu include: Russian fish hors d'oeuvres, roast duck stuffed with meat, consommé with dumplings, mushrooms, baked fish, roast suckling pig, strawberry parfait and apple puff pastries, wines of the rarest brand, golden soviet champagne and caviar made with Iranian Sturgeons - and yes, both extremities living side by side.

The young man's Damascus experience is a social metaphor, which symbolizes these two polar opposites between the exploiters and the exploited. In sadism and in power politics, human beings become objects, which is the ideological basis of the Damascus experience.

The moment by moment analysis designed to bring human-faced attention, hoping that it ushers in producers - producers of human-face activities, which would help bring to light elusive answers to global problems - economic, north and south face-offs.

To the young man, the past was a perversion that was deficient, which thereby requires authentic means of the highest degree to reverse the destruction of hope and will, the humiliation of lives, the self-defeating, self-loathing, self-destructive subcultures in society - a manifestation of past rules of the road, because, according to the men in grey, there has to be a low class and upper class in the warped mindset.

The displeasure of the young man and his audience becomes more overt, knowing that only by showing their discordance, and pushing back, can they be straight with the men in grey. It would not be for exchange of offensive word for offensive word sake, because the other guys used them first; no, for the actions by themselves are uncivilized and barbaric, and contradictory.

They only create atmospheres of acoustic patterns and exchanges, where no one feels offended, because they are all probably so thoroughly offended already, satisfied that the exchanges were of equal value, they then call it a waste of time and energy and call a truce for the good of what they do not know.

But to the young man and his audience, spectators and hopeful occupiers of the new blocks of architectural designs of this new geopolitical terrain, an enlightened block egged on by the hopefuls - knowing that in this new order, one need not believe that if one plays a record backward, and uses tens of thousands of dollars worth of sophisticated electronic equipment, one might just be able to hear the devil say - 'do it, do it.'

The young man, untiring, continued on these philosophical reflections, an odyssey of inner vision, a cathartic journey to rid the soul of bad manners. He believes that the environment and events therein, more than anything else, and much more than we would like to give credit to, are the common denominators most responsible for the output of its citizens - that people in shitty situations, who live in shitty places, eat shitty foods or no foods at all, do shitty works, do shitty things and live shitty lives. Those who cannot imagine a way out for themselves do and resort to shitty-ness.

Elegant Maneuvers...Clever Schemes

"Nigel, there's something I have been meaning to say to you all this time. Please, listen carefully because I will only say this once, and never to be revisited as an initiative by me again. In a relationship like ours, I know a girl is not supposed to ask this, so think before you answer." Uncompromising and touching, in its infinite, I must say.

This has to be it. If the unspoken words and actions don't do it, why not employ elegant maneuvers or clever schemes. At least the conversations in philosophy and the inner vision reflections have gone well and produced diverse guidelines, suggestions, and visions for the new emerging order. Among the bombs and bruises, there was a consensus of what is required to make it a much better place than the previous. So what a better time to find one's position contrasted to one's love project, the relationship one has cultivated the past few weeks, which really seem like an eternity. It is common consent that women tend to be more skilled than men at retooling their lives and accepting reality. Able to free themselves from their shared tragedy, and moving on quickly, when the reality of the situation hits, while he is left behind. It's a type of specialized knowledge you would expect from the daughter of eve, an elegant triumph of craft than satisfying conclusions - sprinkled with a bit more messiness and a bit more passion. Michelle continued:

"You say you love me and all that, but you seem to have a big problem when it comes to commitment and talking about where we go from here. I'm not getting younger, I have no kids, and just like any other intelligent human, I need the security that a permanent relationship accords, the truth is, are we gonna get married?"

If that isn't subtle enough, I don't know what is. You want something you go for it. Why beat about the forest. Especially knowing that the past subtle hints never produced the required response. So, who should fault her for being direct? Let's consider the frame of the question or should I say proposal? 'Are we gonna get married?' is what she said, and not: are you gonna marry me? Which leaves room for preserving a filament of one's dignity, a woman's dignity, since it is not really customary for a woman to say such things to the man. It was definitely essential to employ elegant maneuvers and clever schemes. This woman has spunk - The ultimate bon chic, bon genre. Simply called BCBG in France.

In the kingdom of eve, there are no flawed characters who get stuck in labyrinths of their own design. Residents are groomed to be clever. Doom impends, though it does not always arrive. I looked at the wide brown eyes, imploring me on, taking on the mode of unspoken questions again. This time it was different, more like; it is now or never, Nigel. A not so subtle ultimatum, and who would blame her? I am still the captive, the prisoner of my past, who needs a redeemer. There's a need to act, one way or the other The Facilitator has answered and provided the emancipator, and she beckons, giving insight into the Elysium, as she has done the past few weeks, through thick and thin. The agents of my past, the unseen demons, with long arms, that powerful force that has kept me captive for so long reared its head, and said: 'Not so fast, daughter of Eve, you still have us to reckon with. Don't believe the hype Nigel, she is going to use you and dump you like Jamie, remember Jamie?'

Out loud I said, so I thought: 'Time out everybody, don't I have a say in all this?' Then I realized these were imprisoned thoughts. I couldn't have said them. My mouth was closed, and Michelle was the only one in the room with me. Her composure had not changed from what it was right after she gave her subtle ultimatum. I looked at Michelle and she looked back at me, the wide brown eyes telling me one thing and one thing only: 'this is your last chance, Nigel, your very last chance; you'd better make up your mind, and fast.'

With that, she got up, walked towards the glass window, a habit of hers when she is in this mood, taking solace in the afterglow of the setting sun, unsure of my silence and my delay in answering a very simple and direct question. She looked towards the far beyond, a very determined look, if I have ever seen one. Her white silk frock accentuated her firmly rounded hips and buttocks. Her long legs were melody to my eyes. Her burgundy hair was combed long like a nubile young queen, her feet bare and despite my indecisiveness, I could not help noticing the breasts, which were unsupported and trembled delicately as she moved.

And the Facilitator said: 'Say yes, you fool,' he took me by the arm and led me towards Michelle, whose back is now to me, looking more beautiful, emanating entreaties, invoking memories of the love of the sidekick lover, she who had loved me, who needed me now, she who had been there for me to lean on, whom I had rested on in my long hopeless search for freedom, freedom from my fear of the past. 'Don't ruin it now when the Elysium is at hand, not when you spent your whole fucking life looking for what you've just found... what kind of a man would spend the better part of his life digging for diamond and not seize it when he makes a strike? Eh?'

"No one." I said. This time, loud enough to hear myself, and loud enough to elicit a reaction, if only by the slight body movement.

Just then, the demon, my fear of the past reared its head again, wasn't ready to concede - not quite yet. It said: 'Poor old lover, don't let your overwhelming, all-consuming, all-dignifying love for her blind you, don't let the wenches carry you. Once she has dragged you off to her labyrinth, I won't be there to play big brother anymore. You can have her if you want her, but from that moment on, you've got to find your own reason for living.'

'So which is it? Yes, please or no thank you?', the demon said, 'But before you answer, let me apprise you of one more fact. She is a heavy eater, she goes for the best, think about the big grocery bills, she goes for the best in everything, I mean everything - her fashion is not cheap - D.H. Holmes, Godchaux's, Sak's, Neiman, Cars - she will want a lot and more.'

"Nigel," Michelle shouted, if I may say, furiously. I was certain she was about to say: 'I have had it, I'm gone forever.'

With a quick conspiratorial glance around the room, making sure that the silent voices were just that, silent, and that there were no other living persons in the room, I said:

"She can have whatever she wants," the words were loud enough to hear myself, laced with elements of loyalty. A smile replaced the frown on Michelle's face, and with a movement of the hand, as if pushing the demon out of our way, she surveyed me in her usual familiar manner, reading me my whole life, all its paradoxes, its evasions and its insoluble collisions, and asking what took me this long to make a very simple choice. She may never know, and she really doesn't want to know now that it's over. The sky took a better glow, and it was clearing for me, too.

The past and its demons took a conciliatory tone: 'I never dreamed you had it in you, never dreamed you would make it, Nigel, that's the truth. I must have grown too cynical. Glad she saved you, no point in bitterness. After all, how often do we meet true love, how often do we dig for diamonds and make a strike? Eh? I'll tell you - once in a lifetime if we are lucky, twice if we are Michelle. More than that, this is the emerging new order, where even the old benefactors get the benefit of rehabilitation.'

With that, the old order came to a rest, and the Past, the feared demons of it, was swept with it.

'This is it," Charlie, who had been in the adjoining room with Rowena all this while, said, almost shedding tears, and Rowena resting on his shoulders, in turn leaning on the solid frame of the adjoining door. "My God, this is the big boys' league. I can never aspire to this, never."

Rowena said: "If only Jamie and more people could see this."

"They can," I shouted, "we're getting married, you both can do us the honor...."

"I Nigel, love Michelle, and do solemnly swear that in health and in sickness, in plenty and in scarcity, to uphold this sacred vow till..."

"Oh love, oh love, oh I love you so dearly," Michelle whispered in sobs, if I must say – "Oh Nigel, darling," she sobbed some more -

"You see Michelle," I said to her, "you're the only one I ever loved, the only one I ever had. I mean our savior had twelve, didn't he, eleven were good, one bad, but I have got only you, and so you will have to be right. I needed to take my time. All my failures were made to get to you, I don't need any more failures."

Charlie said: "Rowena, why don't we allow them time to plan their honeymoon?"
"Good thinking, *mon ami*," Rowena agreed

And so in an apartment lifted from the warm and humid cobble stone streets and set above the courtyard that echoes with the old glories of the French Quarter, in a city trembling with the energies of love, decadence and intrigue, in a wide brass bed with a down comforter washed white by the moon, with a view of the Pontalba, somewhere between dusk and dawn, in an hour after great exertion but before intense fatigue, I am alone at last in the inward world of romantic dreams, with Michelle as the emancipator and provider of the Elysium.

She walked towards me, in long strides of her sheer smooth legs. Lit by the striped moonlight through the shutters, she stood at the bed-head whispering, take me. Her body rose like an illuminated goddess out of her fallen clothes. Her plum nipples ripened in the glow.

She paused and let the remainder of her essentials discard, the shackles of unwanted clothing. The daughter of Eve, because of inheritance, discovered nakedness before the son of Adam, she cherishes the opportunity of mutual discovery, the joy the nakedness of the son of Adam and the daughter of Eve can bring in a unifying fusion.

Little Eve floats toward me like some otherworldly presence, calm and cool, as others are flushed and frenetic. She undressed me with gravity, with the ebb and flow of hope and desire - first loosening my tie and lifting it in a loop over my ears not to crush the silk. There were several pauses along the way, with great eloquence, naturalness in this undressing melody, with time out to savor her pleasure, pressing my head against her breasts, my cheek into the silky odorless hair between her closed thighs, arranging me like a love sculpture in the moonlight, commending my dimensions to unseen female friends, calling me kind, and virile, gentle, brave and above all, virtuous. Finally, turning to me the long plain of her back, effortlessly. It was vintage Michelle. She whispered, "Nigel, please Nigel." Imploring me with the half closed eyes, to be a cohabitant with her in this secret flower, in the crevices of slyly concealed forbidden love, and my person is willing, protruding and erect. Will I be a cohabitant with her? It has been my fervent ambition, and even in this unspoken mood, she knew I was able and willing.

She led me to the center of the wide brass bed, encircling my manhood with her long legs - well-manicured fingers drifted back and forth over New Orleans sky. Do I give you pleasure? Should I do it also with my mouth? Absolutely, absolutely, were my unspoken whispers, just the fingers and the pulsating squeeze of the manhood is just fine, thank you. The fingers will do very nicely. A very good addition to the mouth to mouth, my bon bon - Then she opened my leg and traced with her nail's edge the tiny seam that joined me front and back, once, twice, three times. I am saying more, more my *bon bon*, a little please. She kept touching every part of my anatomy that requires attention. Cradling my grateful globes, making the hair on them signal with sharp small sparks, making the skin taut and loving. The half closed eyes asked if it was time to finish it off? I said: 'You know the rules.' There was a mutual melting into the moonlight - it was see you at the alter...

> ...She is boisterous and stubborn....
> And she has grabbed hold of him and
> given him a kiss. She has put on a bold
> face and begins to say to him:...............

'Communion sacrifices were incumbent
upon me, today I have paid my vows. That
is why I have come out to meet you, to look
for your face, that I may find you.'

'With coverlets I have bedecked my divan,
with many colored things, linen of Egypt.
I have besprinkled my bed with myrrh,
aloes and cinnamon. Do come, let us drink our
fill of love with the morning; do let us enjoy
each other with love expressions.................'

She has misled him by the abundance of her
persuasiveness. By the smoothness of her lips
she seduces him. All of a sudden he is going
after her, like a bull that comes even to the
slaughter, and just as if fettered for the
discipline of a foolish man, until an arrow
cleaves open his liver, just as a bird hastens
into the trap, and he has not known that it
involves his very soul...........

And now, O sons, listen to me and pay
attention to the sayings of my mouth. May your
heart not turn aside to her ways. Do not wander
into her roadways. For many are the ones she
has caused to fall down slain, and all those
being killed by her are numerous. The ways to
sheol her house is, they are descending to the
interior rooms of death..........

Charlie looked up and said: 'Cheer up, Nigel; it's not
that bad,
my bible history is limited actually.'

Rowena, with a sly smile, said: "you swear and be
damned it's
the devil's fault; and you think it can't get no worse, but
by the
time a fool has learned to play the game, the players have
dispersed.'
All you have to do, is ask Rashid Abdullah."

To me, it was time to look forward to a period of decompression
from the rigors of the past, the fast moving adventure and the daily
anxiety of waiting, worrying in the game of spying also known as
espionage or cold war...and Michelle, would be part of this period,
not withstanding Charlie and Rowena's anecdotes, the good book
and philosophy quotations. She looked up and became teary-eyed
with emotion as she contemplates what all this would mean to us...

I could not help but reminisce about the 'Hired Killer,' uncle
Baranowsky, the son of the German immigrants. His exploits, his
desires towards the end to make amends, to make good for the sake
of the bigger landscape, the new order he knew was coming. His
sense of anticipation, of events and the blistering bullets and other
missiles were nothing short of remarkable. 'They were his best ones
yet, but it's still not over yet,' is the feeling I keep getting. In a way,
it seems his story just needs one more chapter. It's just a little too
good to end, now...

The Flower Critic

It was in a flower garden;
a raised flower garden,
with a flower show impression
They were flowers of different kinds
– Species and colors and sizes.
Wagner's music played in the background,
and the map of Europe,
with his birthplace highlighted, as a backdrop.
The audience was some young teenage girls,
who were fascinated by the flowers and their unique arrangements.
One stood out vividly.
She could not have been more than eleven or twelve years old.
She was bold, beautiful and bright.
She had an opinion on each flower.
As I stood on the platform and pointed at the different flowers,
she stepped forward from the small crowd,
of no more than five or six,
and gave her opinion or critique, on every flower I pointed to.
Crediting beauty to those she believed deserved it,
and blemish where she sees one in some.
Even some of the ones with blemish, she still ascribed beauty,
just because of the configuration, and the point of the blemish, a
character assignation -
which she says,
makes this particular flower unique and special.
She was quick, firm and polite.
She was also bold and unbiased
She was the beautiful young flower critic in my dream
– last night.

The Beauty Queen And The Evangelist.
The Wrath Of her Philosophy,
An Existential Philosophy...

One of the perks of living in the City in late spring, through early fall, are the street festivals that dot the landscape during this calendar period – festivals that enrich and expand one's soul. Through the nostrils, we glean the aromas of foods from all over the globe. From the fragments of melodies emanating from the bandstands, come signifiers of happiness and the renewal of love. The Ocean, a stone throw, rejuvenation – a newfound interest in life and the abandonment of a habitual tone of detached living. Among these festivals, the union street festival, defined solely on leisure and pleasure, is a transient oases in this desert of human commingling, a source for decompressing, for escape, even for a short period, from the stress, pressures, humanity of pain, suffering, both synthetic and existential. And when all these are factored into the uncertainties of the times, in this mad, bad and dangerous times with its juggling acts of anxieties, where the undercurrents of economic, social, especially social - where heartbreaks and ecstasies coexist, anger and forgiveness, fleeting crushes and lasting relationships are woven in a tapestry of love: producing its own mosaic of vibrant, messy, mysterious, passionate, and enduring canvas: in the mysterious journey of the heart. Where religious, political, racial and historical tensions cut much deeper and labels come easy. Yes, for leisure and pleasure, for decompressing and the ultimate *release* from the daily grind, the Union Street festival is ideally suited for tamping down these vagaries of living. A note of caution: this is purely from my perspective, and I could be biased, because as it is said, every expert opinion is the product of the biases and background of the expert. But I am sticking with it.

What makes union street festival unique? Is it because of the men and women who wear odds and ends reminiscent of other worlds and times, reminding one of places beyond? Hardly. So why is it the best in the city? I will tell you. Again, this is not because it might suit any of my purposes. No. My observations are purely based on the facts and merits, and I can say unequivocally: it is the logistics that make union street festival the best. One. It stretches over ten blocks on a single street, which makes navigation easy, more leisurely and pleasurable. Two. It is adorned with elegant homes with photo-friendly architecture. Three. It has elegant shops and world-class restaurants – These are a few of the perks, hints, why union Street festival deserves the crown of the best Street festival in the city. I hope this alleviates any notion that my bias may have been too tilted. See, in punditry, anytime you try to game it and it doesn't work, then you feel like a complete ass. The basic purpose of punditry should be to examine the great questions, the facts as they are, and not as a signifier of how smart the pundit is. I have got to tell you this: it is the last luxurious job to have.

So, as I looked down from the deck of the Thai restaurant at this summer's festival, the sky promised more sun, the air is fresh, cleaned from the rain of the night before. A lone figure stood out. From where I stood, I would put her height at 5' 7" and possibly 115 lbs in formfitting tank top, and a flared skirt that comes just above the knee. Her hips swayed to the samba beat from the Brazilian band. Her demeanor, that of self-absorbed confidence, that puts her in her own world, a world that is absent all others, all that is going on around her notwithstanding. The calm she radiates is not a natural fit with the festival crowd. Her feet barely moved from the same spot. The body's sway, the slow movement of her hips, embellished by the hip hugging flared skirt, were all that told of a dancer, a manner deeply introspective. Her attitude toward the world around her captivated me: peaceful and sophisticated, fearless and joyful, perfect, but does not preach perfection, warm, not rushed, engrossed in the music, but reacts to it in infinitesimal ways. She is doing her thing and doing it to perfection, even when she does not preach it. She is fully human. For the moment I am swept up. The question becomes: do I just stand here and simply feel the sensations in my body in reaction to her presence, or do I leave the comfort of the restaurant and replace it with the heat and cacophony of the street below; where humiliation could be possible in approaching this mysterious woman. Then I remembered an anecdote from another very beautiful lady friend of mine, from a long time ago: 'It's better to go through fifteen-seconds of humiliation, than a lifetime of regret.' She had told me. The choice became simple: I will take the 15 seconds over a possible lifetime of regret.

The luminous caramel hair cascaded down her shoulders, her eyes were closed, and her lips were slightly parted as she stood still for a moment. Contemplative. She did not look like someone who answers to anything in this merely material world. At the same time, reflecting the image of a young woman who could be sent into ecstasies by a sunset. She pulled the placket of her shirt back, which further pronounced the tank top and bra strap, revealing the top of her breasts and the length of her clavicle. She flexes her chest so the bone is instantly more defined. She is wearing no makeup. A mole is visible at the lower left cheekbone. There was almost a perpetual smile on her face. In this light, natural light, she is impossibly lovely. She looks the way a warm girl looks. She looks beautiful, inaccessibly exquisite. It's as if the sun had dissolved the festival grounds into a single spot - the mystery woman's spot and sets one's soul vibrating. Eruptions of soft longings, and visions of her plump bulbs and of the swells and inlets of her body and of labial purple coils, germinated in several places at about the same time- Emblems of expressive freedom.

She is a bit tanner than those in the crowd, thinking if she might have migrated from Florida or southern California. She was definitely shinier and smoother. The mole, the single most defining characteristic of her face, becomes more pronounced. She looks perfect. Even with the constant smile, the look of sadness was obvious, a little loneliness.

It was impossible to watch and not do something - to not do something in this case would be an actual metaphor for not actualizing the desires and lusts engendered by the spectacle before me. To not do something would be yielding to cowardly instincts, fear and falling into the category of the not-so-red-blooded man. To do something on the other hand, I would walk the few feet that separate the mystery woman and me: boldly introduce myself and say something.

And that is what I did.

"Hello, my name is Nigel, what's yours?"

She gave me the once-over, a from-head-to-toe once-over, with a pause at my crotch, her lips parted briefly into slight smiled, and said: "My name is Zoë, hello Nigel." and resumed her dance, in as much as it can be called that.

I moved a bit closer, mindful of an adequate social distance, wanting to make sure there was no shouting over the din of the samba music while still able to get my point across and said: "You are beautiful."

This time, there was no up and down once-over, from the strikingly refreshing lady, in the midst of the clamor and din, and the ever mounting distractions – the continuous beats from the bandstand, the yelling throngs and solipsistic twittering and profound longings – which reminds one of how easily we forget how much we needed it, the free escape that union street and its kinds provide – which is why sometimes we must rush to fill up, knowing that it is positive and nurturing – so we wait for spring, and we rush to actively seek them – these mundane moments away from stillness, ways so potent they become addictive, even when they are not quite like the magical quiet of swimming under the sea – that which we oftentimes seek for contemplative moments, for regroup and balance. She looked at me straight in the eyes, held my gaze, and again smiled and said, "Thank you. I am glad you agreed with the judges."

"What judges?" I asked.

"I am a beauty queen." She said, matter of fact. "I am the reigning miss Florida, I am here for the miss America pageant."

A new threshold has just been established, prompting the question of the wisdom to continue, or exit the scene gracefully. I stayed on the bold route. Not knowing how to respond to her short biography, confronted with the old problem of what to say and how to say it - I said:

"I would vote for you, if I were a judge. I hope you win." I volunteered.

"Thanks." She said again, and added, "You have confidence and boldness, and I admire that in a man."

"Thank you much, some might call my move futile and overcompensating – borne out of lust and unbridled enthusiasm." I said self-deprecatingly.

"I do not see it that way, and besides, it takes confidence and boldness to make a futile and overcompensating move, even when they border on lust and unbridled enthusiasm as you call it. To me it deserves reward." She said, again, quite matter of fact.

The word 'reward,' played in my head. What does she mean; 'it deserves reward?'
I was emboldened and decided to go for broke. I said: "Would you like to have tea/lunch with me."

She looked at me, again, with the same ritual: eyes locked for a few moments, and said: "Sure, why not, where do you have in mind."

"The Thai restaurant across the street, on the deck from where I first saw you." I braved, and right away became apprehensive of my choice of an ethnic restaurant. What if she does not like Thai foods? That could be a game changer, a deal breaker.

"Good choice, I love Thai food." She purred, and I was relieved and the day seemed a bit brighter, a bit more hospitable, levitating, and 'I can almost do anything,' kind of day. It was that kind of energy the object of my desire or lust engendered, and all we have done is talk, small talk of not much significance. And she has aroused in me feelings only one who experiences it can describe. Could it be that it's all because I had never had or possessed someone quite like this before?

"Thank you." I said.

"You welcome." She responded. "You know, not many men would do what you just did, having the chutzpah to approach and come talk to me. Most men find it intimidating approaching the very beautiful woman; they find it unapproachable. They use the oldest clichéd excuses in the book: she must be married, or she has tons of suitors going after her."

She continued: "the strange thing is, when a man like you makes the move, they come out of the woodworks, trying to upstage you, thinking if you can get me, they also can get me. The superficial woman, the simple-minded types would let it go to their heads, and go with the flash in the pan types. It is why I said you deserve a reward."

She is a philosopher; the beauty queen, the object of my desire, is a philosopher. How about that? She creates poignant subtexts involving fundamental human values and emotions – love, desire, honesty and malice or subterfuge - A graceful pondering by a deeply sensual soul, a consummate lover and free spirit, wrapped in her own fabulousness.

In a world, where we live a life of inconsistencies, our goal is to bring order into areas and situations where order lacks. We could do this singularly, or in our collective experience. Zoë brings her own special kind of order, rewarding behavior that goes against the grain, the untoward in human nature, capable of creating disorder. In so doing, she highlights the fact that, in each other, we find harbor, hope and friendship, perhaps the first true friendship we have ever had, even though we can't quite escape our tragic pasts. It is the existential paradox. Because, however glee from the moment of reprieve, of order, we are apt to pull at the straws of the past, picking at half-healed wounds, our own and those of our friends, even as we mix our grandiose declaration of love with come-ons and slurs – where occasionally, the voices are edged in malice. Friends occasionally hurt each other, and often, we hurt ourselves. But, we still think of ourselves as heroes - flawed to be sure, but we acknowledge we are the best humanity has to offer: It is the beast of imperfection. The outcome, which is a fact, is, our obsessive romance of damage makes us self-indulgent and ultimately unlikable and tiresome. It becomes harder to tell what's fresh from what's rotten, what's artificial from what's true. In recognition of these disorder causing elements, it is no surprise that Zoë, in her own special way, strives to bring order where order lacks, in the best way she knows how. Where she hopes, ultimately, to lead us from out of the ruins into her special brand of nirvana - Where one, hopefully, gains some perspective on time and human pain and effort.

The tea/lunch morphed into an early dinner. Blueberries and whipped cream for desert. Mangoes, banana-foster cupcakes and tiramisu cake that verge exquisitely on the decadent, were wrapped in crinkly paper and packed in bright tins and dripping with snob appeal, to go. We talked about our lives, what is currently going on in them, that is. Zoë, I discovered is a very engaging woman. She is not shy about any topic, a very open-minded gal. There were lots of giggles, laughter and touching, mostly her touching my hands to make a point. I resisted the impulse to reach over and kiss her cheeks. Then out of the blue, she wanted to know where this was leading. I told her I do not know - Even as the little cute arrows were piercing my heart. All before I could even find out the stranger's last name, an obsession was already in the making - An obsession with a beautiful mysterious woman, who may not be entirely available.

Then she gave the affirmation, without any equivocation: "Is this gonna lead to a knock out, drag out sex tonight?" She asked, in a tone no different from when one goes to ask a neighbor for some extra sugar. I almost gagged on my tiramisu. It was very unexpected, pleasantly so, and I felt joy. This must be one of the layers around sexuality as she knows it, the idealization and projections, experiencing the rawness of it without the physical contact – energies entwined, blended in awareness, awareness in what is to come – in its form and emptiness. And as with anything else, it becomes more potent when you are present and alert – in the awareness – where the musings create the environment that allows the participants to be at ease with each other, which manifests a tenderness and care, allowing the actors to merge their beings in a much more subtle way of being deeply loved and accepted; without the shadows of shame and sexual wounding. In its true essence, it becomes a romantic notion of what it would be like, a vehicle for a deeper inquiry into what true completion actually is. The process of corruption is gradual.

Answering her question, I told her from my point of view, a woman has more right to such a prerogative than a man, when it comes to such a question. Question to self: "am I ready to deal with the pain such love inevitably brings?' Even when it fulfills my longings for completion? I had thought that I had mastered the handling of this elusive and tempestuous force called love. If I had grown as I had thought, and developed a modicum of self-possession as I had imagined, I would have stopped to think more deeply about this affair. I did not. I was shamelessly in lust - Hopelessly and pathetically so, inviting the gods and goddesses to smack me silly from this ecstasy of spirit I could not shake, the ineffable state beyond the veil of separateness where what I say to her is different from what she hears - but the thought of her remained constant. She is a cultural provocateur. That is what she is. She looked at me, held my gaze again, and said:

"In my world, all people have equal rights to all things, and I do not prejudge, never." She went further: "All those things," she said, "are personal concerns." In other words, private concerns to people, to do to, what they see fit. Zoë was not done, she went on: "As Margaret Atwood said: 'if you are not annoying somebody, you're not really alive.' I want to be alive, Nigel. If I may quote an old sage: 'there is no right, there is no wrong. There is only what is and what is not'. It's all about breaking up the natural barriers and the synthetic ones - As long as you don't hurt others. But, thank you for your natural instincts, the essential gentleman." I could not prevent from appearing before me, the images of parallel worlds that are unable to intersect. On the one hand, a beautiful cultured gal; obviously bright and engaging, on the other hand, a person who is willing to have a knock out, drag out sex with a complete stranger. However appealing in its familiarity, it feels at once glib and antique, interesting in its presentation, but not lived experience, not in my realm. Still, it did not diminish the appeal. I became even more fiercely attracted to her. It is another hallmark of the times and its characteristics: two sided to an extreme and paradoxical degree. On one side of the coin, we are sober and practical, but on the other, wild and crazy. The beauty queen is a bona fide case study. And I am not mindlessly ebullient about being of the noblest laurel. That has to be earned. There's the saying that people seek in others what they admire about themselves. What does Zoë admire about me that is within her?

Her musings are not congruent with the hallmarks of the age in which we are living, the crackup of traditional categories of morality and values. Purists on either side of the divide will recoil at such statements. In this, there is absolute disconnect - between the topical and the truly long-lasting in the persistent centrality of the trivial in popular value-morality conversation. Where practical thinking rather than ideological and sometimes common sense, is the only antidote to being too judgmental. Leading, hopefully, to uncommon wisdom, an old reflex all its own. Zoë apparently is experiencing a kind of quarrel with the system as it is set up, she is very aware of it smallness and ordinariness, the lack of excitement. She wants to live. Wants to change the things she cannot accept, things that imprison her needlessly. She is quick to say: 'The cruelest prison is the one we build around us.' She does not want to be subjected to any kind of enforced physical and mental primitiveness.

"Tell me about the last time you had an incredible wild sex, in the most unusual place, Nigel?" The first thoughts that came to my mind was that she was trying to butter me up, loosen me to a point where resistance would be minimal. It is why I believed Zoë stayed on the same trajectory, employing the tone used for requesting extra sugar from the neighbor kind. Unabashed. It was an ode to those who distrust absolutes. We are in the garden of good and evil, in the crossfire between their forces. Rumors and innuendoes grab our attention faster than we can say family values, morality and vice – We endeavor and pray for forgiveness, for our sinful desires and secret trysts, for our failures and Un-kept promises. This is just in my head, I thought. Zoë is in a different place, where she is unable to hear my thoughts. It is one hand clapping. But one thing is clear. We need forgiveness. We need someone to blame. I came to a firm conclusion. Zoë was testing me. She wants to gauge my prudishness. She wants to find out how sexually adventurous I am. How sexually creative I have developed. She forgets that the ultimate fulfillment is found by recognizing the empty and transient nature of all things. That using sexuality wisely and abstaining from exploitative sexual practices, recognizing the danger of attachment and desire, contained in it is a virtue: amalgamating desire and sexual exploit, within a moral or ethical boundary, so that we do not harm anyone, including oneself, would be a desirable mantra.

I knew I was fighting a losing battle, even when she could not hear my thoughts. I have to separate the sinner from the sin. That is what I have to do, to avoid it backfiring, because I am too arrogant to own up to my limitations. I have absolutely no influence on the woman while she is acting out the shadow of self and desire. As we all know, desire is not a rational thing. Romance is mysterious. It brings with it life changing decisions. I will let Zoë control the process of negotiating with her shadow, and hopefully find the means to heal the landscape of her own body, heart, and mind and balance her compulsive desires. My goal becomes firm: I have to separate the sinner from the sin. There is a dynamic tension between acceptance and making an effort. If we try to change things without wisdom, we are likely to burn out. And if we try to force people to be how we think they should be, sometimes our effort is misguided. Knowing that we are imperfect can allow us to ground ourselves in the truth of the moment. Because no matter how neatly we arrange things, life's impermanence will always cause them to shift. So, I decided to answers her question with my own question. And I said:

"Is this a trick question?" She said no, that it was not. Then I said: "You first."
"I am cashing in my prerogative, Nigel, oblige me." Zoë responded. Her eyes fixed on me as always. Questioning me. Asking if I was going to chicken out or oblige her this itsy bitsy request. The gaze was a firm one this time. It was absent the perpetual smile. She was trying me, has been trying me, I thought. Yet, I had this feeling of being transported through a world of supernatural flourishes, where I was able to perceive with equal acuity the tiny details of all that is going on and the grand sweep of space and time. It was a quintessential clarity. Yet, there was the nagging question – am I mindful? Would I keep in mind the story about human limitations – all the beauty and value and the need for mindfulness we fail to recognize in our day-to-day lives just because of a flash in the pan – things that become evident, revealed whether we live by plan or by chance. Plan. Chance. Is there really a difference in these complex and complicated modern times we live in? We grasp for solutions,

and realize there are no easy ones. It then dawns on us that the only solution is when we refuse to give easy answers to the hard questions we ponder, allowing us to be a little more attuned to them ourselves. Zoë, it occurs to me, seems a little more mysterious - more infused with some ineffable spirit beyond flesh and blood, which makes her able to alter the spiritual weather of her world, including all others in it. The question becomes, what do I have to lose by jumping into this world, in a moment-by-moment acquiescence? So, I said. "Okay, I will go first but you might be disappointed, it's a boring story. I have to take you back to college, to an experience with my college sweetheart."

This was my story, the story I told Zoë. It was as bland as they come, but I did not promise otherwise: "This is the story of Jamie and me, it happened in New Orleans. Jamie was my college sweetheart at UNO. She maintained a place in the French Quarter, on Saint Ann, and I had a cottage in the Gentily area, not far from UNO by the lake. For expediency and the natural study partnership it afforded, and to save money and time, and bring some discipline into Jamie's life - wean her from the Valley girl characteristics, it was suggested, according to Jamie, by her mother for us to move in together. From what she saw in me, the mother thought I could bring added value to Jamie's life, help her settle down. For me it was not a big deal for I was already head over heels for Jamie, my place was large enough for Jamie's vast belongings and us. She already spends most of her time at my place anyway. For the simple reason that we had the same major, we took the same classes. This was factored into the calculus of her mother. Tuesdays were different. We did not have a class together, and my classes ended before hers, which meant, as agreed, I had to wait for her in the Library, in the quiet section, after my classes ended. Jamie mostly wore ankle length flowing cotton skirts in the summer. Because of the New Orleans heat and attendant humidity, she makes it a point to not add underwear to the mix. Underwear is too constraining, and Jamie believes, makes the heat more unbearable.

So, on this particular Tuesday, in the quiet section of the library, in the quiet view of everyone, the low cubicle divides not withstanding, I felt Jamie's soft hands on my shoulders, massaging them gently. She lowered her head to my ears and whispered: 'I wanna fuck you right here, Nigel.' Before I could respond, she pulled the chair, even as I was sitting on it, back a bit. She sat on me, just as student-love-birds would, their special way of public show of affection. I felt her hands on my zipper as she worked my manhood out. She methodically pulled her flowing skirt a tad from the back, lowered herself on me. She proceeded to ride me, grinding into me as slowly and noiselessly as she could, minimizing the drawing of unwanted attention, reverse cowgirl. Did I say noiselessly, yes, noiselessly to a nicely paced crescendo: in the quiet section of the library." I waited for Zoë's reaction. It was quick in coming. We hold out heaven, and give people hope of achieving it, and then we yank it back.

"You were right, that was pretty lame, at best nominal. Library fuck is two for a penny. But, I can't fault it for being your best." There was a pause. "Besides," There was another pause. Then she said, "Anyway, to say more than that would be counterproductive." All the while, her eyes were on me, with the same fixed gaze, accompanied this time with a slight smile that quickly vanished. I took that as a sign of impatience. She then suggested we take the party, as she called it, to her hotel room. Where she promised she would tell me a story that would blow my mind. Her suite at the Saint Francis was luxuriously appointed. She reached behind her and unzipped the back of her skirt. She had to work it slowly over her hips, and when it dropped to her ankles, she slowly stepped over it. She then peeled off her the rest of her clothes and tossed them, with carefree motion onto the soft beautiful rug, and she turned slowly, not quite full circle, I am thinking this is so I could get a good look at her. This is not an exact science, but the movements seemed designed for my benefit: A modeling of her assets so to speak. She was wearing white bikini bottoms and red bikini top, which is pulled up, revealing the bottom third of her breasts. The skin there is white, and it indicates a non-nudist sunbather. She doesn't talk. She doesn't move. She is expecting me to do something. Without her clothes on, she looks less thin, not the waif-like girl at Union Street. Her stomach is impossibly taut. She has grown somehow. Maybe it is the cleavage. As she lies down on the floor with torso and arms, one of them precisely positioned over, but not covering her breasts. Her hair fanned out behind her. She becomes the northern California girl from Florida. She is no longer covering her breasts in that artful way, no, she is holding them because modesty, some kind of modesty dictates it, I assume. She scowls like an animal. Was that more sign of impatience? With me? She becomes even more gorgeous. Her breathing slowed, and her lips parted. It was cue for me to follow suit, and make the floor our bed. Surprisingly, the rug was as soft as it looked, well padded for such a rendezvous. There was no chance either of us breaking our back. I rested my hand on her stomach and let it rise and fall with her breath. The story, her story, I decided, can wait.

I am not gluttonous by nature, and although I like beautiful things, I have never been greedy or covetous. Friends have often told me of being too careful, not aggressive enough when it comes to worldly pursuits, including but not limited to the pursuit of money and women. It is why my actions, this very moment, defies the conventional me. It goes to show human nature has no bottom. It is as deep and mysterious as free will would allow. I am thinking the frenzy would pass. She would come to her senses and order me out. She did not order me out. It seemed it has all been deliberately planned and executed. At this point, I want to dive in over my head. I have an inspiration. She is lying next to me, on the soft hotel rug: two naked bodies on a hotel room floor.

One would ask: under what circumstances do men and women give in to forbidden desire? Is it when one meets a woman like Zoë, who is so gloriously warm-blooded? - A woman obviously starving for love and affection, who is possibly alienated from her parents. See, in situations like these, the primordial environment shapes the characteristics at play. The revelation that she has these desires is not a particularly shocking one. What makes it interesting is the way by which she embarks on sating them. She is human enough to understand the cost of what she does, but she's too smart not to do it. Her actions lay bare the cynical souls of some of society's familiar traits and paradoxes. She was quick to ask, in her rich, elegant and natural voice, as if reading my thoughts: "which is worse Nigel, giving in to desire or keeping it locked up inside/" She asks from her deep authenticity, acutely aware of the fact that she has more to say, and the fear that she might have less time to say it – in her understated, moody, and supremely intelligent way of presentation – presentation oozing with love and rhythm, a layered effect that actually seems to exude an energy field around her – a kind I want to swim in, even as a multitude of personal disasters loom in the horizon. I can't wait to see how all this come together or implode. To her, keeping it locked up inside is inherently toxic, dangerous to self. Then she probes further, not waiting for an answer: "Tell me this Nigel, if I turn away from the desire, does it mean it no longer exists?" Which to her, can lead to its disaster – emotional or otherwise. Because it can so profoundly attack one's sense of one's own reality, where heaven and earth are shaken to their foundations. And one hopes, from the destructions, there's the possibility of growing beyond the fears, anxieties, and worries, allowing us to touch something within us that is clear and bright. Where we are delivered from the madness of the mind, in the unlikeliest moment, in an ordinary moment.

To balance the dynamics at play, (see, Zoë, in spite of everything you may have heard, believes in balance), she is quick to say: "you go with the flow and let the chips fall where they may," is her way of balancing difficult issues, situations she would rather not over analyze; and she adhered to this dark mantra in an obsessive methodical approach – with the subterranean emotions very obvious to the naked eye – albeit with precision, mystery and beauty interwoven perfectly with the framing of the landscape. The landscape of forbidden fruit and desire – immersive, disturbing, and if you may, spiritual, born ahead of her time – a discovery of a bewitching powerful universe within Zoë's desires: A brilliant, deranged confection of lust, desire and imagination wrapped in dark Vedic hymn of an abandoned soul in pursuit of resistible and moving prey.

She kept telling me to go harder, almost belting me with her up-thrusting hips, as if she wanted to buck me off. A pause. She sensed it wasn't quite getting it done, wasn't getting there. She was on top me, which made it much easier for her to control the tempo. I dipped my index finger into the soft tiramisu and rubbed the fingertip on one of her tart nipples. She smiled at my touch. I got off, and got down on my knees, leaned over and licked the moist skin around the nipple, the familiar taste of the tiramisu making the roots of teeth itch for more. I lowered my mouth and sucked the rest of the tiramisu until all that remained was the familiar saline taste of Zoë and her very own body scent. Then I got astride her again and allowed my tongue to play with her belly button. She arched her back as I worked my arms around her waist. I held on and pushed deeper.

"Buck me back." She commanded. She was beyond rationality. Crazed. I bucked her as hard as I knew how. I close my eyes. I feel nothing but warmth. The river runs deep between the valleys, filled with fire. Yet I see apples, oranges and blueberries. Sometimes, beneath the pleasant murmur and tinkle of cocktails, one does not hear the sound of ice cracking, and the crowd of any age can be deceived. I am of the human race. We always strive to do the right things in spite of our natural inclinations. We strive to always do the right thing and not pause to reflect on self and things around us. Then, the distance accrues between us, and that world; the individual selves we have outgrown. It becomes the best chance to measure our growing up.

"You can do better than that, Nigel." Then she added, "Buck me hard." I buck her harder, fearing my pelvic bones would shatter. Fearing for Zoë's too. She just smiled and pulled my lips to hers, pulled me harder into her, and held me, with her legs wrapped around me, in a tight hold. "Oh my God, yes, yes, yes," She whispered, as if to prevent the guests next door from hearing. Then she began to cry. I am confused, but hoping it is a cry of joy, that the deed was done right. Outside, someone's car alarm went off.

"Thank you, Nigel. That was the release I was aiming for." She said, gradually letting go of me, and collapsed by my side, then went limp. Zoë, my beauty queen, is a mystery wrapped in a riddle. Those who would base their judgment on her exterior, and her large appetite for sex, are bound to miss the true Zoë. They would not like her, and would misunderstand her and have a total misperception of her true makeup, methodology. They would mistrust the very part of her that imagines and dreams – because they do not understand nor share those dreams. These misperceptions become imperfect predicators of who she is or will ultimately become – for they do not offer a clear look at Zoë's style or essence – even as crisp a decision maker as they think they are, they would miss the calm influence on her preys and immediate environment.

Zoë, the woman, defies labels. It would be fair to say that she hates them. Others, especially friends struggle to offer philosophical definition of this free spirit essence – and it leads one to wonder: how many ironies can a single person engender? She has myriads of friends, yet remains detached, while still inspiring fierce loyalties from those who love her – a cool woman who has aroused both warm feelings of affection and a fiery opposition from those who misunderstand her – but in all, she loves to engage – for as she puts it, 'it is the only way to humanize all and all.'

It was two o'clock in the morning, and I was not sure it was the perfect time for story telling, in the uninterrupted hours after midnight, after the sweet intimacy between a man and a woman, an act in the wee hours, the breathless stillness after an exquisite sex; the hush of awe while gazing at God's beautiful creation, a gem of rock glowing in the subdued lighting. Is it enough? There are visions of spinning, shining beyond. Our thoughts are stilled, stripped back, preventing us from gleaning the mystery of that which is greater than ourselves – because we have allowed our thoughts to be smothered by lust and desire – the wages of the sin of the flesh. I would not blame her if she elects to put story telling off till later. Blame, as we know, can be counterproductive.

She was so still I thought she had fallen asleep. I was mistaken. When she recognized what I was about to do, which was to turn in, because the desire to sleep had grown stronger than any other desire. She rose slowly, adjusted the pillows for leverage, and pulled the covers up her bosoms. Shakes out her long hair. With a piercing look of her bright eyes, she began. Her voice was clear, void of any sleep effect. "I will tell my story now," She said softly. "I do like to keep my promises." Then she added: "To understand who I am, and why I am what I am, requires introduction to my background and immediate past, vis-à-vis family and initial environment." She said, then added, maybe for effect: "I am the product of my environment, the sum of all the parts, in both existential and societal influences: the societal aspects mostly accruing from my parents and those who relate to them one way or the other. I never blame T.V. or big brother for anything, charity should begin at home." Then she added again for effect: "As they say, 'the end depends on the beginning.'" Which I thought was a testament to the impossibility of shrugging off one's own beginnings.

Here is what I understand from the introduction. Zoë grew up mostly in the upper east side of New York, with vacation home in the Hampton. Schools were mostly private, boarding, and all-girls. She lived a somewhat regimented cloistered life: sleep, school, more homework, eat and then sleep. She was mostly raised by her nanny in a situation that became her main architecture - most of the emotions that became the driving force of what she is today. A woman who expected more but who got much less from her parents - a rather pampered little brat in a rich cocoon albeit with parents who were distant and inattentive, who lived the life that made it seem she was a mistake, an intruder who crashed their hedonistic life: amoral, narcissist, desperate for success at any cost way of life – and this spanned the globe. The overall impression one gets from

Zoë's narrative is that of someone strong yet vulnerable, fallible, yet not quite ready to take responsibility, viewed at more immediate narrative proximity, less a character and more a living, breathing being, who sometimes slip into her own special cadence, only she could understand – in her own unique permutations.

This neglect created a disconnection between her life, the reality of what was present and what she had envisaged the family position would offer. The nanny, the surrogate parent, was left to provide the last minute redemption and neat resolution to the many messes she found herself entangled in – which, if truth be told, were worthy of reality T.V. Which to her, were but faint stains in the shadow. Her philosophy, as time went by, became more mandarin, and less of the proletarian. She vowed to live life on her terms. She was quick to paraphrasing Socrates: that it is not living that is important, it's living rightly to the benefit of ones soul. What's ironic about the abandonment, her parents' abandonment, is that, even as much as they wanted to run away from her, parts of the endowment they had bequeathed to her through genes, is a combination of what have helped mold the framework of who she is: her father's intelligence and the mother's intellect – she has used them according to the ebb and flow of life; the vagaries of existentialism. As a student of Richard Hofstadter, she knows that the two are quite different: intelligence and intellect. But the most intriguing aspect of her methodology is the way in which she combines her father's gift: intelligence, and her mother's: intellect, in framing and refining her way of life. As Hofstadter argued, intelligence is an 'unfailingly practical quality,' that 'works within the framework of limited but clearly stated goals.' Intellect on the other hand, is the 'mind's creative and contemplative side,' that 'examines, ponders, wonders, theorizes, criticizes, imagines.'

Zoë's intellectually inclined side will turn out to be more dominant, sowing mystery, a mystique veneer cast as a mechanic, an apostle of the dark side of the instrument of thought, but a devout nonidcologue – a free agent. This later became the most intriguing aspect of her makeup – the free spirit.

"Just like you, my story also takes me back to my college days." She began. Staying sufficiently clear-eyed to tell her story. "I had developed this intense crush on a fellow student, unbeknown to me at the time was the fact that he was an Evangelist. He resisted all my moves and whiles. I couldn't believe how such an Adonis could be a religious fundamentalist." She paused momentarily, to collect her thoughts. "My mind was made up, that one way or the other, I was gonna fuck this guy and sate my crush or desire, take your pick." She paused again. "At the time, I wasn't sure how far I wanted to go, but I pretty well knew I would go the extreme length, if I had to, especially since none of my other less drastic methods fell short of accomplishing my goal." All this time, she had been staring at the floor, with the covers held tightly with both hands. The intensity was palpable. To the uninitiated, it would seem as if she was in a remorseful mode, but I knew better. Then she looked up at me, I took it, to gauge my reaction. When Zoë's mind is set, it is set and there's no going back. Zoë's mind was set on the Evangelist, and that was that. A plan was devised to actualize this desire. A crew, in this case, old 'captives' were 'recruited,' 'captives' who had at one time or the other, had fallen victim to her lure. She saw this plan, and the crew she was putting together as a byproduct of the life she had been dealt, and which she now abides, from a purely sophisticated way rather than the commonsensical: the more socially accepted, of which she is no part.

"I had woken up that day, a bit later than I should have. The clock on my bedside table indicated I had less than half an hour before my first Class, which also happened to be a final exam for a prerequisite. I had just enough time to do the most basic of my morning personal hygiene ritual, threw on some clothes and rushed out the door: with book Bag, purse and some other girl stuffs intended to be stuffed in my book bag as I headed out. It happened so fast, so unexpectedly that the next thing I knew I was on my back, on the green in front of my dorm, spread eagled - and this hunk of a man was kneeling besides me, asking if I was okay, apologizing and trying to help gather my belongings now scattered over the place. Due to my rush and mindlessness, I had bumped into him because I had not looked at where I was headed." She paused for a moment. I assumed to gather her thoughts again. Then she continued:

"It was an extraordinary moment. One of those moments when you think: 'if it shouldn't be happening, it wouldn't be happening' kind of moment. I found myself drawn to this boy/man, like I had never been drawn to anyone before – At that moment, it dawned on me, that there is a possibility of a Damascus experience; leading to my growing beyond my fears, anxieties, and worries and touching something within me that was clear and bright. Realizing and helping me see the madness of my mind and its causalities, which I alone was responsible for, and had allowed to infiltrate my consciousness – because I had been acting like a dog sniffing around at all kinds of things, and allowing them to dictate my mood, my emotion, and they had beaten down on my body and spirit, affecting my sleep and energy and my daily relationship with others, guaranteeing that friction will occur. In spite of my self-developed 'skillful means' to thwart them, the blind spots show up, sparking powerful blaze of emotions."

"That collision jolted me out of my complacency and allowed me to give a more skillful reflection on life, especially the last few weeks, and especially those who I invited into it, and what I needed to do to live. I like to live Nigel. The collision gave me a new opportunity, an opportunity to explore my intentions, past and present and possible results. Everything was on the table. I had resolved at that seminal moment, that my past should be confined to the actions of a child, and future actions to reflect a grown woman. Promising that the new me would not just do things for the fun of fireworks and stardust; that inevitably dissolve back into the underlying blackness, because sexual bliss by its nature, is fragile, as is its attendant pleasure – they rise and cease in something that just is." She continued. "I was ready to give it all up for him, to turn a new leaf, become a conformist, play by the rules of the bigger society." "To me, he was like a philosopher's stone, Nigel, whatever he touches, I believed he transforms and blesses, revealing the treasure within. This road to Damascus collision opened my eyes to possibilities I never knew were embedded in my psyche – the search for inner simplicity while juggling all the outer complexities. It was not working. The collision was my wakeup call. It came and provided me with that sacred ground for achieving inner simplicity, for growing wiser. It arose out of perfection, even if the method looked imperfect."

"My attempt at reforming myself was futile. The pain of change is difficult to bear when the objective criterion is elusive and stubbornly so. When I realized the ineffectual nature of my methods, and that nothing else I do would make a difference, it was then I decided on the extreme course you are to find out during my story. Please, bear with me." She continued.

"We each have a body with urges and a mind with desires. My beginner's policy with regard to sexual energy is not to repress it. Sate it, but remind the partners, that they cannot assume that just because I had had sex with them, the two of us are close. There's a serenity that comes from recognizing energy without labeling it as 'good' or 'bad.'" Then she added, "Please remember, this was the policy I had promised to give up after the collision experience." This was a switch that caught me by surprise, sensing the two parallel worlds of Zoë rearing its head. And I am thinking a need for some clarification. Wasn't she just talking about a more meaningful life? Has she forgotten, that what makes sexual contact truly intimate is a quality of presence and mindfulness, of honesty, tenderness and love? That what steals away the sacred and makes sex profane or exploitative is when it is tangled up in feverish grasping without regard for consequences? Yes, in the parallel universe that Zoë inhabits, there are contradictions. And contradictions are acceptable. And Zoë is the ultimate practitioner. It is the two sides of the same coin that she is able to navigate so effortlessly, even as she tries to do the right things. It is the nature of the beast.

Zoë resumed her story telling, her narrative voice resonant and rather serious, rising and falling crescendos that break into almost a mournful song. It was a deep rich sound that enhanced that of the warm night wind. It was a night of love, with drops of bitterness. But it was as it should be. Sometimes, we have to dive headlong into our fears to find happiness: "You have to excuse my digression, Nigel. I do employ the little insights I know to explain what makes me who I am, and why I do the things I do. Without that, it is easy to peg me into a hole I do not fit in. I am not perfect, very far from being one, but I would rather one sees me for my essence, my true essence, and not the adulterated version of someone else." She paused for a moment, sighed heavily and held her face in her hands - as always, I took it as gesture to gather her thoughts, and continued.

"The Adonis was a complete gentleman. He picked me up. Helped, without being too invasive, brush off some of the grass and other debris picked up by my skirt and blouse. He offered to help me carry my backpack and other books not in the bag to my lecture hall - all done and enunciated in serenity. I was impressed. He gave me his telephone number and asked that I call him later to let him know about my condition from the nasty fall." She looked up at me, gauged my reaction, and then continued. "After my exams ended, I called him and thanked him for his attentiveness earlier, and suggested I take him to lunch or dinner as a thank you gesture. He said that was not necessary, that he would have done it for anyone. I was devastated. Can you imagine he would do it for anyone! Here I was thinking we had a connection, and he just blew me off. Thinking he was engaged in the old games of cat and mouse, falsehood and posturing for self-protection and the re-creation of ancient mirages, keeping in mind that change is slow and difficult, I made several attempts after that to see him but all were fruitless. Then I discovered that there was a religious dimension to his position - He was an Evangelist. This compounded the challenge, but I was determined.

See, when I set my mind on something, I allow very little to stand in my way. No man had ever turned me down before, and I believed I had it within me, the capacity to make his mind begin to clear of the fog of old holdings and pretendings, that I was capable of nudging him to let go of obstacles to his understanding me, make him relinquish his grasping, and of his hiding from himself and see the mercilessness of his self-strangulation – to see that every moment is to be lived, cherished as it is, and nothing needs to be otherwise – that religion or philosophy is for self-enrichment and not to self-strangulate. To cut a very long story short, when I realized that his religion had inoculated him against all my methods, including reforming myself for him, to go on the straight and narrow, I then set in motion a plan to get this man alone, by whatever means necessary. I enlisted an ex-lover as a coconspirator. You would be surprised how easy it is to make people do things when money is no object, especially when these persons are lovers or ex-lovers, who still have a thing for you. From the surveillance I had on him, I discovered he was headed to London for some missionary activity, and we packed for London. We, meaning my ex-lover and me: My coconspirator. Our plan was to abduct him, if necessary, handcuff him to a bed and ravage him as my sex slave. I knew it could easily become an unlawful imprisonment. We got the tools we needed: ropes, handcuffs, maps and notations of the game-plan."

There was the usual pause, and then she continued again. "It was an elegant plan, simple, but I knew it was dangerous. Behind its simplicity lie hidden mistakes, unobservable variables and correlations that can provide a sense of security that might end up false. It was a task I had to execute," She continued. "There was a time we thought he was onto us, which would have complicated things a great deal. His movements as we followed him at one point in London did not make any sense. For on this typical April weekday, the Evangelist spends the morning in his glass windowed room, in a small gray house that is completely nondescript save for the huge glass windows with blinds pulled to the sides. There, we assume he was going over the day's planner with his missionary friends. He comes out alone and then takes the tube to London's posh Grosvenor Square and met with three other young men, and a very beautiful young woman - 'A model' that looked like she wore all her faults on her sleeves. This got my heart racing. The question became whose girl was she." She paused and then continued. "They went into the modern dining room of Gordon Ramsay's Maze grill restaurant for what I thought was an eternity. When they finally emerged, the Evangelist again sets off alone and sets off down Oxford Street, a stretch of shops that's swarming with tourists. Picking his way through, on and off his cell phone. He stood out in the maddening crowd, for he was dressed in skinny jeans, black Chuck Taylors, Gucci eyeglasses and a retro zip-up cardigan. This would not be his outfit of choice, so long as he was a missionary, in which case he might change his shoes and throw on a jacket.

It did not make any sense. Why this mode of dress? Why this crowded tourist haven? Was he onto us? Is he trying to lure us into a trap? Back on Oxford Street, he walked by several tube stops, deep in conversation. He acted agitated. Waiting for traffic in the shadow of St. Paul's cathedral, having walked the three miles from Grosvenor Square, he became even more agitated. Nothing made sense. My coconspirator got out of the car, and I took the wheel. He walked up to the evangelist and acted as an old lost friend. We had to act, come what may. I drove close enough and my coconspirator pushed him into our car and we drove off to the rendezvoused place. There were no car chases. There were no blaring sirens. His movements were just that, movements, even though they were of the kinds that did not make sense to us."

She paused again. Looked at me. She now assumed a purely defensive posture - knees pulled to chest, hands clasped around them. The tension between the immediate and the reflective was quite vivid. I am still thinking: "She is gauging my reaction." I had my best poker face on, and hoped it was truly my best, as I find myself overwhelmed by the story of the moment. I had to fight the tendency to assume that I fully grasp the risks and opportunities that lie before me. What would be useful would be the ability to pick the faint stirrings, even when you do not know quite where to look for them. It is said that practical people should open their minds to the opportunities to be seized just as much as to the dangers to be dodged. Zoë is undeniably a contra cultural force. Her story is the stuff of pulp fiction:

A Florida-born beauty queen who moved west, won the Miss USA and went on to college at USC, and became obsessed with an Evangelist fellow student. When that young evangelist resisted her advances, and took a missionary trip to England, the beauty queen hired a private detective so she could locate and follow him. She and a male companion accomplice abducted the 21-year-old missionary as he went door-to-door taking him to a rented 17th century 'honeymoon cottage' in Devon and chaining him spread-eagle to a bed with several pairs of mink-lined handcuffs. There, he was repeatedly forced to have sex with the beauty queen before he was able to escape and notify police. According to Zoë, this was how the press reported the story, but to her, they were half-truths. She said without irony.

Zoë got up slowly, still very naked. Walked to the bureau by the side of the bed. She extracted a black leather briefcase, stood still for a moment, her back was to me, contemplative, then turned slowly and walked back to where I was on the floor. She sat down, still very naked. She opened the briefcase and pulled out some newspaper clippings. She handed them to me. "I have kept these for so long Nigel, and I have never shown them to anyone until now. I am showing them to you. These are the press reports of the time, read them and do what you may with them. I love you Nigel, I do not know what your motives are about me. I do not know what you truly have in mind about us, if really there is an us. I do not subscribe to nineteenth century America, when women were judged by themselves, and their husbands largely by four cardinal virtues: piety, purity, submissiveness and domesticity – the cult of True Womanhood, the code that held that a woman's proper sphere was the home. That is not who I am, it will never be me. If you want me, still want me; you have to take me as I am. I just hope you do not judge me too harshly." Judge harshly? Me? No! No, no, no. I am the one who jumps in head on. I am the one who tries to always do the right thing, when stopping to reflect on the little things could make a difference - No. I am the one in thrall to my idealistic philosophy, caught in a tug of war, a clash between ideals and reality, the flesh and the spirit. In a never-ending quest to always do the right thing.

The sayings of some wise men came rushing in: Homer, Catullus, and yes - Leonard Cohen; their thoughts were all I could think of: Homer. 'There is nothing nobler or more admirable than when two people who agree keep house as man and woman, confounding their enemies and delighting their friends.' Do I agree with Zoë? Would our mutual friends be delighted, and our enemies be confounded? Catullus. 'Give me a thousand kisses, then a hundred, then another thousand, then a second hundred, then yet another thousand, then a hundred.' Okay, I give her this, the kisses are great, truly quintessential, and fabulous, engaged in with a woman wrapped in fabulousness. Leonard Cohen: 'If I, if I have been unkind, I hope that you can just let it go by. If I, if I have been untrue, I hope you know it was never to you...But I swear by this song and by all that I have done wrong, I will make it all up to thee.' This truly sums it up. It would be my pledge to Zoë, if only because I had never had anyone quite like her. So, judge harshly? No! No, no, no. I jump and rush in head on, really! These were just thoughts, private thoughts, none of which was expressed to Zoë. I did not find a need for it. I was sure she knew my type already - you know, the kinds that jump and rush in head on, forgetting to pause for reflection, reflection that may afford one the chance to see the little things one misses when we rush and always try to do the right things...things that could alter the essentials as they are. The refusal to acknowledge them, keeps history on repetition mode, on continuous play. In a clichéd form, it is why some would say to stop and smell the coffee.

I took the press clippings from her and set them to the side, and took her in my arms. We held each other for a long time without saying a word, not a word as we made love, not fuck. It was slow and deliberate with much hunger for a different kind of release and reconnection, a deeper connection with implied expressions of feelings, emotions, and love. Take your pick.

The next day, as Zoë laid asleep, I picked up the reports and decided to have a read. According to the reports, from several international press at the time, during the court hearing, when mobbed by the British press, Zoë said she had fallen head over heels in love with the Evangelist man and acknowledged tracking him to England. She declared for the first time: "I loved him so much," to the judge. Then added: "I would ski naked down Mount Everest in the nude with a carnation up my nose if he asked me." She denied a sexual assault, saying that the young man was a willing partner.

Zoë and her coconspirator spent three months in a London jail before being released on bail. The pair then jumped bail posing as deaf mute actors in Ireland to board an Air Canada flight to Toronto and eventually a bus to cross into the US, where investigators lost their trail. London police later consigned the case to the history books because of the time that lapsed, and other exigencies, not the least being the fact that the Evangelist decided not to press on. The notoriety was something he and the church wanted to mute. There was no way he could have proved that he was not an exuberant participant, navigating the fallout when their experiment particularly in the free-love trial came to grief, not unlike the other men in Zoë's life, and in London. Those details are never less fascinating in this awfully big adventure, where Zoë is the only one looking wise and gentle.

I decided there was a need to rein in my emotions. Not to be judgmental, but to look at the cause and effect, from Zoë's point of view. For one thing, is it necessary to mock them for being naïve enough to believe in their own mythology, in this exploration of personal and cultural hypocrisy and a young person's journey and fearless leap into the unknown, steeped in the unusual and capped with a lacerating final act.

That was her story: appropriately a *mea culpa*. Rich in detail, an exciting excursion to a time and story that I thought I already knew well, but not enough. An honest story well told, for fragile humanity in all its guises. Love is a house with many rooms, to explore one at a time – sometimes with bites sometimes with kisses, even as Venus sits on one shoulder, and mars perched on the other. Sometimes we hit the bull's eye even without trying, and sometimes we find the connubial bliss with just a little exercise and simultaneously open our third eye. They are not randomly arranged. Instead we follow a winding, sometimes treacherous path from the innocence and the impetuousness of young love through devotion, temptation and betrayal and heartbreak and hopefully, forgiveness and mercy. Zoë's story was a moving account of obsession, filial love, and the darker side of the trust fund babe who seemed normal at first blush until she bumps up against the outside of her world with disastrous results. Far away from where she could rub shoulders with the upper crust. And the inevitable question; "how does one rub shoulders with the upper crust?" After all said and done, it boils down to human emotions at their essence. And in this story, two circumstances collide at the same time, constantly alternating, locked in a changing state of sadness and happiness, in which case, life would be unendurable, the alternating mood running between misery to happiness and back again, where she would be driven mad by the emotional instability of her creation. But, to be lying here, on this rug, listening to Zoë, my beauty queen, was kind of harried, exhausting and distracting experience. And I ask again: Is it necessary to mock them for being naïve enough to believe in their own mythology?

This was a new experience for me. When you think you have seen or heard it all, an experience like this makes you have a rethink, about areas you once thought were beyond human reach, unknowable regions of the human psyche; places one thought were beyond the reach of our understanding, that resist exploration, so remote to you to be viewed only in fantasy mode. Yet, it would be a mistake to view her story as an evocation of the struggling mind: Because the images are so powerful and real not to have material resonance. The story itself becomes an invitation into those areas, the unreachable areas. To her, the 'preys' were 'invited' into her life, and they accepted, by the most understanding host, in this case, herself, to experience and achieve the unreachable. That was the lure. Their dilemmas, pains and joys and secrets are then inevitably related to the outside world through the host, again her – who best understands the characters better than they understand themselves – who does not judge them in any way as they might have judged themselves unfairly – ditto the bigger society – an empathy that perhaps they would never have allowed themselves to imagine bestowed by her the host. Because, clearly, to accept the 'invitation' and really enter this world is to make a demanding entrance, a thrilling one, too. That anything one wanted to do could be done: That our possibilities are only limited by our own freewill. My beauty queen cuts a dramatic swat. To her, the transaction isn't complete if you do not participate. Perhaps, because she never expected her actions to be accepted and approved of, and since she is at peace with that reality, she could pursue her chosen lifestyle to its furthest conclusions. To her the dramas of existence are mostly shabby anyway. But looking at her, at the end, there is the remote feeling, the sense of being at once together and alone.

> The sky promises more sun.
> The air is fresh.
> Cleaned, from the rain of the night before.
> Fragments of melodies.
> Tapping feet, enthusiastic revelers.
> Garments of odds and ends,
> From other worlds.
> Reminds of places beyond.
> Discovery of forgotten parts of selves.
> Briefly, existential struggles consigned.
> And the world, from different perspectives.

The sun goes down
The day grays, night beckons.
Down along the cool misty shore. The pacific.
Moon shivering. Glistening blue-green waves.
Into themselves, they disappear,
Rhythmically. A symphonic dance,
In the last red and dying evening.

The Demon, the Liar and the Animal-kind

They are familiar, they are distinctive, they are distinguished and dignified - always with regal performance and bearing, a style and class of exclusivity – they are elusive and have intricate patterns of grandeur. They come straight-faced, have impressive and stately punditry. The expressions are, shall we say, appropriately designed as god-speak. The pronouncements are meant to influence, coded to arouse a certain segment.

Their rhythm, deliberate and symmetrical. Their works and ideas couched in subtlety. Their voice sonorous, with a hint of highfalutin - their movements are startling, with a touch of delicacy, delicacy that does not hide the strength behind the movements. Their power is always obvious, even when not too stated.

It is 1:30 a.m., the eyes are heavy, the Macintosh blinks on and off with a little push of the mouse. The telephone rings. The air is transfixed, in the pragmatic sense. The telephone ring of an odd hour has it's own mind, its own message and translation of what could be. A deprogrammer of a mindset in motion - a messenger, who after long gone, leaves a message that takes on a life of its own - At 1:30 a.m., the messenger and the message take an aura of an electric current, wavelengths that control, but designed to remain unstated.

The importance of having this experience and coming to grip with it, is to come away with the understanding that there is no medium or device, of modern electronic information distribution that will bring one into that privileged position of complete understanding of its nuanced purpose – And then, the ring of a telephone at 1:30 A.M. conjures up all emotions: not the least the resonance, its breath and countering funeral cortege and tragic tone - the elevated and beatific spirit which prevails - the rhapsodic fervent rings - engaging and exceptionally personal.

The message and the messenger, in this case, the telephone device, do not guarantee a satisfying finale - an impression that lingers - long after the messenger's exit.

The line of thought is interrupted, the ovation loud and clear - an eloquent and greatly deserved tribute to the mastermind - the great thinker - No! Wait. There is a solitary voice, a voice of dissent -

"Hello," I said, killing off the stubborn ring

"Hello, it's me, Jamie," the air grew absurdly still - The voice, enthusiastic, curious.

"Hello Jamie," this voice, quite without any emotion, affects nonchalance.

"You're alive, I thought your were dead,"

"Dead! What do you mean you thought I was dead?" What a strange lady, and what a strange thing to say.

"Well, I had this feeling you were dead; so I called you some few months ago, this line was also dead - as in disconnected." Okay! So my telephone was disconnected, but how does that relate to me, I mean my "death," unless of course, I am connected to my telephone, which, in spite of all the advancement in information technology, I do not believe is possible, unless I have been locked away in a cave the past forty some years...

She continued; "I wanted to confirm so that I can pray for you; see, in our organization we pray for the dead."

"If I must offer, I do say that's a strange outfit. You don't pray for me when I'm alive, you pray for me when I'm dead. I'm sorry to disappoint you and your members - as you can see, with the venerable Mark Twain in mind, 'the rumor about my death have been greatly exaggerated.'" My voice was still without any emotion, but not due to any loss of respect for the messenger, but a keen mindfulness to stay alert, a respect for the messenger's prowess. But I did feel it was appropriate to introduce Mark Twain. I am sure he would not mind, especially in the scheme of things. Anyway, I continued:

"My telephone was dead for a while because I had gone to Europe and Africa - a private mission."

I wasn't quite sure where all this was leading. Jamie just does not allow any impetuous instincts to influence her. She does not wake up at 1:30 a.m. and decide to call me long distance without a reason - not after an absence of a lengthy period - this calculating Lassie has something up her sleeves. What is it? See, in our daily pursuits, it's not what a man gets that matters; it's what he ends up giving up. What is Jamie after?

"You know my Mom died?" She said.

"No!" I offered, which was true, I never lie about the dead...

"Yes, she died some few months back."

"Sorry to hear it, she was my friend." She was my friend all right, in spite of our usual mother in-law/son in-law feuds over the usual disagreements in-laws usually have - which is usually because daughter cried home to mother due to an over active imagination of suspecting husband sleeping with other women - and quite possibly with the best friend - mothers don't take too kindly to these sorts of stories, friend of husbands or no friend of husbands - it just have to be investigated, albeit with tact, no one is going to make a fool of their daughters, not especially in the Creole community of New Orleans - the shame it bring to the family, not to talk of the woman in question...

"Yes, she still talked about you even on her death bed. She was hoping we get back together. She couldn't accept me and the other guys, she's just romantic like that."

So! But what's the purpose and import of the latter part of this statement, this very moment, this very hour? What does Jamie really want? Why has she really called me at this odd hour?

"Oh!" Was all I could muster, in the back of my mind, I knew she was on a fishing expedition - she's trying to trap me, softening me up before the kill, the calculating dame! Why is she suddenly talking about the other guys? I wasn't. I never even knew about these "other guys" until now. In the past, we've been polite enough not to introduce the "Others" in our lives. She has just broken the unwritten rule - Now, she is in utility of an artifice to draw me into "their karma." A ruse I found more tragic in tone than in presentation.

"I have a room mate now you know." The sly schemer and subterfuge inventor that she is - she's trying everything in the book, to make me ask the obvious question - and I am going to oblige her, I am going to ask it, not that it matters one way or the other. This is no way to really find out if I still have any feelings for her - but I was ready to indulge her, for all it's worth.

"Oh!" "Male or female?" Again, trying hard to affect nonchalance.

"What does it matter to you?" She asked, in flat but firm voice, with room for more anticipated rebuttal. I can sense it, even over this telephone line. But she was out of luck, my generosity had run out -

its full course, if I may say. At this moment in time, all she deserves is no more than a laconic response, so I said:

"I don't want to rock any boat." Also flat in tone, but more than adequate, a lot more than she deserves.

She is definitely trying to plunge into sexual fervor or a discussion on that trajectory and with typically cool candor - sensual arousal of what lays beneath. Who is the cleverest? Who is strongest? Who has the most love to give, vis-à-vis the immense egos, the idiosyncrasies, the fight for domination and control. Then, aware of all the farce and hollowness that follow, you say: "What was all the struggle for?" "I don't get it, you fight to get somewhere, when you get there, why do you feel a coming out empty, the anti-climatic feeling of it all." Could it be due to the old saying; that too much credit or hope for the goodness of human nature bounds one for a big letdown? At this point, an old proverb comes to mind, an appropriate one for this line of thought. You say: "What does it benefit a man to gain the whole world but lose his center." "Is it better to die, or live to face the chaos that follows?" Then you wonder what the classicist would say to all this?

Do I try to get into his mind? When I do, and succeeds, is it possible I find he says: "The easiest way to find out an answer, is to know all the wrong ones." But which are the wrong ones? And how do you recognize the wrong ones with the package known as Jamie? Who never makes any move without her manipulative mind calculating the cost benefit, which others may call profit and loss - To her, the cost benefit should always be eighty-five percent to fifteen percent in her favor. Never less - in most cases, more is what she calls for, and this, I must assure you, is not an exaggeration - trust me, I was married to this woman for more than seven years - and I was happy to leave with my pants on...This is not an exaggeration. I never lie about things like these.

"And I hated life, because the work

that had been done under the sun
was calamitous from my standpoint,
for everything was vanity and a
striving after wind..."

Even with these thoughts in the back of the mind, the immense ego rears its head, eschewing the acquired precept of egolessness, allowing the fight to dominate and control live. A game that invariably enriches, if we are lucky, our capacity for understanding more about the complex connection between sex and spirit - a game that is radiant with intelligence about the mysteries of passion and creations that propelled life, lives and shimmers of erotic sensibility and naked intensity of the emotions involved - stripping away the puritanical hush that surrounds this most basic of human drive.

What is Jamie fishing for - why after this long hiatus - and then, there is the now Mrs. Peters, Michelle Peters - whose sexual and philosophical awakening were pivotal in getting rid of my fear of the past, a past that Jamie contributed a lot to - Michelle has great respect for my strength as well as weaknesses - an honest and nonjudgmental sensitivity that radiates healing effects - single-handedly replacing old memories with emphasis on the present, the here and now. And memories as we all know, are not easily replaceable. Memory, it can be with you or against you. It is not as perfect as death, but close. See, death never misses, (murder is a different story) - and since we are still on the subject of memory, awareness of the undercurrents in any situation, does some good. And the memories of Jamie are still very fresh on my mind, even with the extraordinary help of Michelle, my friend, lover, sometime sidekick and constant companion - who now bears my name, Mrs. Peters. Memories, you see, are not always easy to erase, and Jamie's are no different....

While Jamie would emphasize the physical possession and simultaneously promote the Don Juan game of seduction, of maddening, of possessing men not only for the physical, but for their souls - always demanding more than the physical - to her the idea to control and dominate predominates - ideally, why she prefers the top position when making love...in the naked bucking of its passion, the footfalls that echo behind the door we never hear open.

Michelle on the other hand promotes mutual respect, egoless-ness, mindfulness, the impermanence of things - that all things are subject to change, which creates the atmosphere for understanding - although carefree and cocky up to a point, no one is perfect, she is drenched in tears when she relives intimate moments that remind her of me, and the elusive and now disappeared uncle, "the hired killer." She is angrily baffled by the lies, and pretension of Jamie - the constant fight to break the emotional hold she had on me, and bemusement as to why it took so long - an enigma to say the least – A product begotten of the demon, the liar and the animal-kind - a brilliantly sultry half child, half whore sexual nymph - a gold digger who yearns for all the trappings of the jet-set: furs, and jewels - who breaks men's heart and makes caricatures of them when they no longer are able to satisfy her appetite - appetite of pathetic self-indulgence.

To Michelle, loyalty is the cornerstone of a good relationship, the rock of stability on which both participants rely on. To Jamie, it's of convenience and her need for stimulations - a beat of the drum that drives them home - to a crescendo - deliriously, a mean to an end.

Michelle has the subtlety to view the contradictory aspects of human behavior - whether it's the crassness or heroism of the "hired killer" or the dilemma of responsibility that is Jamie. - She has the courage to look at many faces of love with grace and sympathy - (even as the misty grey of the Big Easy at dawn gives way to a particularly beautiful and exquisite hue - reflecting the elegant colors of her varied moods, to the erotically charged streets below, the nude dancers in the red-light district of the French Quarter, and the masked artists gleaming in blue body paint, dancing to the beat of African-Caribbean mix.)

The black scant dress, (a first impression of Michelle eons ago, and first impressions are hang-able-crafts, when they are well made0, a good three inch above her knees, the burgundy hair, cropped boyishly, (for the new scheme of things) the staccato voice, barely pausing to catch her breath. Michelle is the embodiment of excitement, especially when she is in love. One suddenly realizes; life's important questions do not come with easy answers, especially when trying too hard to rekindle old glory. Is Jamie trying to rekindle old glory long after the music has finished playing? What would her benefactors say to this? I suspect, the better part of the last couple of years we lived together, she was a stoolie for them.

The benefactors, the men in gray, who sit in deep chairs would see this differently, they would most likely say: "It lacks dignity. It feels dirty; it sounds loud, looks cheap and smells bad. It would probably leave a grimy ring around the edges or on anyone that comes close to it." Just like anyone with puritanical streak would offer. Since we realize these brands of animal-kinds do not have any sense of humor in their stiff-neck mode, we forgive them, or do we?

Michelle, always with the appropriate insertion, would say: "let's go D.H. Lawrence, to see with the soul and the body." In the realm of the dryer wit, an irrepressible sense of the absurd and a sympathetic but unsentimental appreciation for the vagaries of human behavior under duress. Are the animal-kinds under duress? - The last of those to be liberated, who have been for so long imprisoned in juvenile, more like Nigel Peters of old? Who really does not care one bit, right now, the way Michelle is dressed, Scanty dress or not, she is my emancipator...and it might just be the right time to leave the interruption of Jamie, as nothing more than a blip in time, and concentrate on the benefactors, the true demons, liars and anima-kind.

Would they suddenly discover that it is more obscene to dehumanize relationships, the mysterious fabrics that exist between people - would they become more open, willing to know the people and situations around them - the simple realistic things that happen to us all, even when we don't talk about them or agree on them; to listen and talk about the real issues, the commonalties that bind us, the abiding truths – for non-perversions and discoveries – a freedom for the ability to continually question things, the frankness of the story, not the eroticism - nor the obscenity in the raw search for wealth and domination, that is prevalent in the realm of the demon, the liar, and the animal-kind - In this scrutiny of relationships and the experience of the world - the relationship between sinners and salvation, we discover the following:

That is, the shear accident of birth, should not be enough for some to be permanently confined to the "wrong" side of the fence - They should not lose the yearnings of humankind - peace, love, sustenance, justice, and a place in the sun - because no one listens - to the cries, their cries from the other side of the track. No. The band should stop playing and the performers and dancers should listen to the cries sipping through the cracks of the wall... "Hello, hello, Nigel, are you still there?" Jamie's voice brought me back from my revelry. So, I said:

"Jamie, could we continue this conversation another time, at a less godforsaken hour?" I offered, still affecting nonchalance. Emotionlessness, from me, yours truly, whom Jamie assumed she had pussy-whipped, is a sure way to deflate any ulterior move she may have up her sleeves.

"I am sorry you find me such a bother, Nigel." She deadpans. "It is either of two things, you totally hate me, or you have a woman with you. Which is which Nigel?"

I could not think of one time that Jamie had been less transparent or predictable – nakedly obvious. But that was tomorrow's anxiety, and since she has forced my hand, I am happy to oblige her, give her the information I had wanted to ease in slowly to her. I hope she receives this news with the gravity proper to it. My feelings for her had run the gamut during this 1:30 A.M. call, pity to anger to passion. Maybe it was all the same. I had wanted a more appropriate time to break the news about the new Mrs. Peters to her. I closed my eyes, and tried to drink in her old scent, tried to refashion in my mind her self and voice, the old ones. "Tell me what to do," I wanted to say, but I could not say it. I could not say it because the new Mrs. Peters was some few yards away in our bed. I also could not say it because one should not believe that people could be improved in their character in between times or by reason. Beware gentle knight, there's no greater monster than reason, I reminded myself, especially the knowledge about the larceny of time and flesh, which is sweeter for the betrayal.

She held out her hand, and I stepped forward to take it, then I realized it was a dream, a dream one has while awake, of a figure shrouded in that summer landscape: real land and sky, and yet a dream withal. But yet, she stood there with her legs spread and her head down, her small hands resting against her slight waist, and she looked at me with great forthrightness and smiled and put her face against my shoulder, we turned under the lights and a trumpet note guided us on our separate and collective paths – lush green, sunlight of a single intricate design of brilliance, a single bird, a bird of prey, a subtle motion of its own. I woke up. The story has to be told. Jamie has to know about Michelle Peters, no more need to ease it slowly, because nothing could hurt when you do not care and that was the end of the beginning of that. We must all be cut out for what we do, however we make our living is where our talent should resonate. Jamie and I had shared moments, shared past; and a certain work of the cat and mouse sort, albeit sanctioned by the government, invariably, often times, aspects shrouded in plausible deniability; requiring youthful, intense, cold sober approach, work that required that our talents resonate with the assignment of the day. Work we were cut out for. Work of a mindless, mechanical brute-ness, where we observe ourselves observing others we observe, who may in turn be observing us - the dark of what was, of pointless accidents, of irreversible injustice, that take us to the edge of our realms, that is now of no relevance to the new reality, the reality of the world of Michelle Peters, nee Ford; a photo negative of her glorious form staring at me – spread lazily on the divan, her lips slightly open as she stared, the tongue taut, the expression frank and competitive. There was no visible sweat, wearing only panties and bra, exposing her long legs, the left knee cocked and her schoolgirl belly and the dimpled muscles of her thigh, in a room that crackled in the midsummer heat as the moon grew slender in the sky. When light streams in on Michelle, all other objects disappear into shadows. So it goes. Michelle Peters is the single abiding certainty that we would be where we are now.

"Jamie, I have been married for about two years now, and the new Mrs. Peters is some yards away from me, in our bedroom." I told her. Waited for the explosion I anticipated would come, but did not. Jamie has grown some. She surprised me thus:

"Congratulations, Nigel, who is the luck girl?" Jamie said politely, very politely.

"Her name is Michelle, I believe you know her, have met her, an operative in one of the assignments we participated in, I believe in Brussels, some time back, I believe in eighty-eight." I said, also politely, very politely. As they say, one good turn deserves another.

"Looks like you did not have too far to go to get a new wife, you always seem to stay close and within the community." I was not sure what this meant, or the true implication thereof. But I was not going to quarrel with it.

"She is a cute girl, I thought she was kind of young for that gig then, but she did pull through, can see why you would go for her, just like me at one time, I guess." Jamie was not giving any compliments; she was stating facts, albeit understated. Michelle is not cute, she is beautiful, an elegant specimen of what Jamie described. And she did not pull through; she was extraordinary in her performance then.

Everyone saw it and acknowledge it, the precociousness, and the prodigious, absolute remarkable representation she engendered, was nothing short of quintessential.

Like I said, it was not a time to quarrel with Jamie. She has reacted to the news of the new Mrs. Peters as best as she could; better than I had expected. There was no obvious bitterness, no name-calling. I wanted to end this telephone call of a 1:30 A.M. kind, on a civilized note, and refocus on the Demon, the Liar and the Animal-kind, trying to deconstruct them as I possibly can. So I said:

"Thank you Jamie, I will pass along your observation to Michelle. It was nice hearing from you again. Good luck with everything."

"Thanks." Jamie responded. There was a click, and the line went dead. And that was that. As always, Jamie got the last word in, but I was thankful it ended, and that it ended better than I had expected, and I could go back to my thesis, the attempt at deconstructing the demon, the liar and the animal-kind, with a segue to the next day, to a fast moving train, the fast moving train as the stage, and characters representing both sides of the political divide: the young man speaking for the progressives, the old man and the old woman, who is just as old as him, representing the masterminds; where I am an observer observing others who may be observing me. Here it goes.

The Old Man and The Old Woman, The Young Man, On A Fast Moving Train.

The old woman, a family member of the demon, the liar and the animal kind, who is just as old as the male companion, on a fast moving train, disagreed with the aforementioned analyses before Jamie's rude interruption. The old woman believes it is what's wrong with the new generation - they think and talk too much, and bring too much attention to the ills of the world, which she believes should be left in the hands of the "Doctor feel goods," the media lab, technicians of the benefactors - to craft a story, a story that would make everyone feel good. The fact that the stories told by the media men are falsities is of no consequence to her. To her, maintaining stability and security is more important than human rights. When confronted and called on any of the lies, she would rather change the subject - because it is in her character to do so - one of her asides, always said with a sneering contempt is: "Of course, New Orleans isn't what it used to be. It never was. Any young person who praises this place to tourists is decadent and obscene; they should be ashamed of themselves, for contributing to the doom that is bound to befall this once lovely place. They should have been here forty years ago, the glory days, when it was the Queen of the South." George Orwell comes to mind: 'Then the lie passed into history and became truth.') The people now become confronted by two common properties of the healthy mind: easily distracted by the unusual, easily numbed to the ordinary. In this scenario, what does one do? Do people accept these lies as glossy inconvenient attractions? Or make them not some forbidden thoughts, but permissible ones?

The young man, for the sake of clarity, and eager to draw the line that separates the sinners and salvation, and a need to rebut the old woman who is just as old as the her companion, says: "Don't believe the hype, they are the ones that raped the people, perpetuated incest, stripped people of their identities and dignities - created mindsets, they are the demons, the liars and the animal kind, let's embrace Plato, for acquisition and exchange of knowledge is our savior and only hope, because it's always an affair of love, love of our fellow mankind, and it does not have to be physical to be real, change is in the air, the old guard like her would resist it, vigilance is called for friends." The young man looked at the old woman straight in the eyes and said: "We of the new generation lady, are not easily fooled by your kind."

The old man, who is just as old as the female companion, looked around, and then stared deeply out the window of the fast moving train. There was melancholy, there was hopelessness, there was the defeatist attitude of the general who is losing the war, but who is determined to continue kicking and screaming long after the drumbeat has stopped, even though the kicking and screaming is now fainter and fainter - but he himself doesn't know it.

The old man turned around, looked at his companion, the old woman who is just as old as him. He nudged her lightly on the side with his elbow. He said: "I am gonna show these deviants that this country is still a law and order society, I'm gonna show them..." He rose, walked to the Young man. They looked at each other squarely in the eyes...a duel to the finish brewing. The old man broke the stillness of the air, he said -

"I am part of what you have been railing against young man, I am a mastermind, I'm a gatekeeper, and I make performers out of politicians, because society needs it. Without me society would drift aimlessly. The politicians, the leaders, they expect it, they seek it, that's all they are - marketable personas, created in our media-adviser think tanks, and then projected into the collective television mind, because society needs it, otherwise, like I said, people would drift aimlessly; more so after the tiresome era of the gruff, wide-grinning, wimpy, sentimentalist peanut farmer." He paused, expecting a feedback. It was quick in coming. The young man asked:

"Are you saying you and your cohorts are reshaping government into theatrical events?" Apparently bemused at the aggressiveness, the audacity of the old man, who is not acting his age, and who is just as old as the female companion, a representation of an equally vulgar side of the same coin.

"Yes, my boy, yes." The old man said, with an air of pride and satisfaction. He was expecting a fight, an equally aggressive reaction from the young man. He was surprised at the apparent self-control and levelheadedness shown by the young lad.

The young man looked more bemused. He was not quite sure he was hearing it straight; did some thinking and asked -

"Who is responsible for the script and this whole new vocabulary created, I am sure, to match the new mindset being promoted - is it faithful to the reality of our lives or does it just pander to our fantasy?"

This is a trick question the old man thought. Who does this little kid think he is? "I'm gonna get him yet," he thought to himself. To the young man, he said out loud: "It's all in the mind, my boy, it's all in the mind, different strokes for different folks, if it works and is successful, who worries about the semantics and idle questions."

The young man still confused, but holding on to mindfulness, wanting to get all the facts before making judgment, not wanting to act like the foes he detests. To him, hypocrisy is not becoming, not when one wants to be taken seriously. So he pried for more answers and said: "To make this work old man, there have to be lots of coaching, memorizations, role playing, cue cards and contingencies made incase there are lapses, when the script fails to match the event, yes? I am thinking to make this work, would entail elaborate props, preparations and manipulation of facts and people, and might not necessarily be in that order, yes?" The young man broke the facts down, as he saw them, wanting to make sure there was no misunderstanding of the old man's position or points of view. He waited.

"This is exactly what is wrong with the young generation, they think too much. Why worry about what does not concern you. Your role is to absorb the information projected for consumption, and you would be okay." This threw the young man for a minute. He could not believe what he was hearing. This, he thought, had the potential to not only make him forget about the precepts he grew up around, but could make him lose this self-control. He needed mindfulness more than anything now. But above all, he needed to get the facts, facts before judgment.

"It does concern me, old man, I'm part of this society, this vast society, if you need reminding." The young man retorted, enunciated with a cool candor, facts, he reasoned, could only be gotten with condor....

"Okay, if it's important to you, I will break it down some." "It has been constructed to be very elementary so that even the dumb-witted politician can grasp it. You see, when and if something goes wrong on the set, the 'politician' knows he is just the star, a performer. He understands others are paid to worry about the rest of the show. He is just the front man. His assignment, as the actor, is to see things from a single lens, from a point of view created by us – of a very narrow and one-dimensional perspective, that of an entire dramatic cosmos filtered through the eyes of this one person, one of its known inhabitants. He tells one side of the national story, a familiar and uplifting national story, a story much of the 'public' desperately wants to hear - a crafty script, delivered cannily enough to overpower the other sides of the same story - because they were too tired already to make clear judgment, too tired to distinguish between what may or may not be in their best interest – it works because they have become too tired of the wimpy, smiling, wide-grinning peanut farmer's simpering. They need words that convey action and a renewed hope for tomorrow."

"Now, old man, you're truly clever, that's brilliant, and I must give that to you. You and your cohorts have measured the peoples' threshold for tolerance, and had a good gauge of the activities of the wimpy cabinet, yes?" The young man continued, prying for more information -

"Thank you young man. You see; it's so simple. It's like taking candies from a baby." The old man reiterated.

"This is the thing, old man, I want to be sure I understand your premise. What you are saying is that once the politician got to the 'set,' in this case the Statehouse, and siphoned resources meant for human-face activities for toys and gadgets of mass destruction - toys and gadgets that go obsolete before they leave the drawing board due to changing times - and even when you know that these toys are useless, wasteful expenditure of scant resources, you still had a role to play to draw the people's attention from the reality -- the two sides of the same coin - the vagabond-filled streets, the military fiascoes, the collapsing financial institutions and corrupt managers that belied his message of hope and prosperity, strength and leadership, and the paramount nature and place of national security, was the doing of you and your cohorts, yes? – All this was designed to blur the vision and pain of the people - all were, to them, a blur, yes?" they were part of an aggressive political propaganda campaign, instead of the truth just to sell your candidate, yes?" "It was a deliberate decision to turn away from candor and honesty when those qualities were most needed, yes?" It was in essence a culture of deception, where a permanent period of campaign is created, and it becomes all about manipulating sources of public opinion to the candidates advantage, where the media, the press becomes some kind of complicit enablers, a vehicle for the cooked up ideology, by not probing or holding accountable your group and candidate, yes?" The young man inquired. Not giving the old man time to respond to his questions until he was done. All the while, still embracing mindfulness and levelheadedness.

"Now you're talking my boy, now you're talking. And it is yes, yes, yes and yes to all the questions you asked. It is like taking candies from a baby, as simple as that, my boy. That's the beauty of the whole thing. That is the way it is, and that's the way it's gonna remain. How many times does an actor get a chance to play different parts in the same play, how many times? Tell me? Tell me?"

"I kinda think almost none," the boy responded, "unless, of course, he is your student, the politician and you back him up, as you did with the original actor. "

"Yes, right again my boy, right again, unless we back him, as we did with the actor. That was well enunciated. You are a bright boy my boy, a quick study actually, if I may borrow the vernacular of the young generation." The old man continued.

"See, as the masterminds, we have to be able to gaze at the same scene through many successive pairs of eyes. As Shaw once wrote: For the dramatist to do his job, he ought to be able to rewrite a script as many times as there are characters, once from each point of view."

"Isn't that an overthrow of your point of view? I mean, doesn't that totally supplant it? Does it not belie the crux of your game plan?" Unless I don't read you correctly, you're saying he would have to take stands at the intersection of many different truths?" The young man feigned some confusion, and a mild exasperation.

"Life is full of contradictions, my boy, life is full of contradictions - it's what makes it interesting, and that's where the masterminds come in." The old man fruitlessly tried to reassure him.

"Old man, you're actually really very clever, I see what you mean, it's what is called versions of truths, the options and choices we are left with, isn't it?" The young man mocked, but the joke was lost on the old man.

"Right my boy, again right, I'm really getting to like you." Convinced he had gotten the young man on his side. He continued.

"I came here for a fight, look what I got." The old man was impressed with the seemingly cooperative attitude, or non-belligerent tone of the young lad, who previously was filled with polemics, albeit laced

with candor. The old man was in his elements. He was sure he had
a recruit in the making; he needed to close the deal, reel the young
man in. A bright young man like this would be an asset for the
cause. He continued.

"We had to hype him, the actor that is. Make him into a trend, a
messenger, who after he is long gone from the scene, leaves a message
that takes a life of its own. A messenger who would be quoted
and invoked by future politicians, a reference point of currency,
of being cut from the same cloth, political cloth so to speak - It
is the result of the complexities of politics, we just made it simple
and more interesting, highlighting, in other words, underscoring
the fundamental lines of conflict that run through each person,
and package it as something worthy for them to take into their
awareness."

"I see what you mean old man, the message does live on, as the
conservative political doctrine embraced and assigned to the actor
as originator, et al." The young man offered. Still fishing.

"Yes, yes, you're truly a quick study, if I must say so again." The
old man said, unable to rein in his glee, at the apparent success in
capturing a recruit, a candidate for the mindset. He was wrong. He
just couldn't have been more wrong and deluded. The young man
has had him played. He wanted facts, just the facts, nothing but the
facts that would clue him into the mindset of the masterminds, the
demon, the liar and the animal-kind. What makes them tick, what
drives them and got them to where they are.

"Old man, isn't it true that multinational corporations are really the
main players in the new global village, making politicians figure
heads of convenience?"

This took the old man aback for a minute, he had thought he had the
young man pegged, he was wrong. Could the young man have played

him? The glee from a possible successful recruit was diminished, giving room for suspicion and a retreat to the old order.

"That is a dangerous talk, my boy, that is a dangerous talk, we were really doing well, let's stay that course, it's a safer course, it's a safer line, don't you agree?"

"Old man, I really believe you're a very clever kind of a gatekeeper, a true mastermind in the realm the demon; the liar, and the animal-kind, albeit in the veneer of a scholar and a gentleman; but don't you agree that leadership requires skills like no other, an ineffable quality, as Porter puts it, 'the truth that finally overtakes you?' Don't you believe that an ideal leader is one who looks beyond reductive categories, one who calls on us to think past our own individual interests, to envision a world that is better for every person in it? One who combines strength and compassionate elements, a visionary and pragmatic leader – honest, patient and bold?" The young man was not done, he continued.

"Old man, I believe a true leader is one who has a first rate intelligence, and as F. Scott Fitzgerald eloquently puts it: 'the test of a first rate intelligence, is the ability to hold two opposed ideas in mind at the same time and still retain the ability to function.' Do your candidates have this capacity? Can they retain the ability to function while holding opposed views on the multiplicity of issues facing the nation? I believe only a man with self-respect, in the best sense of the word, who is capable of listening to the voices of a divergent group, accepting equality for all God's creation, even the little mermaids among us. Someone who is genuinely enthusiastic about these ideals, an enthusiasm so great that he feels an irrepressible impulse to acquaint the masses with his ideals, is ideally the most suited leader for a nation. Don't you agree with me? " I believe an understanding of the philosophical and ethical underpinnings of American political customs and mores, as the founding fathers constructed, and knew might help as a cathartic elixir. Those old dead guys, the ancient Greeks and Romans thinkers, recognized four absolute virtues: justice, temperance, prudence, and fortitude, it was not that desirable traits like honor, patience, compassion, generosity, honesty, humility, altruism, forgiveness, gratitude are not essential in human relations, they were deemed more situational. But in this discus, I would recommend them all as a starting point for you and your cohorts. They could cleans you of the bad habit, and again, by extension save the electorate of your poison."

The old man squinted his eyes. This young man has been playing him for a fool. He came to fish, not to divulge. He suddenly realized the young man had really not made any solid statements since the beginning of the discourse until now, but has asked questions and flattered him - softening him with kindness - like the mouse who bites away at your sole and blows on it at the same time, to deaden the pain - only the next morning, when you walk that you realize the pain; that mouse's "fan" was a mean to an end. It is called using the weapon of the mastermind on the mastermind – their life of lies, constantly affirming something that can't possibly be true and denying others that are perfectly obvious - this is the belly of the demon, the liar and the animal-kind - and, yes, their masterminds - who expect our leaders to work from a script that has been pre-approved, censored, sanitized - and are eager to conform - thus over and over, we hear them uttering one thing when we know they are really thinking another: propelling us into a period when strangely distorted demands are made on the freedoms of the people. Artists and writers restrained, limiting their ability to write and speak about the unpleasant truths -

In the words of the poet, philosopher, and statesman: "They are empty ideological phrases, ugly and violent rumors that gets whispered among skeptics, they are fears borne out of ignorance and the rare historic circumstance of the shifting times, meant to produce incantations that petrify thought." - it is of inordinate value - whether delivered from the stage or the statehouse, or the king's castle, it's still double speak that wears the coat of dishonesty, duplicity, arrogance, and willful ignorance of the blueprint the founding fathers envisaged in the bill of rights for governance."

The young man was done, and he paused for effect. He was not going to fight, nor engage in any form of belligerency or polemics, he would let knowledge be his tool - "in the new world order, the globe is a small village, actually." He mused to himself.

The old man observed the young man solemnly, shook his head, and with a shrug that could mean anything, walked back to his companion, the old woman, who is just as old as himself; symbols existing outside the realm of the graspable.

"I have long outgrown the naive astonishment accustomed to the animal-kind, that he might have a liking to tofu, and reinvent himself to the point of being like one of us." The young man thought to himself. This portent of contradiction was valid, one of many paradoxes of his character, the character of the 'Demon, the Liar and the Animal-kind,' existing within the framework - the demon, the liar and the animal-kind - moral choices before the young man - Remembering the imaginative freedom of thought, and the reversal, the scattered reactions of raised or glowering brows of the masterminds, thrown in for good measure. Then there is the vibrant overkill, in their zeal to humanize the monster, to produce an acceptable societal icon. Which is, more or less, dressing up human savageness in cooked-up ideological uniforms. And you ask: how does one describe a shadow after calling it black or gray? Does it depend on the hue of the reflection?

We have seen it often, how they succeed in glossing over the fact, the known fact that the mastermind is a twisted and abnormal being. A member of some subspecies of mutants, with character deficiencies in an environment where no holds are barred, the mug shot of a maniac - an aberrance that exists in a collection of individuals, one grounded in the unique features of the animal-kind character and culture - which is derived from their desire to divorce themselves from the main species and all the ordinary traits of the wider landscape - a one dimensional stereotypical demon, who would want you to believe that he is not a part of the flesh and blood-being, who put their shoes on in the morning and took them off at night like the rest of us, a person motivated more by opportunism than by compassion, who advocates ruthlessness for its own sake, a psychopath who come into their own wherever civilized codes of behavior have been replaced by sanctioned brutality, spin, hide and shading of the truth - going the whole way and more - the rest, functional within the necessity of harsh treatment - in dealing with the enemy, especially the ones that are different from them - a chronic myopia of correcting an abstract political and tribal differences.

The young lad's prodigious recollections in amassing and deconstructing the series of contradictions and stratagem of the masterminds, grew greater with the passage of time -- in the realm of the ultimate Faustian...but he would like to let go. He wants to let go. For he knows the toxicity of accumulated negatives on body and mind, an aggregate no reasonable person wants to harbor. But the question is: Would the opposition let go? Are they amenable to change? Can they change? Or. Are they willing to change; in this balancing act, perched on a tightrope of two extremities – in a choice between good and evil, salvation and sacrilege induced final solution. The young man was perplexed, almost overwhelmed by his thoughts. But after this grueling encounter with the icon of the demon, the liar and the animal-kind........."anything is possible..." He thought. "Anything is possible." He smiled as he disembarked from the fast moving train.

And They All Clapped

The slight button-down figure walked into the gray chamber of the "Hall of the People." His bearings were regal, albeit slight, exuding confidence, a face that might have been fixed, irrevocably in stone. His smile, if you could call it that, was measured and calculating.

He carefully surveyed the faces of the people in the great hall, especially the ones of the grey suited men, those who are poised to play god - whether he has the qualifications, demeanor and necessary instincts to serve the vast people of this great land, the People's Kingdom.

He looked around the vast hall and the spectators again, and one more time, scanned his prospective executioners. This was more from habit than anything else; he had no trepidations whatsoever on his preparation. Assurances and guarantees are in short supply in the human realm, but as far as the media handlers are concerned, he was quite confident that assurances are not needed, they did quite well for the actor, and they would do equally well for me, he thought.

Politicians come, and politicians go, but the masterminds and the media lab people remain, they are the ones who make politics interesting. Without them, politics as we know it would be excruciatingly boring. They had, in his case; computer generated the scenarios he might expect and how to navigate them. He has absolute confidence in them. "They never let the actor down, they would not let me down," he thought to himself, again.

He patted his breast pocket to make sure the outline of his opening speech was there. It was there. There is no room for panic now. No one has really impugned his intelligence, knowledge, or capacity as a supreme arbiter. Their quarrel is with his leanings, or what one might call political leaning, his instincts, understanding and sympathy with the dilemmas of modern life, and those of ordinary people - and most especially the little mermaids within this vast kingdom. And, as long as there is ample accommodation for them in his speech, and his answers to the questions posed by the men in grey, he would be okay. The media men are never wrong, just look at what they did with the actor and the oilman.

They have made sure he was well-briefed by the masterminds, and every conceivable scenarios had been played and rehearsed, and he is here now to assure the executors of the laws of the land that they can trust him as an arbiter of moderate instincts, who is able to understand and sympathize with the dilemmas of modern life and those of ordinary people - especially those of the little "people" within it.

He will talk to them about the effect that arbiters have on the lives of people who come before them and about the constitutional rights to privacy and equal protection under the sun.

His main goal in his opening statements is to emphasize and dispel the erroneous image people have of him as this hermit - of a remote small town arbiter, who approaches the law as a sterile intellectual exercise. "Nothing could be further from the truth," he tried to reassure himself. He knows that to be convincing, he would have to play the part well, go deep into his character, because, the success of playing a part is to put oneself into it. There is just too much hanging on this to fail, too many people depending on him, especially after all the talks from the opposition - "And what was all that comparisons to other known judicial quantity?" His thoughts drifted to the brouhaha of the past weeks, the weeks after his nomination.

The "Easterner" was totally flabbergasted by all the comparisons being floated around: the quirkiness in the mold of John P. Stevens comparison, the intellectual rigor of Antonio Scalia, the pragmatic conservatism of Lewis Powell, Jr., and a host of others he cares not to remember - "They just don't know what is coming at them. They are going to be hit with the biggest surprise pack in the history of the Kingdom's confirmation hearing," he thought as he smiled to himself.

"Who gave them the right to play god, and for that matter, the right to label me and compare me to every Dick and Harry that ever was a supreme arbiter? Me, an ascetic and monastic style persona of Benjy Cardozo? Give me a break people, just fu...king give me a break." This really surprised him, he is not known to use such language, nor even think about them in public. He knows he would have to rein in his anger, before it does irreparable damage to his cause. But as much as he tried, he could not help but agonize over the way the press had treated him since the nomination, and all the prehistoric groups that have crawled out of the different rocks, to fight him, and the so-called unknown stand on the issues.

"So I am not in the mold of Billy Brennan in temperament and judicial philosophy, who really cares?" "Do you all think the people of the Kingdom really care?"

He was definitely incensed, and if it weren't because of his need to fulfill a lifelong dream, and to show and prove to these god-playing buffoons, about how wrong they have been, he would reach over and shake them hard. No, that would not be an appropriate decorum of a nominee to the Supreme Chamber of Arbiters.

"I have to control this silly urge, I can't afford to be reactionary now, just what they would expect me to do." No one has said the "Easterner" wasn't a smart man.

He gave one of those smiles, the one that befits the demeanor of this vaunted position he is aspiring to - just as the "doctors" prescribed it, in this case, the media men.

But as much as he tried, he could not help but reflect on the negatives he was subjected to the past few weeks. All falsities, all heresy. To him, concocted by enemies of good - "remote Olympian figure?" "Undeviatingly cottage cheese and apple for lunch eater." "Me? They've got to be kidding. Have they seen the inside of my mini-fridge in the office? What about the croissant, the yogurt, the cup-a-noodles? They really got to be kidding. I'm gonna show them. These god players and media lynch mobs. I'm gonna show them." He was really furious, but held his cool, accommodating the outward demeanor of a prospective Supreme Arbiter - he was not going to lose it now! No, no, no.

As much as he tried, he could not help but fume over the ridiculous accusations and heresy that trailed his nomination. He was glad that all these thoughts were internalized; for he knew he could not afford any externalization of these emotions, at least not now! Since old habits are hard to get rid of, the reflections continued...

"Remote Olympian figure? To me that is what I call crazy talk. What about the wild private parties, the women and booze in the exclusive parties? They are so naive and sentimental, a trait so uniquely them, which is what really distinguishes them from us..."

"I am tempted, I may just invite them over, just to see how wrong they are. No, no, no. I'm not going to give them that satisfaction. It's better the way it is, better for the image, and the decorum ascribed to the supreme AR-bit-traitor. What planet do these people come from? Why would they peg me as a remote Olympian figure, a cottage cheese and apple for lunch man." What a joke, what a joke, ha!" His thoughts, although private, were now bordering on the maniacal - twisting around themselves.

He wasn't going to quarrel or dignify any of the stories anymore, not even the one about how his black judge's robe added color to his attire, nor how he lives alone in a weather-beaten farmhouse, southerly of small city, USA. He would not think about them anymore, no, no, no. To him, that was another crazy or unenlightened juxtaposition, borne of ignorance. "Live alone? Yeah, right! Have they ever wondered about the "Cleaning lady" that comes in, and is never seen leaving until a week later? Marge would be laughing her ass off now.... Oops! Did I say that?" he reprimanded himself, glad that these were just thoughts and not spoken words. Because, ass is not a word a decorous arbiter should use.

"I cannot believe these buffoons, what they cannot drag from the horses mouth, they always make up." He indulged again, in his private thoughts, as if trying to convince himself.

He was amused at the different names they called him: from someone who is selectively and intermittently gregarious, to a storyteller who displays dry wit to those who really get to know him. "What a joke, what a joke?" He thought to himself again - but he quickly realized that this was a new habit forming, a habit he could not afford, and a habit he hoped would fade, and not carry over beyond this hearing. This is not the person he is, he reassured himself.

But he remained very angry. Angry about all the so-called juicy tidbits the media was promoting about him. Yes, he has a right to be angry - because these are all half-truths and innuendos cooked up for lack of any substantive information from their investigations - how can they be so sentimental..."

He was particularly bemused by the fact that the media would even devote time, space and energy to the fact that he can cast aside 'judicial rigor' for a measure of personal warmth. Do they think he is made of stone? He smiled.
Why would they waste valuable ink and paper, which increases their carbon footprint on trivialities: the fact that each Sunday he walks the same elderly woman from St. Andrews, or for visiting his mother at the hospice - "they got to be out of their minds." "Do they really expect me to neglect my mother, just because she's old, and dad is no more? Who wouldn't offer money to a friend to rebuild his

farmhouse after it was burnt down? Any goodhearted person would do that. And why would my walking an elderly woman home after church be a big deal? They are so sentimental."

He was especially disturbed about all the labels they have generated, that they are now dumping on him, vis-à-vis the contradictions - in their quest to demonize him: on one hand, they say he is courteous, loyal, unaffected and upright, "not stuck up and doesn't put on any airs - down to earth." Even with these attributes, they still found him wanting in his nomination.

Then comes the contradictions - the qualms - the concern over his circumscribed way of life - his engagement as a young man to the daughter of an arbiter, whom he never married - which have giving room to fears from both detractors and admirers - whether his solitary lifestyle might limit his empathy or level of human understanding - even though the laconic standard of his small town and his own reticence show otherwise - "they are so sentimental," His thoughts rang out again, albeit confined within self.

He wondered what the condition of his house had to do with anything: the peeling paint, the sagging porch, the clogged lawn with clover and Queen Anne's lace, and the fact that not too many visitors are invited, had to do with the substance of his nomination and the performance of the duties of a supreme arbiter - "How can they be so sentimental," he mumbled under tight jaws - as the steaming thoughts left his brain.

He has no quarrel with what they wrote about his reticence, which is said to vanish behind the bench, nor for the credit they gave him for bringing a new level of fire and vigor to the once-sleepy oral arguments that long characterized the chamber; nor for his acuity and independence -- his squeakier-than-squeaky clean image: most literary, most sophisticated and most likely to succeed; his being witty and in constant demand - he has no quarrel with all that - who would quarrel with such positive attributes? He thought. But he takes offense when they mix them with half-baked Un-beliefs, contradictions such as giving and attending scandalous parties - to his political persuasion or ideology - which are carelessly flung around as if he were some kind of Jekyll and Hyde - but a Jekyll and Hyde who is unfailingly polite and courtly, but who is reclusive and bookish - always the contradictions - this tendency to disclose compulsively every twist and turn in his life, like: "'even though he is not known to be argumentative in a ranting way, he is intellectually insistent'" "'you could set your watch by his comings and goings.'" - "They are so sentimental." He thought to himself.

"It is an odd fate," he thought. He looked up one more time, carefully scanned the history-making hall, and was struck with the realization that the time for him had come. It was time to face the men in gray, those who are about to play god. The big question.is: "Is he, or is he not?" And the man from the East, the slight button-down man was acknowledged by the Chief Gray man - the slight button-down man knew it was time to go before them, these god-players, whose thumbs up or down - or a mere "yea" or "nay" of their voice would decide his fate. He was ready for them. - The professional media men and their toys had worked him through all the motions; the different anticipated twists and turns in this cat and mouse game. He was ready, ready as can be.

He rose to the acknowledgement of the Head-gray man. He walked to the podium. He carefully extracted from his breast pocket the sheet of paper that would cue him through his opening speech. He did the final test before facing the barrages of inquiries and positions on issues affecting the land. He believes the media men have adequately prepared him for this challenge, a once in a lifetime opportunity. He does not intend to lose the moment, not for anyone. He is ready to do whatever it takes, even if he has to resort to pleading amnesia - a tool the media men devised for others before him. It worked then, it's sure to work now.

He carefully rested the piece of paper on the speaker's stand. He nodded politely. And they all clapped!

The slight button-down man from the East smiled in polite acknowledgement - he fingered his tie to make sure it was in place - And he began - in a voice and accent borne of a mix of Eton and Eastern Shore upbringing...

"I came to the notice of probably most of you on this chamber of the people's guardian when I stood next to the king and tried, with great difficulty that afternoon in early summer, to express some sense of honor that I felt, despite the - despite the surprise, and even shock, of the event to me."

The silence in the hall could be sliced with a knife - the slight man from the East emanated humility void of piousness - the gray suited men turned and murmured to their closest neighbor, wrote on the pads before them. The spectators behind the slight buttoned-down man nodded approval - they did not clap...

The nominee continued: "It's equally - it's equally incumbent on me to try to express some sense of the honor that I feel today, in appearing before you, as you represent the chamber of the this great Kingdom, in discharging your own responsibilities, to review the King's nomination. I could only - I could only adopt what Lord Maubneztem said earlier this morning about the - the grandeur of this process of which we are a part." He paused for effect, just as the coaches had advised. He scanned the room, making sure he makes eye contact with those who will eventually pass judgment on his qualifications. It is a prescription from the media men he believes will not fail. Everything has to be followed to the letter.

The gray suited men in deep chairs turned their heads, their faces showing none of the emotions that lie within - the spectators nodded, their emotions outwardly visible - they are with the slight button-down fellow from the East, come rain or shine. But they did not clap, this is not the time to clap, not yet, it has to be just the right moment - the computer is never wrong, it has to be timed to the last mini-second - the professional media men know best - and who is to argue with them. They did not fail the actor and others before him - and they will not fail the slight button-down man from the East.

And he continued:

"Despite the reams of paper and, I suppose, the forests that have fallen to produce that paper, in the time between early summer and now; I would like to take a minute, before we begin our - our dialogue together, to say something to you about how I feel about the beginning that I have come from and about the experiences that I have had, that bear on the kind of arbiter that I am, and the kind of arbiter that I can be expected to be."

More than ever before, the spectators knew that the media men had done their duties as prescribed. The nominee is on track - but the men in gray, the god-players, who sit in deep chairs did not turn their heads this time - they could sense a professionally inspired manipulator, they needed to be on their guard - this is not an ordinary slight man before them. They cursed themselves under their breath for not anticipating this stratagem - a subterfuge that has been used many a time by such candidates in the past few appearances, as a ruse: the hall packed with their fans, every of their moves and statements primed for the television camera - just in time for the evening news - all to be eaten up by the public. The men in grey did not anticipate this; they had not done their homework right. They may have taken the easterner for granted, too much for granted; and if the man from the East was to comment on this, he would say: It's uniquely them, what makes us more superior to them...

The slight button-down figure from the East fingered his tie again - he looked around the hall, exhibiting a grin, a self conscious grin of knowing he was on track - in praise of the media men - if he was expecting some applause, there was none coming, not yet, thought the spectators, they have their own scripts to follow.

"I think you all know that I spent most of my - my boyhood in a small town in New Land, Egret, to be exact. It was - it was a town large in geography, small in population. The physical space, the open space between people, however, was not matched by the - by the inner space between them, because as everybody knows who has lived in a small town, there is - there is a closeness of people in a small town which is unattainable anywhere else."

"There was in that town no section or place or neighborhood that was determined by anybody's bank balance."

They all rose, and there was evidence of glee on the faces - And they all clapped. The slight man from the East was at home, in his environment, the environment created by the professional media men. Their timing was impeccable. "Why are they so good, how come they are so perceptive of the desires of the King and his subjects?" He thought to himself. He has to play the part of being one of them. He cannot lose by playing that strategy.

He continued: "Everybody knew everybody else's business, or at least thought they did, and we were in a very true sense intimately aware of other lives. We were aware of lives that were easy and we were aware of lives that were very hard."

And they all clapped. They clapped, more from empathy and recognition of his humility and avowed humble background, than from the stated script. He is one of them all right. "He is doing good," some thought. "He has the smarts," others thought. "He is putting to shame the anxieties of the opposition," they all agreed.

Since old habits are hard to kill, he fingered his tie one more time, and continued:

"Another thing that we were aware of in that place was the responsibility of people to govern themselves. It was a responsibility that they owed to themselves, and it was a responsibility that they owed to their neighbors. I first learned about that, or I first learned the practicalities of that, when I used to go over to the Town Hall in Egret, N. L, on town meeting days, and I would sit on the benches in the back of the Town Hall after school. That's where I began my lessons in practical government." It has to hit them all at once. They have to feel it - the media men said so. They did not fail the actor. They have not failed the nominee so far. They all rose, and they all clapped...

The slight man from the East was in his true form. He continued, for he was just beginning: "As I think you know, I went to high school in Cord, N. H., which is a bigger place, and I went on from there to college and to study law in Cam, Mass, and O'Ford, E.land, which are bigger places still. And after I had finished law school, I came back to New England and I began the practice of law and I think probably it's fair to say I resumed the study of practical government."

They all rose again, and they all clapped. To them, this slight man was saying all the right things.

"I remember very well the first few weeks and months I spent in a courtroom. I spent representing clients with domestic relations problems who lived sometimes, it seemed to me, in appalling circumstances."

"I began to become familiar with the criminal justice system in my province and in our Kingdom. I met victims, and sometimes I met the survivors of victims; I met defendants, and I met that train of witnesses from the clergy to con artists who pass through our system and find themselves, either willingly or unwillingly, part of a search for truth and part of a search for those results that we try to sum up with the words of justice.... I saw every sort and condition of the people of my province that a trial court of general jurisdiction is exposed to."

And they rose, and they all clapped.

"I had maybe the - one of the greatest experiences of my entire life in seeing week in and week out the members of the trial juries of our provinces who are rightly called the 'consciences of our communities.' And I worked with them and I learned from them, and I will never forget my days with them."

And they all clapped! They clapped more vigorously this time. The slight man from the East, the man with a cultivated Eton accent, was in his elements. It does not take a rocket scientist to figure that one out, and he knew it too - evidenced by the self-conscious grin of a man who knows he's won.

"These were experiences and lessons I learned, experiences and lessons which are with me and remain with me today."

"It is that whatever court we are in, whatever we are doing, whether we are on a trial court or an appellate court; at the end of our task some human being is going to be affected. Some human life is going to be changed in some way by what we do, whether we do it as trial arbiters or appellate arbiters as far removed from the trial arena as it is possible to be."

The audience rose, and they all clapped.

"I learned from these lessons and experience that if we are going to be trial arbiters whose rulings will affect the lives of other people, and who are going to change their lives by what we do, we had better use every power of our minds and our heads and our beings to get those rulings right."

And they all clapped. They clapped much louder than previous.

"And I am mindful of these lessons and experiences when I tell you this: that if you believe, and the Chamber of the Kingdom believes, that it is right to confirm my nomination, then I will accept those responsibilities as obligations to all of the people in this Great Kingdom whose lives will be affected by my Stewardship of the Constitution."

"Thank you, Chief."

And as before, and many moments throughout the day, the hall resonated with applause, none more so than when the nominee ended his opening speech.

With thunderous ovation, in a wave, never seen in this hall before: they all clapped!

And the gray suited - deep-chair-sitters, turned their heads, and murmured to the ones seated next to themselves, and nodded slowly and said: "He is not the best, but he is the best to expect from this King."

And everyone clapped. The audience rose, and did the wave.

And the slight buttoned-down man knew the answer to the question: "It is he." In the twist and turns of life, everyone knows that one who dances with the devil are scorched. The gray suited men, who sit in deep chairs, the god-players, are no different, they knew this slight man from the East would be the best they could expect from the conservative King - so they acquiesced, and the slight man became supreme arbiter - Regarding the trepidations of the grey men and the people of liberal persuasions, only time will tell!

But they all know when the battle is over and when it is time to take inventory of losses and move on - for again, as it is said: one who dances with the devil, eventually gets burned. So, it came to pass that the slight buttoned-down figure from the East got the nod from the god-players to become the ninth Supreme Arbiter.

This is even as reasons abound to the contrary - leaving room to question whether the executors of the laws of the land, the Chamber Committee, the so-called god-players left a clear impression of a jurisprudential mind at work.

The general mood is that the nominee from time to time will disappoint both ends of the two polar opposites, which is to be expected, of course. He has to at least try to reach everyone, every now and then. The game of politics requires it, even though no one can touch him now. Which, as they say, is the beauty of the position.

Some are betting that the slight man will provide a reliable vote to affirm old constitutional values without scoffing the bill of rights. You know, that ten amendments to the constitution, which interpretation is rigorously contested around the halls of academia and other places law pundits congregate -

If it is true that you know or love a man for the enemies he had made, then the buttoned-down Easterner is no different. His friends and the enemies are as plain as they come.

From the gaggle of heavy-breathing super-wives of the god-players, to those of more liberal persuasion, with enemies like these, the nominee definitely will find a thousand friends.

"No," the head wife cried, "I fear the nominee would end freedom for women in this Kingdom."

"He speaks the language of the right-wing," the friend agreed.

"He will tip the Chamber dangerously out of balance," the head of the Kingdom's main woman's group volunteered. "I tremble for this Kingdom if they confirm the nominee."

And the Queen turned to her head-maid and asked: "What do you think of the King's nominee?"

"The who, your royal highness?"

"The slight button-down fellow from the East, you imbecile," the Queen responded, for she has a short threshold for sarcasm.

"Pardon me, Madame, if I must say, I believe he will treat women like second class citizens. Not a shred of evidence indicates his willingness to uphold or advance civil rights for women and the little mermaids among us."

The Queen was taken aback. She never knew the head-maid harbored such strong sentiments.

"Are you saying that this fellow lacks understanding of women and the little mermaids in the Kingdom?" The Queen asked.

"Yes, Madame, if I must say, a regressive traditionalism." She did not forget the occasional contempt glances the nominee shot their way during the hearing - after completely ignoring them and the other emissaries from the Queen. The head maid made sure she impressed this on the Queen, even though it was too late to help their course. - 'There is nothing wrong with winning some brownie points at the expense of this "ogre.'" She thought....

It was no surprise when the verdict was made, they all groaned. They rolled their eyes to the heavens. They shrugged. Because, in the back of their minds, there is just nothing they could do. Not even the Queen. For the King has made up his mind. The gray suited men knew this was the best they could expect from the King - only time will tell - "It is a season of discontent." Charlie would say. And Charlie is my best friend. And Charlie is always right..."

Charlie, my old friend, looked up at me, the unhappiness very evident in the hazel eyes. He wondered out loud: "Why is it true that we pay for the mistakes we made in our youths later in our lifetimes?"

I had no ready answer to that, and I am not exactly known for lose of words!

"I do not know Charlie, I really do not know," was all I could volunteer.

"The Emperors, Kings, Prime Ministers, and other leaders of great powers have always invariably preferred the heady world diplomacy, the judiciary, war, and international affairs to the unglamorous realm of fiscal reform, educational changes, and domestic renewal... it is left to later generations to pay the price." Charlie concluded...

And they all clapped as the nominee was sworn in as the newest member of the Chamber of Arbiters...

The opposition, in defeat, resigned themselves to the mode of "wait and see" - more or less like a prayer, for divine intervention.

And they all clapped...

Cindy Lou's Bald Mound
A Dialogue, A Lover's Dialogue

"Hey babe, do you miss me?"

"Always…" the lover responded.

"How much do you miss me?" She inquired, not quite satisfied with what she considered a tepid response.

Silence, followed by a chuckle, then a huge laugh - actually, a burst of prolonged laughter…the lover was very much amused.

"I was expecting you to say a lot. Say a lot," mildly exasperated.

"You should see my arms, they are spread wide open," the lover offered.

"Great, and that's how it should be," she mused.

"Always, my dear. What is there not to miss…" he reassured.

"You better be a believer, and right - what is there not to miss, am great and you totally want me…" now satisfied with lover's reassurance.

"Of course, I do." He said, knowing that, a happy lover makes for a happy home.

"Now that I am feeling better, don't you think it's about time we move this to the bedroom? I mean, before I have another relapse…? Big chuckle. "No, no, no, just kidding." She purred, to reassure of wellness, her wellness.

Big laugh from lover's end, then he said:

"That's so cool." I think it's about time we take it to the next level, the bedroom."

"I definitely have to be on top, what do you think of top position?" She said, and asked, to get lover's mindset on top position.

"Great." "Top is always good…top is really good." The lover concurred.

"With your shoulder and all, I think I should be on top. And, I do give great back rub." She promised.

"That's so cool, you are so funny, a true riot, and I must give you that." He said into the mouthpiece.

"Why do you like the top position?" She is curious.

"I think women like it better, for obvious reason." He replied.

"What obvious reason?" Still curious, not quite satisfied with lover's response.

"They are able to maintain a relative level of control, some element of it, so to speak. Where they are able to modulate the process… controlling the tempo for instance. The thrust and penetration." He explains himself.

"No. That is so not true. The back position is the best position for what you are describing." She corrects him.

"What am I describing?" Lover, now on offense.

"Do you really want me to repeat it?" Another mild exasperation.

"I mean, are you being bashful here, having a religious, or do I say, some Damascus conversion, that makes pronouncing the word "'penetration'" awkward?" The lover asked, still on offense.

"For goodness sake, penetration, now are you happy?" A slightly higher level of exasperation.

"Nothing to do with happiness, my dear, just wanted to make sure you have not gone timid on me." But, back to your premise, never thought of it that way…" He said, changing the subject, again, mindful that a happy lover makes for a happy home.

"I was riding in an elevator once, and happened to drop my briefcase in the Mercantile Exchange. The guy riding with me, the only other person in the elevator, reached down to retrieve it for me, and our bodies touched as we both were reaching for the same briefcase. It was unscheduled, unrehearsed, totally unplanned reaction by two strangers; that culminated in a passionate do of me…because of the bolt of lightening that went through me the moment we touched. It was that rare of occasion, when two bodies of chemical forces meet and sparks of passion are witnessed, from a fused attraction, that might never be repeated again. I just bent over and allowed him to take me. Totally ravished, but loved every moment of it." She longwindedly offered; more or less to dispel any notion that she might have gone timid on her "way to Damascus." Unbeknown to the lover, a narrative that would become seminal.

"Were you wearing pants or skirt?" The lover asked.

"Skirt, I wore skirts mostly to work. From Burberry's." She said, emphasizing Burberry's.

"Of course." The lover acknowledged.

"Do you think you may ever run into this guy again?"

"I may, you never know."

"Would you recognize each other?"

"Mmm, I don't know…"

"That's one for the ages!" It was not a cant. It was a compliment – the lover, ever the connoisseur.

"Yes, and not likely to happen again." She finished.

Two Days Later
Driving Across The Big Bridge

"Hey babe, are you glad I have a great rack?"

Driving across the big bridge to the city, with its beckoning lights, always heightens the sassiness of Cindy Lou. It conjures up all kinds of emotion, not the least, the river that flows down there. This instance was no different, and driving with all that is going on, made it a bit tenuous – the big bridge can be treacherous to the uninitiated, especially the ones who take it for granted, especially with the bay winds and all that, a good focus is required, on the big bridge. To Cindy Lou, caution is an inhibition, a weakness of character.

"Babe, the tiny downy hairs down there are rising sharply – the river between flows ever so gushingly - it's the shock and excitement of undressing in your car, the naked body, the cool of the leather seats against the heat of my skin!" Please babe, take the Island route, the Treasure Island, not Yerba Buena – I need the long way to the restaurant, to give me a suitable recovery time." The lover swung the car off the main road onto a smaller, winding hilly road, then onto an even smaller road, to give suitable recovery period for the greater good.

"Lay on your back. Watch everything am doing and how am doing it. Show how you feel with every move or action..." Cindy Lou instructed.

"I thought you said you were gonna totally f my brains out?" - The lover, not quite impressed.

"Hello! You have your cock in my mouth!" Cindy Lou, Un-amused.

Silence, followed by a tremendous burst of laughter, from the lover, that is. It was truly ironic. He just could not help the situation. He knew he deserved that. So, he said: "sorry babe, like you always say, "patience is a virtue," and you are doing good, continue."

"You can also show your pleasure, if you're enjoying it, like by being verbal, talking to me..."

The lover acquiesced; there were lots of noise.

"You can come in my mouth. I do want you to come in my mouth..."

"Don't wanno come in your mouth..."

45 minutes later

Attention was given to the rack, the belly button and areas in-between. Lover moves slowly to the mound. The lover looks up at her. The face, a question mark...

"I bet you were expecting a bush down there?" Yes?" Cindy Lou answered the obvious question on the lover's face.

"I was..." The lover agreed.

"I had it waxed, I always have it waxed." She explains.

"Where do you wax it?" The lover is curious.

"At the saloon." Matter of fact.

"Who does the waxing?" Lover wants some explanation.

"Some Asian Lady." She is not quite sure where all this is going.

"She must have an eye full…" The lover, a bit more comfortable.
"I am sure she does…don't you like it?"
"No." Said with finality.
"Do you want me to grow it back?"
"Yes,"
"How about a bikini wax."
"Acceptable. Yes, when you gonna wear bikini in the summer."
"I will grow it for you, just for you…"
"Great." Why did you have it waxed in the first place?"
"It's more comfortable when I masturbate."
"Oh!'
"You are really big, truly well hung…"
Silence, bashful silence…
"I did not mean to make you uncomfortable. But, you are really big.
I have not had sex in months. You gonna love it, because time has a
way of making it more tight…"

"I can't wait, oh please put it in now!" Cindy Lou begged the lover
to do her, another irony, remarkable in itself. "One supposes that I
am striving for satisfaction, an ease of the pressure, yes?" She purred
breathily into the lover's ear – the lover was not sure – was this a
question or a statement? With Cindy Lou, one never knows. "One
would be right." Again, she purred breathily, as she answered her
own question/non-question – It's all about the universal truism,
life's journey - the board game of life – in this game, it is each to
her own, and Cindy Lou, the sassy girl who had an encyclopedic
knowledge of fabulousness; a woman of tomorrow for today – has
always made it clear that you have to live life by your own terms and
you have to not worry about what other people think – and above all,
have the courage to do the unexpected. She possesses a rare ability
to read the imperatives and possibilities of each new moment and
organize herself and whoever she is with at the time to anticipate
change and translate it into opportunity. – She is tremendously
smart – has original voice, with provocative opinions –she always
does her best up on the high wire – with imagination and intimate
knowledge of variety of subjects – she is an evolved product not

buried in traditions or culture – she creates and refines her style toward ultimate simplicity, functionality and elegance in bare bones minimalism – quintessential bare bones chic infused into her fashion repertoire – always a struggle to find a balance between the present state of things and something of slightly better quality – she thinks of what she wants and why it doesn't exist, and begins from there: she knows how to write new plays and do things in new ways – yes, she is the ultimate woman of tomorrow for today: her genome is global in outlook, her mind is innovative, her world networked - She knows what is in, what is on its way out, who is worth knowing, and she always looked spectacularly, exquisitely, just-this-minute fashionable, is full of surprises. Since surprise is a relative term, we ask: do we really truly know anybody? And for that matter, how much do we really know of ourselves?

The End.

Lot: The Ultimate Outcome.

As far as the eye can see,
beyond the palm trees,
and the once open lush green field.
In the far horizon, the
great water, the Mississippi.
Parts muddy, parts clear.

Atop the world,
At the very apex.
As far as the eye can see.
The immensity of concrete
and steel molds, desolation.
No life in sight.

Standing on the precipice,
in the not too distant horizon,
great molds of concrete and steel -
parts obstacle, parts bridge.
Neither, a true solution.
The cascading water and its mangled molds.
As far as the eye can see.
Hypnotic brain drain.
Sensory deprivation.
But wait, a pulse,
mystical stimulation of nerve activity
in brain.
Electro magnetic waves.
Brain activity stimulated.
Being controlled, not knowing how.

Need to cross the crevice,
not knowing how.
Too far to jump,
too far to leap.
A deep drop,
sure death?
Behind too is sure death.
Raging flames devouring all in its path.

A miracle.
There he comes,
Joy of innocence,
Sweet mate for life.
Ancient love.
To understand all is to forgive all.
Dream? Have we met before?
Would be so offensive,
not to have met before.
God can only beget God.
Penetrating and ethereal at once.
Peace equals heaven and earth uniting.
What can I expect of you?

Paper tigers floating over unseen halos.
Sometimes slipping between us.
The colors captured inside themselves.

There was a dull piercing, not like the stars.
It was a night when only rose petals
fell from my lover's lips.
A dream? An imagination?

This was a bright darkness, this night.
But my words were only ragged rocks,
scalping my lover's ears...enough to beg.

Striding along with sure long steps,
no fear in his eyes.
No doubt whatsoever.
Take my hand lady.
He said.

Jump with me.
He said
Real enthusiasm filled the city,
its noise hates me.
Its roar pretends to kiss me.
Licorice eyes don't shift or turn away.
Seeing your taste through a fleeting glint,
gives me life for an hour, an eternity.
An hour I would never have without you.

I look longingly at him.
I put out my hand.
I take it back.
The flames are so close.

Keep thoughts struggling up.
Remember Isaiah.
"Thou will keep him in perfect peace,
whose mind is stayed on thee, in all thy ways,
acknowledge him, and he shall direct thy paths."
"In quietness and confidence shall by thy strength."
Proverbial.

The cascading flames rage closer.
In the far horizon, the great water of the Mississippi,
parts muddy, parts clear,
moves the mangled molds of concrete and steel.
He jumps,
he turns and looks at me,
disbelieving.
I look on helplessly.

The raging flames, palpable, right behind me.
I jump,
hurtling through the air.
Hope is eternal…

Sibylla's Rain,
That Night In San Francisco

It was one of those rainy nights in San Francisco, I found myself alone with a dearth of available choice companions, and rainy days, especially one accompanied by thunderstorms, and especially on a weekend, is not the best time to be alone. The rain smashed against the translucently fogged huge French windows, drips down, creating its own canals, which converge downstream into bigger oases. One cavalcade, undeterred by the whistling and hissing wind rolled between the pool of wetness until it reached the bigger opening - images of rapture, bodies, hard-bodies merged in a Eucharistic coalescence - with the fires and waters of passion - and the crackling sound from the fireplace reminded me of my immediate need, the need for a warm-body to share this most unique experience, that fire and water create.

The situation becomes desperately urgent. It is a war between my desire for safety on one hand, and the need for adventure on the other - and the adventure realm looms large, roaring, gushing, voluptuous torrent of geysers, unlike anything I have experienced before. There is nothing else to do but pull and dig into my old school "black-book," that is, if a woman is "allowed" to call it that, especially one brought up with the affectations of New England gentility, or should I say sensibilities.

I traced along the edges of the "black-book," allowing my fingers to flow and be the guide, until it led me to the "C" section, and there! There it was! Calderon! Past childhood observations resurfaced, thoughts of adult duplicity, or simple indifference, intimations of that blurred boundary between affection, love and lust - in this arena nothing is stated, nothing is listed, everything is implied - in choices between conventional domesticity and the wider life. Calderon! Portraits of two bodies in the back of the Buick flashed right before my eyes, which was actually no more than a mere pleasant encounter in our ambitions and longings, which one might not want to hang out over tea and talk about - instinctively, the address book found itself lodged between my thighs, as I curled up in the soft sofa, watching the Latin girl, what's her name? She is always delicious to watch. Women envy her, and she obsesses over their envy. What's her name? No! I'm not quite sure what, maybe she was not Latin at all; maybe it was Whitney Houston, sitting on Arsenio Hall's lap on my 45" Trinitron...yes, right here in my den - in this physical world, the atmosphere is vivid and precise; images of salt air, motorboats leaving tiny froth of trails across a glimmering ocean.

There's a conflict, an empathetic traction, stuck somewhere between character and caricature. Where characters are reduced to internal binaries that feel schematic: love pitted against ambition, selfishness pitted against empathy, and one can feel all the social forces, pressures, stereotypes, and misconceptions collecting and waiting to ambush one, if one is not so careful, in the clamor of an unforgiving social carousel. Where more continuous area is needed for the ambiguities of a fractured self to survive, fester - where more space is needed for the dense silence of an abiding social loneliness, inherited from Adam and Eve - an unsavory cast of characters, in a play written for two people - not unlike the one about an adulterous housewife who exudes a halo of sexual energy and the not-so-trust-worthy butler. Am I being selfish? Am I allowing my ambitions to blind me to the fact that there is a man in my life? Why am I enabling, encouraging this insatiable passion. That it did not work with Calderon was a disappointment. Yes, but, as one knows, disappointment is part of growing up, learning to accept a less-than-perfect outcome, to tolerate ambiguity. Yet at the level of personal experience we resist this fact.

It is only when we realize that life isn't always going to go our way, that we start to see these ambiguities in their true forms: that in life, there are always loses as well as gains, whether we like it or not. And if we can just relax with that, we will have no problem, like the one I am now wrestling with, because I fell into the category of those who use escapism, sexual escapism and other daily activities as a shield against the fundamental ambiguities of our situation, expending tremendous energy trying to ward off impermanence and boredom - in the daily grind, in the complexities of modern living, the pain of getting what we do not want.

To tolerate ambiguity, and accept the less than perfect outcome is inherent and to live our lives from this understanding is to create the causes and conditions for happiness. And I said, without uttering any words; "physician, heal thy self." Why can't I act like I preach? Why do I not take my own counsel? Especially knowing that we suffer, get into the funk and boredom, not because we are basically bad, cursed or deserved to be punished, but because of the tragic misunderstandings we have about those things we cannot control about life, when we destroy ourselves in order to find temporary relief. It is only when we realize that there are no cures to the facts of life, that we regain our balance. And I said, again: "physician, heal thy self."

Calderon, why does that name conjure such passion, and the funny feelings between my legs? Could it be the legend about that first sexual tangle, in the back of the "Buick," – the notion about the indelible mark it leaves, especially if it was otherworldly good? And school never was the same after that, and Sibylla, that is I, never was the same at home either, I had just tasted the forbidden fruit started by the mother of all mothers, Eve, and crossed into womanhood. It is a realm of no return, where people act with the directness of a kiss that turns into a bite, and Sibylla, me, loved the way it her felt.

Calderon, I hear he is now with a high priced law firm in the city, but still lives in the family house. My fingers did the talking again, and the dreadful answering machine reared its head. But then, who expects anyone to be home at this hour, unless he or she is curled up with the opposite number, and Calderon never lacks available companions. In my smoothest, silky voice, I said: "Hello Calderon," see, we called ourselves by our last names then, it was being different, the iconoclastic set. But this time, I decided to use my first name only, in a game, I hoped would not backfire: "This is Sibylla, from pacific heights, call me if you remember me, I am in the phone book..." I was not going to leave my full name and number for his amusement and those of his playmates, and that was that

... A man who does not remember our first tangle in the backseat of a Buick, does not deserve me, dearth of available choices or not, he does not deserve me if he cannot remember me...

My strategy worked, and the legend lives: I was made a believer - it is true, people never forget the partner in a primordial sexual escapade...he called back. He was so long-winded, and we were on the phone for such a long time, I was beginning to wonder if this was the same especially unattainable guy from school that would have required the proverbial last-woman-on-earth status before I had a chance; notwithstanding the fact that I was among the so-called in-crowd of drop-dead-gorgeous-babes in school. It was just that, the keyword being "one of." There were just so many drop-dead-gorgeous-babes that one had to practically stay in line, if one wants to land the gorgeous hunk with capital T, and being the proverbial last one, becomes the right metaphor - but I was loving every minute of it - he remembered everything about me after all these years. I kept reminiscing on the attraction I felt for him seven years ago, albeit animalistic, and what others might term juvenile infatuation, but call it what you may, it was a different chemistry this hunk generated in me when I met him for the first time, in our humid gym class. It was like an unexplained chunk of meteor, brave and vigorous, clear thoughtful eyes, with a certain intellectual chic - slightly florid cadence, inviting a walk on the wild side.

I have always said that, if a man does not do it for me the first time, there is no chance it might ever happen, I believe in love at first sight - and the beauty of it all is that, I sensed that he felt the same for me too. We talked endlessly, touched constantly to make a "point," and found ourselves the only couple left in the steamy complex. The temptation was there, all the elements were present, but we did not do it in the steamy gym class, we decided on his father's Buick - which, to me, should belong in the Smithsonian...

"You know, it is strange how things workout, when we do not pay attention to the ambiguities and impermanence of daily life, when we make assumptions about things we do not know, or understand, especially about things one felt unattainable, in spite of one's hubris and station, and the doting from all the others of same ilk. Ilk in this case being the beautiful things." He continued.

"The point is, I had watched you for some time. Your almost ghostly blond hair, light dusting freckles, blue eyes and narrow nose. I had expected this type of beauty existed, and upon finally achieving visual confirmation in the gym that day, I felt reassured that other great and glorious things imagined but unseen also existed in the universe. To me, to say you were part of any crowd would have been to insult what I felt was an exalted status I placed you. I thought you must view our school with an air of mild contempt, because of the family history, the old money behind you and the fact that you could have gone to any other "it" school in the city and you chose our school." He stopped. I was flabbergasted. What he had just said was a facsimile of how I felt about him. It goes to show, nothing is, as it seems - That we should pay more attention to the ambiguities and impermanence of daily life. Yes, he was from new money, the Internet millionaire dad. But I felt he was cultured, and much more refined than some of our contemporaries then. He continued.

"In the class we took together, even though you seemed to enjoy my company, I thought it was purely a cordial relationship of limited potential. With your wealth and this other guy, what's his name? The Pelosi guy, who was occasionally photographed with you in the celebrity pages. Funny how things work out." "When I talk to friends about you, they ask if you were my girlfriend. I tell them "girlfriend" is a sophisticated term college people adopt after much deliberation. That I would not call you that yet, which I knew was an exaggeration, but a young man had his pride, especially someone with the kind of following I had in school - especially among the babes. It was then I discovered the previously unknown depth of character and creativity that lurked in me." I did not know what to say. I did know some guys were intimidated by the aura I presented in school then, I never knew Calderon was one of them. It is funny I felt the same thing about him. Again, it goes to show, does it not? About all the assumptions we make, especially about things we do not fully know or understand.

The large tank-like Buick was parked on the parking lot, which incidentally was on the roof of the gym building, which connected by way of a bridge to the bluffs overlooking the marina, on the pacific, not the bay side. When he opened the door, I could feel some sort of current run through me. We hugged and I let his hands linger on my backside. I was always impressed with the way he comports himself in class, and during ball games - the sleek panther of a man, leaves the floor, spins 360 degrees in the air, achieves the aerodynamically impossible, and sinks the ball with only a whisper from the net. The packed auditorium explodes, and earthquake shakers resound in areas you would not imagine...and I am quite sure, now that I think about it, he felt the same way about me. But now, I was not sure of how to control my fatal obsession, see, I love to take my clothes off. He was patient, playing my game of carnal brinkmanship. Will he undress me? How do I get my clothes off? He reached inside my bra and felt my little titties, and I wished they were much rounder for him. I pulled down the straps of my chemise, and allowed his hands to roam about my very silky, firm hard purple nipples. I wiggled out of my bikini panties and he put his hand on my furry cutty-sac, and I knew right there and then, that if questioned, I'd lie. If caught, lie. If interrupted in the act, lie. I have come to call it, the etiquette of preserving one's virginity, or should I say, dignity?...because, acting is making the audience believe who you say you are...

I do not know how it happened from then on, but it felt so natural that at one point I found myself sitting on him, turning to each other, and exchanging easy kisses - openmouthed, with tongue. We are suddenly transformed so that finally I can see the stars and the moon in their true essence, and the view of the marina and the coastal night-scape became more vivid, precise and familiar - the cars rushing by on the boulevard down below. Taillights glowing through the fog and sea mist. I finally saw them all for what they were: beautiful. I pulled him in with my legs wrapped around his waist so that we were pressing hard into each other. We kept it up, enjoying this game of capture. I reached behind him and pulled him in deeper. It was the culmination from the miracle of mutual seduction, unfolding before our eyes, and the stars and moon as the only light we needed. Outside of the fact, the pain that comes with the "first" time, it was actually effortless; it felt like we had done this a thousand times. It did feel like we made love a thousand times that day.

C.C. was more experienced than I was. He asks me to feel the skin, he strokes the inside of my thighs, and I'm naked inside this tank of a car, nipples distended and scarlet... "Spread your legs," he says, "no," I replied, not liking the command tone, "just a little bit, please," that sounds better, I thought. He slips his hand between my thighs and pushes them apart... I hug and hide my breasts, preserving the last shred of my virginity, ergo dignity, but hot and wet with fear and hunger, watching fingers in the curly hair of the cutty-sac, I giggle. "No." "Yes," "No, don't." C.C. pulls me onto him; kissing me frantically, I felt excruciating torture. He has me pinned against the car seat, pushing his thing into me, pushing against bone, hurting, tearing against flesh. "C.C., I mean it, stop C.C.," but no, he had passed second base, now into third, a realm of no return...and I have lost my virginity forever, to Charlie Calderon...but relieved in my thrust into womanhood...

Now, back to the present. I kept thinking that he was staying on the phone for an unnecessarily long time and was apprehensive about where this was all leading - one thought, one purpose, one magic, a non-primitive approach to love in the 90's. It's all about couples becoming one and staying one, which, will be safe to say, is the enhanced individualism of the 80's, which broke us apart, giving way to the 90's closeness and de-emphasized individualism, which hopefully should bring us together, with enough left to sink our teeth in - (falling in love is easy, staying in love is the hard part...)

"I've seen some of your work, you know, and rumors have it that you may well be the next female Calvin Klein, but in a more revolutionary way. It really does not surprise me, you're outstanding in our art and design class, even back then - very different, iconoclastic and avant garde...need I say more...."

Say more, more, more, go on, C.C., say more, a woman never gets enough of it, I thought in my private ecstasy...I was flattered, too absorbed to focus on what's in front of my face, preoccupied with the lust of the present, a byproduct of fire and water, it's life in the 90's, and I hoped I was not running out of imaginations, because what makes us wise also makes us rich. But this was eating away at me like a Chinese water dropper, it keeps dropping and my soul was receptive, yes, it is the taste after the buildup, the explosion, a magical place, kingdom of dreams, love, lust, gushing...

"In my private moments, in those early days of our acquaintance, I would allow my imagination to get very creative - I would picture you, as a canvas on an easel, and I as the artist, studying and refining the straight lines of your slim figure dressed in various designs of my creation. You would often lay in your neat bed with your back to me, and I studied the dip in your waist, the discernible climb of your hips and your feet arranged, right heel tucked into the arch of the left, like the yin snug inside the yang." He stopped, and I was impressed with his prose, which actually was more like poetry. I did not know what to say after that very flattering review, from a man, I especially thought was unattainable. I told him: "Thank you, C.C., you are the best, the very best."

A love affair is like a football game, it has halftime, to review the past plays, actions, positions - it allows one the luxury to make the determination as to which to keep, change, upgrade, or give up - plays and actions within the parameters of the mutually prescribed code of conduct, Calderon and I may have just ended a seven-year half time, and it took this long, all because, the man wants to live several lives, but he forgets he can't, because he only has one life, and something is worth only what people are ready to pay for it. We don't fall in love with people, we fall in love with our ideas of them, because there is a time under the heavens, for every purpose...

He had been following my work and progress, and in the competitive world of fashion design, it is Milan today, Paris tomorrow, and London, probably the following day, and I thought I was going to have a hard time snaring him. What do you know? Which really goes without saying - but then, another legend has just been vindicated: the quickest way to a man's heart is really not through food, but through good sex, that is hard, loosely tight, different, and filled with variety styles and positions, different from the "others," - it leaves indelible marks, and he never forgets you. Such memories are hard to forget, they are the ones that hunt us, the ones that sometimes set us free, because the body rebels when you deny it its basic needs...

Charlie Calderon, (CC) wanted to know if I would design an outfit for him and I said I would pause and seriously consider it. "Does everything really have a price?" He asked. "It's called how to keep the eyes down even when you are looking at the sun, learning to protect the center," I replied. Calderon paused, then he said: "I kind of like you, you still have your charm," "Thank you. And if I may say so, it comes naturally, my parents are from Boston, remember?" "All I am trying to say is that you don't miss a well until it's run dry, how come you never tried to contact me all these years?" I was certainly playing the hard-to-get to the hilt. "Give me a break, Sib, what's absent in the eyes, is present in the heart." He said. I was quiet, more for effect, then I said: "Okay, I'll design your outfit, but with one catch," "Just name it," he said. "If you will allow me to take the measurements,"

"You're the designer, you name what you want me do, Sib, and if you don't mind me saying it, that was one heck of an elaborately staged professional affair," and who says Eve was not the wiser one...

I then asked him to call me when he was ready and got another shocker that made my apprehension go into high gear. He said we should do his measurements that evening, which goes to show, a scar is a scar, no matter how much you wash it, C.C. still got it, and it makes me tingle all-over, and love is a beauty you never haggle over... I guess I was so frightened, or should I say, overwhelmed by the rapid, or accelerated movement of this passionate reunion, that I did not realize he had wanted to go to dinner as well that evening... the frantic nature of my preparation, to make everything perfect, was making me "dizzy," I had to change my panties, or should I say underwear, several times, just from the anticipation...and I was not sure if I could handle what I had just started. Have I gone beyond my head? I had vowed never again to let any man chew me up like a piece of chewing gum, and spit me out after the sweetness or nectar is gone - Am I being too easy? Should I change my strategy? These were questions I could not answer because I had been smitten by love-bites, and love is a beauty one does not haggle over...or is it?

When I got home from the shop that evening, Adele, my roommate told me that C.C. had called and she had asked him if he was calling to cancel our date. Adele explained how he screamed no! Which was a little consolation, knowing that I was not the only one giddy from all this. I was getting more apprehensive by the moment. I hoped I was not getting a man on a rebound...

While I was getting ready, (see, I had to buy all new underwear, in lacy bras, filmy negligees, diaphanous, and flattering - I figured diaphaneity should be the order of the evening - all baptized by fire and water, caused by a lonely night in San Francisco...) Pierre and Anne showed up. Pierre was a buyer I had a fling with after a showing that went through the roof a while back - it was one of my best showings. In the glee of that moment, and with all the accolades and Champaign flowing, (I love accolades and Champaign), we did do it, and a couple of times after that night, and then I dumped him. He's been hounding me since then, practically stalking me. In his desire to make me jealous, he came to my house with another mutual friend of ours, Anne, whom he's now dating, and made up a story about my calls to him. He asked that I stop hounding him, and asked that Anne save him from me.

I laughed and asked what planet all this happened. I told Anne to get him out of my house. While I was walking them out, I saw the Jet-black S-500 drive up and I prayed that C.C. would be well dressed and look handsome. Well, I got my wish and blew past Pierre and Anne without a backward glance! Save him from me indeed!

Well, C.C. was very hungry and so was I, especially after the charade of Pierre and Anne, who wouldn't be hungry...so we left right away. He commented that I looked "nice," in my jacket. I told him that I designed it. He took the long way to the restaurant and admitted that it was by design, and not a coincident. He wanted to spend more time with me and enjoy the view I presented. See, I had worn under the black jacket, a very short red skirt, which showed a lot of skins, legs, complimented by a three-inch pump, which further enhanced the thighs and legs. C.C. is a legman, that I knew. I was starting to relax when he made a comment and placed his hand on my knee. Usually, I would not have made anything of it, but it was the way that it was done and the way I knew he was feeling. Trust me, a woman knows these things, it made all the red signals go off in my head, and I remembered the story of the chewing gum, a victim of lost sweetness and nectar, just because it was too easy... no, I have to be patient, go slow, make this work, because I had no intention of allowing this to disturb the equilibrium of my life.... "You are making me weak, don't make me beg," he said, "you're strong enough to be weak," I replied, ignoring the begging part, the distance between the restaurant and the bedroom is astronomical, but it's worth it.

We had a wonderful dinner and got back home rather late. While at dinner, it was established we had mutual goals, to rekindle the love lost seven years ago, even though we played our angles differently. It is called love-gimmicks, and a gimmick is an angle, an angle that works for you, and makes you work not as hard, which I must say, excited both of us...from a certain perspective, all this talk, the touching to make a point, and the foot-romance under the table, seem silly, but from a close up, I find myself dedicated and uncritically sincere...I'm sitting here, definitely here, watching us through the camera eye, studying that self-conscious moment of realization, from a twilight zone of vulnerability and animal abandon on a feast of Oysters and Mushrooms....and I'm dreaming, breathlessly shuddering, a violent climax, body jerking, eyes rolled back, rhythmic groans, C.C. collapsing besides me, his face in the pillow, one thigh fallen over my thigh........

We sat there. Silence. He is staring at me, rubbing an ice cube between both palms... I am dreaming again - he shrugs into my purple terrycloth robe and follows me into the bedroom, I can hear Adele in her room beyond mine, talking back to the television...his nakedness inside the robe makes me nervous...and I was glad about the Macy's beauty facial, the long hours of deep sleep, the numerous leg lifts and sit ups and touch-toes in anticipation...there were the manicure, Pedicure - I've pumiced and plucked and waxed and buffed and creamed with the richest moisturizer available...all that was needed were the close-up and reaction shots from C.C. and I'm totally relaxed and ready for anything, anything - the waiting has been debilitating enough already - chewing gum adventure or not... from the moment he clicked into my consciousness again, I knew we were fated for bed....

His hands, just like the first time in the Buick, knew my body like he invented it. I put my hand on his thigh, he takes it and moved it onto a remarkable bulge in his pants, and I'm the sex-bomb of my generation - the dreamscape, my erotic fantasies became cognizant to C.C., I come, and come again, and when he knows I can't stand it anymore, C.C. grabs the soft little hill of my cutty-sac bone, and does tingle, tingle, tingle till I'm nothing but a cutty-sac on fire. Out of head and into the cutty-sac - that glorious sense of insanity, just one screaming millimeter this side of unconscious - it got to be what good sex is all about...he goes on for hours nonstop. Remind me not to go to bed with his friends or his enemies; it might be their commonality...

His thigh presses against me, it stays - this is not an accident, this is no more a dreamscape, but I have climaxed so many times, exhaustion has set in. He should have had me when I was deliriously hungry, now I'm full, from all the comes, from the heat generated by the fire and rainwater combo, on a lonely night, on a rainy day in San Francisco...I've decided not to compromise the equilibrium of my life, my new found freedom...